I. D. Roberts was born in Australia in 1970 and moved to England when he was three. From a young age he developed an obsession with war comics, movies, Tintin and James Bond. For the past decade he has been the film writer for a national listings magazine. After living all over the country and buying a farmhouse by mistake in Ireland, he finally settled in the south-west and currently lives in rural Somerset with his wife Di and their chocolate labrador, Steed.

www.idroberts.com

By I. D. Roberts

Kingdom Lock

KINGDOM LOCK

I. D. ROBERTS

Allison & Busby Limited
12 Fitzroy Mews
London W1T 6DW
www.allisonandbusby.com

First published in Great Britain by Allison & Busby in 2014.
This paperback edition published by Allison & Busby in 2014.

A CIP catalogue record for this book is available from the British Library.

10 9 8 7 6 5 4 3 2 1

ISBN 978-0-7490-1613-5

Typeset in 10.5/16 pt Adobe Garamond Pro by Allison & Busby Ltd.

Printed and bound by
CPI Group (UK) Ltd, Croydon, CR0 4YY

For Di

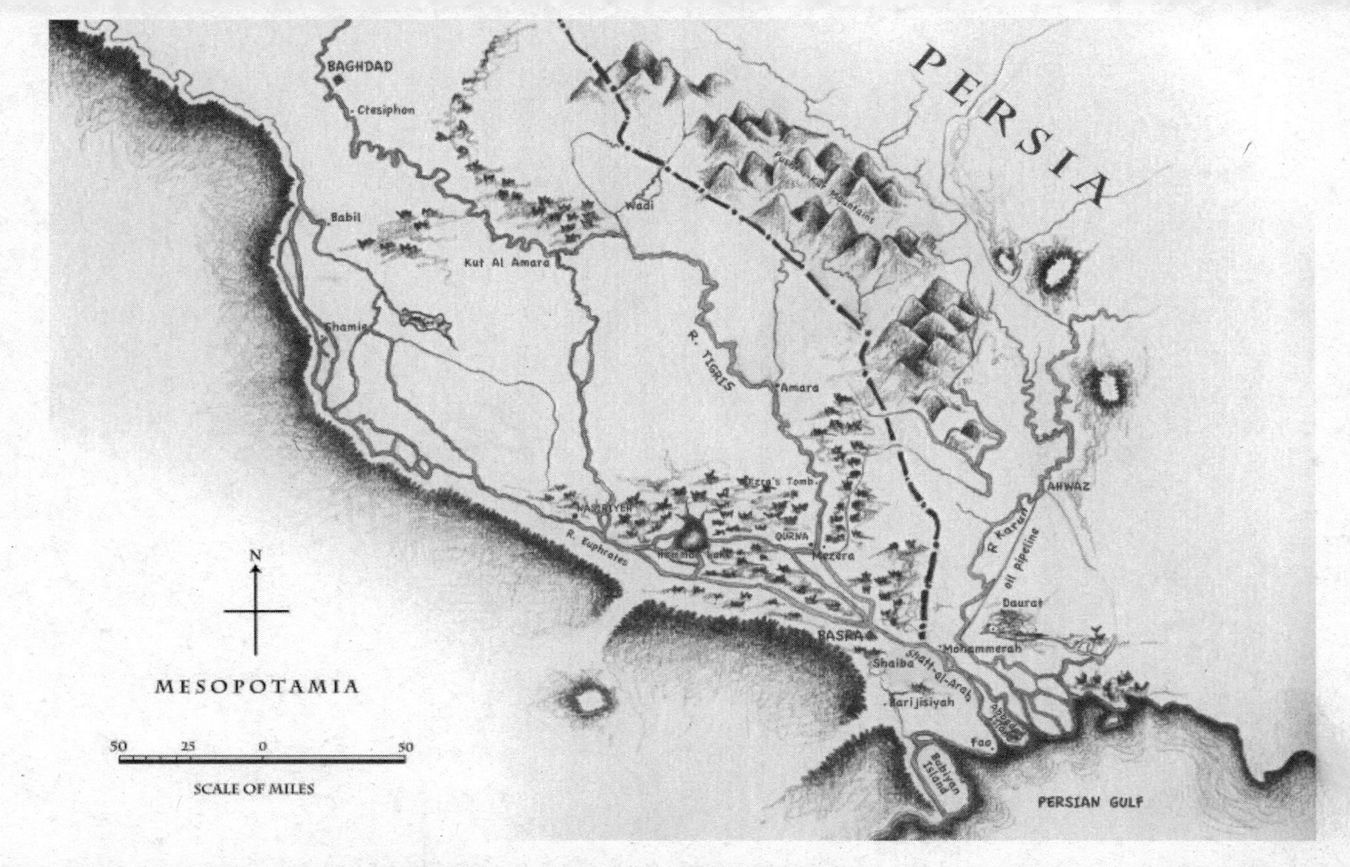
PERSIA
BAGHDAD
Ctesiphon
Babil
Kut Al Amara
Wadi
Shamia
R. TIGRIS
Amara
Ezra's Tomb
R. Euphrates
QURNA
Mezera
BASRA
Shaiba
Shatt-al-Arab
Barjisiyah
Fao
Babiyan Island
AHWAZ
R. Karun
oil pipeline
Daurat
Mohammerah
PERSIAN GULF
N
MESOPOTAMIA
50
25
0
50
SCALE OF MILES

PROLOGUE

The Hindu Kush near the North-West Frontier
December 1914

'You must. If we stop, we die.'

'I need a moment . . .' the girl said, and slumped down in the snow.

The young man halted, and turned round. The girl had removed her lambskin Kalpak hat and was pulling at her bootlaces.

'We don't have time . . .'

Amy Townshend raised her head. Her face was ivory white and drawn at the corners of her small mouth. But her emerald eyes sparkled defiantly.

'I have a stone,' she said. 'In my boot. Besides, I haven't seen any sign of our pursuers for a while now. I think we may have lost them.'

Kingdom Lock stared down at her. He knew India and safety were no more than a few days' hike away, but they needed to press on. How close their pursuers actually were, he wasn't sure. But he knew they hadn't lost them.

'Hurry then.'

'Go ahead. I can catch you up.' Amy's face disappeared behind a curtain of matted, long auburn hair as she continued to struggle with her laces. She tutted and put her rag-bound fingers to her cracked, full lips, winced, and began to pull at the pieces of material with her teeth.

'I won't leave you, miss,' Lock said, his eyes fixed to the top of her head, a splash of chestnut red amongst the crisp whiteness of the landscape around them.

'I'm perfectly capable of looking after myself,' Amy said.

Lock turned his gaze away and began to scan the snow-covered mountain range that filled the horizon. A bitter wind stung his face as it whipped at his tattered coat. He glanced over his shoulder and squinted into the milky sun.

'The border is just over that ridge.'

Amy didn't respond. She was concentrating on inching her foot out of her boot.

'Jesus, miss!' Lock said, and knelt down. Despite Amy's foot being bound, he could see it was badly swollen and bleeding.

'It's nothing. A stone I tell you,' she said.

'That's more than a stone, miss,' Lock said, taking hold of her foot and peeling back the bloodied rags. 'How long?'

Amy winced and shook her head. 'A day, maybe more.'

'Why the hell didn't you say something?' Lock said, and before she could protest, he quickly ripped a strip of material from the hem of her skirt.

'I'm fine,' Amy insisted.

Lock ignored her and slowly unbound her foot. He then began to wash the blood and pus away with snow. Amy kept jerking her foot back, but Lock held firm and started to re-dress it with the strip of clean material.

'We need to get your boot back on or your foot will freeze. This will hurt, miss.'

Amy glared back at him. There were tears in her eyes, but she nodded for him to go ahead. 'Your left eye, Mr Lock, the green one . . .' she said, clearly trying to distract herself from the pain as Lock forced the boot back on as gently as he could. 'It goes almost brown when you're angry.'

'I'm not angry, miss. Just concerned.'

Amy squirmed and cried out briefly, but the boot eventually passed over her ankle. Lock tied it loosely, then got to his feet and held out his hand.

'I can manage,' Amy said, pushing the offered hand away.

'If you say so, miss,' Lock said. He gathered his coat about him, hitched his scarf back up around his head and took one last look back the way they had come. Bugger. His eyes followed their erratic footprints clearly marked in the virgin snow. That was bad.

'We haven't lost them, have we?' Amy put her hat back on her head and shakily tried to stand.

'I can't see them. But they're there, somewhere.' Lock gripped Amy's coat and lifted her tiny frame. She tried to protest, but Lock was firm. 'You can't walk, so I will carry you.'

Amy didn't protest, even when Lock hoisted her unceremoniously up onto his back and started walking.

'This is your own fault, you know, Mr Lock,' she said.

'What is, miss?' Lock said, adjusting the weight of the girl on his back.

'This situation. We should have done as I said, taken a boat and headed north across the Black Sea.'

'The ports and the waterways are heavily patrolled, miss, otherwise I would normally agree. This way, east and south, across country, means we have a better chance of avoiding capture.'

'Well, that's not looking so bright, is it?' Amy said. 'How long have those riders been on our heels? Nearly four weeks now? Never deviating, always close behind.'

Lock didn't answer her. But she did have a point. Their pursuers had stuck with them.

'I didn't need your help, you know. I was perfectly capable of escaping from that internment camp.'

'Perhaps you were, miss. But I'm just following orders.'

'That's what my father always tells my mother when he gets things wrong.'

'Does he often get things wrong?' Lock said.

'Frequently. He left me behind in Constantinople, didn't he? Thinking there would be plenty of time for me to finish my schooling and then follow him and *maman* to India.'

'Be reasonable, miss. How could he know that the Turks would declare war when they did?'

'It's his job to know, Mr Lock.'

'I think that's being rather unfair,' Lock said.

'Maybe,' Amy sniffed.

Lock trudged on in silence. The cold was beginning to creep up from his already numb feet, but he had to ignore that. He had to just keep moving. But after a few paces, he paused. He could feel the tremor of Amy's body through his back and realised that she was laughing softly to herself.

'Miss?'

'Oh, it's nothing, just a childish thought . . .'

'Go on,' Lock said, 'talk. It will keep us alert.' He continued walking.

'I was thinking that this is not how I expected to see in the new year, that's all.'

'What, a relaxing hike in the mountains?' Lock said. 'So what would a typical new year be then, miss?'

'Oh, some damned dull party. Father and Mother love to entertain. Always a full social calendar for them, no matter where he's posted in the world.'

'I'm sure they'll want to throw a big party when we get you safely back to India. To celebrate.'

Amy grunted. 'Yes, I expect so.' She fell silent again and Lock drifted off into a kind of trance, just listening to his breath rasping in his throat and to the scrunch of the snow beneath his feet.

'Tell me,' Amy said after a while, 'have you done this before?'

'Done what, miss?'

'Rescued a woman?'

'On occasion.'

Lock laboured onwards.

'Do you . . . kill? To order, I mean?' Amy said, breaking the silence once more.

'On occasion.'

Amy paused. 'What about dancing? Do you dance? And don't say "on occasion".'

'Dance?'

'Yes, you know, at balls and parties.'

'I can't say I've been to many balls, miss.'

‘Well, I think you are right, my parents will probably throw a party,’ she said. ‘Will you come? If it was more than just a celebration of my return, if it was, say, my birthday?’

‘Will it be? Your birthday?’

‘Not until March. I’ll be eighteen then. Can’t avoid a party on one’s eighteenth, I suppose.’

‘True.’

‘I’d like you to come, if I do have a party. Would you, Mr Lock?’

‘We’ll see, miss.’

‘I’d like to dance with you.’

‘It may be a while before you dance on those feet, miss,’ Lock said.

‘Oh. Yes, I suppose . . .’

‘But what about your beau? Won’t he be jealous if you danced with me?’

‘That’s an indelicate question, Mr Lock,’ Amy said. ‘But, if you must know, yes, I suspect he would be. Anyway, I shall decide whom I dance with.’

‘Good for you, miss. Spoken like a true suffragette.’

‘Don’t be facetious, Mr Lock.’

‘I meant it as a compliment, miss.’

‘Did you?’ Amy sounded dubious. ‘Besides, Casper can go to blazes if he has a problem with the men I choose to dance wi—’

The ground in front of Lock kicked up a spray of snow. Moments later a gunshot rang out, echoing loudly off the mountainside. Lock felt Amy tense as he staggered and turned.

On the furthest ridge behind them, no more than a mile away, there were now three men on horseback.

'Bugger!'

Lock turned away and laboured on. He tried to think only of their escape and not the impact he would feel when the expected bullet pierced his body ending his mission. Not long now, a voice in his head whispered, it won't take long for our pursuers to cover the gap between us on horseback. Hide! We need somewhere to hide, his subconscious screamed. But he could see nothing, only a barren, harsh, unforgiving landscape.

Suddenly Lock lost his footing, and both he and Amy fell to the carpet of snow.

'I can't . . . believe . . . you just dropped m . . . me!' Amy lifted her head and scowled. She pulled herself to her feet, brushed herself down and hobbled over to Lock's side. He was hauling himself up and she helped to steady him. 'We're done for, aren't we?' she said.

'Don't say that.'

'Just be honest with me,' Amy said. 'We can't run, we can barely walk. And I won't let you keep carrying me.'

'I was asked to get you home, and home is where I'm going to get you, miss.'

'If only we could find some shelter,' she said.

Lock shook his head. 'I told you. If we stop . . .'

'We die. I know.' She tried to force a smile. 'But . . . Look, we could hold them off for a while. Maybe even scare them away. See.' She fumbled in her coat pocket and produced a pistol.

'Where the hell did you get it?' Lock could see it was a good weapon, a Browning FN Model 1903, the sidearm favoured by the Ottoman police, and it was lighter and easier to use than the British Webley he carried. Only his gun was useless now. He'd used the last of its cartridges some time back.

'My servant smuggled it to me at the camp,' Amy said. 'I do know how to shoot.'

'I'm sure you do, miss. But shooting a man is very different to shooting a squirrel.'

'I'm well aware of that, Mr Lock,' she said.

'And you've had that all this time?'

'Of course,' Amy said.

'And you didn't think it important to let me know?'

'No,' Amy said. 'Why should I? If the time came, I could produce it. As I have done so now.'

Lock shook his head. 'Besides, how many bullets have you got in that thing?'

'Two.'

'There are three of them.'

'Well, we can get them to line up,' Amy waved her hand to and fro, 'one behind the other. Only need one bullet then.'

Lock snorted and turned his attention back to the ridge. It was snowing now, but he could still make out the darker shapes of their pursuers, and they were getting closer and closer by the minute. 'But you're right,' he said. 'We need to find shelter.' He scanned the landscape in front of them. 'There are some rocks just a little way ahead. Do you think you could make it?'

Amy stuffed the pistol back in her pocket, straightened her skirts, and nodded up at the towering figure of Lock. He opened his coat and she stepped into its protective veil. Amy hooked her arm around Lock's waist and they slowly stumbled on towards a small grouping of boulders fifty yards ahead. The snow was falling thickly about them.

The two fugitives edged forward, and with every passing

minute Lock knew that their pursuers were closing in. He glanced back once but couldn't see anything through the curtain of snow.

Amy pulled up suddenly. 'Stop!'

Lock halted. Now what? Amy was pointing ahead. Lock strained his eyes but he still could see nothing but whiteness and the darker mass of the boulders.

'We . . . we will have to go around,' Amy winced.

'Why? We haven't the time—'

'Crev . . . crevasse.'

'Where?' Lock stared into the snow.

'That slight dip in the ground . . .'

Lock looked again. He could see it, yes. It seemed to be quite wide just in front of the boulders and ran for a good distance off to their right. 'How do you know?'

'Mother took my sister and I skiing . . . in the Alps last winter. We were taught to . . . recognise the signs. The snow is so light . . . acts like a little blanket over a ditch. But one wrong step, and . . . whoosh!' Amy made a diving action with her hand.

'Christ, that's all we need.' Lock stared blankly ahead, through the snow that was now cascading around them in huge, pregnant flakes. To his right the indentation in the ground appeared to widen out and stretch as far as his vision could see. To the left, it seemed to stay about as wide as he was tall. He checked behind him again. If he didn't act now then they were done for.

But Amy was beginning to flag. She was limping worse than before.

Lock heaved her upright.

'We're going to have to jump, miss. Do you hear? It's not too far across, over to our left there.' The boulders were perhaps ten feet away, maybe a little more, on the other side of the crevasse.

Amy nodded.

'Together,' Lock said, gripping Amy's arm tighter. 'I help you, you help me.'

Amy raised her head and peered over at the boulders. She nodded again. 'Very well, Mr Lock, for you,' she managed to smile.

They shuffled a little over to their left, to where Lock hoped that the crevasse was narrower. After a few paces they stopped again. Lock pulled himself free of Amy's grip and inched forward tentatively, tensing himself should the ground suddenly give way beneath him.

'Far enough!' Amy said.

Lock stopped. He unwound the scarf from his head and neck and placed it at his feet, then turned and cautiously made his way back to the girl. They both stripped off their heavy coats, and Amy pushed her hat in one of the pockets. Lock walked back to the scarf marker, transferred Amy's pistol to his own pocket, and threw the coats as far as he could across where he imagined the crevasse to be. They landed about seven feet away. He limped back to the trembling girl.

'Ready, miss?'

Amy stretched up and kissed his mouth. '*Pour la chance*. For luck,' she said, and hooked her arm into his.

Lock took a deep breath and cursed – cursed his luck, cursed his life, but most of all he cursed Major Ross and his bloody White Tabs for getting him in this situation in the first place. He'd had enough of this hero work in China, little more than eight weeks previously. And that had proved to be a disaster. He was tired, he was angry, but most of all he was cold.

They ran.

As they reached the scarf, Lock, with his arm gripping Amy's delicate waist, hauled them both across the crevasse. He suddenly thought that they weren't going to make it. The pile of coats was too far away. Lock yelled, but they crossed the gap and landed in a heap about a foot from the nearest coat. He gave out a cry of pain and grabbed his knee, then lay still for a moment, breathing deeply and grinding his teeth. But it didn't matter; they'd made it.

Lock wiped the snow from his mouth and moved forward to help Amy to her feet. But just as she reached out to take hold of Lock's hand, the ground beneath her gave way. Lock lunged out, seizing Amy's wrist just in time, and fell forward. The crevasse below was a gaping black hole with no end that Lock could see and Amy, eyes wide with panic, was frantically kicking at the wall of blue ice trying to get a foothold. But the more she struggled the more Lock's grip on her tiny wrist slackened.

Lock strained to anchor his weight and punched his toes into the snow. As he tightened his grip on Amy, the sweat of the effort began to sting his eyes. He checked for the pursuers. Still no sign.

'I've got a foothold . . . pull!' Amy yelled out and Lock gritted his teeth and heaved. The muscles screamed in his arms with the effort, but he finally dragged the girl out of the crevasse and onto firmer ground.

Amy lay still, staring up at the white sky, gasping for air.

Lock scrambled to his feet and snatched up their coats. 'Miss, are you all right?' He shivered, quickly pulling his coat back about him and helping Amy on with hers.

Amy nodded and smiled weakly. She was shaking uncontrollably, but there was colour in her cheeks again. 'You could do with a shave, Mr Lock,' she said, rubbing her lips. 'And a haircut.'

'Come along.' Lock helped her up.

They staggered over to the boulders and crashed to the ground behind one of the rocks. Lock took the Browning out of his pocket and checked the magazine. It did only hold two bullets. He handed the gun to Amy.

'Stay here, miss.'

'Where . . . where are you going?'

'Just stay put. Please.' Lock got stiffly to his feet and hobbled away from the boulders, along to the wider edge of the crevasse.

Thankfully their leap hadn't caused the entire covering of snow to fall in on itself, and the crevasse was still hidden from view for most of its length. The snow continued to fall and with each passing minute it was making the dip look less and less defined. Lock hoped that it would stay that way. He followed the crevasse until he was a good fifty yards from where Amy was sheltering. He glanced back to her and could see her hat-covered head bobbing up above the edge of the boulders. Lock waved her down. When she didn't respond, Lock pointed off in the direction their pursuers were coming from. Amy looked over that way, then signalled her understanding and stooped down out of sight. Lock wrapped his scarf around his head and laid himself down in the snow and waited.

After a while, his ears rang as they strained to make out the approaching horses. But all he could hear was the sound of his heart pounding in his chest and the creaking of the snow underneath his body when he shifted his weight. Every few minutes he wiped the snow from his eyes and tried to see into the blankness ahead. How long before he became snow-blind and couldn't see a bloody thing in front of his eyes? What did they call it? White-out?

He could feel the cold seeping into his bones, though, and worried that when the moment came he would be too numb to move. He turned his head and stopped still. About a hundred yards ahead of him, emerging out of the whiteness, were three horses.

Lock rubbed the snow from his eyes again. The riders were definitely Turks. He could now make out that all three wore the distinctive kabalak hats of the Ottoman cavalry, as well as the huge shaggy fur coats that were common among Anatolian peasants.

Lock knew that the riders couldn't see him. Not yet, anyhow, not with the heavy snowfall. And he must be well camouflaged by now, too. Just let them get a little closer, he thought. But not so close, that they would spot the crevasse.

Just a few more yards.

Now!

Lock burst to his feet, yelling. The lead horse whinnied in surprise and reared up on its hind legs. But its rider was an expert and, with a yank of the reins, immediately brought his steed under control again.

Lock fled as best he could, first to the side, and then away, away from the crevasse. He prayed that his plan would work and that his knee wouldn't give out.

He turned his head to see the two lead riders kicking their heels into their horses' flanks. They shouted into the wind and galloped towards him. The third rider was trying to steady his horse as he raised his rifle. Lock knew it would be a difficult shot as the wind and snow were buffeting him from behind, so he just ran on as best he could. He stole a glance over his shoulder just as the third rider pulled the trigger. Lock saw the weapon kick back but he felt no impact and heard no whistle from a passing bullet. The rider thrust his rifle back into its saddle holster and with a kick of his heels set off in pursuit of his comrades. Lock lumbered on. He looked back again just in time to see the first two horses step onto the covered crevasse. The ground beneath them collapsed and they vanished in a cloud of white powder. There was no sound, no shouts, no screams, nothing. Just one minute they were there, then the next they were gone.

Lock stood still, his lungs burning as he gasped for breath.

The third horse pulled up sharply and reared, its rider desperately dragging back on its reins. He peered down into the abyss before him, then up at Lock. He shouted something, but it was snatched away by the wind. Then, turning about, he trotted a little away to his left, until he came to the point at which the crevasse became narrower. He glared across at Lock again then turned the horse, went back a few paces, turned again and charged forward.

Lock ran in great galumphing strides, swinging the leg with the injured knee swiftly out to the side, hurrying back towards the cover of the boulders and to Amy's precious pistol. He checked over his shoulder once more. The pursuer's horse gave a great whinny and, in one graceful movement, leapt across the crevasse.

Lock stopped. To continue to run was pointless. He'd never make it back to the rocks now. He pulled out his empty Webley and, brandishing the revolver like a club, turned full on to face the horseman. 'Come on then, you bastard!'

The rider drew his sword, extended the blade and charged forward.

Lock could smell the musky, rank stench of the rider's fur coat now and the stale, acrid saddle sweat of the horse as it thundered towards him. He waited until it was less than a foot away, then at the last moment swung the Webley at the Turk's leg and dived to one side. The horse's front hooves barely missed him. Lock caught a glimpse of the Turk's blade swinging down in a low, sweeping arc, and felt a blow to his stomach.

Lock sprawled heavily to the ground. He felt as if all the wind had been knocked out of him. He was lucky; the horse's rear leg had caught him, not the rider's sword.

He lay dazed on the frozen ground. Snow fell onto his face and he tried to catch his breath. In the distance he could hear thunder. He turned his head.

The horse was coming again. Lock cursed and forced his body up. Pain seared through his injured knee, but he ignored it. He had to get to his feet. He raised the Webley once more.

A gunshot cracked through the air and Lock instinctively ducked. Then, with the horse no more than a few feet away from him again, a second gunshot rang out and the rider arched his back and fell forward in his saddle. The horse slowed to a trot and as it careered off to the left, Lock could see Amy standing, legs astride, with the raised pistol in her hands.

'Miss? Miss!' Lock shouted, stumbling towards her. She was beginning to sway unsteadily. Just as Lock got to her she let the pistol fall from her grip, her eyes rolled back in her head and her knees gave way. Lock caught her and laid her carefully down.

'Miss? Miss?' Lock brushed the hair from Amy's ashen face. 'Miss?' His eyes fell on her pale, chapped lips. He hesitated, then leant forward and kissed them lightly.

'Amy?'

Lock glanced back at the horse. It was standing still and shivering, head stooped, its dead rider collapsed beside it, one foot still caught in a stirrup. Lock lay Amy carefully down and made his way over to the horse, making gentle cooing noises as he approached. The horse raised its head and snorted nervously, but Lock reached out and caught its bridle. The horse tried to pull away. Lock held firm and stroked its muzzle reassuringly. 'There, boy. Steady, steady.'

The horse calmed and Lock edged around to its flank, gathered the reins and yanked the dead rider's foot from the stirrup. He stripped the rider of his thick coat, then turned the horse about, and walked it over to Amy. Lock helped the girl to an upright position, wrapped the dead Turk's coat about her, and then gathered her in his arms.

Amy's eyes flickered open. 'Hello.' Her voice was barely a whisper.

'Hello, you,' Lock said softly.

'Did I get him?'

'Yes, yes you did.'

Amy smiled weakly. 'You're right, Mr Lock. It is different to shooting a squirrel.'

'You did what you had to, miss.'

'Did I?'

'Yes. You saved my life.'

With an effort Lock raised Amy up onto the horse and then climbed up behind her. He clicked his tongue and turned the horse about and trotted away from the crevasse.

'I feel so . . . dizzy,' Amy said.

'We need to get that foot seen to,' Lock said. 'It may be infected.'

Amy pressed her head against Lock's chest and sighed softly. 'Mr Lock?'

'Yes?'

'Do you have a Christian name?'

'Kingdom.'

'Kingdom?'

'Yes, miss.'

Amy fell silent again and Lock wondered if she had passed out. But then the girl stirred. 'I like it,' she said. 'May I call you "Kingdom"?'

'Yes, miss.'

'And you must call me "Amy".'

'Yes, miss.'

The horse trotted on.

'Kingdom?'

'Yes?'

'Did I faint?'

'Yes, miss.'

'Oh, how embarrassing,' she said.

The horse snorted a protest, its hot breath steaming out of its nostrils and Lock thought that was ample comment. He leant forward and patted its neck reassuringly.

'Kingdom?'

'Miss?'

'Did you just kiss me?'

Lock didn't reply straight away, he just continued to concentrate on the snowy landscape ahead of him. He thought about not telling her, if it was best that he didn't tell the truth. But then he realised he needn't worry. She had passed out again.

'Yes, miss,' he said. 'I believe I did.'

CHAPTER ONE

Karachi
Twelve weeks later

The horse-drawn carriage turned into a sweeping gravel-lined drive and jarred to a halt directly opposite the main entrance of an imposing Victorian residence. All of the homes were grand in the Clifton district of Karachi, but this particular one was a palace. It was one of those Anglo-Indian constructions built in the early days of the Raj, and, as appeared to be the fashion, was lit up like an opera house. The carriage door opened and Kingdom Lock stepped stiffly down onto the greasy path. The rain had eased off and the chilly night air was carrying the sickly sweet aroma of spices and tea up from the distant docks. Lock brushed his hand through his thick, sandy hair and placed his dark-brown fur felt fedora on his head. He handed a coin up to the driver, who bobbed his head with thanks, and watched as the carriage rattled its way back around the drive. Lock glanced up at the sky. The stars were beginning to show through the thinning clouds and there was an ominous sickle moon glowing to the east. He smiled softly to himself: even the gods saw fit to constantly remind him of the Turks and the threat of the Ottoman Empire.

'We shall see,' he muttered and turned to the house.

Outside the front door, at the top of a set of stone steps, two sepoy sentries were standing erect under a pair of yellow gas lamps. They were as oblivious of the cloud of moths and crickets that danced above their heads as the insects were of the certain death offered by the flickering flames. Both soldiers were dressed in long red parade tunics, with blue trousers tucked into white spats, and on their heads they wore the distinctive pagri wrapped around a khulla cap. They didn't even give Lock a second glance as he ascended the steps. Before he even got to the top, the main door opened and a smiling Indian servant greeted him with a bow.

'Good evening, sahib.'

Lock pulled an invitation card from his dinner-jacket pocket and handed it over to the servant. 'I'm a little late. Took me an age to find a carriage in this rain.'

'Very good, sahib. Welcome.'

Lock stepped inside and removed his hat. 'Take good care of that, won't you?' he said, handing it to the servant.

'If you will kindly follow me please, sahib.'

The servant led the way across a cool and dark entrance hall. Opulent portraits of forgotten dignitaries and unmemorable royals gazed down on them from high up on the walls. Their footsteps echoed loudly as they crossed the stone floor and made their way past a grand marble staircase and over towards a set of highly polished wooden double doors. Lock could hear muffled voices and soft music from the other side.

'Have I missed dinner?'

'Not dinner, sahib, a buffet,' the servant replied, and he opened the double doors.

A rotund, bewhiskered regimental sergeant major, resplendent in dress uniform, greeted Lock with a stiff nod of his head. He took the invitation card from the servant and turned to the grand room before him. He cleared his throat and bellowed in a rich voice that held the merest hint of a Teesside lilt, 'Mr Kingdom Lock.'

A few eyes looked across to see the late arrival, but most of the guests continued with their light chatter.

Lock waited by the doorway at the top of three wide steps that led down into what he presumed was a ballroom. There were about fifty people there, of all ages, and all dressed in their finery. The majority of the men were uniformed officers, with bright polished buttons and shining leather belts. The women were a dazzle of satin, silk and sparkling jewellery. A ripple of laughter floated across the room like a wave on a sandy shore. A band was over in the far corner playing light classical music, but it was nothing Lock recognised. Here and there a waiter wafted through the throng with a tray of filled glasses balanced on their upturned hand.

Lock adjusted his bow tie, and was about to descend the steps, when a sudden voice called from amongst the crowd.

'Kingdom! Kingdom!'

Lock stopped and looked up. Amy Townshend was weaving her way through whispering couples and gossiping groups. She put her hand up and waved, calling again as she pushed her way politely on. Lock raised his hand in recognition, and descended the steps. The nearest people to him, a middle-aged British colonel with a yellow-grey walrus moustache and his sour-faced, overweight wife, gave him a disapproving glance, but Lock ignored them and moved on towards the approaching Amy.

The girl, a vision of pink silk and lace, her auburn hair piled deliberately on top of her head, was slightly out of breath when she reached him, and threw her arms unashamedly around his neck. 'Oh, I'm so very pleased to see you!' she beamed, embracing him tightly. There were a few disapproving glances and mutters from those guests nearest them.

Lock gently pulled Amy away from him. 'Miss . . .'

Amy caught the embarrassed look on his face and laughed. 'Oh, tosh! Don't let these stuffed shirts bother you. I don't care! They're not *my* guests. I'm just so pleased *you* came.'

'Well, I promised you, didn't I?'

Amy scowled, as she looked Lock up and down. 'You look very handsome in that . . . dinner suit . . . However, I just bet you'd look even more dashing in uniform.'

'Now, miss, let's not spoil the evening.'

'Well, *I'll* have a uniform soon. I'm to be a nurse.'

'Really?'

Amy nodded. 'I've signed up with the VAD. Father isn't happy about it, but *maman* supports me. She's a nurse, too, well, a sister actually. And we must all do our bit, *mustn't* we, Mr Lock?'

'Amy . . .' Lock warned. He wanted to advise her not to go against her father's wishes, that he had done something similar at her age, nearly ten years previously, and still regretted it. But now wasn't the moment, and she wouldn't listen to him anyway. It was the girl's party, her birthday, and she looked happy. In fact, if he was honest, she looked absolutely beautiful.

'Here, perhaps this will suffice?' He fished a small packet out of his pocket and handed it to her. 'Happy birthday.'

Amy narrowed her eyes suspiciously and tore open the box. She paused, then burst out laughing.

'Oh, how very sweet, a tin soldier. Thank you, Kingdom, I shall treasure it.'

'Well, you do go on about men in uniform. So now you will always have one.'

'You are a tease, Kingdom.' Amy's face broke into a smile.

'So, how is your foot?'

'Well, I avoided the celebratory party upon my triumphant return, as you so astutely predicted. But it's better now, thank you.'

'For dancing?' Lock smiled.

'Yes. For dancing. Shall we get a drink?'

Lock nodded. 'A splendid suggestion.'

'Come along, then,' Amy said, grabbing his hand and pulling him back through the crowd.

Amy smiled sweetly at a white-haired general who was muttering with two other uniformed officers and a smartly dressed Indian merchant as she and Lock weaved by. Lock nodded affably, but was met with cold, steely stares.

'I don't know who half these people are, you know,' Amy called back to Lock.

'What about your beau? Is he around?'

'Who, Casper? Somewhere. His regiment is off to Mesopotamia the day after tomorrow, so all his chums are here having a last hurrah, too,' Amy said, as she continued to lead Lock towards the far end of the ballroom where a small group of officers, ladies and merchants were gathered around a tall and suave older officer.

'There's Father,' Amy said, 'holding court as usual. No doubt telling another of his *boring* stories about his and *maman*'s social circle back home in Paris. At least he hasn't brought out his banjo. Well, not yet. It's still early.'

'Banjo? Are you being serious?'

Amy nodded. 'Deadly.'

One of the officers, a stocky man in his forties, with a dark, round face and a thick chevron moustache, who was standing to the right of Amy's father, caught Lock's eye and gave the subtlest of nods.

'Do you know Major Ross?' Amy said.

'Oh, yes,' Lock said. 'He's the man who asked me to get you out of Constantinople. I wouldn't have come if I'd known he was going to be here.'

'Oh. Well, in that case, let's steer you away and find Casper. I've told him all about you.'

'Good idea. But I'm afraid we're too late, he's coming over.'

'Bother.' Amy put on a false smile and waited for Ross to get to them.

'Ah, Lock, there you are!' beamed Ross. '*Mademoiselle* Amy, many happy returns. And may I say you are looking divine tonight?' He raised the glass of champagne he held in his hand.

'You may, Major, thank you.' Amy gave a short, mocking curtsy. 'But I have been eighteen for nearly a whole week now.'

'How's the knee, Lock?' Ross said, his voice soft with a subtle Scottish accent.

Amy put her hand to her mouth. 'Oh, *mon dieu*, Kingdom. How rude of me,' she said. 'I never even thought to ask.'

'It's quite all right,' Lock smiled. 'On the mend. A little stiff in the evenings, that's all.'

'Jolly good,' Ross said, and turned to Amy. 'Do you mind awfully if I borrow Mr Lock for a moment?'

Amy glanced at Lock and tried to conceal her disappointment.

'I shan't keep him long . . .' Ross said.

Amy smiled politely. 'For a moment then, Major.'

Ross bowed his head and Lock watched as Amy weaved her way through the blur of uniforms and dresses, and over to the French doors on the far side of the band, where a number of young officers were chatting to some young ladies. She was a lovely creature and it troubled him that he thought so. He really had believed that his passion had died on that field in Tsingtao when he watched his love die in his arms. Was he really ready to embark on the chase again? So soon.

'Glad you made it tonight, Lock. I was beginning to worry about you. It's been nearly three months. Did you not get my messages?'

Lock turned to face the major, surprised at how annoyed he felt at being distracted from his thoughts. He grabbed a glass of champagne from a passing waiter's tray.

'I've been busy.'

'Have you, indeed?' Ross narrowed his hazel eyes, looking after Amy, and sipped at his champagne. He took hold of Lock's arm and indicated over to Townshend and his audience. 'There are some very important men here tonight, Lock. You'd do well to take note.'

'I came here to see Amy.'

Ross ignored his remark. 'You see that short, balding fellow with the silver moustache and irritable, impatient eyes?' he continued. 'That's Lieutenant General Sir John Nixon. He's the

Commander-in-Chief of India's Southern Command. And the distinguished-looking chap next to him, with the chiselled face and bushy moustache? That's Lieutenant General Sir Percival Lake. He's the man London have sent over to protect our oil interests in Basra.'

'I have no oil interests in Basra,' Lock said.

'Tisk, Lock. Be quiet and listen,' Ross said, 'you may learn something. He's here to finalise negotiations with the Shah over buying up the majority stock in the Anglo-Persian Oil Company before the Russians and the Germans get too influential. Russia I'm not so worried about, but Germany's on the march, as you well know, and the bloody Shah' – Ross paused and raised his glass to a passing major – 'is totally incapable of keeping foreign intrusions at bay.'

'Foreign?' Lock said. 'Like His Britannic Majesty's representatives?'

Ross shot Lock an irritated glance. 'It's not a matter to be trifled with, Lock, the future of our nation is at stake. Lake is ambitious and I've heard rumour he'll be staying on as the new Commander-in-Chief of the Indian army. It's hard to keep up, but one thing's for certain, oil is going to be the new power base, Lock, in this troubled world of ours, and I have my suspicions about this bloody war.'

'Meaning?'

'The assassination of the Archduke Ferdinand.'

Lock choked on his champagne and coughed.

'You can't be serious?'

'Think about it. Take him, over there.'

'Who?' Lock looked in the direction the major had jerked his chin. It was at the only person, beside himself, who wasn't in uniform or native dress. He was a rather grey, sallow-faced man in his mid-to-late forties, clean-shaven, and wearing round spectacles perched on a straight, thin nose. 'The gentleman in the dinner suit, with the glasses?'

Ross pursed his lips. 'Yes. Lord Shears . . . A bit of a mystery, really. So far, all I know is that he's an oil tycoon, Anglo-Persian's man. I wager he's here to ensure that APOC maintains its interests in the region, no matter who wins the war. They're only interested in self-preservation. He arrived on the steamer from the Cape with a letter of introduction from Lord Crewe himself, and it is not just any old businessman that has references from the Secretary of State for India, Lock. He's apparently "to advise" as to the best way to protect the oilfields on Abbadan Island and the pipeline that runs through neutral Persia. He has a lot of influence with the government in London, more so than Sir Percival, in fact. But I do know for certain that he'll be travelling with us to Basra.'

'Excuse me?' Lock turned in surprise to Ross.

But before he could get a reply, General Townshend broke away from his conversation and stepped forward and held out his hand to Lock.

'Major, is this him, is this your man?' he beamed, looking at Lock with a glint in his eye. His voice was velvety and warm, with no hint of an accent, just pure aristocratic English.

'Major General Townshend, may I introduce Mr Kingdom Lock,' Ross said.

'Delighted, sir, absolutely delighted,' the general said, pumping Lock's hand. 'I don't know where to begin to thank you for getting Amy out of that damned internment camp. You saved her life, Mr Lock.'

'She actually saved mine, sir,' Lock said.

The general gave a chuckle of laughter and patted Lock on the shoulder, and continued to shake his hand. 'She's her father's daughter all right. A crack shot and a stubborn streak as long as the Lyari River. Just like her mother.' He turned and called back to his wife, 'Alice, *chérie, s'il te plaît*!'

A handsome woman dressed in pale green excused herself from the group and glided over to the general's side. She was a little younger than her husband, tall and slender, with a soft, rounded face framed by lightly curled brown hair that, like her daughter's, was piled up upon her head. Lock could see Amy's beauty in her mother's face, the same piercing emerald eyes full of mischief and determination.

'Alice, this is the young man who rescued our darling child from the lair of the enemy.'

Lady Alice held out her hand. Lock wasn't sure if he should shake it or kiss it, but Lady Alice just held his grip and studied him intensely. He returned her gaze, and what he saw there was genuine warmth.

'Mr Lock, Amy has told me so much about your gallantry,' she said, her French accent as soft and delicate as a waterfall. 'I am indebted to you, as is my husband, for returning her safely to us.'

'Well, my lady, I think the Turks were rather glad to get shot of her, to be honest. I know I was.' Lock bowed his head.

There was a moment's awkward silence and then Townshend slapped his thigh and laughed. Lady Alice smiled brightly and was about to say something more when Amy burst forward with a young blond officer in tow.

'Here he is! Kingdom . . . I mean, Mr Lock, I'd like you to meet Lieutenant Casper Bingham-Smith.'

'Lieutenant Smith.' Lock held out his hand.

The blond lieutenant was tall and slim. Lock was immediately impressed with how fit he looked and guessed he rode regularly, probably hunted, and perhaps he did a little boxing, too. His face, though admittedly handsome, had a certain cruelness about the eyes. 'It's *Bingham*-Smith, actually,' he said, looking down his nose at Lock, 'with a hyphen.'

'Casper,' Amy hissed, 'don't be so rude.'

Lock lowered his hand. 'A hyphen. You must be so proud?'

'I note you're not in uniform, Lock?' Bingham-Smith said.

'Very observant of you,' Lock said.

'Too good for the military are we, Lock?'

'Casper, stop it,' Amy insisted.

'May I ask you something . . . personal, Mr Lock?' Bingham-Smith said, ignoring Amy's pleas. Lock shrugged. His patience was wearing thin, but he let the insolent young officer continue, having seen his manner was affecting Amy and her opinion of her so-called fiancé-to-be. A selfish act, perhaps, but one worth playing out.

'Your eyes . . .'

'Casper!' Amy growled.

'What about them?' Lock said curtly.

Bingham-Smith snorted. 'Don't be like that. I'm sure we've all been dying to ask. I've never seen eyes two different colours before – not in a person, that is. It's heterochromia, isn't it?'

Lock nodded.

'There was a mangy old sheepdog in our village . . .'

Bingham-Smith paused, frowning. 'And I do believe Alexander the Great had the . . . erm, similar . . . eyes, I mean . . .' he smiled, insincerely. 'Is it a birth defect?'

Lock didn't reply straight away, sensing the growing discomfort amongst the small group, but also noting that they were all waiting for his answer.

'No. A fight. When I was a boy.'

Bingham-Smith nodded his head. 'A scrapper, eh? What did you do?'

'Do?' Lock said.

'To the person' – Bingham-Smith waved his hand in front of his own eyes – 'who did it?'

'Set fire to his bed.'

'What!?' Bingham-Smith spat. There was a murmur of surprise from the others, but Lock noted how uncomfortable Amy seemed, and he suddenly regretted letting the line of questioning get this far.

'Did you . . . kill him?'

'No, Lieutenant. Bastard wasn't in it at the time. More's the pity.'

Bingham-Smith was about to add something else when the general stepped in.

'I think, Amy, you and Casper should return to your friends,' Townshend said. 'Mr Lock and I have some business to discuss.'

Bingham-Smith cleared his throat and glanced nervously at the general. 'Only jesting, sir,' he said. 'I'm jolly grateful to Mr Lock for rescuing my Amy.' He held his hand out.

Lock took it graciously, but it was limp and clammy and the look in Bingham-Smith's grey-blue eyes was one of contempt.

'Monsieur Lock, I really cannot thank you enough for bringing our eldest back safe and sound,' Alice said, trying to lighten the prickly atmosphere. 'If there is anything Charles or I can ever do to repay you, then do not hesitate to ask.'

Lock shifted his attention from Bingham-Smith and smiled at Lady Alice.

'Just doing my duty, ma'am.'

Bingham-Smith snapped a quick salute to the general, and taking Amy by the arm, gently, but firmly, escorted her away.

'Casper, how could you be so rude?' Amy fumed.

'If you'll excuse me, too, Monsieur Lock, I must continue to circulate,' Lady Alice said. 'Perhaps I will see you a little later? I have a small token of gratitude to give to you.'

Lock bowed his head again. 'I'd be delighted, ma'am.'

'Yes, quite right,' Townshend said. 'You'll have to forgive young Casper, Lock. Can't be easy for him. All Amy talks about is you. I think he's feeling a tad inadequate.'

Lock gave a non-committal grunt, as he watched the young couple get swallowed up by the crowd. 'I thought your daughter had better taste, sir.'

Townshend frowned. 'Major, if you'd care to escort Mr Lock to the library, I'll join you directly.'

Ross nodded and, placing a hand on Lock's arm, led him in the opposite direction.

The library was dimly lit and smelt faintly of stale cigars and brandy. Books lined every wall from floor to ceiling. There was a drinks trolley next to a pair of deep and inviting worn blood-red leather armchairs. An oak table stood between them, empty except for a leather-bound folder and a green-shaded reading lamp that spilt a circle of light into the shadows. Opposite was a marble fireplace. A fire was burning away in the open grate. Ross made his way to the drinks trolley and poured himself a glass of brandy, then went and stood beside the fire. Lock was scanning the shelves. He pulled one large volume out, a blue leather-bound book with gold lettering on the spine, and opened it. An elegant carriage clock set on the mantle chimed the hour. Lock was surprised to see that it was ten o'clock.

'Do you like Napoleon?'

Lock looked over as General Townshend came into the room.

'I remember your daughter telling me about his strategies, sir.' Lock closed the book and put it back on the shelf.

The padded library door made a soft click as Townshend closed it behind him. 'Yes, Amy may be a trifle . . . free-spirited, but she's got a head for military manoeuvres. Not like her younger sister, Audrey. She's just obsessed with society and marriage.' The general drifted off for a moment, staring into space. 'Amy should have been a boy really,' he mumbled, then clearing his throat, he focused back on his two guests.

'Well, gentlemen, sorry to have kept you, got cornered by that Shears chap. Right, a drink and then let's get down to business.' He rubbed his hands together and walked over to the trolley, fixed himself a brandy and soda, picked up the leather-bound folder, and went to stand next to Ross. 'Have you told him?'

'No, sir,' Ross said.

'Hmm. Now, Lock, the major has filled me in on your background,' Townshend said. He placed his glass on the mantle, opened up the folder and started to leaf through the papers within. 'You were born in . . . Australia? Really? You don't have an accent.'

'I was brought up in India and schooled in Somerset, sir.'

'You joined the army at sixteen,' Townshend read, 'the British army, and were with the British exhibition to Tibet and fought under Major Younghusband at Lhasa in 1904 . . .' He looked up as if for confirmation. Lock nodded. 'Promoted regularly until you made platoon sergeant . . . And then this.' Townshend shook his head slowly and tutted. 'Dishonourable discharge, and after such an exemplary record, too.'

'I was a young lad, sir,' Lock said.

'Not when you were kicked out, you weren't,' Townshend said.

'I was just twenty-one, sir, and, as I have explained to the major—'

'How old are you now?' Townshend interrupted.

'Twenty-six, sir.'

'Five years to gain maturity! Pah!'

'Sir, he's one of my best agents,' the major said.

Townshend chewed his lip thoughtfully and turned another page in Lock's file.

'You were working as a civil engineer,' he continued, 'supervising the laying of telegraph lines across Turkey, for the *Société Ottomane des Téléphones*, when the major recruited you into the White Tabs . . . is that correct?'

'Sir.'

'And then you had a stint in the Far East . . . Tsingtao?' Townshend raised a questioning eyebrow at Ross.

'It's a former German port on the east coast of China, sir.'

'Really? Never heard of it . . . and then you returned to Turkey after we had declared war on them . . . and what did you do?'

'I set about sabotaging the telegraph lines.'

'He also did a little snooping for us, sir, until he was asked to get your daughter out of Constantinople,' Ross said.

'Quite, but ther—'

'He has considerable experience, sir, that's what counts,' Ross said.

Townshend brushed his carefully manicured English moustache thoughtfully and stared at Lock. He was clearly attempting to give the illusion that he was mulling over what to do, even though Lock knew he had already decided. Otherwise, Lock told himself, he wouldn't be here. He remained cool and turned his gaze to the flames. The wood spat in the hearth and the clock softly ticked away the evening.

Townshend closed the folder and put it to one side. 'I've been discussing your situation with Major Ross, Lock. He insists that given your background, your knowledge of Turk and Arabic languages and their customs, having lived and worked amongst them for a number of years, not to mention my daughter's gushing tales of your resourcefulness in a tight spot,' Townshend smiled briefly, 'that you would be the perfect man for work . . .' He paused and glanced at Ross.

'. . . of a special nature,' the major said.

'More rescues? More snooping?' Lock said.

'Well, not exactly,' Ross said. 'We were thinking more about . . .'

'In the field?' Townshend offered.

'Precisely!' Ross said.

'What field would that be, sir?'

'You'll have to have some official status, of course,' Townshend said, ignoring Lock's insolence. 'So we thought a commission.

Besides, there's a war on and it would only have been a matter of time before you would have been called up.'

Lock was momentarily taken aback. 'But, sir, as you have already pointed out, what about my army past? Won't that be a problem?'

Townshend laughed. 'I don't mean in the British army. No, no, that would never do.' He paused once more and looked to Ross. 'The major and I feel it would be more prudent for you to be commissioned into the army of your birth nation. In case of . . .'

'Complications,' Ross said.

'I see, sir,' Lock said.

'So, you'll be part of the general's 6th Poonas and still be working for me,' Ross said. 'But in Australian uniform.'

'Well, Kingdom my boy, how does that sound? Interested?' Townshend raised an expectant eyebrow.

Lock didn't respond immediately. He just held the old man's gaze. He didn't want to join the army again, he'd had his fill of military service, of saluting. He liked the White Tab work, being his own boss, if he didn't count Ross. Besides, he was thinking of making a little trip home, back to Australia. To get away for a while, recuperate, take in the desert air of the outback. But then there was Amy and he suddenly realised everything had changed. For the first time since he lost Mei Ling in Tsingtao, he felt alive again, inside. And that was thanks to her, to Amy. He still felt the loss of the Chinese girl deeply, but the scars were healing. The war wasn't going anywhere soon and it was only a matter of time before it caught up with him. He looked to Ross, then back to Townshend. He was going to regret this, he thought, but what choice did he really have?

'Very well, General . . . sir, I accept.'

'Bravo, my lad, I knew you wouldn't let me down.'

The two men shook hands vigorously.

'When do I leave, General, sir?'

'Keen to get on, eh? That's the spirit! You'll have to watch this one, Major, eh?' he winked.

Ross nodded slowly. 'Aye, I already am.'

'Now, I know you have an army background, Lock,' Townshend said, 'but being an officer and a gentleman is a very different matter. There's an officer cadet training camp in—'

'Sir,' Ross said, 'I think we can dispense with all that nonsense. Lock is an experienced man, nearly five years' military service under his belt. It's all there in that folder you have. He's adept at weaponry, close-order drill, marksmanship, scouting, tracking, elementary tactics, and that sort of thing. Not to mention the last five years he's had with the *Société Ottomane*. Team leadership under pressure is a given. Besides, time is of the essence. You've said so yourself.'

'I . . .' Townshend was clearly uncertain, but from the look on Ross's face there was no argument to be had. 'Hmm . . . it's just not the done thing, Ross . . . Could cause a bit of an upset with the other young officers coming through, don't you think?'

'All the more reason for his commission into the AIF rather than a British regiment, sir. Better cover if – when – he bumps into other new officers who've never seen him at OTC,' Ross said, pulling an envelope from his breast pocket. He gave it to Lock. 'Here, it's official, signed and agreed to by General Bridges.'

Townshend plucked at his moustache. 'Very well, Major, but on your head be it.'

'Naturally, sir, isn't it always?' Ross knocked back his brandy and put the empty glass on the mantle. 'Well, sir, we must be off. A visit to the tailor's for young Lock here, and I have some paperwork to catch up on.' He held his arm out for Lock to lead the way out.

'Sir, I did promise Miss Amy a dance. She'll be very disappointed if I leave without even saying goodbye.'

'Won't be the first time, Lock, and it won't be the last,' Townshend said. 'And I think you've riled young Casper enough for one evening without whirling his girl around the dance floor to boot, what?' he grinned. 'I'll explain to Amy. She'll understand.'

'Very well, sir. Goodbye.' Lock, unsure whether to salute the general or not, half lifted his arm then dropped it again and followed Ross over to the door. He would get a message to Amy later, arrange to meet her before he set sail.

'Oh, and Lock . . .' Townshend called after him.

Lock stopped and turned. 'Sir?'

'Go see a barber and posh up, there's a good chap! Even Bridges' Australian Infantry Force has standards, I believe. Chin-chin!' He raised his brandy glass in salute.

Lock smiled wryly and followed the major out.

CHAPTER TWO

Two days later, Lock felt strangely self-conscious as he approached the wharf, dressed as he was in officer's service dress, consisting of a pale khaki shirt and an irritatingly restrictive olive-drab necktie, a dark-khaki open-collar tunic, light-coloured cord breeches with brown leggings and ankle boots. As well as the smart sunburst badge and the Mendips' three hills on each collar point, both arms bore the bronze shoulder title 'Australia' and his shoulder straps the single brass pips of his rank. The patches below them were a bit of a mish-mash, however, being the plain block of purple signifying the 1st Div. Engineers, as a nod to his civil engineering experience in Turkey, but with an additional white square, for the White Tabs, in the centre. It would add a little confusion, Ross said, but would also stop any cases of mistaken identity. Lock doubted this greatly, but what did it really matter? He was just another young officer amongst many. He tossed his half-smoked cigarette aside, hitched his haversack up on his shoulder, and adjusting his slouch hat, followed the train tracks that ran the full length of the dock to the towering cranes in the distance.

As Lock strode on, his mind drifted to Amy. He had tried to see her, get word to her, but all his efforts had been blocked. She either wasn't at home, had gone sailing, or he had just missed her. If he didn't know better, he would say she was avoiding him. He had left countless messages, but all had gone unanswered. Surely she couldn't have been that angry at him for leaving her party without saying goodbye, for not giving her that promised dance? And now time had run out.

Lock walked on and to his left, looming large, black smoke billowing out of its two funnels, was the monstrous form of the RIMS *Lucknow*, the 650-foot-long, 19,500-ton troopship with steam turbines and three propellers that would be steaming him to Basra and the war. All along its length was a hive of activity as Arab and Indian dockhands worked the cranes and pulleys, busily loading supplies into the ship's hull. And stretched out before Lock, surrounded by piles and piles of trunks, kitbags and sacks, milled hundreds of British and Indian troops. They were doing nothing more than hanging around, waiting. Some were smoking and laughing, others just sitting quietly, eyes wide as they took in the sheer mass of the *Lucknow*, noses flaring at the heady mix of brine, coal and oil. And despite the early hour, the air tingled with a mood of anticipation. Lock caught snatches of conversation as he wormed his way through the men, most of it relating to rumours about Indian troops from Egypt and France having been ordered to Mesopotamia, and whether or not there were German officers in Baghdad.

Lock moved on towards a large stone warehouse situated to the right of the wharf. It had been converted into a makeshift embarkation hall and inside it was claustrophobic, moist and fetid, heavy with the stench of sweat, tobacco and gun oil. He followed the moving crowd and made his way to the far side where there was a row of wooden desks. Soldiers and low-ranking officers were queuing up waiting for their papers to be checked. Lock joined the officers' line and waited patiently for his turn. When he got to the front he put his haversack down and was greeted by a gruff sergeant with cropped grey hair and a neatly trimmed bristle moustache. Lock tried to lighten the mood by asking the sergeant if there was hot water in his cabin.

The sergeant didn't even smile. 'Very funny, sir. Haven't heard that one before,' he said, holding his hand out for Lock's orders.

A couple of regular Tommies lounging nearby laughed at the sergeant's sarcasm, but swiftly went about their own business when Lock caught their eye.

'Lock, K., Second Lieutenant, AIF . . . Hmm . . . attached to the 2nd Mendip Light Infantry . . . Ah, yes. Here we are, sir. Compass flat. Sign here.' The sergeant held out a dip pen and swivelled a thick ledger round for Lock to put his signature next to his name on the immaculately written list.

Lock dipped the nib in the bottle of ink on the desk. His hand hovered over his name. 'Compass flat?' Lock knew the journey up the Persian Gulf to Basra would take about six days, and the prospect of spending it all out in the open didn't thrill him in the slightest.

The sergeant cleared his throat. 'Compass flat, right at the top, behind the funnel, that's for NCOs and officers under the rank of major, sir. Most of the ordinary soldiers will be on the forecastle and upper deck, some on the saloon decks, and some in the hold. The top brass, they get the promenade deck, mid-ranking officers the boat deck up to the midships, then the aft of the boat deck and the saloon deck, including the poop deck, that's for the lasses.' This was clearly a conversation the sergeant was well versed in.

'Lasses?'

'VAD, sir, nurses for the military hospital. The best cabins, all gone to the top brass, as well.' He leant forward a little. 'That Lord Shears has taken two.'

Lock held the sergeant's gaze for a moment, then flashed a smile and scribbled his signature. 'Of course. Thank you, Sergeant.'

He handed the pen back, picked up his haversack and moved away. He stopped and turned back, much to the irritation of the lanky British captain who was next in line. 'Excuse me a moment,' Lock said to the officer. 'By the way, Sergeant, has Major Ross, political officer, boarded yet?'

The sergeant glanced back at his ledger, running his finger down the alphabetised names. 'Yes, sir. He signed in an hour ago. You'll find him on the promenade deck, sir, cabin 22.'

Lock gave the sergeant a jovial salute with a finger, nodded his apologies to the captain, and made his way back out of the embarkation hall. As he crossed the wharf, Lock spotted a shiny black motor car parked beside the gangplank. When he got to within a few feet of the vehicle, the driver's door opened and a uniformed chauffeur, a man in his late sixties with a flushed complexion and watery eyes, stepped out. He turned and opened the rear passenger door. From the darkness within a familiar voice called out.

'Kingdom?'

Lock stopped in his tracks. 'Amy?' He peered into the passenger compartment and the chauffeur stepped discreetly aside.

Amy's face loomed out of the shadows, radiating warmth, all smiles and sparkling eyes. 'You left without saying goodbye, without giving me that dance you promised,' she chastised.

Lock grinned down at her. 'I'm sorry. My knee was giving me trouble.'

'Nonsense,' Amy said. 'You left because of Casper. How that boy infuriates me, sometimes. He was so rude to you.'

'Yes, he was a little curt,' Lock said. 'But jealousy will do that to a man.'

Amy scoffed. 'I'm beginning to have second thoughts about him. Here.' She held out her hand and Lock helped her to step out of the automobile.

'I don't believe it!' Lock said, looking her up and down.

Amy was dressed as a VAD nurse, in a dress of mid blue with a stiff white collar and cuffs, a white apron with the distinctive red cross on the chest, a stiff white cap and a navy greatcoat.

'Don't act so surprised, I told you I'd signed up as a nurse. But look at you, a soldier. And so handsome, too.' She gave a stiff salute.

'I thought I'd upset you,' Lock said.

'Why on earth would you think that?'

'You never replied to any of my messages.'

Amy frowned. 'What messages? Damn my father, always interfering.'

'I see. But you're here now,' he smiled.

'I'm here because I'm sailing on this very ship with you.' She indicated over Lock's shoulder.

He turned and further down the quay he could see another

gangway where about fifty other VAD nurses, all dressed as Amy was, were milling about waiting to climb on board.

'I've been posted to the military hospital at Basra,' Amy said.

'Are you certain this is what you want? Running away is not the answer.'

'I'm not running away,' she snapped. 'It's my duty to go to war. As it is yours.'

Lock grabbed hold of her hand. 'I know more than you think. I lied about my age to join up, too. I know nurses are supposed to be twenty-three, to serve near the front lines, but I guess you managed to convince the right people. I was only sixteen when I ran away to war.'

Amy stared up into his eyes, and Lock could see the spark of anger had faded.

'Is that true?' she said.

'Yes, and I've regretted it ever since.'

'Why? What do you mean?'

'I'm in uniform again, something I vowed I'd never do.'

'But Kingdom, this war is too important . . . For all of us. Listen . . .

And only the Master shall praise us.
And only the Master shall blame.
And no one shall work for money.
No one shall work for fame.
But each for the joy of the working,
And each, in his separate star,
Shall draw the Thing as he sees It.
For the God of Things as They Are.

‘I memorised it,’ Amy said. ‘It’s a poem given to all nurses from Katharine Furse, the Commandant-in-Chief of the Women’s VAD. It’s very profound, don’t you think? Besides, how handsome you look, particularly in that hat.’ She paused, frowning. ‘It’s a strange uniform.’

‘Australian.’

‘Why, Mr Lock,’ Amy smiled, ‘you’re a colonial!’

Lock laughed. ‘And you’re wonderful.’

An awkward silence fell between them.

Lock glanced up at the ship and the faceless officers staring down at the wharf.

‘I had better be getting on board.’

Amy pulled Lock down to her, quickly looking to her left and right. She then kissed Lock fiercely, open-mouthed, and he found himself responding. She tasted wonderful and he felt his body tense with desire as their tongues met. He pulled away, despite wanting to pull her closer.

‘You’re a better kisser than Casper,’ she whispered.

Lock stared down into her pale emerald eyes, aflame with desire. He put his hand to her soft white cheek and pushed a loose strand of her hair behind her ear.

‘Miss, you’d better be getting along.’ It was the chauffeur. He was holding Amy’s haversack for her.

‘Yes, thank you, Hector.’ She turned back to Lock. ‘Perhaps I will see you on board?’

Lock nodded. It would be difficult. Nurses would be segregated, particularly with so many eager, lusty young men on board. But he liked a challenge. ‘Yes,’ he said. ‘Perhaps.’

She kissed him again, quickly, on the lips, stuffing something in his pocket, then taking her bag off Hector, hurried off towards her fellow nurses.

'Good luck, miss. Be safe.' Hector waved after her. Amy glanced back and smiled.

'She'll be all right,' Lock said.

Hector turned to face Lock and smiled. 'That I don't doubt, Mr Lock, sir. I've known Miss Amy all her life . . . headstrong, stubborn, if you don't mind me saying so, sir, and fiercely determined. Maybe it's the French part of her, from her mother. Her father was furious when the miss announced she'd joined the suffragette movement last year, and he's none too pleased about this little venture, I can tell you. Still, better a nurse than a soldier. She'd be in khaki if she could find a way.'

Lock laughed. 'Well, I must report myself.' He hoisted up his haversack. 'Goodbye.'

'Oh, Mr Lock, sir,' Hector called. 'Before you go, I have a message for you.'

'A message?'

'Yes, sir. From the general's wife, sir.' Hector handed Lock an envelope.

Now what? Lock thought as he put down his bag again and tore open the message. The note was short and had clearly been written in a hurry. The ink was smudged and it had been folded at an angle.

Dear M. Lock,

Amy is determined to go to war against her father's and my wishes. I know no matter what I do she will find a way, so I have arranged for her to be posted to the British Hospital at Basra. I shall be travelling to the same place myself at a later date, but I would ask you a great favour. Please watch out for her in the meantime. I know this is a lot to ask given your duties, but you have already proven yourself a more than capable guardian and I would ask you to be so again.

Je tiens à vous exprimer notre gratitude,

Lady Alice Townshend (née d'Anvers)

'Any reply, sir?' Hector asked.

Lock shook his head. It was ironic that he had been asked to look out for Amy. Guardian, indeed! If only Lady Alice knew his true feelings towards her daughter, would she still ask him then?

'Just tell Lady Alice that I will do what I can,' he smiled thinly.

'Very good, sir. The young miss has always been a handful, sir. But I can see that she likes you.'

Lock nodded, gathered up his bag and, stuffing the note in his pocket, made his way onto the gangplank.

'Good luck, sir,' Hector called and got back into the automobile. The engine coughed into life and Lock glanced over to the VADs. He couldn't make out Amy amongst so many similarly dressed young women, but he told himself he would find a way to see her later.

As he trotted up the gangplank leading to the saloon deck of the *Lucknow*, the sound of men singing filled the morning air.

We are Fred Karno's Army,
The Poona Infantry.
We cannot fight,
We cannot shoot,

What earthly use are we!
And when we get to Berlin,
The Kaiser he will say,
'Hoch, hoch! Mein Gott,
What a bloody fine lot are
The Poona Infantry!'

A cheer rose up and more voices joined in as the ditty was repeated. Lock watched the Townshend motor car pull away and manoeuvre slowly through the sea of troops. He then remembered that Amy had stuffed something in his pocket and putting his hand in, he pulled out a lace handkerchief. He pressed it to his nose, breathing in her scent. But as he turned from the gangway and stepped onto the deck, he bumped heavily into a soldier standing directly in his path, and dropped his haversack and the keepsake.

''Ere, 'ere, mind yerself!'

Lock could feel the goosebumps rise on his skin as he bent to pick up the handkerchief and his bag. He knew that voice from a lifetime ago, from a life he had buried, had forgotten, had hoped had forgotten him.

Sounds of gunfire, of burning buildings, of women and children screaming, of English voices jeering and egging others on filled his mind. And that voice, sneering and grunting.

'Oh, beg pardon, sir. Didn't see you was an officer.'

Lock slowly straightened up and lifted his head so that his face was out of the shadow thrown from the brim of his hat. The man he had collided with was a stiff, short, red-faced and bristly-whiskered sergeant major.

The NCO's eyes narrowed. He didn't say anything at first as he stared back into Lock's eyes, first the left and then the right. The corner of his mouth started to twitch, and then it broke into a sneer.

'Well, well, well. If it ain't Private bloody Lock,' he spat. 'Fancy seein' you 'ere.' His voice was trembling with barely controlled rage. 'Bet you thought I'd forgotten you?'

Lock held the NCO's glare. 'Corporal Underhill. How are you?'

Underhill thrust his chin forward. '*Sergeant Major* Underhill,' he hissed, spraying Lock with spittle, as he tapped the stripes on his upper arms.

Lock smiled thinly. '*Lieutenant* Lock.'

Underhill scowled and his eyes quickly took in Lock's uniform. His brow furrowed deeper still as his gaze rested on the 'Australia' flash on Lock's shoulder.

'No salute, Sergeant Major? How very . . . ill disciplined of you,' Lock said. 'I may have to put you on a charge.'

Underhill's eyes flicked up to Lock's. He was biting his lip and the vein on his forehead was throbbing.

Lock shook his head in mock disappointment and gave a deep sigh. Now wasn't the time to renew old acquaintances. Time enough during the voyage, and this little man wasn't worth the trouble. If he saw him again maybe he would settle old scores, maybe he would even kill him. But for now he had someone else he needed to talk to. So, he shouldered his haversack, stuffed Amy's handkerchief back in his pocket, pushed roughly past Underhill, and went in search of Ross.

Lock was seated in Ross's compact but comfortable cabin perched on top of the major's trunk, next to a tiny cabinet upon which rested a washbasin and water jug. A raised bunk with drawer space underneath ran the length of the wall opposite, directly beneath a small porthole. To the right was a racked shelving space full of books. Below this was a fold-down desktop, open, with one chair pushed underneath it. On the surface was a chessboard, an ashtray and, much to Lock's pleasure, a new bottle of rum and two glasses.

Ross closed the door and made his way over to the desk, pulling the chair out and sitting down. He frowned. 'Whatever's the matter? You look like you've seen a ghost.'

'I think I have,' Lock said.

Ross waited for Lock to elaborate. He didn't.

'You can smoke if you like. Rum?' Ross raised an eyebrow.

'Thank you, yes.'

Ross pulled the stopper from the bottle and poured out two generous measures. He handed Lock a glass then placed his tobacco pouch on the tabletop and began the ritual of filling his pipe.

'It's time I let you in on what our mission actually is,' Ross said.

Lock nodded. About bloody time too, he thought, as he lit a cigarette and tossed the match into the ashtray. 'Go ahead. Sir.'

'Johnny Turk is massing around Qurna, as you know. But I don't think they are just reinforcing their new border. Oh, no, they want their land back and the Germans want our oil . . .' He paused, taking a sip of his drink.

'A Turkish army left Amara, that's a little place on the banks of the Tigris in Mesopotamia, and set out east, marching across the border into Persia, according to Arab sources in the area,' Ross said.

'How reliable is the information?'

'That, as is always the case with our Arab friends, is open to question. But Command HQ has heard nothing from the British garrison in the area to corroborate it.' Ross lowered his voice and leant forward conspiratorially, as if worried that someone might be eavesdropping. 'Brigadier General Robinson has been assigned by the current head of the troops in Basra, General Barrett, to lead a reconnaissance-in-force to assess the situation in Persia. He's also to clarify whether the reports that there is a large Turkish and Arab army already gathered to the north of there are, in fact, true. Barrett wants Robinson's force to counter any invasion and to make sure the local Arabs, the ones we've been paying to guard the pipeline,' Ross said, 'don't switch sides . . . you know, join the Turks.'

Lock knocked back his rum and Ross leant over and topped him up again. He struck a match against the tabletop and lit his pipe. 'There is a man who I keep hearing about, a spy based somewhere in Persia. A Boche called Doctor Wilhelm Wassmuss. Do you know the name?' Lock didn't. 'He speaks Persian like a native,' Ross continued, 'and we believe that he is planning on working his way through the centre of the country, weaving his magic, fixing at pushing German influence in the area. If he succeeds in uniting the various warlords and tribes then we may as well pack up and forget this part of our empire for a hundred years. And if that happens, Lock, then our credibility in India will come tumbling down like a house of cards, too.' He stopped to let his words sink in.

Lock gazed down at his rum. 'So you're sending me after this man?'

'Precisely!' Ross said and sat back puffing away thoughtfully. 'You know, Lock,' he said after a brief pause, 'he's very similar to you.'

'Sir?'

'In his abilities, his proficiency with the Arab tongue, their customs.'

'I wouldn't say that, sir,' Lock said. Christ, Lock thought, he liked the Arab people, particularly the Kurds, but he wouldn't say he was any expert. He'd only lived and worked among them for five or so years.

'Come, come, stop being so modest,' Ross said. 'You are so similar to Wassmuss that I feel you are the ideal man to stop him. I believe you could get inside his head, think like him, feel like him. Yes, I admit that he appears to be always just out of reach, that elusive figure in your periphery vision, the fleeting glimpse, just a sense of a presence.'

'A ghost,' Lock said.

Ross nodded in agreement.

'The elusive pimpernel,' Lock added.

'Let's not get carried away. He's a villain, Lock, pure and simple. A jihadist with one aim, to destroy the British in the Middle East by hook, but mostly, I wager, by crook.'

'Do we know what he looks like?'

'No.'

'Do we know where he is?'

'No.'

'Jesus, Major, do we know anything?'

Ross sucked on his pipe and shrugged. 'Not a lot. But what I've gathered so far, and some of this has been corroborated by my men in the field, is that this Wassmuss devised a plan, a feasible and foolproof one, so the German High Command believe, and they've given him all the gold he needs to implement it.'

'Implement what?'

'To organise revolts. To bribe, blackmail and cajole the desert tribes of Persia. And not just here, but in Afghanistan and maybe even the North-West Frontier in India, too. All of Islam could be pulled into a holy war on the side of Germany and the Ottoman Empire. Total carnage.'

'But the British are really here because their navy, not to mention the German fleet, will be needing oil for their warships,' Lock said.

Ross smiled brightly. 'Bravo. Yes, and if the Head of the Admiralty is championing the need to secure the oilfields of Mesopotamia and Persia, then you can be damn well sure that it will be done.'

'Shears?'

'No, he's APOC's man. I mean Churchill. But yes, Shears is after the same end, I just doubt he's got Britain's interests at the top of his list.'

'You don't think Wassmuss is somehow connected to APOC do you? His activities I mean?'

Ross shook his head. 'I think not. He's Germany's man, after all, and as I said APOC want the oil for APOC, no matter which sovereign nation owns the land the oil spews from. Still, now you come to mention it . . .' Ross trailed off, and his face changed into a glazed expression.

'But, this uniform,' Lock said, pulling at his lapel, 'a good disguise, yes, but can I move freely among the troops? I doubt it, and I'll need to if I'm to track this Wassmuss down.'

'Quite so,' Ross smiled brightly. 'I'm setting up a special task force to enable you to do just that.' He paused. 'Well, within reason. The regiment you're going to be attached to as cover, the Mendip Light Infantry, is part of General Townshend's new division, the 6th Poona. It's a small, private regiment raised around the time of the Boer War by some pompous ass called Godwinson, a self-promoted lieutenant colonel who just so happens to be a wealthy landowner in that district of Somerset.' Ross puffed on his pipe again before continuing. 'If you're unlucky, you'll get to meet him one day. But the good news is that I've been given the Mendips to enable us to do the job properly.

'Now, the 2nd Battalion of the Mendips were all but wiped out recently at Qurna, and their 1st Battalion, back in England, has been earmarked for France. Therefore, new recruits and replacements for the 2nd were made up from other decimated units in the Basra theatre, or recruited from India. While you were rescuing that fair maiden from the evil Turk, I was reinforcing the 2nd Battalion and securing the authority to use it for White Tab work. I have a difficult job to do, Lock,' he said, jabbing his pipe forward, 'keeping one step ahead of Johnny Turk and his Arab conspirators, and the Mendip Light Infantry are going to jolly well help me do that job properly.'

'An army of spies?' Lock smiled to himself.

Ross shook his head. 'The battalion is still a military one under Godwinson's command. But I plan to influence its direction and to use a company from within its ranks when and where I need to.'

Lock took a deep draw on his cigarette and shrugged. 'So where do we start?'

'We'll get to Basra and then head north, past Qurna, up the Tigris,' Ross said. 'It's as good a place as any to begin.'

'We?' Lock raised an eyebrow in surprise.

'I shall be accompanying you part of the way. I just doubt I will be taking an active part in the field. More observation.' Ross's face turned serious. 'But for now we have more important matters to sort.' He leant forward, pulled the chessboard towards him and began arranging the pieces. 'Black or white?' he said with a wry smile.

CHAPTER THREE

It was a good few hours later when Lock pulled himself away from the major's cabin and took himself for a stroll. He was actually glad to get away from Ross's chessboard and the major's constant fretting over how a jihad would affect the state of the Empire. But it was just as uncomfortable outside. The hot day had given in to a humid night and, though sticky, there was at least a mild breeze, the ocean was calm and the stars were out.

He made his way along the promenade deck to the forward companionway and climbed the stairs up, past the bridge, to the navigation deck. It was dark now and relatively quiet up there, with only a few officers stargazing, and a sailor on watch. Lock moved to the guard rail and stared down at the upper deck below him. It was a heaving mass of men. Every available space, right up to and including the forecastle deck to the very stem of the bow, was occupied by a soldier of His Britannic Majesty's Indian Army.

Lock could make out th

the low hum of their ch

was too dark for cards or

for fear of attracting the a

the glow of countless ciga

in the night.

'Christ,' he muttered t

own and lighting it. 'And I

Lock realised how luck

There weren't that many

comparison. Perhaps he wou ... one of the ten lifeboats that were lined up along both the starboard and port sides, for a little bit more privacy. But he should do that sooner, rather than later.

He drew a lungful of tobacco and, as he exhaled, his eyes drifted out to the surrounding ocean. He could just make out one of their warship escorts, a little way off, a dark shadow keeping guard over them.

Lock glanced at his wrist and at the new watch Lady Townshend had given him on the night of the party, a thank-you gift for saving her daughter's life. It was a beautiful piece, a Swiss-made Omega with a distinctive red twelve o'clock on the face indicating it was an officer's watch. The hands read 10 p.m. It was time for a visit. Amy would have settled in, been fed and was probably, hopefully, doing as he was, looking for a way to meet.

Lock tossed his cigarette butt over the side and made his way back down the companionway, down past the promenade deck where Ross and the other senior officers and Lord Shears had cabins, on down past the boat deck where the mid-ranking officers were [illegible] saloon deck. There were cabins along [illegible] crew had those. Lock made his way aft, [illegible] alkway, which was surprisingly busy. Soldiers [illegible] ut chatting, smoking, staring out to sea. He tried [illegible] to tread on any prostrate limbs. There were a few curses [illegible] pes, but Lock muttered his apologies and stumbled on past [illegible] gangway, now barred by a barrier should some fool step out into open air and plunge down into the waters below. Beyond this was another companionway and Lock guessed that on the other side would be where the nurses were. They had been given the rear section of the *Lucknow*, as far as he could gather, and it had been segregated from the rest of the ship.

Lock stepped into the companionway. Up was dark and he could make out the muffled chatter of yet more men, officers more than likely; below was darker still and smelt of oil and stale sweat. That was the realm known as 'below decks'. He glanced behind him, then dog-legged past the stairs, and came to the aft section of the saloon deck. This walkway was almost deserted. At the far end was a lone figure, a guard perhaps? Lock couldn't be certain. He fished out his cigarettes and matches, cupped his hands to hide the flame and struck a match. Then, as nonchalantly as he could, he began to stroll towards the lone figure, softly whistling 'Waltzing Matilda' as he went.

As he got closer, the figure turned to face him and Lock could see that he was an armed guard and that behind him was a gate barring the way further on.

'Evening soldier, everything all right?' Lock said.

'Yes, sir. Sorry, sir, this section is out of bounds. I'm afraid I'm going to have to ask you to turn about.'

'It's quite all right, Private . . . ?'

'I'm sorry, sir, them's my orders. Please go back.' He swung his rifle from his shoulder, keeping it low.

Lock took another drag of his cigarette and leant against the guard rail, glancing down to his left and right. He quickly assessed if there was another open walkway below – there wasn't – and then turned to the sentry again.

'Excellent work, Private. You are as vigilant as I had hoped, protecting the honour of our fair nurses. Well, goodnight to you.' Lock gave a nonchalant salute and turned on his heels. He strolled back the way he had come.

'Goodnight, sir,' the sentry said.

Lock stopped at the entrance to the companionway and turned to face out to sea. He drew on his cigarette and watched the sentry out of the corner of his eye. The private lowered his rifle and sat back down, looking out to sea himself. Lock remained where he was, then stepped into the shadow of the companionway.

'Come on,' he muttered, keeping his gaze on the sky. It was bright, but there were clouds and Lock was waiting for one particular formation to drift its way across the moon. Lock looked back towards the sentry. There was no sign of movement, but then he caught the faint glow of a cigarette end. He turned his attention back to the sky and watched as the cloud began to inch in front of the moon.

Suddenly, what little light there was had gone and the gloom intensified. Lock trusted that the sentry would at that same moment glance up to the sky himself. He sprang forward, hitched up onto the guard rail and swung himself over and down. He paused. There was no shout of alarm. So far, so good. He hadn't been seen.

He was now dangling down on the outside of the ship, clinging to the lower rung of the guard rail. When he had stolen a glance over the edge earlier, he had spotted about five feet below a narrow ridge running the length of the ship just below the line of portholes on the next level. Below that, the waterline, then nothing but ocean.

Try not to think about that, Kingdom, he said to himself, and cautiously edged his feet down the greasy topside until he felt the ridge firm beneath his feet. He allowed the pressure to build on the sole of his boots. It would hold. He was in an awkward crouching position, but was out of sight from the walkway above.

He began to move, pulling his right hand off the rail, and as soon as he did, he felt his weak knee throb and lost his footing immediately. He snatched for the rung, gripped and pulled his weight back up.

His heart was pounding.

'Bugger,' he gasped. 'You'd better be waiting for me, Amy.'

He decided now to keep most of his weight supported by his hands and, pushing the edge of his boots hard against the hull, began to edge and haul his way aft again. He listened to the ocean below as the *Lucknow* cut through the water, and told himself not to.

'Just think of Amy, Amy . . .' he muttered. 'Soft red hair, sparkling green eyes . . .'

Lock inched on, patiently, until he came to the point where the sentry would be sitting above him. Here, the guard rail ended and became a smooth bulkhead for, Lock estimated, four feet. This was where the gate was keeping the soldiers from the nurses. Lock paused and peered down at the black water beneath him and at the white foam churned up by the ship's movement. He took a deep breath and was drenched by a sudden burst of sea spray.

Was the sea getting rougher? He must keep moving.

Lock pulled himself ever so slightly up and peered through the bottom rung. He could make out the figure of the sentry, his back to the gate now. There was the glow of a cigarette where his face would be, facing down the length of the walkway. Lock lowered himself down again, then leant his body out.

Could he swing and jump?

Too risky?

He couldn't lean over and stretch, it was just out of reach. He'd have to go lower. He looked down again. He let go his left hand and slowly crouched until he could feel the ridge beneath his fingertips. It was wet but rough, with plenty of grip. He glared up at his right hand. It wouldn't obey him and release its hold.

A booming voice from above made him freeze.

'You there, what do you think you're doing?'

There was a scuffle of movement above Lock and something fizzed past his face.

'No smoking on duty! Do you hear?' the voice called again.

'No, Sergeant. Sorry, Sergeant,' the sentry replied.

'Come 'ere, me laddie!' the sergeant called.

Lock released the grip from his right hand and dropped his body lower, feet dangling in open air just above the waterline. He shimmied himself along, counting the distance, 'One foot, two foot . . . three . . . four,' and gritted his teeth as he pulled himself up by his hands. He lifted his body so that his chest rose above the ridge, then stretched his hand up the topside feeling cool rough metal slide beneath his palm, until his fingers felt, then gripped the rung of the guard rail again. He let out his breath in a great gasp and realised he'd been holding it in for a good while. He hauled his body up, found a foothold, then pulled himself to the edge of the guard rail, looking first to the gate on the other side a little way down the walkway.

The sentry had his back to him and was still being chastised by the sergeant. Lock peered down the length of the walkway on the nurses' side of the ship. It was dark, quiet and mercifully deserted. He pulled himself up and over the guard rail and landed like a cat on the walkway. He stood and pressed his back against the bulkhead, glanced once more through the gate. He brushed his jacket down, and straightened his hair. He rubbed his sore knee, then turned and walked silently aft. Now, where to find Amy?

Lock came to the astern companionway. He was about to go down when a voice whispered out from above.

'Kingdom?'

'Amy?'

She stepped out from the shadows and embraced him. Their lips met and they kissed long and hard, Lock pulling her close and feeling her breasts crush softly against his chest.

'How did you know I'd be here?' Lock said, pulling his mouth gently away and moving his lips to her ear.

'I knew it would be when it got dark,' Amy said. 'So I waited. I must have smoked ten cigarettes wondering if you would show.'

She grabbed his hand and led him up to the top level where she opened a door out onto the poop deck at the very stern of the ship. They moved over to the far guard rail. The moon had appeared from behind the clouds again and Lock could see the ship's wake foaming away into the night.

'Did you have any trouble slipping away?' Lock asked.

Amy shook her head. 'Looks like you did, though. You're soaking.'

'A little light acrobatics, that's all.'

Amy's pale face frowned up at him. She looked very smart in her uniform, Lock thought, and he put his hand to her cheek, brushing the same piece of loose hair behind her ear again.

'I'm confused, Kingdom,' she said.

'About what?'

'This. Us. Casper.'

'Casper's not here,' Lock said and leant forward and kissed her.

She responded, then pulled away and turned to gaze out to sea. 'This is wrong.'

'Perhaps it is, Amy. But it feels right to me,' Lock said. 'For the first time in months, I feel this is allowed.'

'You mean because of that girl?'

'What girl?' Lock was genuinely mystified as to what Amy was getting at, and then he remembered. On the Hindu Kush, with a weakened and semi-conscious Amy in front of him in the saddle of the dead Turk's horse, he had mentioned Tsingtao. 'You're talking about Mei Ling?' Lock said, and pulled her round to face him again.

Amy nodded. 'What happened to you in China?' she said scowling up at him. 'You never talk of it, always avoid the subject.'

'I do not,' Lock lied.

'Tell me, were you hurt so very much?'

Lock shook his head. 'I told you that was the past. This is now. You, me, here.'

'And the future?'

'And the future.'

'But it's impossible, Kingdom . . . My parents . . .' Amy averted her gaze.

'It's your life, Amy.'

'This is different.' There was anger in her eyes now.

'How so?' Lock pressed. Although he already knew the answer to that one. Amy was talking about tradition and status and how things had always been. She was aristocracy, he was nothing but an uncouth colonial. They, in the eyes of society, could never be. Her parents would never stand for it.

'Piss on tradition,' he said.

Amy frowned. 'It's not as simple as that.'

'When this war is over we should be together,' Lock said. 'Come with me, to Australia, to South America, to wherever you desire.'

A sudden noise from the port companionway distracted them both. It sounded like a metal door opening and then closing again. Lock and Amy hesitated, waiting for the inevitable footsteps.

'I must get back before I am missed,' Amy said. 'Same time, same place tomorrow? We need to talk about this. And I need to think.'

Lock smiled. 'Of course, although I shall seek out an alternative route to get to you. Tonight was a little . . . salty.'

Amy lifted up on her toes and kissed Lock's mouth. 'Don't get caught. *Bonne nuit.*' She made her way to the starboard companionway, paused as she listened for movement on the stairs, and then was gone.

Lock put his hand to his lips feeling the memory of her there. What the hell are you doing, Kingdom?

Footsteps were approaching from the port companionway. Lock made to go the way Amy went, but stopped in his tracks.

There were voices coming from the darkness of that companionway. Had Amy been caught? Caught doing what? She was alone. But if he bumbled into the situation then things would get awkward. No, he needed an alternative exit, and fast.

He ran back to the guard rail and peered down. Could he face another climb down, clinging on for dear life? Sod that. He looked up. He could scramble to the compass flat, along the gunwale to the rear lifeboat. Yes, that would have to do. If his knee would hold. He jumped up onto the guard rail, pulled himself up, and was met by a scream that was cut short. It was more a scream of surprise than of fear and was quickly followed by suppressed giggles. Two nurses, young ones for all Lock could tell in the moonlight, were huddled together sharing a cigarette on the roof of the poop deck.

'Ladies,' Lock said, doffing his hat and moving swiftly on.

He hauled himself up onto the first raised lifeboat, scrambled across the taut canvas stretched across as a cover, leapt onto the second, then the third, and stopped. He scanned the open part of the boat deck. He could see the dark figures of many nurses sat below and could hear their gentle chit-chat. He didn't want to jump down in the middle of them, too conspicuous. The line of lifeboats continued to stretch along the roof of the promenade deck. The beginning of the men's section of the ship was about six foot higher and a good ten feet over to where he was now.

Lock looked down then shrugged. 'Ah well, the things I do for love.' He walked back a few paces, to give himself a run-up, then sprinted forward and leapt up and across. His hands grabbed the first lifeboat as his body slammed into its bow with a thump. Lock cursed and winced and then pulled up onto the canvas cover of the lifeboat. It was thankfully unoccupied. He glanced back the way he'd come and at the two shadowy figures on the flat of the poop deck. They waved. Lock waved back. He pulled out the handkerchief Amy had given him before the *Lucknow* had disembarked, and mopped his neck. He then leapt to the next lifeboat, and made his way to the compass flat. He needed a nightcap now, and what better person than the major to provide one, he thought, and made his way to the companionway and back down to Ross's cabin.

For the next four evenings Lock kept up a similar routine at night. He would go for a stroll after the evening meal and later, when it was much quieter, would make his way to a rendezvous with Amy. They never had long, always someone would disturb their increasingly intimate time together and Lock would have to slip quietly away again. He was careful never to be seen and found an easier, though more time-consuming, route to get to her. It involved negotiating the service areas below decks, making his way past the engine room, through the shaft tunnel that ran between the tanks, and which eventually led to the steering engine room. From there he could climb up to the poop deck and to Amy's warm embrace. They talked of dreams and plans and places they could travel, to see the world away from war and family and tradition. Although Lock encouraged this talk, he never really believed it, always his mind recalling their first conversation about the class divide. But he enjoyed her company, the holding hands, the taste of her mouth, the smell of her hair, of her skin. He wanted her more than he thought possible and soon the ghost of Tsingtao and Mei Ling began to fade.

Then, on the fifth night, everything changed.

Ever since they had hit the Oman coast three days earlier,

where they passed the beautiful old Portuguese fort at Muscat, the temperature had been increasing. Despite the fact that it had been raining continuously for twenty-four hours, the heat was unbearable and the men had become short-tempered and irritable, too. Lock noticed the change in the atmosphere and it made moving about the troopship hazardous. Petty squabbles broke out over the smallest things, noses got bloodied, eyes blackened. Lock, not trusting himself to keep his own temper at bay, spent more and more time visiting with Ross in his cabin.

The major poured over maps of Persia as he tried to second-guess the German Wassmuss's next move, whilst Lock buried himself in a book he'd lifted from Townshend's library about Napoleon's strategies. It was actually rather dull and he would often find himself reading the same paragraph over and over and drifting off. If only he could visit Amy in the day, spend time talking with her, to make love with her. But he knew that was impossible.

Night was better. The temperature dropped and around 6 p.m. Ross would put his charts away and get out the rum and the chessboard. Rum and chess was an odd mix, but both men seemed to revel in trying to see who could remain focused the longest. Added to which, they would be drinking on empty stomachs. Both had agreed that it was just too damned hot to eat.

'Checkmate!' Lock grinned.

'Well, you've bettered me again, my boy,' Ross said.

'You'll win next time, sir,' Lock smiled, as he scraped his chair back and staggered to his feet.

'Where are you off to?' Ross's words were slightly slurred as he held his pocket watch close to his eyes. 'It's only just gone eleven!'

Lock squinted at his wrist. 'Bugger, I'm a little late.'

Ross looked up at him. 'You be careful, Kingdom. You are playing with fire meeting up with that girl.'

Lock was taken aback. He thought he'd been discreet. 'Sir?' he said slapping his slouch hat on his head.

'Don't "Sir" me. You know damned well what I'm talking about. Nothing good will come of it, my boy. What if her father finds out? Or her fiancé, come to think of it.'

Lock shrugged, as Ross rose unsteadily and fell back on his bunk.

The major had drunk quite a lot over the course of the evening and the evidence was scattered across the table in front of him. An empty bottle of rum lay on its side gently rocking to and fro with the movement of the ship.

Lock, sensibly, had paced himself, and although very merry, felt surprisingly clear-headed. He opened the cabin door and a cool, sobering spray hit him square in the face. He jerked the second bottle of rum he held in his hand up in a gesture of farewell and stumbled out.

'Cheerio!' Ross called. 'Give Miss Townshend my reg—' His voice was cut off.

Lock hesitated outside the major's cabin. He stifled a belch and grimaced as the acid rose in his throat. He really should cut down on his drinking, he thought as he stood swaying, letting his eyes adjust to the gloom. It was mostly deserted on this side of the ship now. Lord Shears had complained earlier about junior officers swearing and lazing about outside his cabin, so everyone, bribes or no bribes, had been ordered to move off the promenade and boat decks and cram in with the rest of the troops on the saloon or upper deck.

The warm breeze was getting stronger and the ship was

beginning to heave and pitch like a child's see-saw. Lock could hear the steam engines chugging away, and feel them pulsating beneath his feet. Perhaps he shouldn't see Amy tonight, he thought. He'd make it up to her, get a message to her via the MO. Best hit the biscuit. He wiped the sea spray from his eyes and pulled himself away from the major's door.

The deck was slick underfoot and, despite the moonlight, Lock carefully began to weave away from the cabins towards the companionway that led up to the compass flat. He was about to put the bottle of rum to his lips when he was yanked violently from behind. The bottle fell from Lock's hand as he was spun around and his arms were pinned behind his back. A fist smacked him squarely on the jaw, the force of the blow knocking his slouch hat off as his head jerked to one side. Salty blood filled Lock's mouth. His head was reeling, but before he could clear his mind, he was punched again in the belly. He folded up and crashed to the deck, the wind knocked out of him. Lock wheezed, gasping for air and a boot kicked into the small of his back. A lightning stab of pain raced up and down his spine and he rolled over, his brain trying to tell his body to protect itself.

'Filthy colonial scum!' The accent was clipped and educated.

Lock felt hands patting and searching through his pockets. Then something was pulled from one of them and the search ceased. As he lay there listening to a mutter of conferring voices, he tried to concentrate, to bring himself to his senses. He reached his hand out across the clammy wood of the deck for something solid to grab hold of, and found the bottle. He clasped it tightly by the neck.

A figure loomed close, breath reeking of whisky. 'I saw you on the wharf, Lock, and you've been seen on the poop deck. You stay away from my Amy, do you under—'

Lock swung his arm out. There was a scream and a spray of blood as the bottle smashed into his assailant's face. Lock twisted and slashed wildly at his second attacker. The jagged edge caught against something and he heard a tear of cloth and a gasp of pain. Lock scrambled to his feet, wielding the bottle like a dagger, his back to the companionway entrance.

A portly officer, a lieutenant, was standing a little away, cradling his injured forearm. Lock didn't recognise the officer but he knew the insignia on his collars. They depicted the three hills of the Mendips, the same as Lock wore. The second officer Lock knew from his voice. It was Amy's fiancé, Lieutenant Bingham-Smith. He was sitting on the deck, hand pressed to his bloodied, broken nose, moaning in pain. Then Lock noticed Amy's handkerchief in Bingham-Smith's hand, wet with blood.

The fat officer moved a step towards Bingham-Smith to help, but Lock jabbed the broken bottle at him. The fat officer hesitated.

Just then a nearby porthole banged shut.

'Gingell,' Bingham-Smith groaned, 'help me up.'

The fat officer, Gingell, glanced nervously at Lock as if asking permission. No one moved.

'Gingell!'

Lieutenant Gingell stared wide-eyed at the bottle in Lock's hand and edged his way towards his friend. Lock watched Gingell like a hawk, but didn't stop him from helping his bleeding chum to his feet.

'We'd best get the MO to look you over, old chap, nasty cut there,' Gingell said.

'You haven't heard the last of this, Lock,' Bingham-Smith snarled. Lock stabbed out with the bottle making both Gingell and Bingham-Smith flinch.

'Get lost!' Lock said, spitting a glob of blood to the deck.

Gingell put his arm around Bingham-Smith's waist and helped him to shuffle off.

'Stay away from Amy Townshend,' Bingham-Smith called over his shoulder, before the two officers were swallowed up by the shadows of the companionway.

Lock let out a heavy sigh. He stepped over to the guard rail and closed his eyes against the spray. He stood listening to the howling wind, to the crash of the waves against the hull below and to the straining hum of the engines. He took a deep breath, cursed softly, and opened his eyes.

A movement to Lock's left made him snap his head to the side, broken bottle raised in readiness. Despite the gathering clouds and the fading moonlight, Lock could make out a figure by the companionway, watching.

'Who's there?' Lock slurred.

The figure was still, and then stepped forward into the moonlight. It was Amy.

'How could you?' she whispered, her face a mask of despair.

Lock turned to her. 'Amy. I'm sorry, I—'

'You're sorry? I've just seen Casper. His face. He told me what you did.' Her eyes were dark with anger. Lock moved towards her, but she put her hand up to stop him. 'Don't touch me!'

'Amy, what are you doing here?' Lock's mind was swimming with confusion.

'You were supposed to meet me, remember? However, I'm just

as capable of slipping past the sentries as you are.' She glared at the bloodied broken bottle Lock still held in his hands. 'But it appears that fighting like a common soldier, a drunken fiend, is more to your liking this evening.'

'Please, Amy, listen to me.'

Amy shook her head. 'No, Kingdom, I will not. I think it best you sleep it off. As for poor Casper—'

'Poor Casper!' Lock spat before he realised he'd said the wrong thing. 'Amy, I—'

But it was too late. She'd turned and, without another word, disappeared back into the companionway. Lock cursed under his breath. He thought about going after her, but decided that it was best to leave it until morning.

He put his hand to his mouth and realised that he was still holding the broken bottle. He frowned, then tossed it over the side. He was exhausted and his head was swimming. He needed to lie down, to sleep. He turned and, scooping up his slouch hat, made his way to his sleeping space on the compass flat.

CHAPTER FOUR

Lock awoke to the sound of roaring furnaces, an overwhelming smell of burnt oil, and an intense throbbing in his temples. His mouth was dry and his body was stiff. The thin, lumpy mat beneath him did little to disguise the hard deck he was lying on. He couldn't feel his left arm. He rolled onto his back and waited as the blood rushed back into the numb limb, and he tried to ignore the tender spots and the complaining muscles, his body's memory of the skirmish he'd endured only a few hours earlier. There was a dull ache in his side and he felt certain that a rib was cracked. He lifted his arm and studied the face of his wristwatch. The glass was splintered but he could still make out the hands. They read five-fourteen. He groaned and swallowed dryly. He needed water. He rubbed his face and made himself sit up.

Lock put his hands over his ears. The dull throbbing in his head faded. He took his hands away again and the sound returned. He was momentarily confused, and then he smiled wryly. It was the bloody engines! He paused and then pulled himself to his feet and gingerly moved away from his fellow soldiers, a mass of sleeping, snoring bodies, and staggered to the navigation deck, which was thankfully deserted. He gripped the guard rail and took in deep lungfuls of air. But it smelt foul and made him retch. He put his hand to his moist face and realised that the weather had changed. The storm had passed and the air was bone-baking dry. He noticed the water was different, too, and guessed they were now well into the Shatt al-Arab canal. They were close to the shore and were moving dead slow.

As Lock watched the sun rise above the horizon, a monotonous spiked skyline came into view. Buildings with ugly chimneys and vast boilers belched thick, toxic smoke into the heavens above, and a mass of iron pipes wormed their way out towards the quays. The ship glided on and Lock could now see a camouflaged Admiralty oiler docked close by, loading fuel. The canvas pipes that fed into its side reminded him of the tentacles of some nightmarish underwater creature. It was as hideous as it was fascinating, like nothing he had ever set eyes on before. Then his spirits sank and he cursed, remembering that there was still an uncomfortable one-hundred-mile chug towards their final destination, Basra. Then he remembered the night before. Amy!

'You look dreadful, young man.'

Lock turned in surprise. Lord Shears was beside him, looking out at the shore. Lock tried to compose himself and stand up straight.

'At ease. No need to be formal.' Shears held out a canteen. 'Here!'

Lock took it and drank heavily, spilling water down his chin and onto his shirt as he did so.

'It's Lieutenant Lock, isn't it?'

Lock nodded as he lowered the canteen again.

'I saw you briefly at the Townshend party. We weren't introduced.' He stuck out his hand. 'Shears.'

Lock shook it. It was limp and dry. 'I know who you are, sir,' he croaked, then turned his gaze back to the passing port. He could now see the rear of the complex where two iron pipes ran out of the refinery into the open desert beyond.

'Where the hell are we?' Lock started, realising he'd spoken aloud.

'Why, Abbadan, the oil refinery in Persia,' Shears said, matter-of-factly. 'From this point,' he continued, pointing at the complex, 'those two pipes, each no more than fourteen inches in diameter, snake north over the ground to the oilfields of the Anglo-Persian Oil Company at Maidan-i-Naftum, one hundred and twenty miles away. Incredible, don't you agree?'

Lock didn't answer. He kept his eye on the refinery until it disappeared from view, then he turned his gaze out across the land beyond.

It was a lonely strip of country, bordered by a thick belt of palms that lined either side of the canal. Unlike the land by the oil refinery, which was bleached white and looked dead, this was thickly planted with date groves and seemed to be cultivated. Beyond the palms lay a nondescript khaki belt. It was hard to make out with the naked eye, but it appeared to Lock that it divided the desert from the sown area. Further on still, he could see through the gaps in the trees that, after a mile or so stretching inland, there was nothing but a flat, bleak and, he imagined, unprofitable wilderness.

'Christ, what a hellhole,' he said to himself, taking another draught of water.

Shears took a deep breath. 'Ah,' he exhaled, 'the very seat of civilisation! Can you smell the history, Lieutenant Lock?' He sounded like an excited schoolboy. Lock could smell something, and it wasn't history. 'Tell me,' Shears asked enthusiastically, 'have you heard of the Roman Emperor Justinian?'

Lock shook his head and handed back the canteen. 'No, sir, can't say that I have. Thank you.'

'Well,' Shears said, placing the canteen on the deck and taking a silver-and-pearl cigarette case from his pocket, 'in the time of Justinian, Mesopotamia was one of the richest wheat-growing countries in the world.'

Lock grimaced. He was in no mood for a lecture. He just wanted to find Amy. Explain to her, make amends. He put his hand to his chest and held in a belch, wincing at the bile taste that rushed into his mouth. He focused on Shears' thin lips. They were moving, but Lock couldn't hear the words. He closed his eyes and pulled at his loose shirt, which clung to him like a second, damp skin, and wiped his brow with his rolled-up sleeve.

'. . . destroyed it,' Shears was saying, 'putting its cities to fire and sword. Then, in 541 AD, if I remember correctly, the Roman General Belisarius, the soldier who gave a last flicker of glory to the fading Eastern Empire by retaking Rome and North Africa from the Barbarians, also partially retook Mesopotamia into which he descended as far south as the fortified city of Ctesiphon.'

Lock nodded, as he guessed he was supposed to. But he wasn't listening. He put his hand up to wipe his face and froze. It was caked in dried blood. He dropped it down again and his mind suddenly returned to the night before, to Bingham-Smith and Gingell. He closed his eyes and shuddered. He saw Bingham-Smith's bloodied face. He remembered Amy's handkerchief being taken. He saw it covered in blood, pressed to Bingham-Smith's bleeding face. He would have to get it back. And then he saw Amy's disapproving face, the hurt in her eyes.

Shears had stopped talking for a moment and was lighting a cigarette. Lock patted his pockets, feeling that a smoke would help clear his nausea. No, he cursed under his breath, they must be in his jacket, which was back on his bed mat, rolled up as a pillow.

'Now, today, contrary to popular belief,' Shears said, 'the Arab threat there is far more significant than many of our commanding officers realise. Back in November our forces captured Basra and the Fao Peninsula. But British command refused, stupidly I might add, to make a clear declaration of support for local Arab independence. Do you know, because of that stupid decision, we have turned their friendly neutrality into widespread hostility?'

Lock winced and pinched the bridge of his nose. Christ, where was Bingham-Smith now? And that fat bastard? He should try and find out. He turned his face away and stared down at the dirty waters below.

'. . . Turkish soldier is no fool,' Shears said, blowing sweet smoke in Lock's direction. 'He is a hardened fighter and has been battling over Mesopotamia and Persia since the times of the ancient Greeks, probably earlier. He is used to guerrilla warfare, as are his Arab cousins, and his faith, as we know from the Muslim uprisings and unrest in India, makes him a formidable foe. We also know that high up the Turk chain of command are German officers, and those German officers have been training the Turkish troops for a number of years now.'

Lock nodded in agreement as he tried to concentrate on controlling his stomach, taking his mind off it by thinking about how the sweat was running down his back.

'. . . will be to our peril if we regard them as such,' Shears droned on. 'It's clear the Ottoman government has their own agenda that often conflicts with that of the Germans.' He turned away from the rail. 'Why, Lieutenant Lock, even the Kaiser recently declared himself a convert to Islam so as to call all the Muslims out in a holy war against us and our allies.' Lock gave a non-committal grunt and imagined diving into the canal below and letting the water envelop him.

'It's total hogwash, of course,' Shears said, 'but I pray that the Turks and the Muslim Arabs and, indeed, our Muslim Indians, are not foolish enough to believe it. What a mess we'd be in then, heh?'

Shears fell silent again and Lock wondered if he was supposed to reply. He looked across at him, but he was still staring out at the passing landscape.

'History will repeat itself, Lieutenant Lock,' Shears said, tossing his cigarette butt over the side. 'You mark my words! For we are a fading empire—'

'Yet, maybe we can stop that from happening,' a familiar voice interrupted, 'as we will fight where Belisarius fought!'

Lock and Shears turned to see Major Ross approaching. Ross nodded courteously at Lord Shears.

'Possibly, Major. Possibly,' Shears said. But all the passion was gone from his voice.

'Good morning, Lord Shears,' Ross said.

Shears smiled thinly. 'Lieutenant Lock and I were talking history.'

'So I heard, so I heard.' Ross turned to Lock. 'Did you learn anything?'

Lock didn't respond and just closed his eyes. Ross grinned and slapped him on the back. 'Come along, time for your briefing. There's some coffee brewing in my cabin. I think you had best have a cup or two. If you will excuse us, Lord Shears?'

'By all means, Major. Good day to you, Lieutenant Lock. Perhaps we can continue our discussion another time?'

'Yes, sir. Thank you, sir,' Lock croaked.

'Oh, and Lieutenant Lock?'

'Sir?'

'I would be grateful if you would refrain from conducting your . . . little moonlit debates from outside my porthole in future.'

Lock managed a weak smile and nodded politely. He turned away from the guard rail, leaving Shears to his dreams of ancient history.

Ross's cabin bore no resemblance to the mess it was in the night before. Everything was spick and span, bunk made, chair straight, all in order. If Ross had a batman, Lock had never seen him. But someone had been hard at work. A pot of coffee was steaming on the tabletop. It smelt wonderful.

'Sit down,' Ross said, closing the door and moving over to the tabletop. He poured two cups of coffee and then took a seat opposite Lock, who perched on the trunk again.

'You should cut down on the booze, my boy.'

Lock grunted and put the coffee cup to his lips. It was hot, bitter and strong and burnt his tongue as he sipped at it.

Ross pulled his pipe out of his pocket and tapped it against the chair leg. 'There's some hot water in that jug next to you. When you've had your coffee I suggest you wash that blood off your hands.'

Lock peered over the rim of his coffee cup at the major and pondered if he should tell him about last night.

'Guess where I've been?' Ross said. 'No? Sickbay. Seems there was a little bit of trouble last night. Lieutenant Bingham-Smith was brought in by his friend Lieutenant Gingell and a nurse. Appears Bingham-Smith walked into an open porthole. The medical officer doesn't believe a word of it, of course, and neither do I, but I've told him to keep quiet and leave it to me.'

Lock gazed into his coffee while the major spoke.

'His face looks pretty messy, Bingham-Smith I mean. Nose flattened and split, cheek lacerated, one eye hidden behind a swollen lid.' Ross sat forward and Lock's eyes flicked up. 'What exactly happened when you left here last night?'

Lock took a sip of his coffee avoiding giving an answer. He needed to get out of here and find Amy. The major sighed and sat back in his chair.

'Gingell corroborated the story when I confronted him. Seemed a little shaken, though. Still, it's a good job you and I are disembarking at the next port.'

Lock nearly choked on his coffee. It couldn't be, he thought. 'Are we not going to Basra?'

'Change of plans. We're getting off at Mohammerah.'

'Why? What's there?'

'Your new platoon.'

Lock frowned. His mind was tumbling with thoughts. How long did he have before they jumped ship? Would he have time to see Amy? Could he even get to her in the day?

'I've set up a unit within the Mendips, nominally under your command. The main bulk of the 2nd Battalion is in Basra, yes, but two of their companies have been earmarked for Ahwaz. A section of our forces are moving up the Karun, following the pipeline to the oil-pumping station at Ahwaz. Things are hotting up, Lock. There's intelligence that a substantial Turkish force is moving towards there, and I need to take a look.'

'And me? There's something else, isn't there?'

Lock could tell by Ross's agitated body language, the way he kept toying with the folded piece of paper on the desk in front of him, that there was another reason for this earlier disembarkation.

Ross stopped messing with the paper and looked at Lock. He smiled.

'Quite right, my boy.' He tapped the paper. 'The real reason is this. I received a cable from Mohammerah half an hour ago. A German spy has been captured by a pro-British tribal leader at one of the settlements along the pipeline.'

Lock could see the excitement in Ross's eyes. 'Wassmuss?'

Ross's smile broadened. 'It's a strong possibility, yes. But we can't be certain until we take him – you take him – into custody.'

Lock nodded, put down his coffee cup and went over to the jug of water. He began to wash the blood from his hands and face. 'How long?'

'Fifty minutes, maybe less.'

'There's something I need to do.'

'Write her a letter. I'll see she gets it.'

Lock picked up a towel and patted his face dry. 'I need to see her, sir. There's something I must—'

'No, Lock, that's an order. Pack your stuff and meet me down at the gangway on the saloon deck. You've got half an hour.'

An hour later, as the little launch bounced its way towards the port of Mohammerah in the south-west of Persia, Lock watched RIMS *Lucknow* take up steam and slowly crawl away from them, continuing on her journey up the Shatt al-Arab to Basra.

He had disobeyed the major and gone straight to the nurses' section of the ship only to be met by hostility and stubbornness. They wouldn't even try and find Amy for him. And, by the time he'd hurried back to the compass deck to gather up his belongings and then got himself to the gangway and the waiting launch, he realised that he had forgotten to even write a note for her. He had not had the chance to find Bingham-Smith either or, indeed, retrieve Amy's handkerchief. But he had a sickening feeling that he would get another opportunity to confront the young officer again soon.

Ross was next to him, and on the other side of the launch, much to Lock's disgust, stood Sergeant Major Underhill, the soldier from his past whom he had bumped into on the gangway at Karachi. Lock glared at him, but Underhill kept his eye on the ever-nearing port. Lock looked to Ross, who was concentrating on lighting his pipe against the breeze. As the tobacco caught, he puffed away contentedly, and then pointed the pipe over Lock's shoulder. Lock turned to see a second launch a little way behind them. It began to peel off to the right. He wasn't sure, but he thought he could see the distinct figure of Lord Shears standing at its stern. Was it just a coincidence that the oilman had disembarked also? Or was there something else Ross wasn't telling him? Lock turned to ask the major that very question, but instantly changed his mind. Their own launch was slowing down and it came to a rest against a steep wooden staircase rising up to the quayside.

'Welcome to the Sheikhdom of Mohammerah,' Ross shouted above the noise of the launch's spluttering engine.

'Not Persia?'

Ross pulled himself onto the greasy staircase and turned back. 'Well, technically, yes,' he said, 'but we call this bit Arabistan.'

Lock followed Ross up the stairs, looking up at the quayside towering above him as he climbed. At the top he was greeted by a dry, hot wind full of sand and a cacophony of noise made by machinery, animal cries, and thousands of troops. It was a daunting sight, seeing so many bodies in such a small space, more so than the dockside at Karachi. But he didn't mind, and as he moved off the final step, he was just glad to be on terra firma once again. Underhill stopped a few paces away, pulling off his heavy topi, and wiping his wet brow. Lock dropped his haversack and turned to say something to Ross, but the major had disappeared into the crowd.

Lock lit a cigarette. 'Do you know where he's gone?'

Underhill's eyes snapped towards Lock. 'Sah?' He almost spat the word out.

'The major?'

Underhill shook his head.

Lock blew smoke through his nose and scanned the dock. A first-class gunboat was berthed at the far end, belching thick black smoke into the stifling air. Soldiers were moving about everywhere below it, but it was impossible to tell whether they were embarking or disembarking. The odd shout raised itself above the general chatter as NCOs tried to form some kind of order. Lock spotted a hawker up ahead, weaving his way through the crowds, selling chai to the parched troops. Lock threw his half-smoked cigarette into the slimy water lapping at the quayside and licked his dry lips, then put his fingers to his mouth and let out a harsh whistle. The hawker waved his bony hand, and trotted over to where Lock and Underhill were standing. He quickly set about pouring Lock a glass of chai from the urn strapped to his back, and then waited patiently for him to drink up.

The sergeant major cleared his throat. 'Give me one of those, you black bastard.'

Lock quietly sipped at his milky drink, while the hawker nervously poured Underhill a tea.

'Sod this,' Lock said, and downed the rest of the chai. He gave the hawker a couple of coins, handed the glass back, and began to walk off.

Underhill put his hand out to stop him. 'Sah. We're to wait 'ere.'

Lock turned sharply back. 'So you *do* know where the major has gone?'

'No, sah. I do not. 'E just instructed me to wait.'

'You.'

'And to keep you 'ere with me.'

Lock glared at Underhill. 'You're one of his, aren't you?'

Underhill stared blankly back and sipped at his chai. The hawker stayed a few paces away. He fidgeted nervously, averting his eyes from the two men, and waited for the return of his other glass.

'You bloody are! I should have known,' Lock said.

‘Maybe ’e’s gone to check on the whereabouts of your platoon. Sah.’

‘Wouldn’t he send you to do that, Sergeant Major?’

‘No, no ’e wouldn’t. Sah. The major . . . ’e likes to do things for ’imself. I imagine ’e will be trying to locate some brass ’at, too.’

‘You imagine?’

‘Sah.’

Lock fell silent again. What Underhill said was probably true; after all, it was clear to Lock now that the sergeant major knew Ross better than he had originally thought. He nodded grudgingly and moved over to the edge of the quay, and sat down with his legs dangling above the fetid, brackish water below. He put his face to the sun and closed his eyes. ‘So we wait.’

The sergeant major finished his chai and handed his glass back to the hawker, along with a coin. The Indian nodded his thanks, then scuttled back to the throng of the troops. As he pushed on, calling out his wares, Lock spotted Ross emerging from the crowd.

‘Ah, there you are, my boy. Sarnt Major,’ Ross called. ‘Come along, no time to dawdle. We’ve got a mission to get underway.’ He gave a broad smile, and turned and led the way back along the quayside, with Underhill marching briskly along beside him.

Lock pulled himself to his feet, hauled his haversack up onto his shoulder and followed. Ross had obviously said something to Underhill for the sergeant major was nodding in response. Lock quickly caught up with them and noticed that Ross seemed more preoccupied than usual.

‘Any news, sir?’

‘Hmm? News? About what? Oh, yes. Well, appears we have a problem.’ Ross fell silent and rubbed his moustache thoughtfully.

'Sir?'

'There have been developments. Not only does it appear that your platoon is not here yet, but worse still, our captured spy is no longer in captivity.'

'Sir?'

'That's if he ever was in captivity in the first place. Seems communications are a trifle fuzzy. The telegraph lines are continuously cut and although a rider was sent, the message was so garbled that it just didn't make sense.'

'So we don't even know if it was Wassmuss?' Lock said. For the first time he was beginning to have doubts about Ross's organisation. This seemed to be so very haphazard.

'Don't look so worried, Lock, it's war. These things happen. I'm just as unhappy about it as you look. But you'll have the sergeant major with you. A good man in a tight spot. He's to be your number two.'

Lock gave Underhill a sidewards glance. Man, maybe. A good man? Never. 'Major, I think I can man—'

'Orders, Lieutenant!' Ross snapped. 'I give them, you follow them. Now, the prisoner was being held at a small settlement called Daurat al Qaiwain, sometimes called Darkhoveyn. It's a little east of the river and the pipeline, on the road to Shadegan. I want you to go there and see what the hell is going on. If they have a captured spy, if they ever had a captured spy, if they've ever seen a spy.'

'Wassmuss,' Lock said.

'Let's hope so,' Ross said. 'If he's there, bring him back. If he's not, find him. You should be there in two days, just follow the troops.'

'Sir?'

'The march, join the march.'

'March?' Lock was not keen on the idea of a long tramp. 'What about a boat, sir? The pipeline follows the river most of the way to Ahwaz. We could hitch a ride part way.'

Ross shook his head. 'We missed the last one by a good six hours.'

'What about that one?' Lock pointed to the gunboat berthed at the end of the quay.

'Doesn't sail for two days. And even I can't force them to hurry up. Takes time to load troops and supplies. Besides, they're heading the other way, to Basra.' Ross paused. 'There's nothing for it than to set out on foot. The 4th and the 7th Rajputs and some of the 2nd Dorsets are already marching, following the pipeline north. Just not enough river transport. Still, it's not too far. Like I say, you'll be there in two days.'

'You not coming with us, sir?'

'I have a little business to take care of here. I'll be waiting, hopefully with your platoon. On arrival at the settlement seek out the tribal leader there. Here's some gold.' The major tossed a small hessian bag tied with string. 'Bribe him if you must.'

'I thought he was pro-British sir?'

Ross grunted. 'He was. Doesn't mean he still is. But that bag of coin may remind him where his loyalties lie.'

After a few more paces, Ross stopped. 'Well, I'll leave you here. When you get back, look for me at the army encampment north of the town. You'll pass it on the way out. Right. Cheerio, then. See you in a few days.' Ross nodded to Underhill, who snapped a smart salute back, then the major waved his hand, turned on his heel and disappeared in an instant amongst the crowd.

Lock and Underhill remained where they were in silence for a moment as if waiting for someone else to come and collect them. Lock dropped the haversack at his feet and turned to face Underhill. 'What do you want here?'

Underhill frowned back at him. 'Want, sah? I was assigned.'

'Don't give me that. You're a base-wallah, you like a cushy number at camp. You don't want to be out in the field. Do you?'

Underhill looked away. It was clear to Lock that the sergeant major was eager to say something in return, but he remained tight-lipped.

Lock stepped closer. 'Did you put Bingham-Smith and his fat crony up to that . . . business last night?'

Underhill still kept his mouth shut, but there was a smile upon his lips again.

Lock angled forward and glared into the sergeant major's twitching face. 'Don't think I've forgotten what you did in Lhasa, Underhill,' he said softly. 'I know the kind of man you really are, even if Ross doesn't.' He then smiled and backed off. 'Bring my haversack with you, there's a good fellow!'

Underhill muttered a curse and unclenched his fists, but he didn't rise to the challenge. He picked up his own haversack, as well as Lock's, and as Lock walked off, Underhill hurried after him.

Lock pushed on through the hot, sweating crowd of troops, and continued to worm his way along the quayside to the far end of the dock. The heat and the flies were a mild irritation he could easily ignore, but it was difficult to do the same with the sand in the wind. It was getting into everything; his eyes, his nose, his mouth, even his ears. He glanced back at Underhill, huffing and puffing and shoving his way on with the two packs on his back. Lock smiled to himself and moved on through the sea of men, passing the plain wooden custom halls, hoping that soon he would come to the end of the docks and find some space to breathe.

'Good God! This is worse than Karachi,' he said, scanning the body of Indian and British troops swarming near to the sentry posts and the checkpoint at the entrance. They were at the edge of the city itself, a festering, crumbling collection of mud-brick buildings and stinking piles of rubbish, and very little charm. But it wasn't just soldiers they needed to cope with now; there were just as many camels, horses and oxen carts to deal with, as well as local merchants, street hawkers and the inevitable beggars.

'There!' Lock said above the noise, pointing to a motor vehicle not one hundred yards away. It was parked under the shade of a palm tree, next to an official-looking building.

'Where are you goin', sah? The major told us to join the march,' Underhill panted, pulling up next to Lock.

'You really want to walk all the way? In this heat? For two days? A motor vehicle will get us there in a few hours,' Lock said.

Underhill scowled at him, brow contorted in thought. He nodded reluctantly.

'Good,' Lock said and pushed forward, crossing the rough track of a road.

As they got closer, Lock could see that the vehicle was a Rolls-Royce armoured car, with an enclosed cab and a gun turret. There was a barrel of fuel loaded in the open flatbed at the back, but it still offered plenty of space for possible passengers. A scrawny soldier of about twenty-five, with a square face and small, furtive eyes, was slouched nearby smoking a cigarette, sheltering from the sun. He sported a single stripe on his arm and a peaked cap with a pair of tinted goggles pushed up over the band.

'Ah, Lance Corporal . . . this yours?'

The soldier drew on his cigarette and studied Lock and the panting, sweat-soaked sergeant major beside him with suspicion. 'Aye, what of it?' He spoke with a thick Irish accent.

'Nice rig,' Lock said, nodding at the turret. 'Looks frightful.'

The soldier narrowed his eyes suspiciously. 'You just off the boat, then?'

'Yes. I'm Lieutenant Lock and this is Sergeant Major Underhill. We're newly attached to the 6th, but we urgently need to get to Daurat. It's on the road to Ahwaz.'

The soldier was nonplussed. 'I know where it is, sir,' he said. 'I've heard all the begging stories from new arrivals wanting a free ride to spare their boot leather.'

Lock could see by the twitch at the side of his mouth that Underhill was itching to step in and use some parade-ground tactics on the Irishman. But Lock knew that this man needed some gentle persuasion, not aggression. 'You not heading for Ahwaz yourself?'

'Nope. Just back from patrol. Been refuelling.' He patted the barrel.

'Patrol?'

'Aye. Keeping a look out for bloody Abduls trying to wreck the pipeline. The road to Daurat's a particular trouble spot.'

Lock nodded. 'I see. Well, Lance Corporal, that's what we're doing. Sergeant Major, my bag if you please.' He held out his hand expectantly.

Underhill hesitated before handing Lock his haversack.

'I have the authority from Major Ross to requisition this

vehicle. Somewhere . . .' Lock began to rummage in his pack. He pulled out a book and then a pint bottle of brandy. 'Hold this a moment, would you?' he asked absent-mindedly as he continued to hunt for the mythical orders.

The lance corporal's face lit up when Lock passed him the brandy bottle. 'Orders, you say?'

'Yes. Look, be a pal. We don't have time for this. The major has gone to square it with your captain . . .'

'Flannigan,' the lance corporal said, his gaze fixed on the brandy bottle. He gently shook the bottle and ran his pink tongue along his dry lips as the liquid sloshed about seductively inside.

'Yes, Captain Flannigan. So let's not dilly-dally.'

The lance corporal rubbed his chin, still uncertain. 'I'll just check with the captain.'

'No time. Orders are to leave now. Keep the brandy. I've plenty more,' Lock said.

The lance corporal's eyes shot up. 'Sir. Well, thank you.'

'Splendid! Let's get off then!' Lock heaved his bag into the flatbed and hauled himself up next to the spare barrel of fuel.

'You sure about the captain?' the lance corporal said, dropping his cigarette and popping the brandy bottle in his pocket.

Lock smiled down as Underhill clambered up onto the flatbed next to him. 'I told you, it's an emergency.'

The lance corporal hesitated, uncertainty still clouding his face.

'What's your name, Lance Corporal?' Lock said.

'Connolly, sir. Seamus Connolly.'

'How long will it take, Seamus? To get to Daurat, I mean?'

'About five hours, sir.'

'Good. Well, stop worrying and let's get a move on. These

orders come from Major Ross. He will back you up if there's any trouble, isn't that right, Sergeant Major?'

Connolly looked to Underhill as if for confirmation, but the sergeant major just grunted non-committally and sat down opposite Lock. Connolly shrugged, pulled his tinted goggles down over his eyes, then clambered up onto the turret, opened a hatch and climbed into the cab.

'Stupid Micks, all the same,' Underhill muttered. 'Do anything for a tipple. Drunken, bog-trotting sons of whores.'

The engine kicked into life sending out a belch of black smoke that startled a passing team of camels. Then, with a crunch of gears, the armoured car lurched off.

'Hey, you there! Stop! Where the hell do you think you're going?'

Lock glanced back to see that a young captain, clutching a pair of goggles and a sheaf of papers in his hands, had appeared from the official building.

'Orders, from Major Ross, sir!' Lock called back. 'We need to borrow your vehicle!'

The captain trotted after them. 'Orders? What bloody orders? Who the hell is Ross? Connolly? Connolly? Stop this instant!'

But Lock knew Connolly would be unable to hear his captain's shouts above the noise of the engine. He cupped his hand around his mouth. 'Major Ross, sir,' he shouted, 'you'll find him at Command HQ.' He sat back again, grinning to himself and gave a cheery wave as the armoured vehicle picked up speed. The captain threw down his goggles in anger and stood, hands on hips, watching them pull away onto the main road and join the troops marching north away from the dock.

'Think you're real smart, don't ya, sah?'

'I got us a ride, didn't I?' Lock shifted his weight and faced away from Underhill. But yes, he had to admit, he was rather pleased with himself.

The road they were travelling along was rocky and full of potholes and followed, as did the River Karun, the course of the oil pipeline. Lock thought how ridiculously vulnerable the raised iron tubes appeared, helpless and exposed to attack from anyone as they stretched out across the stark desert. He was then struck by the fact that Persia wasn't a desert at all, in the traditional, romantic sense. What he remembered from the *Arabian Nights* tales he read as a child was that deserts were all soft sand and oases of palm trees. This was an arid terrain, with a vast rocky plain bleeding off to the bleak horizon.

Lock's eye was distracted by the wind whipping up dust clouds in the distance and his thoughts turned to how devastating sandstorms could be. He'd never witnessed one, only heard the tales, and hoped that they wouldn't have to go through one any time soon. The dust and sand kicked up by the wheels of the armoured vehicle and by the marching troops was bad enough. It was beginning to catch the back of his throat and he was feeling a thirst coming on again.

Lock glanced at Underhill. The sergeant major was dozing peacefully, with his topi pulled down over his eyes, oblivious to the bone-shaking ride and the heat of the sun baking down on them. Already the flatbed was hot to the touch. How had he ended up alongside Underhill again after all this time? Lock thought he'd seen the last of him in Tibet. How many years ago was that? Ten? The man was as odious as ever. He shook his head. Best watch your back, Kingdom, he told himself.

Lock unpinned the upturned left brim of his slouch hat and fished out his packet of cigarettes. He held his jacket up over his chin to protect the match flame from the wind, and then tossed the spent match over the side of the car. As he smoked, his mind was filled with the rhythmic march of the soldiers, clearly audible above the rattle and hum of the Rolls-Royce engine. He couldn't believe how many men there were here, snaking behind him as far as the eye could see, all the way back to the dock.

There were hundreds of them; the English boys in their short KD trousers and topi helmets, their faces, arms and bare knees already red with heat and sunburn, and the Indians, all in similar uniforms, but with a bewildering variety of headdress styles all according to the individual's religion, race or caste. Some wore turbans, either bound directly around the head or around a pointed cap known as a khulla. Each man was marching in the same direction, and each man looked hot and exhausted, as the heat sapped his energy with every step. There was no colour to be seen as everything was caked in dust, save for the odd flash of red from a sepoy's turban. It was a khaki, faceless mass tramping on, on to meet the Turk and to shake hands with death.

They passed a camel train and Lock was amused at the sight of 'the ships of the desert' plodding along, their riders sitting high above their fellow soldiers, just glad, no doubt, as Lock was, to save on boot leather and blisters.

The Rolls slid to a halt, throwing Lock and Underhill to the floor of the flatbed.

'Now what?' Lock said, pulling himself to his feet and peering over the edge. An ox-drawn gun carriage had lost a wheel and spilt its load, crushing three sepoys who must have been marching close behind it. 'Jesus!'

A number of soldiers were frantically trying to shift the cannon but were finding it hard to get a foothold in the marshy ground between the river and the road. Two of the sepoys beneath the collapsed gun were dead, their upper torsos crushed to a pulp, but a third had his lower half pinned underneath the gun's barrel. He was screaming in pain as an English sergeant tried desperately to organise five men with wooden joists, ripped from a nearby fence, to lift the gun. He was shouting at them to take the strain but was barely audible above the trapped sepoy's cries.

'Shut up, soldier! Do you hear me?' the sergeant bellowed at the trapped Indian before turning to his men again. 'Lift, damn you! Lift!' But the gun would not shift. Then the sepoy stopped screaming altogether. He convulsed. His mouth oozed blood, and then he was still. The sergeant and his men hadn't noticed and continued in their vain attempt to heave the gun up.

Lock sat down again as the Rolls jerked back into life and slowly manoeuvred around the carnage.

'There'll be worse to come,' Underhill said.

Lock ignored him. He'd seen enough sickening sights in his time already. But Underhill was right. There would be worse to come. He went to relight his cigarette and noticed that it was broken. Prising it away from his bottom lip, Lock tried to straighten it out again, but it just broke up in his fingers. 'Bugger.'

Underhill chuckled and, pulling his topi back down over his eyes, settled back down to sleep.

CHAPTER FIVE

'I don't suppose you'd be having any eggs in that pack o' yours, Lieutenant? Fresh ones?' Connolly said, wiping his hands on an oily rag. He was staring forlornly down into the engine cavity of the armoured Rolls. Steam was smoking out from the overheated radiator and water was spilling at his feet and quickly evaporating into the bone-dry ground.

'Eggs?' Lock nearly laughed.

'Aye,' Connolly said seriously. 'Crack a couple into the radiator, once it's cooled, and they'll fill the leaks.'

'Really?'

'As God is my witness, sir.' Connolly peered back down at the leaking radiator. 'Hose has split, too.'

Lock sighed. 'So we walk.'

The Irishman closed the inspection hatch of the Rolls' engine with a loud clang. 'Aye, looks that way. Sorry, sir.'

'How far is it?'

Connolly peered down the rocky, empty road. He shrugged. 'Ten miles. A little more, a little less. Can't be certain.'

'Four, five hours' march.'

'Aye, sir, but it'll be getting dark in a few hours.'

Lock surveyed the length of the road, the way they had come. It had been hours since they passed the head of the marching troops and they too would soon be looking to set up camp for the night. He turned to the direction of travel. The sun was still burning down on the barren road and the shimmering horizon appeared as harsh and unforgiving as always.

'You'll still get there ahead of the lads,' Connolly said.

'I know.' Lock smiled thinly. 'Where's Underhill?' He walked to the flatbed at the back of the Rolls. His and the sergeant major's packs were still there, but not the sergeant major himself. 'Underhill!'

'I don't like leaving her, sir,' Connolly said, a touch of unease in his voice. 'The Abduls'll strip her naked if they find her.'

'Well, you're not staying here. We march together. You can get the parts you need at Ahwaz later and come back. Underhill!' Lock called again, agitated this time, as he continued to scan the landscape. 'Under—'

'All right, all right!' a shout came from the left. Lock spotted the sergeant major scrambling over a nearby ridge, spade in hand. His face was red with anger. 'Can't a man have a shit in peace?' he growled to himself, throwing the spade into the flatbed with a loud clatter. 'So has the Mick fixed it?' He glared at Connolly.

'We're walking. Grab your stuff. We only have a little daylight left so I want to get as far along the road as possible,' Lock said, hauling his haversack from the back of the armoured Rolls and hitching it up over his shoulders.

Underhill grumbled to himself as he pulled on his haversack, and when Connolly gathered up his own bag and his SMLE rifle, they set off leaving the broken-down Rolls to her fate.

Connolly patted the vehicle. 'Sorry ol' girl. Take care.'

They made their way along the road, which mirrored the course of the river to their left. The form of the oil pipeline loomed over them to their right, stretching off into the distance. Underhill, moaning and muttering under his breath, soon dropped behind, whilst Lock trudged along ahead with Connolly at his heels.

'So what brings you here, Connolly?' Lock said after ten minutes of listening to his boots scrunch 'A-my, A-my' along the dusty, rocky road.

'Orders, sir, like the rest of us.' But there was a glint in the Irishman's eyes.

Lock smiled. 'Well, that's something we have in common.'

Connolly grunted and fell into step with Lock. He jerked his head back. 'You known the sergeant major long, sir?'

'Too long. How did you know?'

'Ah, sir, you can smell genuine hatred a mile off. It's like love, sir.' Lock scoffed. ''Tis the truth, sir. My ma said you can only truly hate if you truly love. Both's four-letter words.'

'I know another four-letter word and you're talking it, Lance Corporal.'

'Aye, that's what my father said about Ma's philosophy, too.'

Lock laughed. 'So, really, why are you in the army?'

'Better than starvin', sir. There's not much work in Skibbereen these days.'

'You enlisted?'

'That I did, sir.'

Silence fell between the two men and Lock returned to listening to the taunting of his boots. Bugger his luck; if only he had explained to Amy what had happened. If only she hadn't seen. If only Bingham-Smith didn't exist.

Lock paused to take a sip of water and stared up at the harsh iron tubes of the pipeline. They were like two giant snakes caught in the baking heat of the day. He wondered how much oil there was inside at that precise moment, rushing past on its way downriver for a hundred miles or so to Abbadan Island. Maybe there was no oil? Maybe they were empty and Wassmuss wasn't ever held captive in a dank cell in Daurat. Maybe the Arabs had blown the pipeline to the north of Ahwaz already? Maybe they had taken over the oilfields at Maidan-i-Naftum? 'Bollocks,' he muttered, before moving on.

It was dusk by the time the river began to worm away from the pipeline and the road. Lock stopped. His eyes scanned the run of the oil pipes, which continued on until they melted into the distance. The sun was now a burnt-orange orb hovering above the horizon to their left. The heat of the day was cooling fast and Lock could feel the chill start to pinch at his naked arms. Connolly tapped his elbow and held out his goggles. Lock nodded his thanks and put the tinted goggles down over his eyes and stared west directly into the sun. He watched as a flock of birds flew majestically across the pinking sky. He felt his spirits lift. It was a beautiful country and the distant mountains to the north were now bathed with the reflected sunlight. Lock guessed that they had less than an hour left before they would be forced to set up camp for the night. He was about to carry on when something on the ground a little way along caught his eye.

Underhill came up beside him panting heavily. He squinted in the direction where Lock was staring. 'Sah!' He pointed at the object.

'Yes, Sergeant Major, I saw. A body?'

'Could be,' Connolly said, his hand shading his eyes as he squinted.

Lock fumbled in his pack for his field glasses. He flipped the goggles up and strained to focus on the object. 'It's not moving.' He raised the field glasses again and followed the line of the land all the way up a slight slope to a rocky ridge that was about five hundred yards ahead of them.

The three men set off again, and as they got closer it didn't take long for them to recognise the object.

'It's a dead sheep,' Underhill grunted.

Connolly trotted on ahead and knelt beside the carcass. He touched its side. His hand came away red with blood.

Lock paused and scanned the empty terrain thoughtfully. Something wasn't right. Could there be Turks in the area? So far behind the British lines? He eased his haversack off his aching shoulders and lowered it to the ground. 'We'll set up camp by the river back there.' He indicated in the direction they had come. 'I'm going to walk up that ridge to see if I can see anything on the other side.'

'Sah?' Underhill said.

'The thing is,' Lock said, 'where there's sheep, there's bound to be a shepherd.'

He moved on. There were three more of the animals lying dead along the way. But when he came to a fourth, he stopped. This one was slumped at the foot of the ridge, bleating mournfully, its hindquarters a mass of bloodied wool. Lock took his Webley out of his holster and approached the animal. It jerked on sensing his approach and struggled to stand. Lock knelt down beside it and stroked its muzzle, trying to soothe it. He pulled back the hammer of his revolver and levelled the gun at the sheep's head. He bit his lip, hesitating, and slowly eased the hammer of his gun back into place. He cocked his head slightly.

As the day cooled the wind had picked up and was now blowing towards the ridge. Lock waited, listening. Then the wind changed direction. He could hear rushing water on the other side of the ridge, but there was something else, another sound. Faint, but familiar, not unlike the whining of a wounded animal. It too was coming from the other side of the ridge.

Lock spun sharply, Webley raised. Connolly had crawled up behind him. Lock put his finger to his lips.

The Irishman frowned, listening, then nodded his head. He drew his knife and made a quick cut in the injured sheep's throat.

'What are you doing here?' Lock said, keeping his voice low.

'The sergeant major told me to come and fetch you, sir. He's found fresh tracks. Horses.'

'He has, has he?' Lock said. 'Well, they'll keep. Where's your Enfield?'

'Back by the river, sir.'

Lock shook his head and Connolly shrugged. 'I'll be all right with this blade, sir.'

'Come on.'

Both men crouched low and crept up the scraggy ridge. The

breeze kept changing direction, and as they got nearer to the top, they could clearly make out the sound of the rushing water. There was also the distinctive smell of burning wood, and cooked meat now, as well as voices behind the whimpering.

'Turkish!' Lock said.

They reached the top and peered over the edge. Beyond, the ridge sloped down for one hundred and fifty yards, before levelling out again for another hundred yards of scrub grass until it hit the rocky bank of the Karun River. There it dropped to the rushing waters themselves, moving fast in a natural trench cut through the rock.

'Sir!' Connolly whispered, pointing off down to their right.

Amongst a group of boulders, a small campfire was dancing in the breeze, and around it sat four men. Lock was unable to make out their attire, but one had a kufiya on his head and another was wearing what seemed to be a sheepskin tunic. Lock was almost convinced that the men were shepherds until he saw their rifles, propped up in a neat stack of four the way soldiers are taught to do so. The men appeared to be arguing. Every now and again the odd word of harsh Turkish would be carried on the wind, but Lock couldn't make any sense of what they were saying. A little way from the fire was an upturned cart. A dead mule, still in its harness, lay next to it. On the other side of the cart there was something else . . . Lock squinted against the setting sun. Something . . . a body was lying there. But it was moving, he was sure of it. Then the mournful cry came again.

Lock went to lower the goggles to take away some of the sun's glare, then stopped himself. He couldn't risk the light reflecting off the lenses and giving their position away. He ripped the goggles from his head and gave them back to Connolly. 'Let's get closer,' he said.

Connolly nodded and, staying on their side of the ridge, both men crept off to the right. They stopped a few yards on, behind a group of boulders. Cautiously they peered over to see that one of the men, most definitely a soldier, judging by his khaki jacket and trousers and the puttees around his shins, was shouting as he approached the snivelling creature. Lock was shocked to see that it wasn't a dog tied there after all, but a child. As the soldier stooped over the child, pointing angrily, his comrades broke into laughter. The soldier spat and kicked out at the prisoner, then returned to sit by the fire.

Lock paused for a moment. 'I think it's just the four of them, Connolly! Let's go,' he said. The Irishman followed as Lock scrambled over the rocks, Webley at the ready.

Keeping low and moving as carefully as they could over the uneven ground, Lock and Connolly wove their way down the ridge. Loose rocks made the going tricky and Lock tensed, all the while thinking one of the soldiers would hear them. But as they got further and further down the ridge, the sound of the river increased, and the more hidden from view they became.

At the foot of the ridge they paused.

The soldiers' voices were more distinct now. Lock wondered if they had stumbled upon a patrol. Could there be more soldiers nearby? But what the hell were they doing so far into the British lines? Could this be a scouting party from the larger force Ross had said was encamped north of Ahwaz? Well, only one way to find out, Lock said to himself. He signalled to Connolly and both men edged towards the upturned cart. It was now about twenty yards away. The carcass of the mule blocked their view of the child.

Lock and Connolly dropped to their bellies and lay flat, hardly daring to breathe.

One of the soldiers was up again and walking in their direction, but his head was turned away as he was still talking to his comrades by the fire.

'*Kes sesini!*' the soldier yelled at the child.

Lock heard the slap of hand against flesh and a cry of pain. But the wailing continued. The soldier cursed and hit the child again. Lock had seen enough. He sprang up, gun in hand.

But Connolly was quicker. His knife fizzed through the air and thudded into the soldier's spine. The soldier gave a muffled cry of surprise and sank to his knees, before collapsing, face first, to the ground. Lock gave Connolly a look of surprise. It was a good throw.

Connolly shrugged. 'Skibbereen's a dangerous place after dark.'

They scrambled over the mule and there, with her hands and her feet tied, and with a rope around her neck tethered to the broken axle of the cart, was a naked girl of no more than eight or nine years of age. She let out a scream.

A second soldier rose to his feet to see what was going on. His jaw dropped as Lock ran at him. But he didn't have a chance to shout a warning as Lock pulled the trigger of his Webley. The revolver kicked back in his hand and the soldier froze, a third eye having suddenly appeared in the middle of his forehead. He slowly sank from sight.

Lock kept running. His heart was pounding in his chest as he rounded the cart. The other two soldiers were just getting to their feet, crying out in alarm as they made a grab for their rifles.

Lock fired again, wildly. He instinctively adjusted his aim in a split second and pulled the trigger once more, this time hitting the third soldier in the shoulder, spinning him to the left. The soldier's rifle flew from his grip. Lock fired a fourth bullet and the side of the soldier's head exploded in a spray of red, and he fell sideways in a heap. The fourth soldier had his rifle levelled, ready to fire at Lock, when suddenly he arched his body and cried out. Blood burst from his chest and his eyes rolled up in his head. He crumpled to the ground, revealing Connolly standing behind him, one of the Turks' rifles raised.

Lock nodded his thanks. 'If I ever get there, remind me to ask you to show me around Skibbereen.'

Connolly grinned, then knelt down and turned the head of one of the bodies towards him. 'Turkish Kurds, sir. A patrol maybe? Or deserters?'

'I don't think so, Connolly,' Lock said. He picked up one of the saddlebags by the fire. It was heavy. Inside were papers, a notebook and what looked like coin bags.

Just then the child cried out again.

'The girl!' Lock said, dropping the saddlebag.

As Lock rounded the other side of the cart, Sergeant Major Underhill rose to his feet. He was standing over the girl who was shaking and whimpering uncontrollably. Her head spun round on hearing Lock approach. Her eyes were full of panic and her neck was raw as she strained against the rope tied around it. She made to scream again.

'Get away from her!' Lock said, shoving Underhill in the chest. The sergeant major grimaced and stepped away. Lock glared at him, then looked at the girl. He holstered his Webley, and opened his hands out reassuringly as he crouched down. 'Shhh,' he said. 'There now, we mean you no harm . . . British . . . Does she understand?'

'I was just tryin' to tell the little bint that, sah,' Underhill said.

'She must be a nomad, one of the Persian tribes. Qashqai, Bakhtiari or Lur, sir,' Connolly said, approaching.

Lock glanced up. Connolly was carrying a flaming piece of driftwood in his hand. Lock turned back to the girl. Her long dark hair was matted, her tear-streaked face was cut and swollen, and her thin body was bruised black and blue and filthy with mud, dust and dried blood.

Lock shook his head. 'No, the Lurs are mostly in the Zagros mountain area, on the other side of the Karun, I believe. Qashqai?' he said, turning to the girl. But she just began to whimper again. He put his hands up. 'No, no . . . we British,' he said, waving his hand back at Connolly and Underhill. '*Breetaanee*. Me, Australian, *Ostraalee*.' He pointed to his chest. 'You, Qashqai?' He pointed at her.

She shook her head faintly.

'Bakhtiari? Lur?' Lock said, but the girl just whimpered and drew her legs tighter to her body, hiding her nakedness. '*Esmee* Kingdom. *Esmak ay*?'

'You're wastin' yer time, sah. She's clearly dippy. You fanti, lass?' Underhill shouted down at her. ''Ey?'

'Shut up, Underhill!' Lock said, as he removed his service jacket and offered it out to the girl. 'Please,' he said. '*Tafadal*,' he repeated in Arabic, inching forward. He hoped the language would be common enough for the girl to know some words. If she were a nomad, then Arabic would be familiar to her from the traders her people would come across. The Qashqai spoke a form of Turkish, but he knew no Luri.

The girl nervously glanced at Underhill, and then she focused on Lock again and sniffed.

As the light from Connolly's torch flickered over her face, her eyes momentarily transfixed Lock. They were a stunning turquoise, like two oasis pools in a burnt desert. Maybe that was how people regarded his own eyes, how he was regarding hers now, with surprise and wonder. He smiled softly, holding out the jacket. He inched closer and closer, then carefully placed the jacket over her bony shoulders and moved back. The girl sniffed again, continuing to watch the three men with suspicion.

Lock glanced at Connolly, who was looking to his right at the dead soldier with the knife between his shoulder blades. The Irishman walked over to him, kicked him, then leant down and tugged the knife out. It made a sickening, sucking pop as it came free. He made a show for the girl of wiping the blood on the dead soldier's tunic and spitting at the body again.

'We should get out of 'ere, sah,' Underhill said.

'Why, Sergeant Major?' Lock said.

'I count four dead soldiers and there's four 'orses tied over there.'

Lock glanced across at the animals. 'So?'

Underhill nodded to the mule cart. 'If I'm not mistaken, them there's snout bags.'

'Your point, Sergeant Major?' Lock was beginning to get irritated.

'There's five.'

Lock frowned and Connolly quickly scampered over to the cart.

'He's right, sir. And all have fresh oats in.' It meant there was another rider out there somewhere.

'Right. Connolly,' Lock said, 'gather the horses. Sergeant Major, those saddlebags by the fire.' He turned back to the girl, raised his wrists but held them together as if they were tied. He then pulled them apart. '*Tafadal?*'

She understood and jerked her head up and down. Connolly approached with the horses and stood watching Lock and the girl. Underhill came up and threw the saddlebags over one of the horses, then mounted upon another.

'Come on, sah, before we lose all the daylight.'

'Connolly, your knife.' Lock held his hand out, and the Irishman slapped the blade into his palm.

Lock got to his feet, delicately, approaching the girl. She was terrified and was unable to pull her eyes from the glistening blade. '*Tafadal*,' he repeated softly. The girl held out her trembling wrists and Lock slowly lifted the knife and cut her bonds with one slice. He cut her bound feet and finally, he sliced the rope from around her neck.

Lock stepped back and handed the blade back to Connolly. '*Wa howa ka-zaalek!*' he said, 'Good!', and he thought he saw a faint smile play on the girl's lips. He remained perfectly still and watched as the girl struggled to her feet and pulled the jacket around her properly. She was shaking so much that her fingers couldn't button it up.

Lock dropped to one knee and extended his hand. '*Taa hena*,' he said, 'Come here.'

'Sah,' Underhill repeated impatiently.

'All right, Sergeant Major,' Lock hissed.

Underhill and Connolly waited as the girl, never taking her eyes from Lock, shuffled forward and let him button up the jacket for her. It swamped the child's tiny frame, covering her hands and reaching down to her knees. Lock rolled up the sleeves until they were above her wrists and straightened the lapels.

'*Afdal be-katheer!*' he said, 'Much better!' and then saluted.

The girl stared into his eyes. Something registered there for she threw her arms around his neck and held him tight. Lock raised an eyebrow to Connolly. Underhill indicated for them to move, so Lock put his arms around the girl, and lifted her up.

'A moment, sir,' Connolly said, tossing the dying torch aside.

Lock waited as Connolly rushed back to the campfire. He moved to the second Kurd Lock had shot and stripped the soldier's sleeveless sheepskin tunic from his body. He stamped the campfire out and jogged back to Lock.

'What's the sheepskin for?'

'You, sir. It'll be mighty cold tonight.'

Lock helped the girl climb up onto his horse, then, pulling on the foul-smelling sheepskin tunic, he hauled himself up into the saddle behind her. Connolly mounted his own horse, then they circled and followed Underhill back to where they had made camp, further down the river.

CHAPTER SIX

The sun had sunk below the horizon and a final strip of pink and purple filled the sky as the twilight began to spread over the land around them. They rode in silence and it took little more than ten minutes to cross the plain where Lock had first seen the dead sheep, and hit the pipeline again running beside the road. From there they directed the horses onto the loose rock of another ridge down to the wide riverbank below.

Lock eased himself out of the saddle and helped the girl down. She clung to his arm whimpering. 'Connolly, you'll take first watch. Put yourself a little up this ridge where the ground levels out. Sergeant Major, get a fire going!'

Connolly dismounted, left his horse with Lock and removed his peaked cap and goggles. He placed them on the girl's head, winked, then grabbing his rifle, marched back up to the pipeline. Lock tethered the horses and, with the girl at his side, he gathered up Underhill's and his own canteen, and walked down to the river. He unfastened the leather strap from his belt and tied the end to the hook at the top of one of the canteens and lowered it down the two-foot drop from the rocky bank into the flowing waters of the Karun. He yawned and rested his eyes for a moment until the weight of the full canteen tugged at his arm. He retrieved the canteen and gave it to the girl to hold and then repeated the process with the second canteen. He trudged back to the fire, with the girl gripping his hand, and dropped the canteens beside Underhill.

The sergeant major grunted his thanks. Lock sat down with the girl curled up beside him, and watched as Underhill finished building a small circle of stones. The sergeant major then set about filling it with driftwood and dried twigs collected from the riverbank. He struck a match, coaxed the flames into life, and then balanced a tin pan on the stone circle ready to boil some water for the inevitable cuppa.

Lock pulled a blanket from one of the haversacks and handed it to the girl. He then pulled the saddlebags to him and opened them up. There was little of interest in the first, just some clothes, a lump of hard brown bread and a box of rifle cartridges. The second contained explosives: sticks of dynamite, wires and charges. In the third, the one he had seen earlier, were papers, a map, a leather-bound notebook held together with string, and the two bags of coins. Lock opened one up and, as he suspected, it was full of gold. He fished one coin out and turned it over between his fingers.

'Got you, bastard,' he said softly to himself.

The coin showed a crowned eagle, with wings spread, and the legend '*Deutsches Reich* 1914, 20 Mark' around the edge. The other side depicted Kaiser Wilhelm II.

The girl's eyes were wider than ever as she watched the coin glinting in the firelight.

'Here,' Lock said and tossed the coin to her. It landed with a tinkle in front of her. She picked it up, face transfixed by its lustrous gleam. Lock opened up the notebook. It was crammed with letters and numbers, broken by the occasional sketch or crude map, none of which meant anything to him. He pondered for a moment. Codes? Perhaps. Ross would know. He closed the notebook again. He then leafed through the papers. There was a map of the Karun River, with the pipeline clearly drawn out and points along its length marked with a red cross, a number and a short note in German. Lock had limited knowledge of the language, so was not sure what it said. The other papers looked to be receipts, itineraries and lists of supplies. Lock hesitated. He felt his mouth go dry and the hair prick on his neck. He leant closer to the fire.

Amongst the pile were two letters with broken wax seals bearing the crest of the Ottoman Empire. Lock opened the first. It was typewritten in Turkish, a language he did have knowledge of, extensive knowledge, and it contained the usual rhetoric about God and Honour and Glory. But as Lock read on, he saw the hidden message within.

Baghdad
Miralay Mahomed Pacha Daghistani

My Heroes! My Soldiers!
Brothers march across the rooftop of Persia to stand shoulder to shoulder with you as the full moon swells in the fight that is to

come at the place where the land bleeds black. The enemy is to be pushed back to the sea, to be expelled from the open veins of our motherland.

It is now that we must coordinate and expedite our movements and in so doing confuse and split the attention of our enemy from Miralay Subhi Bey's offensive at the shadow of the crescent moon. I appeal to the energy and the initiative of you, your commanders and of their troops to make decisive the results obtained in triumph.

Let those of you who are to die a martyr's death be messengers of victory to those who have gone before us, and let the victory be sacred and the sword be sharp of those of you who are to remain in life.

In the name of Mehmed Reshad and Hadji Mohammed Guilliamo, I salute you.

Birinci Ferik Khalil Pasha

Lock read the letter a second time and slowly lowered the paper, staring down into the flames. 'My God!' he said.

'What is it?'

Lock looked up to see Underhill watching him, a steaming mug of tea in his hand. ''Ere.' He passed it to Lock.

'Thank you. I'm not sure. But Major Ross needs to see this.' He waved the letter.

'So we 'ead back to Mohammerah at first light?' Underhill asked, barely disguising his eagerness to return to the safety of the British-controlled port.

Lock sipped his tea. It burnt his tongue and tasted metallic.

It was disgusting, but a welcome warmth. 'Not yet. I still want to check out this so-called captive at Daurat.'

Underhill scoffed. 'You really think there's any point? I don't believe they've got a prisoner. That girl there, she's the only prisoner round 'ere!'

Lock glanced at the girl. She was sleeping now, her thumb in her mouth and the coin clutched in her other hand. 'Maybe, but those are our orders, Sergeant Major.'

He put the mug of tea down and unfolded the second letter. As he read it, he felt a tingling of excitement rush through his veins. There was no name, no addressee, but Lock knew whom it was intended for. It had to be.

Constantinople. Time is of the essence. Daghistani will strike and you must prepare Mohammerah for his arrival. Abbadan is to be brought to chaos. Proceed to Basra. Your contact will have further instructions.

In the name of the Kaiser.

G

Lock's mind was reeling. He's here, Wassmuss is here, close by. The Turks they'd killed with the gold, the explosives, these letters, the notebook, they must be Wassmuss's men. And Wassmuss must be the owner of the fifth horse! Lock glanced back into the night around him.

Where was the German now? He would surely return to his camp, find his men dead, his gold and his papers gone. What would he do? Would he panic? Yes, he must do. How could he know just two men attacked his camp? Surely he'd have scouts, spies working nearby? He'd know by now that the British troops were marching this way. And what the hell did the girl have to do with it all? If she was a Lur, then what was she doing so far south? Had she been captured when Wassmuss and his men crossed into Persia and passed through the Zagros Mountains? And where did the sheep come from?

Lock put his hand to his head and cursed. So many thoughts. If only it was morning.

'Why don't you get some kip? I'll take second watch,' Underhill said.

Lock nodded. He folded the second letter and moved over to the girl. Checking that Underhill wasn't watching, Lock stuffed the two letters and the notebook into the breast pocket of his jacket that the girl was wearing. She whimpered in her sleep but didn't wake, and Lock pulled the blanket up to her chin. He then closed the saddlebag and, using it as a pillow, he lay down and pulled a blanket around himself. He felt his eyelids getting heavier as he watched Underhill fuss with the fire, then pour more water into the tin pan serving as a makeshift kettle.

Lock wondered what Amy was doing at that precise moment, whether she was perhaps waiting for a cup of tea. Maybe she was standing on the poop deck of the *Lucknow* thinking of him as she looked up at the blanket of stars in the night sky. Lock smiled as he saw himself standing behind her, hands on her hips, kissing her neck. She turned to face him and their lips met in a long embrace.

'I love you,' she whispered, and he suddenly saw his own reflection in her eyes. Only it wasn't his face he saw, but Bingham-Smith's.

Lock opened his eyes, bewildered.

It was dark. The fire was little more than burning embers. Underhill's kettle was still perched on one side. He could feel the air was cold now, rasping in his chest. He pushed his blanket aside and sat up. He reeled at the sudden waft from the sheepskin tunic he was still wearing. His hand shot to his holster. It was empty. He slowly pulled himself up to a crouch. The girl was gone, too.

Lock strained his ears, but could hear nothing but the crackle of the fire and, beyond that, the rushing of the water of the river below. He was alone. He looked back to his pillow, the saddlebag. He moved over to it. Empty. Where the hell was Connolly and that bastard Underhill? There was no sign of the horses either, or the other two saddlebags. He opened his mouth to whisper the sergeant major's name into the night, but decided against it.

A piece of wood popped. Lock started and ducked down. It was just the fire, he reassured himself, keeping his eyes on the shadows beyond. No, there was something else.

Lock scanned the campsite and spotted the three haversacks stuffed behind some rocks to the left of the fire. He paused, straining his eyes and his ears for any sign of movement, then scuttled over to the bags. He stopped, listening again. Still there was nothing. He opened the bags. But after a hasty rummage through, he could find nothing of use as a weapon. 'Bugger.' He reached out for Underhill's tin kettle. It was empty and only lukewarm to the touch. How long had he been asleep?

Keeping low, Lock moved off up the ridge until he was enveloped by the night. He stopped and peered back at the fire, a speck of light in a black, inky well now far below him, then turned and carried on as quietly as he could. But as he slowly inched forward into the darkness every footfall seemed to crunch deafeningly in his ears. Despite the rushing water in the river below, he felt that he could be heard all the way back in Mohammerah. He paused to let his eyes become accustomed to the blackness, and waited. Where the hell *were* Underhill and Connolly?

Lock breathed softly and tried to pick some other sounds out of the eerie emptiness around him. But he could still hear nothing but the flow of the river. There was no moon above him, only the occasional glimpse of the star-speckled sky through the gaps in the canopy of clouds. As he looked down again, he was convinced that there was a darker mass not ten feet ahead. Surely that must be the pipeline? He crouched down and momentarily closed his eyes, trying to decide what to do. Should he call out? No, he could be right on top of a group of Arabs. Or Wassmuss? Christ, was the German here? Had he found them? Come back for the girl? His papers? But why, Lock wondered, was he still alive if that was the case? Why was his throat not cut?

Lock opened his eyes again and stared into the gloom. He shifted his head slightly in an attempt to get a clearer picture of what was up ahead from his periphery vision. There was a slight variation between the blackness of the ground and the deep grey of the sky, and he knew then that the dark mass in front of him was indeed the pipeline.

After a few more moments, Lock took a deep breath, pulled himself to his feet, and crept on. He edged forward, taking one tentative step at a time, then stopped after ten or so paces and crouched down again, listening. Still there was nothing but empty silence. He couldn't even make out the river any more. His eyes were adjusting to the gloom with each passing minute and he was beginning to make out the odd form on the ground around and ahead of him. He tried to see if he could pick out Connolly or Underhill crouched nearby, but it was impossible. He hesitated. There *was* a shape up ahead. It appeared to be a kneeling figure.

Lock felt around for a small stone. He picked one up and tossed it at the shape. Stone struck stone with a gentle click. The shape was nothing more than a boulder. He moved on. More shapes became clearer; a bush here, a larger boulder there, but still there was no sign of Connolly or Underhill, or of the Arabs he knew must be nearby.

He swore bitterly. This was a fool's errand. He couldn't possibly find anything in this darkness, and his mind raced with thoughts of what was the best course of action: go back to the fire? Or keep searching?

Lock put his hand out and it fell against the cold, rough metal of the pipeline. The sensation jolted him into action. He must make for the troops. He turned on his heels, crouched low, and scuttled as quietly and as quickly as he could back the way he had come. He stumbled, kicking against something hollow and metallic, and landed heavily on his hand. Cursing through gritted teeth, he lay still, breathing heavily, listening. If there was anyone around then he must have surely given his presence away by now. But there were no other sounds, no movements, no click of a gun's hammer or of a bolt being pulled back, nothing but his own heart beating like a drum in his ears.

Lock felt around until his hand came across the smooth surface of a tin mug. He picked it up and put it to his nose. Brandy! Connolly? It had to be the Irishman's mug.

Lock made to stand, but his foot was tangled in something. He slowly sat up and felt down his leg to his boot. A thin cable was caught around his heel. He pulled the cable free and felt along its length. It seemed to stretch off back over towards the pipeline. He gently tugged at it. There was no give. He felt along its length in the other direction, away from the pipeline, and pulled again. This time it moved.

Lock pulled again, harder, and heard a soft dragging sound in the near distance. Something heavy was attached to the other end of the cable. He pulled a third time and the object on the other end toppled over with a dull thud. He felt his way along the length of cable until he came to a metal box. Blindly he studied the object in his hands. The cable split and the ends were screwed to two terminals. In the centre was a thick handle, depressed. It was a detonator box, he was sure of it.

Lock wiped the sweat from his brow, and sat for a moment, thinking. Then he pulled the cable violently from the terminals and stood with the disconnected detonator box in his hand. At least he could delay their work.

There was a sudden pain in Lock's left side and all the breath was forced from his lungs. The detonator box went flying out of his hand, crashing to the ground nearby. He couldn't move. A huge weight was on top of him fighting to push his flailing arms away. Lock threw out a punch and hit something hard. There was a clang of metal a little to his left. He tried to throw the weight off again, but a terrific pain filled the side of his head. His ear began to sing. He grunted and desperately tried to hit out again. His hand was slapped away and then he felt his throat gripped by rough fingers that kept on squeezing.

Lock threw his body left and right, but the weight on his chest wouldn't shift. He coughed, choked, and could feel his lungs begin to smart. He bucked again and brought his right knee sharply up. It connected with something soft and his assailant cried out in pain. The grip around Lock's throat slackened and he punched into the dark above him again. He felt a sting in his knuckles and heard a crack of breaking bone and his assailant fell off to the side. Lock scrambled into the darkness after him, grabbed out and raised his fist ready to strike again.

The whole night lit up around Lock and a terrific clap of sound filled his ears. He flinched and stared at the cloud of orange flames rising into the night air over to his left and at a figure not ten yards away, an Arab judging by the shape of the silhouette, running from the burning pipeline. Lock stared down at his assailant.

'What the . . . ?'

'You broke me bleedin' teeth!' Underhill spat, trying to shake out of Lock's grip.

'Just what in hell's name do you think you're doing?' Lock said, pulling himself and the sergeant major up.

Underhill rubbed his jaw. 'Thought you were 'im, the bloody saboteur!' he said, stooping to pick up the knife Lock had knocked out of his hand.

'Christ, come on! We can't let him get away!' Lock said, and ran after the fleeing Arab. Underhill cursed and followed.

'Where's Connolly?' Lock shouted back.

'Dead,' Underhill panted. 'I went to relieve 'im . . . found 'im slumped by the ridge . . . 'is throat 'ad been cut.'

They ran past the point where the pipeline had been blown. Twisted, charred metal was strewn all over the ground. The oil burst into liquid fire as it gushed out of the wrecked pipeline, and the heat from the flames was immense. Lock and Underhill's shadows danced ahead of them as they ran on, away from the burning oil and after the Arab. But soon the darkness closed in on them again and Lock pulled up. He grabbed Underhill's arm and dragged him down to a crouching position. Both men waited, breathing, listening to the dark.

It was Lock who broke the silence. 'The girl?' he hissed.

'Search me. She was sleeping when I left you.'

'Give me your gun.' Lock held out his hand.

'My what?'

'Your Webley. I see you've acquired Connolly's Enfield. So you won't be needing a sidearm, will you?'

Lock waited, staring at the dark shadow of Underhill's form. Then he felt the cold metal of a revolver slap into his outstretched palm. Underhill started to complain again, but Lock hushed him. 'Quiet! Listen!'

A little way ahead of them they could hear movement and then the distinctive jangle of a horse's bridle, followed by the sudden pound of hooves galloping away. Lock pulled the trigger of the Webley and fired into the gloom. The muzzle flash momentarily lit up the landscape ahead like an eerie photograph. As the crack of his gunshot echoed around him, Lock spotted the tail end of a horse in the distance. But it was pointless to shoot a second time and, as quickly as it was illuminated, the gloom engulfed them once more.

'Now what?' Underhill said. 'We can't stumble about in the dark chasing that soddin' Abdul!'

'I know. But I've got a good idea where he's heading. Shadegan's about fifteen miles north-east at the edge of the marshland. I saw it on the map earlier today. Connolly mentioned we might get supplies from there to fix the armoured Rolls. The locals are supposedly pro-British.'

'All the locals are supposedly pro-British,' Underhill spat. 'I bet that bugger ridin' off in the dark with Connolly's blood on 'is blade is pro-British. We should forget 'im. Get back to the road and wait for the troops.'

'No,' Lock said. 'We've got a spy to catch, remember? And I think that's him!'

Underhill stared into the dark. 'Our troops'll only be a few miles back,' he said, sounding more and more to Lock as if he was pleading. 'We could go and get some 'orses, some 'elp, and 'ead back 'ere, try and pick up the saboteur's trail.'

Lock shook his head. 'It'll be too late by then.'

Underhill grunted his scepticism, but Lock knew what their best bet would be. Dawn was coming and already a thin strip of light grey was breaking up the dark horizon ahead.

'We go back to the campfire, grab our haversacks, pick up that detonator box I disconnected on the way back, then head after the saboteur. If it's not Wassmuss, then I think he'll lead us right to the German himself. Now move!'

Lock scrambled to his feet and both men ran back in the direction of the burning pipeline.

'Wait.' Lock suddenly pulled up. 'There!' He pointed to a section of undamaged pipeline where there was a stopcock. 'Help me close the valve!'

Lock and Underhill gripped the wheel. It was hot to the touch.

'Jesus!' Underhill flinched back, shaking his hand.

'Come on!' Lock yelled at him and began to put pressure on the wheel. His muscles started to scream and the sweat broke out on his head as he put all his effort into turning the wheel. Underhill gripped the other side and began to push. He swore and cursed and it looked to Lock as if the vein that throbbed on the sergeant major's forehead would burst. But then, with an ear-piercing squeal of rusty gears, the wheel juddered, and then moved.

Lock and Underhill turned and turned it until it was closed fast, and slowly the flow of oil ceased and the flames died down.

'Let's move, Sergeant Major!' Lock said, and ran down to the campfire.

CHAPTER SEVEN

Well over an hour later, with the sun rapidly rising over the surrounding hillside, Lock and Underhill came upon signs of life. Both men, crouching behind some scrub bushes, stared down into a small settlement nestled in a shallow valley. Despite the early hour, there was a lot of activity down there, and Lock followed the line of a well-traversed dirt road with his naked eye as a team of goods-laden camels were led into the town. 'Must be market day,' he said. 'No sign of our rider. But I think we should take a closer look.'

'We're never gonna find that bleedin' saboteur down there!' Underhill said.

'Maybe not, but this is where those tracks have led us,' Lock said. 'And I say we go and take a closer look.'

Underhill grabbed Lock's arm. 'I say we 'ead back, pick up our troops. They can't be far off.'

Lock glared at Underhill. The sergeant major let go of his arm.

'I'm giving the orders here, Sergeant Major, and you'd do well to remember that. And if you can't do that, then remember Major Ross's orders.'

It was a challenge to Underhill's military conditioning, and Lock knew that the sergeant major would find it hard to go against that. No matter how belligerent and stubborn he was, Lock had no doubt about the unquestioning respect Underhill held for a superior officer, and that it was something he prided himself on upholding. The problem was, though, that Lock doubted the sergeant major regarded him as a 'superior' officer.

Underhill hacked and spat into the sand. But he didn't say anything else.

'Glad that's settled,' Lock said. 'Leave yours and Connolly's haversacks here, and just take the saddlebag with the detonator.'

'What the 'ell for? Ain't this place Daurabat?'

'Daurat,' Lock corrected, hauling his haversack onto his back.

'Who bloody cares how you say it? What I mean is, ain't this the pro-British place?'

'Yes, but as you said yesterday, what the hell does that mean anyway, out here, in the middle of the Persian desert? So do as I say and bring the detonator as insurance.'

Lock could see more and more traders arriving as he and Underhill scrambled their way down towards the town. There were old men with staffs herding goats and sheep, donkeys laden with rich and deeply colourful rugs and jangling brass pots, and more tribespeople with horses, camels and ox-drawn carts, mostly loaded up with caged chickens.

Lock, with his holster unclipped, and Underhill, with

Connolly's rifle slung low and the saddlebag over his shoulder, joined the procession and marched on into the town, passing the watchful, suspicious eyes of two guards stationed at the town's entrance. They, like most of the other men, Lock had noticed, wore a distinctive felt hat of a neutral colour. It had stiff flaps raised over the top which, he guessed, could be pulled down over the ears during blizzards or sandstorms. Their clothes were the usual combination of Pirahan, Shalvar and Jameh, but the wide kamarband belt was replaced on the guards by a hefty cartridge belt. They weren't challenged as they passed, and the traders paid them little heed either. But Lock knew that news of their arrival would spread like wildfire.

As they walked on into the settlement, Lock and Underhill found themselves on the edge of a sea of crudely constructed, open-sided tents, made up of rough canvas sheeting, animal hides and blankets thrown over basic pole frames. The air was alive with human shouts of conversation and sales pitches mixed with plaintive animal cries and snorts. Lock led the way, passing foul-smelling animal pens already beginning to fill up with livestock.

Traders had set up their stalls of fresh dates, figs and vegetables. The smell of tea, coffee, herbs and spices wafted across the square, and the early morning sun dazzled on the trinkets of brass and tin. One man was attempting to sell a number of books that gave the impression of having been recently unearthed from some damp cellar, so mouldy, dusty and dog-eared were they. A circle of old men stood smoking in silence, studying goats in a pen. Tribeswomen dressed in colourful robes stood with pots balanced on their heads, while children stopped their games and stared as Lock and Underhill passed by. More women were bent over a flat rock preparing food and kneading dough, while others were scraping animal hides. There was a large, sweaty Arab standing in front of a stall bursting with rugs, hundreds of them, in all sizes and colours: vibrant blues, deep reds, golds and greens. Next to him were two more women, again adorned in colourful flowing robes. Both had long black hair topped by a headscarf. They were spinning wool. A mangy dog, ribcage protruding, was snuffling around. It growled at Lock and Underhill as they approached.

'Even the soddin' mutts 'ate us,' Underhill said. 'I tell you, we'll get no 'elp 'ere!'

'This way!' Lock said, leading off to the far side of the market. Mud-brick buildings edged the square, in the middle of which was an open-fronted pavement cafe already buzzing with customers.

The cafe was rustic, but deceptively large inside. A rough wooden bar ran along one wall, with a number of tables scattered about beyond it. There was a beaded curtain covering a doorway at the back, which Lock presumed hid the horrors of the kitchen. A couple of flyblown oil lamps hung from the greasy walls. Outside, under a ragged awning that ran the length of the open frontage, were more tables. Lock headed to an empty one on the far right. It offered a good view of both the cafe interior and the market square beyond.

A portly Persian, whom Lock guessed could be anywhere between thirty and fifty, bowed as they approached.

'*Sabaah al-khayr*,' he said, greeting them in Arabic. His fleshy, round face was moist with sweat. '*Eftaar?*'

'He means "breakfast",' Lock translated.

'Ah, *Engleezee*,' the proprietor beamed. 'I speak leetle Engleezee. Hallo! Seet!' He lifted the felt hat from his oily football of a head in salute, before pulling out a couple of chairs and beckoning for Lock and Underhill to take their places at the table.

'We 'aven't time for this,' Underhill said. 'We'll never find that bleedin' saboteur amongst this lot. Let's get back to the troops while we can.'

'Just take a seat, Sergeant Major. I'm told Persian cafe owners are like priests; they know everything.' Lock sat down, dumped his haversack at his feet, removed his hat, and smiled up at the proprietor. '*Baydah maslooqah, khobz, qahwah saadah, law samaht.*'

The proprietor bowed his head, and with a waft of his flowing robe, disappeared into his cafe and through the beaded curtain at the back.

'What the 'ell you ask for in that jibbajabba lingo?'

'Boiled eggs, bread and coffee.'

'Coffee?' Underhill eyed Lock thoughtfully. 'What's "sweet" then?'

'*Sukkar zeyaadah.*'

Underhill leant back in his chair and shouted after the proprietor. 'Oi, Abdul! Sooker zayadu! Compree?'

The proprietor popped his head through the curtain and waved his understanding with one chubby hand, before disappearing again.

At the table next to them an ancient old man with a face as lined and cracked as the desert floor was seated playing Alquerques. He glanced up from his game, but hurriedly averted his watery gaze when Lock caught his eye.

Lock turned to Underhill. 'You're an ignorant bastard, aren't you?'

Underhill grinned back at him, showing his newly broken tooth. 'These rag'eads are the ignorant ones. Sah.'

'He's wearing a felt hat.'

'Looks like a bleedin' tea cosy to me.'

Lock shook his head.

Underhill just smirked, lifted the saddlebag onto his lap, and opened it up. 'Right, now let's see what we 'ave 'ere . . .'

Lock leant forward. The sergeant major was studying the detonator box they had taken from the pipeline. 'Recognise it?' Lock said.

'Give me a chance . . .'

Lock moved his attention to the market. A group of young boys caught his eye. They were swarming around a shiny white motor car parked about fifty yards away, just inside an open-sided barn. The children reminded him of the boys who buzzed around the traders at the Saddar Bazaar back in Karachi. The way they weaved in and out of the stalls, laughing and pushing one another. A good ruse to distract traders while one of their number quickly helped themselves to a piece of fruit or a trinket they could sell. His mind snapped back to the moment. A shiny white motor car! It was too far away for him to make out the model, but it was very much out of place. He nudged Underhill. 'Over there!'

'Huh?' Underhill said, looking up from the saddlebag, frowning. Then he too spotted the car. 'What the 'ell's that doing 'ere?'

'My thinking exactly. The local khan's perhaps?' Lock said.

'I thought they preferred 'orses? I'd wager that's a white man's car,' Underhill said, returning his attention to the detonator box.

Lock began to scan the crowds as if they held the answer to the mysterious presence of the motor vehicle. His eyes fixed onto two Bedouin Arabs dressed in abas and kufiyas, wandering over to the cafe. Nothing unusual in that, as there was a number of Arab traders in the marketplace already. These two were deep in animated conversation, but fell silent once they reached the entrance. One of them stole a quick look at Lock, before both men stepped inside. The proprietor emerged from behind the beaded curtain and they greeted him with hearty '*salaam*'s'. After a brief, whispered conversation, the two Bedouins made their way further into the cafe to an already busy table where they appeared to be greeted as brothers. The two Bedouins seemed innocent enough, but one of them caught Lock's attention. He wasn't particularly remarkable, yet his attire was markedly different in two aspects. The first was that he wore a pair of tinted goggles. Not that unusual, perhaps, a good device to own if riding in a sandstorm. But the second pricked Lock's suspicions. He wore a pair of leather riding boots. But not just any old pair of riding boots, but what looked to Lock as extremely well-crafted and expensive riding boots. More than that, was the mud they were caked in. The same mud that was splattered up the side of Lock's and Underhill's boots; oil-soaked mud. A very distinctive colour and sheen. Lock wasn't a betting man, but he'd wager all he owned, not much admittedly but he'd do so, on that Bedouin being their saboteur.

Lock opened his mouth to make the same point to Underhill, but as he turned his gaze away, the proprietor approached carrying a wooden tray laden with food. Underhill quickly closed the saddlebag and lowered it to his feet. The proprietor grinned and nodded, and set about placing a plate of freshly baked flatbreads, half a dozen boiled eggs in a basket, and coffee on the table in front of them. He bowed. '*Bel-hanaa' wash-shefaa*'. Enjoy meal.'

But before he could move away again, Lock reached out and took hold of his arm. 'We're seeking a man.'

The proprietor frowned. '*Ma afham*,' he shrugged.

'You understand perfectly,' Lock said. 'He came riding through here ahead of us. A stranger, perhaps.'

The proprietor shook his head and waved his hand at the traders' camp beyond. 'Many riders come, *as-sayed*. Many strangers.' He smiled and glanced nervously back into the cafe, before lowering his voice. 'But, *as-sayed*, all riders head to the camp of Khan Jenaab Ahmad Omid Esfahani.'

Lock tried to see who the proprietor had looked back at. But his view was obscured by the man's bulk as he leant in closer, close enough for Lock to smell his stale breath.

'He is local khan, *as-sayed*. Very powerful Qashqai.'

'Qashqai?'

The proprietor bobbed and grinned again, patting his chest proudly. 'We Qashqai peoples, *as-sayed*.'

'Is that the khan's motor car?' Lock asked, pointing at the parked vehicle.

The proprietor lowered his eyes. 'I know not about such things, *as-sayed*.'

'I'd like to speak with this Ahmad Omid Esfahani.' Lock removed his hand from the proprietor's arm and placed a gold coin on the table. It glistened in the morning sunlight.

The proprietor didn't even pause to think as he snatched up the coin. 'You are indeed fortunate, *as-sayed*. Jenaab Ahmad Omid Esfahani is honoured customer today.' He bowed and moved quickly away.

Lock watched the proprietor weave his way toward the back of the cafe where the two Bedouin had gone to join a group of older Qashqai. The men were sat in a haze of tobacco smoke. A larger, bearded Persian loomed up, stepping in front of the proprietor. He was obviously a bodyguard, judging by his build and the way he stood, arms folded, like a formidable statue, blocking the way to the table. The proprietor began gesticulating wildly and, after a moment, the bodyguard let him pass.

'I thought you'd lost that gold?' Underhill said, as he began to peel an egg.

'Not all.' Lock had wisely hidden the gold Ross gave him elsewhere about his person than in his haversack.

Lock could see that the proprietor was bent down, talking rapidly to a white-bearded Persian. The man was staring directly across, and as the proprietor talked, he too kept glancing back over to Lock. The white-bearded Persian gave the faintest nod of his head and the proprietor stood, bowed, then waddled quickly back over to Lock.

'The most esteemed Jenaab Ahmad Omid Esfahani would welcome you to his table. You would perhaps wish to share his shisha?' His voice was trembling and he was sweating profusely.

Lock nodded. '*Shokran*. Sergeant Major, you wait here!'

Underhill stuttered a protest through a mouthful of egg. 'Where you goin'?'

'To meet our saboteur.'

'But this fat Abdul don't know anything,' Underhill said, wiping his mouth and jabbing a thumb at the proprietor.

'Perhaps not. But I'll wager the Qashqai Khan does.'

Lock rose to his feet, but Underhill pulled him back by the arm. 'And what makes you think 'e'll give 'im up?' he hissed, voice low.

Lock shrugged the sergeant major off. 'Because I'll tell him that there's an army of British troops marching this way. He won't be that stupid.'

'What if 'e is? You know nothin' about 'em!'

'I know what Ross told me.'

'Bah! You can't trust these Buddoos, other than to slit yer throat as soon as look at yer. I keep tellin' you that. Too risky. What if it's a trap? Let's scarper,' Underhill said, as he glared at the proprietor hovering a few feet away.

'Isn't this what White Tabs do, though, Sergeant Major? Take risks?'

Underhill shifted his gaze back to Lock's.

'Well?' Lock said.

Underhill narrowed his eyes. 'Aye. Sah. But I don't like it.'

'It's not about whether you like it. Now, sit still and keep that rifle ready. We may need to make a hasty retreat.'

Underhill glared back for a moment, then nodded reluctantly.

'If I call, raise up the saddlebag for all to see.'

'Why?'

'Just do it! And save some of those eggs for me,' Lock said before turning and making his way over to the rear of the cafe.

A low murmur started up amongst the clientele as they eyed the proprietor leading Lock to the table at the back.

There were seven men sat there; four Persians, all of a similar age, around sixty, all quietly watching as Lock approached, the two Bedouins and the khan. But Lock was not intimidated and immediately fell into the correct etiquette. He knew no Farsi, but greeted each man in the common Arabic, shaking him by the right hand in turn, starting with the most senior and ending with the youngest.

'*As-salaam alaykum.*'

When Lock had finished, he turned back to the elder, white-bearded Qashqai whom the proprietor had been conferring with earlier, and bowed his head slightly. 'You do me a great honour, *ya ostaaz sayyid* Ahmad, inviting me to your humble table.'

Ahmad Omid Esfahani held Lock's gaze for a second more than was comfortable. '*Wa-alaykum as-salaam. Khosh amadid.* Sit.' His voice was croaky and rattled with phlegm. He clapped his hands and ordered coffee.

The proprietor, who had been shifting around the edge of the group in a mist of nervous sweat, bowed and quickly scuttled off.

There was silence again after Lock sat himself down opposite Ahmad Omid Esfahani. He was older and frailer than the other men, perhaps closer to eighty than sixty, but his grey eyes were bright and his face lined with decades of wisdom. The shisha was passed slowly around the table and it eventually made its way to Lock. He smiled politely to the Qashqai elder to his right, and then began to puff away at the sweet-scented apple tobacco. The proprietor arrived carrying a tray laden with a large terracotta coffee pot and eight small clay cups. He placed one cup in front of each of the men, then poured the thick black coffee. Lock passed the shisha on, then took up his cup and sipped at the coffee. It was hot, sweet and strong.

'I like your motor car,' Lock said.

Ahmad Omid Esfahani puffed contentedly on the shisha. 'What is it you desire?' he asked, ignoring Lock's obvious probe about the car.

'Esteemed *ya ostaaz* Ahmad,' Lock began, clearing his throat. 'I am here at the behest of my leaders, Major General Townshend and Major Ross of His Majesty's Most Britannic 6th Poona Division. I have travelled many miles in search of a man who is determined to taint the friendship of our great countries with the poison of hate and intolerance.' He paused, wondering if the Qashqai leaders would believe his flowery waffle. But no one interrupted or laughed or scoffed.

'I am on the trail of a German spy who is known to be at work in this area,' Lock continued, 'stirring up unrest and inciting young men to rise up and not only to attack your British friends, but to attack the very oil pipeline that brings wealth and prosperity to your people. I was led to believe such a man was held captive here.'

The men at the table remained silent when Lock finished, and all eyes were on the Qashqai chieftain.

In the time Lock followed the proprietor to Ahmad Omid Esfahani's table, greeted the elders, sat down and shared their shisha, took coffee and then told the tribesmen why he was there, he had subtly unclipped his holster, removed his Webley and placed it on his lap under the table. No one had mentioned it, no one had made a move for him, and Lock was sure no one had noticed.

After a long, drawn-out pause the old khan put down the shisha pipe. 'You have entered our great country,' he said, 'uninvited and you ask for our help? Help in stopping the rising where my people will push infidels from our land to the south and from our land to the north. You British say you extend the hand of friendship, brotherhood and loyalty, but you take our oil, you poison the soil, and you let our people starve.'

Ahmad Omid Esfahani paused, but Lock wasn't certain

whether he was expected to respond or not. He glanced around the men at the table. They were all staring at him. He opened his mouth to reply.

'You are no better than Ottomans who rule in west,' the old Qashqai khan said before Lock could speak, 'who make our brothers suffer in Mesopotamia, so why you think I will help you? Will your generals and your majors support our call for independence? Will you give equal share of oil production?' Esfahani stared challengingly into Lock's eyes. 'Of course you will not! For you British are as corrupt as rest of empire builders. Where were you British when the Russian troops massacred my people at Tabriz? Old men and children killed, our women raped? Answer me this! You say you want to catch German spy. I know no such man. I know only friends who wish to help our struggle for freedom.'

Lock felt a chill creep up his spine as the old Qashqai spoke. He had hoped that he would find a friend and an ally, some help in tracking this Wassmuss down, but he had gravely misjudged the attitude of the locals. He now knew that he really had no idea what he was doing. He did not understand the true feelings of these people and no wonder, as he had never given them a second thought up until now. He didn't even know about them. They just lived here, where the oil happened to be. And the oil belonged to the British Empire, didn't it? That's what Ross had said. Lock knew that his life was in danger the longer he stayed where he was.

In a swift, fluid motion, he pulled his Webley out from under the table. The Qashqai elders made no attempt to move; they didn't even flinch. The huge Persian guard stepped forward, but Ahmad Omid Esfahani raised his hand. The guard stopped where he was, sword half drawn, eyes boring into Lock's face.

'I'm sorry to spoil our little chat, gentlemen,' Lock said, 'but I know you are just as aware as I am that the German spy Wassmuss is sat at this very table. And I am taking him with me. Dead or alive.'

Lock's accusations were met by a stony silence. He moved the gun away from Ahmad Omid Esfahani's general direction and trained it at the Bedouin who was sitting to the Qashqai Khan's right. He was the Arab wearing the goggles and the well-tailored boots.

'You are under arrest, Herr Wassmuss,' Lock said.

The Arab didn't move at first, his expression didn't change. But then he sprang up, pushing Ahmad Omid Esfahani away from him, and made to pull his pistol from the holster at his waist. Lock pulled the trigger of his Webley. There was a deafening crack as the hammer slammed into the bullet sending it racing down the chamber and tearing through the Arab's throat. The Arab made a gurgling, choking noise and slumped back in his seat. He seemed surprised, as if that wasn't quite what he was expecting to happen to him, and then he crashed face first down onto the table, his head making a terrible smack as it hit the terracotta coffee cup in front of him. Blood was pulsating from the wound in his neck and began to slowly spread out through the broken pieces of pottery and across the tabletop. Lock adjusted his aim but felt a terrific sting of pain as the Qashqai elder next to him smashed the shisha pipe down on his wrist. The Webley clattered from his grip, and he was seized from behind and wrenched up from his seat.

'Enough! Let him be!'

The voice came not from Ahmad Omid Esfahani but from the second Bedouin Arab. The entire cafe was deathly silent now and Lock could see Ahmad Omid Esfahani hesitating. Then he nodded at the man who held Lock. The grip was released and Lock glanced over his shoulder to see the huge Persian guard glaring down at him.

'Sit, Lieutenant, gentlemen,' the Bedouin said, clapping his hands. 'More coffee. And clear this up!' He waved in the direction of his dead companion. The proprietor, who had been cowering behind a table, slowly rose to his feet. He bowed unsteadily and rushed back to the kitchen muttering prayers to Allah.

The chatter started up again and the cafe returned to how it was before. Lock stole a glance to where Underhill was seated, and passed a hand through his hair. He saw the sergeant major briefly nod his head in understanding. Lock turned back to the Bedouin.

'Very clever, Herr Wassmuss.'

'What is, Lieutenant? Having my assistant dress how you would expect me to dress? In goggles and a pair of expensive riding boots? Why, Lieutenant, I find that . . . insulting.' He smiled and held his hand out. 'Sit, please.'

Lock looked around the table at the other Qashqai men who were all focusing on Ahmad Omid Esfahani for guidance. And when their khan finally sat, they too sat. The proprietor arrived with fresh coffee and three young men. Two dragged the body of the Arab Lock had killed away, whilst the third set about wiping down the table of all evidence of the man's demise.

Lock took his seat again and felt the presence of the large Persian guard looming over him. For the moment he would see how this played out. He glanced down at his gun still lying where it had fallen.

Wassmuss followed Lock's gaze and smiled. He leant forward, picked up the Webley and levelled it at Lock. 'Bang!' he shouted and laughed. Lock didn't even react. Wassmuss tut-tutted his disappointment, quickly emptied the shells from the Webley, then tossed the gun back to Lock.

'Put it back in your holster, Lieutenant,' he said, pocketing the bullets, 'I have plenty of superior weapons of my own.'

Lock caught the gun and did as he was told, stuffing it back in his holster. What the hell was Wassmuss playing at? he thought, studying the man properly for the first time. His disguise was remarkable, in that he looked totally *un*remarkable. His clothes, a mixture of Persian and Bedouin Arab attire, were brown and black in colour, and ragged and dusty. He wore a kufiya wrapped around his head and a cartridge belt across his shoulder. But it was his face that Lock really saw for the first time. There was a thick blond-brown beard hiding fleshy lips below a straight, flared nose. He was rather thickset – stocky, really – and shorter than Lock by a good four inches. It was hard to tell his age as the angular face was grimy, tanned and weathered, but Lock reckoned he would be in his early-to-mid thirties judging by the way he held himself, just the confident side of arrogance. But what was really remarkable about him, Lock thought, was his piercing eyes. He couldn't believe he hadn't noted them before, as they weren't the ubiquitous brown of the Middle East, but were the sharp, piercing blue of Northern Europe. And his voice. Authoritative, yet gentle, and with barely a hint of an accent.

Wassmuss chuckled, as if reading Lock's mind and noting his surprise. 'I imagine, Lieutenant, that your eyes attract a similar interest to my own.'

Lock didn't respond.

'Oh, come, Herr Lock, no need for the silent response. We are all good friends here!' Wassmuss said, extending his arms at the Qashqai seated around.

'To German gold,' Lock said.

Wassmuss tut-tutted again, then took a sip of his coffee. 'That reminds me, Lieutenant, you have some items that belong to me. May I have them, please?'

'I don't know what you are talking about.'

'You sleep very soundly, Lieutenant. You must have been exhausted last night,' Wassmuss said.

Lock tried not to look surprised. He knew he had failed for there was a spark of triumph in the German's eyes. He had thought it was the girl who had taken his gun, the gold and the papers from the saddlebag. The notebook and the two incriminating letters with the broken Ottoman wax seals would still be where he put them himself, inside the pockets of the jacket she wore. But now he had a horrifying feeling that this German bastard had emptied the saddlebag. He imagined that after Wassmuss had slit Connolly's throat, set the charges on the pipeline, and sneaked down to their campsite, somehow eluding Underhill, he had stood over him. Maybe he even put a knife to his throat, before he had taken back his documents and his German gold. But why had the German not killed him?

And then Lock cursed himself. It was all a bluff. None of it was true. All right, you bastard, he thought, I'll let you keep thinking that I believe everything you say.

'So any questions?' Wassmuss said.

'What did you do with the girl?'

'Pretty little thing,' Wassmuss smiled. 'Found her at the foot of the Zagros with her brother, tending sheep. Lur nomads. They made a good disguise to get through the British patrols north of Ahwaz. They served their purpose, until the boy tried to run. So, alas . . .' Wassmuss shrugged. 'A bit of a bloodbath. My men were bored. The girl . . . a necessary distraction. But as to her whereabouts now, I do not know. I do not have her. I wish I did. Why, Lieutenant, did you take to her? Like you took to . . . Now, what was her name? The Chinese girl? Although she was more of a woman than a child.'

Lock was stunned into silence. What had Wassmuss just said? The Chinese woman? How on earth could he know about . . . ?

'How in the world could I know about Mei Ling? you are asking yourself,' Wassmuss sneered. 'We've met before, Lieutenant. Although, I doubt you will remember. No? It was last year, in Tsingtao.'

Lock studied Wassmuss's face as he racked his memory, but he couldn't place the man. Yes, then that part of China was full of German officers, soldiers and merchants, but . . . Besides, he doubted whether Wassmuss wore Arab garb at the time, if he was truly there.

'Perhaps, if you took that ridiculous get-up off, I may be able to place you,' Lock said.

'And you think you look less ridiculous in that sheepskin and that slouch hat you wore when you came in?' Wassmuss scoffed, glaring back at him. 'It is of no matter. But remember this, Lieutenant, I know a lot more about you, your White Tabs, and your Major Ross than you do about me.' His voice had gone up a pitch, the German accent more profound now, and his eyes ablaze with irritation. 'Now, where is . . . *mein* notebook?' He slammed his hand down on the table, making some of the listening Qashqai elders start.

Lock smiled ruefully. A chink in the armour; this German was touchy. He shrugged. 'I have no idea.' It was true, although he knew who did. He needed to find that girl again, and quickly, before she ran into more trouble.

'Perhaps our friend there,' Wassmuss said, indicating to the large Persian guard behind Lock, 'can prick your memory? *Ja?* Shall we ask him?'

'I think not, Herr Wassmuss,' Lock said, rising to his feet. He immediately felt a powerful hand on his shoulder. But as quickly as it landed there, Lock snatched it away, twisting it and bending the fingers back against their joints. The guard yelped in pain, but Lock kept forcing the hand up and back. There was a snap like a twig breaking, and the guard dropped to his knees. Lock brought his own knee up to meet the hefty Persian's jaw. There was a terrific crack and the guard slumped to the floor like a sack of potatoes. He was out cold. Lock turned back to face the table and was staring down the barrel of Wassmuss's pistol. The cafe was again deathly silent as the clientele watched the khan's table with captivated awe.

'Are you as stupid as you look, Lieutenant? You are going nowhere!' Wassmuss hissed, the spittle spraying across his beard.

'My, we are tetchy,' Lock scoffed. 'Sergeant Major!' he called.

Underhill sprang to his feet at the far end of the cafe, and raised the saddlebag so that Wassmuss and the others could see it.

'A little insurance, Herr Wassmuss,' Lock said. 'One of your detonators, primed and ready. It won't be a huge explosion, but it'll be big enough to take out this cafe and everyone in it.'

'You would not dare,' Wassmuss sneered.

Lock raised an eyebrow. 'A challenge? My mission is to stop

you. Yours, to carry on. I would say this is a . . . stalemate. Check, if you like?'

Wassmuss glared back at Lock, keeping his gun level. Lock watched as the German's facial expressions changed. He was clearly mulling the options over, trying to size up what Lock would actually do.

'Sergeant Major Underhill is a bastard,' Lock said. 'He hates me as much as he hates Persians, Germans, other human beings in general, really. If you know me as well as you claim, Herr Wassmuss, then you'll know that he won't hesitate to throw that bomb just on the off chance of killing me. Now, he's not the most patient of men either . . .' Lock shrugged.

Wassmuss glanced over in Underhill's direction, then back at Lock. He glared at him a moment longer, then his face broke into a smile and he lowered his pistol.

'I mean to get my notebook back, Lieutenant. And I shall.'

'Perhaps,' Lock said, and turned to Ahmad Omid Esfahani. 'Your Excellency, thank you for your hospitality.'

The Qashqai elder looked up at him with a stony expression. 'Go, young man. Your safety is no guarantee if dwell here,' Ahmad Omid Esfahani said with a dismissive wave of his bony hand.

As Lock left the table, he noticed that four Qashqai tribesmen, all holding long-barrelled rifles, were standing near to the tables under the awning, watching him with cold, black eyes. Lock caught Underhill's gaze and the sergeant major instantly understood the danger and slowly got to his feet, rifle at the ready and swinging the saddlebag over his shoulder.

Lock bowed his head. 'Gentlemen,' he said in English, 'I bid you good day.' He moved away from the table, pushing past the frightened-looking proprietor and swiftly made his way over to Underhill.

'Let's get the hell out of here!' he said, picking up his haversack and slapping his slouch hat on. He grabbed a piece of flatbread and a couple of eggs.

'And the saboteur?' Underhill asked, knocking back his coffee, and slipping the saddlebag over his shoulder.

'There are no saboteurs here, only heroes fighting for Arab independence.'

Underhill scoffed. 'Told you we'd get no 'elp from these 'eathens. By the way, it's an 'Un one all right.'

'What's a "Hun one"?'

'The soddin' exploder! The detonator box!'

They quickly made their way over the busy square and darted down one of the passageways between the brightly coloured canvas tents. It was dusty and oppressive, and lined with open pots. In such a confined space, Lock found the air chokingly thick with heat and the heady aroma of overbearing spices. He glanced behind to see that the four armed Qashqai tribesmen were hastily following.

He pushed Underhill on ahead of him. 'We need some transport, and quick! We'll never make it out of here on foot.'

'Are we finally leavin'?' Underhill said.

'Yes. But we need to find that girl.'

'What? What bleedin' girl?'

'The child!'

'The fanti lass? You mad? She could be anywhere!'

'I know, but she's got something vital and Wassmuss wants it too!'

'Wassmuss? The 'Un spy?'

'Our saboteur,' Lock said.

'You're kiddin'? And you let 'im go?'

'We were lucky to get out of that cafe alive. And we've still got to get out of here!'

'I saw some camels over that way.' Underhill jutted his chin to the left.

'Got anything to barter with?' Lock called to him.

'I've got me gun!' Underhill snarled.

'What about that detonator box? Can you make it work? Set it off?'

'Not without explosives.'

Lock pulled his haversack up and, fishing about inside, produced an oily package and quickly unwrapped a stick of dynamite. 'From the pipeline.' He slapped it into Underhill's outstretched hand.

'Jesus! Careful! Was that in there all the time?' Underhill said. 'It looks so bloody old, bound to be unstable. All right then, won't be needin' the detonator box. Got no blastin' cap, anyhow. Or safety fuse. But I'll rig one up with these,' he said, snatching up a handful of candles as they passed a store stocked with them. He quickly broke the wax apart, yanking out the wicks. The storeholder called angrily after them, and Lock tossed the man a coin, and pushed on quickly through the crowd.

'Hurry!' Lock glanced back over his shoulder again, but he could no longer see their pursuers. He weaved his way on through the milling traders and shoppers, barely registering their faces as they went about the business of buying and selling.

The passageway widened out onto an open area and Lock felt his hand instinctively go to his Webley. He came alongside Underhill, who was still frantically working with his knife and a candle wick to set up a crude fuse for the dynamite.

'This stuff's pretty brittle!' the sergeant major said.

One of their Qashqai pursuers emerged from a canvas passageway a little ahead of them. 'This way!' Lock shoved Underhill to the left, pushing by a man holding out an animal hide for their inspection, and down another narrow passage. Lock could hear shouting behind him, but he didn't look back.

They rounded a corner and came to the open-sided barn where the white motor car was parked. It was a handsome vehicle, with an open-top body and a plush green-leather interior. Lock now recognised the model. It was a Rolls-Royce, and it looked even more out of place at close quarters. The thought flashed across Lock's mind to hijack the vehicle, but he quickly dismissed it as foolish. The terrain wasn't ideal for an automobile, and escape across the hills would be better by four legs than four wheels.

'Ready?' Lock asked, glancing over his shoulder once more. He could see one of their pursuers pushing angrily through the crowds and knew that it wouldn't be long before gunshots broke through the general melee.

Beyond the Rolls, past the open barn, was a flat area of rocky sand and scrub enclosed on three sides by crumbling, ten-foot-high mud-brick walls. Here were the camel traders. Inside the enclosure, twenty or so camels were picking at the ground, and nearby, four Bedouins sat in a circle drinking mint tea. Lock could smell the distinctive scent from the moment he rounded the corner.

'Done!' Underhill said, and he held up his crude dynamite bomb.

'Keep that handy and keep an eye out for our pursuers.' Lock turned to the camel traders. '*Sabaah al-khayr!*' he beamed as he approached.

The four Arabs rose to their feet. Three were very young, little more than boys, and Lock thought they looked extremely wary, shifting on their feet and tugging at the worn cloth of their grubby abas.

'I need two camels, gentlemen, saddled,' Lock addressed the older Bedouin man, who wore multicoloured robes, sandals and a grey turban.

The man pulled at his long greying beard and bobbed his head. 'We have many fine camels, sayyid.'

Out of the corner of his eye, Lock could see Underhill leaning against the wall at the entrance to the enclosure, rifle raised and ready.

'I can see that you have, but two is all I require,' Lock said.

The old Bedouin nodded again. 'Come, sit. Have mint tea. We discuss.'

Lock cursed to himself. He knew that the proper etiquette was to sit, haggle and finally, after maybe half an hour, agree on a price. But he didn't even have half a minute. He had two options: make a threat or a ridiculous offer. Threat was the best option, but he was surrounded by enough enemies as it was. He scrutinised the three boys again. They were scared. He undid his wristwatch and held it out. It was all he had to offer. '*Haza ahsan sear.*'

The old man took the watch and put it close to his eyes. Lock was momentarily distracted. He could hear shouting getting closer and closer. When he looked back, the old man was staring at him. His watery brown eyes moved to the sound of the approaching commotion, then back to Lock's face.

''Urry up!' Underhill called. 'What ya bloody doing? Just shoot the bastards!'

'*Min fadlak*,' Lock pleaded.

The old man's brown eyes dropped to Lock's holstered Webley and then darted across in Underhill's direction. He snapped some quick instructions to the three youngsters at his side. They quickly scuttled off to the camel herd and came back with a couple of mangy-looking beasts, but both were saddled.

'Underhill!' Lock called, as one of the young men coaxed the gurgling camels slowly down to their knees.

''Bout bleedin' time!' Underhill said, and shouldering his rifle quickly, he scrambled up onto one of the camels.

Lock climbed up onto his beast, and the young Arab egged both animals up again. 'You ever ridden one of these?' Lock called across to Underhill.

'Once. Filthy bloody things! Flea-ridden. Got bitten to buggery. But they can't 'alf move! Hut-hut!' The sergeant major kicked his heels into his camel's side and it shot forward.

Lock indicated his thanks to the old Bedouin and quickly made off after Underhill. There was a shout from behind and he instinctively ducked down as a rifle shot cracked through the air. Lock twisted in his saddle to see not only one of the young camel traders aiming a rifle at him, but the four Qashqais giving chase. Lock gave a shout of encouragement to his camel, kicking his heels hard into its sides.

'Throw that dynamite!' he yelled to Underhill. But the sergeant major was one step ahead of him, and Lock ducked again as the makeshift bomb came fizzing over Underhill's shoulder.

Seconds later the dynamite exploded in a cloud of dust and

fire. There was an almighty crack and Lock's ears rang. His camel faltered but kept on galloping forward.

'Bastard!' Lock shouted.

They rode hard and fast towards the east, Lock thinking that they would double back for the river and the road to Mohammerah once they were out of sight of Daurat. The British troops wouldn't be far off and he knew Wassmuss and his Qashqai allies wouldn't risk running into such a formidable force. He glanced over his shoulder, back at the settlement. There were people gathering, gesticulating wildly, but no horsemen on their tails yet.

He pushed on up the rocky ridge that weaved towards the horizon. Then he heard Underhill curse and saw him yank back on the reins of his camel.

Lock pulled up beside him.

At the top of the ridge lining the horizon directly ahead of them were a number of horsemen silhouetted by the morning sun.

They were trapped.

CHAPTER EIGHT

Lock turned in his saddle. They couldn't double back through Daurat, not now. It would only be a matter of time before Wassmuss persuaded Ahmad Omid Esfahani and his Qashqai warriors to come after them. He still believed Lock was in possession of his precious notebook, after all.

Underhill levelled his rifle at the silhouetted riders and cursed. 'Shitty place to die.'

But just as he pulled the trigger, Lock smashed the butt into the air sending the bullet harmlessly up into the cloudless sky.

'Wait!' Lock snapped.

'Are you out of your bleedin' mind? I ain't just gonna sit and let them take me an' skin me and bugger me corpse!' Underhill snarled.

'Trust me.' Lock had seen something in one of the silhouettes, the only short figure among them, something familiar about the shape of its head.

Underhill snorted and swore.

'Shoulder your rifle and follow me,' Lock said, kicking his heels into his camel's side. The beast gurgled and lumbered forward.

'You ar—' But Underhill's words were cut out by his own camel's guttural complaint at being urged on again.

As they got closer to the men on horseback, Lock counted twenty riders, a fierce-looking bunch, unsmiling, with weathered, mostly bearded faces. They were all wearing distinctive large round felt caps and long, bulky cloaks. He could also see that they all carried long-barrelled Muscat rifles.

'As I thought, they're not Qashqai,' he said. 'Bakhtiaris perhaps? No, I think they're Lurs, I'm sure of it.'

The two men stopped about twenty yards from what appeared to be their chief, a man with a scarred face. He was sitting astride the only horse that wasn't black or brown. His was a beautiful white stallion.

Nobody moved for what seemed like an age, and then the scar-faced Lur tapped his heels and his horse trotted forward. He came to within five feet of Lock and Underhill, and then began to circle them.

'Well, I'll be . . .'

Lock glanced at Underhill to see that he was nodding to the left of the main group. The girl they had rescued was sitting behind one of the riders. She was still clothed in Lock's service jacket and had Connolly's cap on her head and his goggles over her eyes. Lock couldn't help but smile. That was the familiar shape he'd recognised, the cap.

The Lur saw the expression and glanced behind him. He looked back at Lock quizzically. '*Min an to?*' he said. '*Almaanee?*'

'*Ostraalee, wa Breetaanee*,' Lock said.

The Lur turned his horse, which snorted impatiently, and continued to circle them, but now in the opposite direction.

'My daughter tells that you save her from Turkish devils.'

Lock glanced at Underhill and raised an eyebrow. The Lur had switched from Arabic to English.

'This is truth?' the Lur said.

'Yes,' Lock said, 'but I wish we had found her sooner. I am sorry.'

The Lur yanked at his horse's reins, trying to still the beast. He patted its neck, then trotted closer until he was face to face with Lock. He studied Lock's features in silence for a moment; Lock took the opportunity to do the same.

The Lur was in his forties, judging by the flecks of grey in his beard. His skin was dark and weathered and a scar ran from his left eye, which was blind and opaque, down to his neck. His good eye was bright and fierce and never blinked. He was dressed in a black cloak with a brown tunic underneath and two bandoliers criss-crossed over his shoulders, forming a showy waistcoat of cartridges. He wore a pair of deep-red baggy trousers with a green sash tied around his waist, and on his feet were a fine pair of leather riding boots. He brought to mind a circus performer crossed with some bandit from a penny Western novel.

The Lur suddenly broke into a toothy grin and his arms flew up in the air. '*Bismillah hir rahman nir raheem!*' he shouted.

The horsemen on the ridge raised their rifles in the air and cheered Allah as one.

'*Esmee* Lock, Lieutenant Kingdom Lock of the Australian Imperial Force.'

'*Wa-alaykum as-salaam*,' the one-eyed Lur bowed his head

slightly. 'I called Aziz Azoo. I of Bala Garideh Lurs. I am eternally in your debt, ya sayed Kingdom Lock, for life of my daughter.'

'What is her name?' Lock said.

Aziz looked back towards the girl. She was staring over at Lock and smiling. 'It is Fairuza,' he said.

'Ah,' said Lock, 'the colour of her eyes.'

Aziz grinned. 'She tell of her rescue. And how she escape and find me, her father who had been tracking her for days. We were on other side of river when she find us, then bring us back to you. She knew you would need assistance.'

'Lock, I don't wanna break up your little tryst, but . . .' Despite his usual belligerence, Underhill sounded concerned.

Lock turned in his saddle. Underhill was shielding his eyes and looking back down the ridge towards the town. Lock pulled his field glasses out of his haversack and steadied his camel. He could see Daurat clearly. There was a thin line of dust running from the western entrance, and at its head something glinted in the early morning sun.

'Looks as if that fancy motor car is heading for the Ahwaz–Mohammerah road,' Lock said. He turned his gaze to the eastern entrance and to what, he presumed, Underhill was worried about. A band of about forty riders were heading straight for them. Their rifles and swords, raised above their heads, glinted in the sunlight that penetrated the huge dust cloud created by the pounding of their horses' hooves.

Aziz Azoo trotted alongside Lock, a large elaborate brass telescope pressed to his one good eye. He was still grinning. 'This is good, ya Kingdom Lock. The Qashqai dogs want your blood. But they shall not have your blood. The only blood they shall have this day is their own spilt upon the desert floor.'

Lock lowered his glasses. 'What do you mean? You have only twenty men. What about your daughter?'

Aziz Azoo folded his telescope away and stuffed it inside his tunic. 'She is a warrior's daughter, ya Kingdom Lock. She is a daughter of the Bala Garideh Lurs, the most fearsome of all the Lurs. We have a reputation to uphold. It is said that we have habit of preying on both our Lur and not-Lur villages. I do not want to disappoint the storytellers!' He put his hand out to Lock and the two men gripped each other's forearms. 'I thank you again for the life of my daughter. It shall never be forgotten. I will have a man collect your tunic and cap from her.'

'No, ya Aziz Azoo. They are hers to keep. I ask only for the notebook and letters in the breast pocket.'

Aziz Azoo nodded. 'You are most kind, ya Kingdom Lock.' He then pulled his horse about and trotted back to his men.

Underhill came up alongside Lock. 'What the 'ell's 'e up to?'

'I think he means to charge our pursuers.' Lock clicked his tongue urging his camel to move on up the ridge towards Aziz Azoo and his men.

'Eh? Why not go?' Underhill said, following on.

'Religion.'

'Come again?'

'The Lurs are Shi'a; the Kurds who held his daughter prisoner were Sunni. The Qashqai . . . I don't know, but honour is at stake, too. They helped the men who violated his daughter.'

'Bloody 'eathen loonies, if you ask me. Still, it'll make a good diversion while we make our escape, them chargin' down the 'ill and all.'

'No. I can't let them fight our battles, Sergeant Major.'

'What do you mean?' Underhill said, pulling at Lock's arm. Both men came to a halt again.

'I mean that I don't let other people fight *my* battles.'

Underhill stared at Lock, frowning, trying to make sense of what Lock meant.

But Lock had made his mind up. Stupid, yes, he thought, but he was an honourable man, too. Besides, what guarantee did he have that the Lurs would succeed? He couldn't just leave them while he and the sergeant major sneaked away like cowards. The Lurs lived in the Zagros Mountains. If he proved himself brave in battle, then their allegiance to the British could be sealed. They would be a useful ally to have along the borders of Northern Mesopotamia, keeping a watchful eye for Ottoman invaders.

'Jesus!' Underhill spat. He understood what Lock intended now. 'This isn't a suicide mission, Lieutenant! What if you get killed? What about them papers, eh? Best give 'em to me!' He held out his hand.

Lock shook his head. 'Oh, no, Sergeant Major. If I buy it, you can find my body and fetch them yourself. I'm not asking you to join in. You can always sit and keep Fairuza company.' He gave a patronising smile. 'If we fail, scuttle back to Ross and tell him what I did. Besides, I don't have the papers . . . yet.'

Underhill glared back, his face reddening. 'I may just do that,' he spat.

'It is time,' Aziz said, trotting up to them. He handed Lock Wassmuss's notebook and the two letters with the broken wax seals. 'You head east on towards Shadegan. About five miles there is trail used by sheep-herders. It heads south back to road to Mohammerah.'

Lock put the German spy's papers safely away down the top of his boots, avoiding the heated glare of Underhill. Then he pulled his Webley from his holster and, pushing open the cartridge drum, began to reload the empty chambers. 'If you don't mind, I think I fancy a spot of shooting practice before I leave.'

Aziz Azoo narrowed his eyes. Then he threw his head back and laughed. 'You are like Lur; fierce and bloodthirsty for a fight! It would be honour to have you at my side. And your soldier with the red face?' Aziz addressed this to Underhill.

'He'll wait with Fairuza and head back for Mohammerah.'

Aziz Azoo's expression changed to that of a man who had stepped in dog excrement, an expression that Lock knew would rile the sergeant major.

'Not on yer life, you tinpot bleedin' emperor. I'm gonna be there, rifle at the ready,' Underhill snarled, and pulled back the bolt of his SMLE.

Aziz Azoo laughed again. 'Good. I like your anger, Under the hill. You will be a valuable addition. Do not fear for Fairuza. If we die, she will return to our camp and tell of our heroics here today. They will sing songs and write poems about us!'

'Poems?' Underhill scoffed.

Aziz pulled his horse about and took a moment to assess his men. He then turned in his saddle and thrust his sword to the heavens. '*Allahu Akbar!*' he cried, pulling his horse onto its hind legs.

The tribesmen all called out Allah's name in unison and Lock glanced back at Underhill. The sergeant major nodded stiffly in reply. Then, with a blood-curdling screech, Aziz shot forward, with his men close behind.

With a yell and a kick of his heels, Lock was with them, thundering down the hillside, kicking up a plume of choking sand as they raced at the Qashqai horsemen.

Lock whooped with sheer adrenalin and pointed his Webley at the approaching Persians. He had often wondered as a boy, playing with his toy soldiers and horses, what it would be like to take part in a cavalry charge. He had tried to imagine the feel of blood pumping in his ears, and how his heart would pound in his chest as the beast beneath him would snort as they thundered onwards to their target. And now he knew, because here he was, on top of a camel, admittedly, but alongside real riders, tribesmen and warriors who had spent generations fighting on horseback.

It was as exhilarating as it was frightening, but Lock felt elated. He glanced to his right at the Lur tribesmen who aimed and fired their rifles haphazardly. Even Underhill had his blood up. Whether it was fear or sheer hatred written across his face, Lock couldn't tell, but when the sergeant major caught his eye, he was reminded of the murderous man he knew ten years previously in Lhasa. And Lock knew he'd have to be extra vigilant with Underhill close by in battle. To Lock's left Aziz, eyes ablaze with bloodlust and revenge, was screaming and cursing as he charged on, his own sword circling about his head.

The moment of impact took Lock's breath away.

One minute they were pounding as one towards a screaming, seemingly faceless mass; the next they were amongst them. Qashqai faces contorted in rage, fear, surprise, agony and death. Lock was close enough to reach out and touch them, close enough to smell their earthy odours, to see the sweat dripping from their creased foreheads, to pick out the intricate designs of their colourful tunics and their saddlecloths.

And the noise! Never had Lock heard such bedlam, such power, as metal struck metal and sparks flew. Men yelled and cursed as blood flowed and blade cut flesh, crunched bones and crushed skulls. Shots rang out deafeningly close, muzzle flashes stung Lock's eyes, and the dust choked at his already dry throat. Everywhere there was dust, kicked up by the horses, horses whose own eyes rolled white as they salivated at the bit, turning this way and that. Soon everything became khaki. All except for the blood, fresh and deep red, spilling and spraying onto man, beast and ground.

Lock's first bullet found its target at close range. One minute a yelling, bearded face was upon him, the next it exploded into a mist of scarlet. Men fell, horses stumbled, limbs were severed. But on and on Lock rode, they all rode, Lur and Qashqai and Underhill, turning, shooting, maiming and killing.

Aziz's sword swung suddenly into Lock's periphery vision and he turned to see a Qashqai rider, headless, slump forward in his saddle. Aziz grinned manically at Lock and then he was gone again. One of the Lurs yelled out and tossed a sword towards Lock. He snatched it from the air and swung to his left, staying a killing blow from a Qashqai blade. Then the Qashqai jerked as a sword embedded itself in his chest. The tribesman's hands grabbed at the blood-soaked blade, a look of disbelief on his face, and then he toppled from his horse to be lost under countless hooves.

A bullet whistled past Lock's ear and when he snapped his head around he saw Underhill. Their eyes met. Underhill had his rifle pointing in his direction. Then there was a flash to Lock's right and he instinctively raised his sword again and stayed another blow from another Qashqai blade. He parried and thrust and the Persian fell away mortally wounded. When Lock looked back, Underhill was gone, lost in the mayhem.

And then it was over.

One minute the Qashqai seemed to be everywhere, a choking, swarming nightmare, and then they were gone. All Lock could see now was a thick blanket of dust. The odd riderless horse walked into view; a Persian, arm severed at the shoulder, staggered and fell. Lock trotted on, eyes scanning for Underhill.

As the dust began to settle, Lock could see that the Qashqai were retreating back to Daurat.

Aziz emerged from the dust cloud and trotted over to Lock.

'Ya Kingdom Lock!' he said. 'You ride well. Your Under the hill ride well!' He waved his hand in the air. 'The Qashqai dogs have fled. They are poor sport.'

Lock nodded. 'They'll regroup, bring reinforcements. We'd better not hang around here.'

'This is true. I have lost five men. Now I must get my daughter safely home. Come, we will escort you back to river.'

Then Lock saw Underhill again. He had a bleeding gash above his left eye, but was sitting still, his camel picking at a scrawny bush.

'Sergeant Major, time to leave,' Lock said.

The Qashqai didn't appear again and they saw no one as they travelled the road to Shadegan, or as they made their way down the sheep-herders' trail that weaved south. They continued on until eventually the pipeline loomed up ahead of them. And there it was, the road back to Mohammerah and the Karun River, as empty as before. Lock had thought that they might come across the marching British troops, but there was no sign.

‘Do you think we’ve missed ’em?’ Underhill asked.

Lock looked north. There was a large dust plume on the horizon. ‘Maybe,’ he said. ‘But not like you missed me.’

Underhill frowned, but made no comment.

Aziz Azoo trotted over. ‘This is where we must part, ya Kingdom Lock.’

Lock held his hand out and he and the Lur leader gripped each other’s forearms once again in farewell.

‘This is not my war,’ Aziz Azoo said, ‘but I promise you this, as Allah is my witness, we will, from this moment on, wage war on any Ottoman that crosses our path. They shall not find the Kerkha River to the north a safe place to travel!’

Lock bowed his head. ‘I am unable to express my thanks to you and your people for what you have done.’

Aziz pulled his horse about. ‘No thanks are needed when one performs a duty. *Mak toub*,’ he said, switching to Farsi.

‘*Maa as-salaamah*.’ Lock held up his hand in farewell.

‘*Ensha Allah*, ya Kingdom Lock, *ensha Allah*!’ Aziz nodded to Underhill, then galloped away north with his tribesmen and his daughter, who waved back, a smile upon her lips.

‘God willing indeed,’ Lock said, returning Fairuza’s wave. He removed the sheepskin, folded it neatly and stuffed it behind his back on the saddle, and then rolled up his sleeves. It was going to be another hot day.

As Lock watched the Lurs go, Underhill cantered up. ‘Mohammerah?’

‘Mohammerah,’ Lock said, wheeling his camel about.

‘About bleedin’ time,’ Underhill said.

CHAPTER NINE

The day was already half over by the time a dusty and saddle-sore Lock, with a weary Underhill at his side, rode up to the army encampment. It was pitched in a godless spot, an open space of fly-ridden, barren and scorched, rocky earth outside Mohammerah. A number of tents and campfires had been set up near to the river, whose muddy brown water ran indifferently along the western perimeter. There was more open, colourless land beyond, and to the north and east of the camp dusty hills scant of vegetation squatted like broken giants.

Lock and Underhill handed down their passes to the Indian sentries on duty at the entrance barrier, which was little more than a simple hinged pole, painted red. It was balanced across an opening in the crude wooden fence that enclosed the eastern perimeter.

'Christ, what an 'ole!' Underhill said to nobody in particular.

'A home from home then, Sergeant Major.' Despite his tiredness Lock couldn't resist the jibe. Underhill grunted, but even he seemed too jaded for another verbal duel.

'I wonder if Ross is around,' Lock said, lighting a cigarette. He turned to one of the Indian sentries. 'Where can I find the Mendip Light Infantry, Corporal?'

The naik gave a quick salute. 'Mendips, sahib?'

'There's a battalion from the Somerset Regiment here, I believe.'

The naik's face lit up. 'Ah, yes, sahib. Try the 2nd Dorsets. Down the slope a little way and over to the left. The camel enclosure is just there also, sahib. Follow your nostrils!'

Lock saluted nonchalantly, then he and Underhill urged their camels onwards and slowly lumbered their way down through a series of bivouacs, all neatly lined up, row upon row. As they passed through, Lock saw soldiers engaged in various activities to either keep themselves busy or to just while away the time. A few were stripped down to the waist and were playing cricket; others were meticulously cleaning their rifles, whilst some spent their time writing, reading letters or just lazing in the sun. Lock steered his camel on past the kitchens where a number of Indian natives were surrounded by steam and smoke, cooking fish caught from the river. Lock's stomach grumbled and he realised that he had eaten nothing in the past twenty-four hours but a piece of bread and a couple of eggs.

A few yards further on, they found the camel enclosure where a frustrated lance corporal was shouting and cursing as he desperately tried to get one of the beasts to lower itself down. Nearby, watching with amusement, were two Tommies. They were sat cross-legged, attempting to outwit one another at cards. Lock and Underhill dismounted and left their camels with the flustered lance corporal, who was less than pleased to have an additional pair to add to his worries.

Lock stretched and rubbed his backside. 'You the Dorsets?' he called to the card-playing Tommies.

'Blimey, is that an Aussie officer?' one of them said a little too loudly. They both got to their feet and saluted. 'Yes, sir! We're with the Dorsets,' they said in unison. The Tommies looked like farm labourers, big lads in their late teens, with rugged faces and rough hands. One of them, Lock could see, was red-raw with sunburn.

'I'm looking for the Mendip battalion. Where can I find them?'

'Sir, about four rows down,' said the sunburnt Tommy, accent thick with a West Country drawl. 'Bright flag outside a big tent, that's the Mendip battalion commander's quarters. Can't miss it.'

Lock nodded, and with Underhill following close behind, continued on.

'Did you see that officer's eyes?' Lock heard one of the Tommies mutter.

'Bloody weird,' the other said. 'Come on, your deal.'

Passing another section of tents, Lock soon spotted the flag, a gaudy green-and-gold pennant with the familiar Mendip insignia, three hills, emblazoned across it. As he and Underhill approached, a fresh-faced sergeant of about twenty-three, who was seated at a trestle table by the entrance flap to the tent, rose to his feet.

'Can I help you, sir?'

'Yes,' Lock said, 'is this the Mendip Light Infantry?'

'That's right, Lieutenant. Well, part of it. C Company, Second Battalion.'

'Good. My name's Lock, this is Sergeant Major Underhill.

We're here to report to the company commander. Is he here?'

'Down at the mess tent, sir,' the sergeant said, taking in Lock's Australian slouch hat. 'If you'll follow me, I'll escort you.' He stepped forward, hand open.

'You'd best wait here, Sergeant Major. Guard the bags,' Lock said.

Underhill was about to protest, but Lock turned on his heels and followed after the sergeant. They walked a little way through a row of canvas to an open-sided tent. Here a group of rowdy junior officers, all of a similar age, in their early twenties, were seated around a long wooden table, eating, and discussing, Lock gathered very quickly, the finer qualities of polo. There was a raging fire nearby where an Indian cook was standing over a large steaming cauldron. The smell of spicy food made Lock's stomach growl.

'Who the devil are you, sir?'

Lock turned to the major at the head of the table, whom he took to be the company commander. Lock raised his hand in salute, but his reply was cut short by a familiar voice.

'Ah, gentlemen, let me introduce Lieutenant Lock.'

From the other end of the table, Major Ross pushed his chair back and stood up. The officers broke off their conversation and nodded politely, although Lock could see amusement written across their faces.

'Did you bring Captain Flannigan's motorised patrol vehicle back? He's not a happy chappy, I can tell you!' Ross said.

There was a general chuckle across the table and Lock felt a twinge of irritation, wondering if he had been the butt of Ross's jokes for part duration of the meal.

'So this is the young colonial who rescued Major General

Townshend's daughter?' the major said. His barking voice was monotone and, despite his distinguished, albeit greying face, Lock guessed that he was in his early forties, judging by the touch of silver in his neatly trimmed brown hair. He had an air of aristocratic arrogance about him, from the way he held his knife and fork, to the way he was looking down his thin, straight nose.

'He is indeed,' Ross said. 'Lock, this is Major Janion, C Company commander in the 2nd Battalion of the Mendips. And this miserable lot,' he added, waving his hand over the table, 'are his platoon commanders.'

Janion chuckled, placing his knife and fork down and dabbing at his mouth and bushy moustache with a napkin. 'Quite, quite. And you, Lieutenant . . .' He twitched his nostrils. 'Good God man, you stink to high heaven! And shirtsleeves in the mess . . . it's just not done. This isn't the outback now!'

The officers sniggered and whispered between themselves.

'Yes, sir. Sorry, sir. That will be my camel—'

'Filthy things!' Janion said, clearing his throat, something he did repeatedly when he spoke. 'Can't understand why the blasted things are used. Horses are much faster!'

'Aye, but camels are smarter,' Ross said.

'Rot!' Janion spat. 'A camel is a horse designed by committee, and well you know it, Ross!' He screwed his face up and waved Lock away. 'Step back a pace, will you? Now, Captain Carver there is the senior platoon commander. What say, Carver?'

Lock's gaze met the hazel eyes of the young man seated at the far end of the table. The left side of Carver's thin mouth curled up into a mocking smile, made all the more elaborate by the obligatory officer's pencil moustache resting above his top lip.

'That's correct, sir,' Carver said, voice resonating with impeccable diction, as he passed a hand through his pristine, silky mop of brown hair. 'Our Mister Lock here . . . well, I think it best we give him Green Platoon for the time being, sir. Rather apt, I thought, as he's an inexperienced man.'

Janion let out a snort of laughter, joined by the other officers. 'Jolly good. Cheer up, Lock,' Janion said. 'Green was the late Lieutenant Peters' platoon and he was a brave officer. We miss him. But you have got . . . How many?' He turned to Carver for help.

'Eleven, sir,' Carver said. 'But all fully dressed, I can assure you.' Again there were a few guffaws from amongst the officers.

'Quite,' Janion said. 'Eleven good men under you. Mostly bloody idol-worshippers,' he added almost apologetically, 'but I believe your sergeant major . . .' He paused again.

'Underhill,' Ross said.

'Yes, yes, Underhill,' Janion scowled. 'He'll soon beat them into shape for you. It's little more than a section, I'm afraid, but that's all I can spare for this business Ross has been going on about.' He picked up his knife and fork again and returned to eating, nodding in satisfaction as he chewed. He stopped suddenly and made an elaborate performance of wrinkling his nose again. He glanced at Lock. 'You best run along and get cleaned up. The AIF may tolerate dirty, smelly, half-dressed officers. But you're in the Mendips for now, and we most certainly do not!'

Lock saluted Janion, who dismissed him with a wave of his fork before returning to his meal. The conversation started up again and Lock, much to his annoyance, became invisible once more.

'I'll catch up with you in a while,' Ross said.

'He knows.'

Ross frowned.

'Wassmuss. There's a rat wearing white tabs.'

'Not here,' Ross said.

'And you'll want to see what I have,' Lock insisted.

Ross pursed his lips. 'Very well, give me ten minutes to make my excuses.' Lock must have inadvertently shown his exasperation, for Ross tutted. 'Manners, dear boy! I'll be with you in a wee while. You'll find your belongings in your tent. Trunk arrived from Karachi.'

'I say, Lock?' Carver called, smirking. 'What say you about polo?'

There was a general snigger from the table.

'I've only ever played with the hill tribes of the Himalayas,' Lock said. 'Gets a little messy when the ball starts to fall apart.'

'Fall apart?' Carver said, curiosity aroused.

'Yes, there's only so much a severed head in a Hessian sack can take.'

There was a stunned silence. Lock nodded to Ross and, with a wry smile, he exited the tent.

The sergeant was still waiting for him outside.

'I took the liberty of fetching you a jacket from the quartermaster, sir. It's a British SD jacket I'm afraid, but it's all he could find.'

Lock grunted and pulled the thick serge tunic on. It was tight across the shoulders and a little short in the arms. But at least it was the correct rank.

'You look fine, sir. Now, if you'll follow me, I can take you to Green Platoon.'

Lock paused to light a cigarette. The laughter increased in the tent behind him and, with a glance back, he swore under his breath. Bloody aristo officers. Always the same. Arrogant, cocky, belligerent. Well, they were in for a mighty shock if the evidence he had in his boots was true. He waved for the sergeant to lead the way back to the command tent and the waiting Underhill.

Having collected his bag, Lock and Underhill followed the sergeant down through the bivouacs to the very end of the encampment site.

'Here we are, sir, Green Platoon,' the sergeant said.

'Thank you, Sergeant. I can manage from here.' Lock returned the sergeant's salute and waited for him to walk back the way they had come. He then dropped his bag and turned to observe the platoon.

He counted nine turbaned sepoys, all of whom were sat chatting, sipping from tin mugs. A gaunt Indian in native dress was deep in discussion with a skinny, pale white corporal as he served tea to him from a black kettle. The Indian stopped pouring, having noticed Lock and Underhill watching, and nudged the corporal. He looked up, cursed and jumped to his feet, tripping over a rifle strap as he clumsily approached, sending a neat stack of the firearms crashing to the floor. He bent down to pick them up, but was all fingers and thumbs.

'What the bleedin' 'ell are you doing?!' Underhill bellowed. He threw the saddlebag to the floor and marched over to the clumsy corporal's side, falling straight into his parade-ground guise. As he did so, the sepoys all put down their tea mugs and scrambled to their feet.

The corporal dropped the rifles and jerked to attention, shaking. Underhill was standing almost on top of him, his face pressed close.

'Well? I asked you a question, soldier,' Underhill barked, spittle showering the corporal's flinching, acne-ridden face.

'Sor-sorry, Sergeant Major. I . . . just tripped . . . rising to greet the ne-new loot—officer.' The corporal could barely raise his voice above a whisper.

'Speak up, man!' Underhill said. 'You're a bloody corporal according to them stripes on yer arm. 'Ow the bleedin' 'ell did you get to be a corporal, eh?'

'Captain Carver, Sergeant Major,' he said.

'You gave a touch to an officer, did you, sonny?' Underhill was clearly enjoying himself.

Whilst the sergeant major chastised the corporal, Lock turned his attention to the sepoys. One in particular stood out. He was a big man, well over six feet tall, broad and obviously physically powerful. His uniform, which bore a single stripe upon the arm, gave the impression of being two sizes too small, the seams clearly struggling to hold his muscular frame in check. The Indian was sorting the other nine sepoys into a line of inspection, and even the man in native dress was now standing to attention, a ladle held stiffly up in his hand as if it were a rifle. The tall sepoy stepped to the end of the line and remained at attention, eyes front, kirpan sword drawn and resting on his shoulder.

'Corporal?' Lock cut in above Underhill's bullying.

The corporal looked from Underhill to Lock and then back to the sergeant major. Underhill kept glaring at the soldier. There was a moment's pause, then the corporal swallowed hard, tore his eyes away from Underhill's and faced Lock.

'S-sir?' he said.

Lock smiled and stepped forward. 'Introduce me to the men, if you please.' He kept his tone calm but stern, knowing that this was a battle of authority between himself and Underhill, and one that he must triumph in. Lock walked on and went to stand opposite the first Indian sepoy. He glanced back at Underhill and the corporal. The sergeant major had placed his foot on top of the corporal's boot.

Lock stood and watched in silence. Bugger you, Underhill, he thought, why must I always have to deal with your crap?

But before he could react further, the tall sepoy with the single stripe on his arm stepped forward a pace, stamped to attention and saluted.

'Lance Naik Siddhartha Singh of the 2nd Mendip Light Infantry, sahib.'

Lock turned his head and narrowed his eyes. The tall sepoy's face showed surprise momentarily. But as his eyes met Lock's he quickly moved his gaze to a point in space just beyond Lock's left ear, held his salute steady, and waited. Lock adjusted his posture to face Singh. Behind the black, neatly groomed beard, the Indian's face was like that of a classical statue, youthful and chiselled. His nose was large and straight, and below thick eyebrows a pair of brown eyes shone brightly. Lock was struck by how wise they seemed, as if they belonged to an ancient soul.

Lock returned the salute. 'Lieutenant Lock of the Australian Infantry Force, attached to the 2nd Mendips.'

Singh lowered his arm but remained at attention.

Lock glanced back at Underhill and the corporal. They hadn't moved an inch.

'Forgive my ignorance, but isn't lance naik . . . a lance corporal?' Lock said, turning back to Singh.

'Yes, sahib,' Singh said.

'I asked for the corporal, did I not?'

'My humble apologies, sahib. I did not hear correctly.' Singh still kept his gaze away from Lock's.

One of the sepoys choked back a laugh and Lock whipped his head around. Enough was enough. He needed to prove his authority to these men and what better way than by putting Underhill in his place? He briskly marched back over to the sergeant major and the corporal.

'Name, Corporal?' Lock shouted, making the pimpled youth jump and breaking him from Underhill's spell.

'Dun-Dunford, sir. Algernon Dunford.'

'Well, Algernon Dunford, what gives you special privilege not to be standing in the line of inspection? You are part of this platoon are you not? You can carry on your private chat with Sergeant Major Underhill later. *Now move it!*'

Lock bellowed the last words into Dunford's ear and the young man was so visibly shocked that he yanked his foot away from beneath Underhill's boot. He grabbed a rifle from the collapsed stack, stumbled over to the line of sepoys, and snapped to attention at the far end.

Lock leant in close to Underhill so that the others couldn't hear what he was about to say.

'Don't you go getting all cocky with me, presuming that we're equals after our little adventure earlier.' He paused, daring Underhill to reply. But the sergeant major just remained still, listening, eyes fixed to Lock's.

'I know you took a potshot at me during that little cavalry charge we took part in. Hoping I'd be fatally wounded, were you? Then you'd collect Wassmuss's notebook and the letters and slither back here to inform Ross how tragically I had met my maker, but that you had escaped by the skin of your teeth. And not before you'd wrestled vital information from the German spy—' Lock stopped abruptly, as a faint smile had formed on Underhill's lips.

Lock leant in closer still, putting his own boot on top of Underhill's toe, and applied pressure. 'Don't push me too far, Sergeant Major. I will break you. That's a promise.'

Underhill glared back, the smirk still fixed to his face. He turned his head and spat on the floor.

Lock stepped back and put on a false smile. 'Come, Sergeant Major, we had best introduce ourselves properly to the lads.'

Underhill continued to glare at Lock for a moment longer, then gave the slightest of nods. 'Whatever you say. Sah.'

A quarter of an hour later, Lock was alone in his sparse tent. A camp bed ran along one side, and opposite was a small table and chair, with an oil lamp hanging above them suspended from the roof supports. Lock was sitting at the table, dipping a cut-throat razor into a bowl of milky water, and slowly shaving the two-day stubble from his face. His left foot was perched on his trunk, which had been sent on ahead from the wharf at Mohammerah. There was a knock on the wooden support from outside.

'Come,' Lock called, scraping the last of the soap from his jaw. He raised his head as Singh entered. 'Ah, the Indian with the hearing problem.' Lock dropped the razor and picked up a towel from the back of his chair and got to his feet. He returned Singh's salute. Singh remained at attention, staring ahead.

Lock studied the Indian for a moment. Could this man be a friend? It was difficult to tell. He needed someone on his side within the platoon if this was going to work and he had lived and worked with Indians before. Underhill was never going to help, not really. He just could never truly trust the sergeant major.

'Stand at ease, Lance Naik. I want to thank you for earlier.'

'Sahib?'

Lock didn't respond as he rubbed the towel over his face. 'Is that for me?' He indicated to the bayonet that Singh held in his hand.

'Sahib, yes, from Corporal . . . I mean to say, Private Dunford told me you requested one.' Singh handed Lock the bayonet.

'Yes, could have used this the other night. Still, never mind now. I'm sure another occasion will rear its ugly head.' Lock put the bayonet on the table and moved over to the trunk. He opened it up and began to rummage about inside. 'Is that cocoa I can smell?'

'It is, sahib. Cocoa and biscuits is on the menu for supper.'

Lock paused. 'Is that all?'

'Cook does the best he can, sahib.'

Lock rubbed his chin. 'But we brought fresh supplies from Karachi. I can't understand it.'

'Yet supplies are still sparse, sahib. Well, they are for us. The men are often hungry, if I may say so, sahib.'

'Who's your . . . our cook?'

'Bombegy, sahib. Fine cook, good Sikh.'

'I'd prefer a good cook and a fine Sikh,' Lock said. 'Call him.'

'Sahib.' Singh saluted, opened the canvas flap, and shouted for Bombegy in his native Punjabi.

The gaunt Indian with the ladle hurried into the tent. He crashed to attention and saluted. Lock nodded and bent down to the trunk again.

'Here,' Lock said, handing Bombegy a number of packets. 'There's real coffee, rice, a little sugar . . . and some dates. It's not much, but use them . . . for the men. Oh, yes, and these . . . tinned peaches I think, though the labels have come off. I will try and get you some eggs, courtesy of Major Ross.'

Bombegy's face fell into stupefied bewilderment as Lock piled the packets into his arms.

'Go on, then!' Lock said, and Bombegy scuttled off. Lock glanced at Singh. 'Do you eat meat?'

'Well, sahib, strictly . . . no. But . . . in times of war we indulge . . . if it is *jhatka*, sahib. Except for beef . . .' Singh trailed off.

Lock nodded and turned back to the trunk. 'Good. I'll try to get some buckshee chickens as well, live ones. Now, how about a glass of wine?'

'No alcohol, sahib. It is forbidden.'

'Really? When I was a boy growing up in Assam, the servants all used to drink. And I don't think it was tea.'

'Sadly, there are Sikhs who partake in alcohol, sahib,' Singh said.

Lock pulled a cloth bundle from the trunk and laid it out on the table. He carefully unwrapped it to reveal a straw package. From inside this he produced a bottle of wine. He bent back down to the trunk and again pulled out a smaller cloth bundle. Inside this, also wrapped in straw, were two glasses. 'Amazing!' he whispered to himself, pleased that they were undamaged. He poured the wine until one glass was on the point of overflowing, and then poured water from his canteen into the other glass and gave it to Singh. He raised his glass in a toast.

'What shall we drink to? War?'

'To peace, sahib,' Singh said.

Lock eyed the big Indian for a second. 'To peace.'

They touched glasses with a gentle tinkle, and then Lock gulped down his wine greedily.

'Tell me, Singh . . . what of the men?' he said, pouring himself another generous glass of wine.

'Sahib?'

'What are they like?'

'Like, sahib?' Singh said. 'Good men; good soldiers. Excellent shots also, sahib.'

'Are they all Sikhs?'

Singh nodded.

'What about that cook, Bombegy? He looks old enough to be your father!'

'Sikh, sahib, as I said. His name is Singh also.' He frowned. 'But we are not related.'

'And Corp . . . Private Dunford, what of him?' Lock sat down on the edge of his camp bed. He placed his glass down and began to pull his boots off. 'A white private in an Indian platoon?'

'We were originally with two separate units, sahib. His was wiped out; mine had just nine men left. Major Janion joined us together and put us in Lieutenant Peters' platoon. That is Green Platoon, sahib, now your platoon. Lieutenant Peters was killed. As Dunford was the only other Englishman left, sahib, the major promoted him and made me a lance naik. But we are little more than a section. Only twelve men now, including your good self, sahib. And the sergeant major.'

'Let's not forget the cook.'

'Thirteen with the cook, sahib,' Singh said, with a smile and a bob of his head.

Lock was disappointed. It wasn't much of a force. He sat down on his bunk, then stretched out and closed his eyes.

'We are all now Green Platoon, sahib,' Singh said again.

Lock couldn't be bothered to talk any more; he was dog-tired. He really needed to sleep. Just for a while. He could tell that Singh was hesitating, then he heard the Indian place his glass on the table, turn and pull the canvas flap of the tent aside to leave.

'Ah, Lance Naik. Is Lieutenant Lock in there?'

Lock groaned.

'Yes, Major sahib,' Singh said.

Lock kept his eyes closed as Ross entered the tent. There was a moment of stillness, and then Lock felt his feet being prodded. He opened his eyes.

Ross stared impassively down at him. 'A little early for wine, isn't it? It's not even six o'clock.'

Lock grunted and sat up. 'I don't suppose you've got any of that curry with you?'

Ross shook his head and patted his stomach. 'All gone.'

'I thought you'd never come.'

'Sorry. Been chinwagging with the brigadier general and then with that ass, Major Janion. Bound to get indigestion, having had to suffer his conversation over a meal. So, what do you have to report? Did you collect the prisoner?'

'There was no prisoner, sir.' Lock lit a cigarette.

Ross looked crestfallen. 'I feared as much.'

'However,' Lock said, pulling out the notebook and the two letters, 'I did come across these. Here.' Lock handed Ross the documents taken from the Turkish Kurds. 'They belonged to Wassmuss.'

The major frowned. 'How do you know?'

'He told me.'

'What?!' Ross tore open the first letter.

'He was there, sir, but he was no prisoner.'

'Meaning?' Ross said as he scanned the letter.

'Meaning, he was their guest. At least, he was the Qashqai Khan's guest. Wassmuss was well disguised, as an Arab, and has been overseeing the systematic sabotage of the pipelines himself. Only he's rather careless with his personal effects. I found those, and a hell of a lot of gold, German 20-mark coins, at a campsite near Daurat.'

'But that's well within our lines!' Ross said.

'I know, sir. But they're on their way, the Ottomans I mean.'

'Blast it!' Ross spat, pulling the chair from the desk and sitting down heavily. 'And what's this nonsense about a rat in white tabs business?'

'Wassmuss admitted as much, sir,' Lock said, 'that he has knowledge of what you, we, the White Tabs are up to. He even said he'd met me before, in Tsingtao.'

Ross whistled softly between his teeth. 'I had no idea his web spread so far.'

'Do you have any idea who it could be, though, the rat?'

Ross shook his head. 'Maybe someone at HQ in Karachi.' He scowled, then opened the letter again.

'Reading between the religious rhetoric and the sabre-rattling, sir,' Lock said, 'the first alludes to this second army you were worried about marching across the Persian border to the north and joining the troops already gathered near Ahwaz. They plan to push us from the oil-pumping station all the way down the pipeline to here, Mohammerah.' He paused, before adding, 'I think they plan to overrun the garrison and then split and march on Basra. Our forces in Mesopotamia won't be expecting an attack from the east, not from within neutral Persia.'

Ross pursed his lips. 'I agree. And I'm willing to bet that they mean to arrive at Basra on the fourteenth, or thereabouts.'

'Sir?'

'The message says: "*Miralay Subhi Bey's offensive at the shadow of the crescent moon*".' He stroked his moustache. 'What was the moon last night? A half, if that? I'd say the attack on Basra is planned for when the moon is almost full. That's around the fourteenth of April, three days from now. Colonel Subhi Bey has twenty-five thousand Turks encamped at Hammar Lake to the west of Basra. I'd say that was plenty of distraction to keep the garrison's eyes from the east, wouldn't you?'

He opened the second, shorter letter. 'Good God,' he muttered. 'It *is* him!'

'I think he's to command this army it talks about, for the march on Basra.'

The major nodded in agreement. 'He's proving to be a real thorn in my side.'

'It's signed "G", sir. Does that mean anything to you?' Lock said.

Ross frowned. 'Perhaps. There's a high-ranking German officer, a Lieutenant Colonel von der Goltz, who is Vice President of the War Council under Enver Pasha. He could be this "G".' He folded the letters away and began to flick through the notebook. He started to chuckle. 'This is a gold mine, Lock, a gold mine. In code, maybe, but I wager it's all we need to put a stop to his network!'

'There's something else, too, sir.'

Ross put the notebook aside, fished out his pipe and tobacco pouch, and began the familiar ritual of filling it. 'What?'

'While I was in Daurat I saw a motor car.' Lock paused.

'And?' Ross didn't look up from his pipe.

'It just seemed so out of place.'

'Lots of these local chieftains have elaborate motor cars. We *are* in the land of black gold, after all.'

'Yes, but something wasn't right . . .' Lock fell silent, struggling to find the right words to express his concerns about the car.

'What make was it?'

'A white Rolls-Royce.'

Ross looked up from his pipe with renewed interest.

'Tell me, was it a Silver Ghost model?'

'I believe so, yes.'

Ross popped his pipe in his mouth. He struck a match, and puffed away in silence, frowning.

'So, now what, sir?'

'Well, we need to get some transport. We have to get to Basra and warn the garrison there, warn them to watch the east!' He scooped up the notebook and stuffed it, along with the letters, in his pocket.

There was a knock on the outside of the tent.

'Come,' Lock said.

A messenger entered and saluted stiffly. 'Major Ross, urgent signal.'

Ross took the paper and tore it open. 'Thank you, Private,' he said to the messenger, dismissing him with a salute.

When the soldier had left the tent, Ross turned to Lock. 'You best come with me into town, Lock. Seems we shall all be needing to get out of here sooner than we thought.'

'Sir?'

'Ahwaz has fallen,' Ross said, handing the signal to Lock. 'That Ottoman army my informants told about, the same army we've just been discussing . . .'

Lock looked up from the message. 'Wassmuss!'

Ross nodded. 'Aye, lad. It's on the march.'

'Jesus,' Lock said. 'How long?'

'A few days. Robinson's been forced back.' The major shook his head. 'We're on the run, Lock, the British . . . We're on the run.'

CHAPTER TEN

Mohammerah was in a state of organised panic as the town busily prepared itself for a possible siege. Everywhere Lock looked, soldiers were piling sandbags in doorways and in front of windows. Instructions were shouted as barricades went up on street entrances, and Lock wondered how the watching native population felt about their liberties slowly disappearing behind a wall of barbed wire and wood. Lock had to step out of the way three times when the sandbags started to be piled up by the entrance to Military Command HQ where he was waiting for Ross. The major was inside somewhere and had been so for some time.

Lock rubbed his forehead. There was a stabbing pain behind his eyes, but he tried to ignore it, putting it down to the fact that he hadn't eaten properly or slept for more than an hour or so for some time now. Perhaps his irritability showed, for passers-by were giving him a wide berth.

'There's a courtyard out back, sir. Looks over the river. Lot quieter there,' one of the English soldiers constructing the barricade said, throwing down another heavy sandbag with a grunt.

Lock stamped his cigarette out. 'Good idea, Private.'

'I'll tell the major where you are, sir,' the sentry on guard duty added.

Lock thanked the sentry, turned and made his way along the building to the end of the street where it met the river. He rounded the corner and found a wrought-iron gate, beyond which a path ran the length of the military building along the riverbank. The gate opened with a teeth-jarring squeal. Lock closed it behind him and lit his fourth cigarette of the hour. He gazed out at the river and the docks a little further up the bank, watching as still more troopships, filled to capacity with Brigadier General Robinson's men, local civilians and oil workers, arrived at the port from Ahwaz. The retreat was in full swing.

Lock tossed his match away and continued along the path until it came to an open cobbled courtyard. It was cool and quiet here, just as the private had said it would be. Dark windows stared down disapprovingly from the surrounding walls, but Lock could see no sign of life behind any of them. There was a rear entrance to the building here, at the top of three stone steps, with another bored-looking British private on guard duty. The sentry nodded his head stiffly in response to Lock's nonchalant wave.

At the far side of the courtyard was an open gateway with a barrier across. Two more sentries, sepoys this time, were on duty there. But what struck Lock the most was the pristine white automobile parked on its own over on the far side of the courtyard. It was strangely familiar. There was a dozing figure in the driver's seat. Lock couldn't see his face, though, as it was obscured by a chauffeur's cap and driving goggles.

'I wonder . . .' Lock muttered. But as he was about to investigate, the sentry at the entrance snapped his heels in attention and Lord Shears came out of the door. He hesitated on seeing Lock, then smiled thinly, and taking his cigarette case from his pocket, lit up and made his way down the steps.

Lock tossed his own cigarette aside and crossed the courtyard, his boot heels echoing loudly against the walls. 'Hello, sir. I presumed you would have left by now.'

'I will be, Lieutenant,' Shears responded flatly, blowing smoke from his nostrils. 'But I have a few loose ends to tie up here. Tell me, is Major Ross with you?'

'Yes, sir. He's inside trying to rustle up some transport to get us to Basra.'

'Oh? I would have thought that you would be staying here to help fend off the Turkish hordes,' Shears said.

'No, sir, it appears not.'

Shears gazed out at the river. 'The retreat from Ahwaz is still in full flow, I see.'

'A strategic withdrawal, sir,' Lock said with a smile. 'At least, that's what Major Ross told me. There was a danger that Ahwaz could be cut off and surrounded. Supplies were low and there weren't proper facilities to treat the wounded at the oil-pumping station.' Lock shrugged. 'Best to abandon the position and make for here.'

'I suppose you are right, Lieutenant. But it will have to be a last stand, will it not, if the Turks push further south? Very troubling.'

Both men fell silent. Lock tried to read Shears' face, but his eyes were, as usual, hidden by light reflecting off his spectacles.

'Do you like my limousine, Lieutenant?' Shears said, nodding at the white motor car.

'I . . . yes, sir,' Lock said, thrown by the innocuous question.

'It's a Rolls-Royce,' Shears said, guiding Lock over to the automobile. 'A 1909 40/50 Silver Ghost. Not actually mine, sadly. Belongs to the Sheikh of Mohammerah. I would offer to take you for a drive but you have pressing matters of your own.' The smile across his lips appeared forced.

'Yes, I'm afraid so, sir,' Lock said. 'Still, it's very gracious of the Sheikh to loan you his car.'

'Oh, it's not his only one, Lieutenant. He has a fleet. All the same colour, all the same model.'

Lock studied the car closely. Could it be the same as the one he'd seen in the market at Daurat?

'Been driving around long, sir?'

'Oh, not really. But it's good business from the Sheikh's point of view.' Shears lowered his voice in mock conspiracy. 'He thinks it will reflect well when Churchill hears about his generosity.' He chuckled as if it was some great joke.

Lock didn't understand, but, then again, he was certain that he wasn't supposed to. More Admiralty business to do with the oil rights to Persia, no doubt.

Shears took a final puff on his cigarette, and dropped it to the floor. 'Well, Lieutenant, I wish you a safe journey.'

Lock took Shears' limp hand in his. 'Thank you, sir. And to you.'

Shears turned and waited as the Arab chauffeur stepped out from the front of the vehicle and opened the passenger door. Shears climbed in and the chauffeur closed the door behind him and got back into the driver's seat. Shears leant forward.

'By the way, Lieutenant, I am reporting now to the Sheikh about the situation at Ahwaz. The pipeline . . . Tell me, this German spy, Wassmann, that the major told me ab—'

'Wassmuss, sir,' Lock said.

'Ah, yes, Wassmuss. He is stirring up a lot of trouble in these parts and the Sheikh and I are deeply concerned about pipeline secur—'

'Don't worry about him, sir,' Lock said. 'The net is closing in on our German friend.'

'Really?'

'Yes, sir. We had a stroke of luck a while back,' Lock said, lowering his voice. 'A valuable piece of information came into our possession.'

'How *very* fascinating, Lieutenant. Well, until we meet again.' Shears tapped on the driver's shoulder, signalling for him to move on. The engine coughed into life with a clatter of metal that echoed deafeningly around the courtyard, startling a group of brooding pigeons into flight. The engine settled down to a gentle purr and, with a crunch of gears, the motor car glided off.

Lock rubbed the leather of his holster and watched the Rolls manoeuvre out of the courtyard and onto the main thoroughfare. The sound of approaching footsteps made him glance back towards the building. Ross was making his way across the courtyard.

'A penny for them,' he called.

'Do you remember the white Rolls-Royce I told you about? The one I saw parked in Daurat?'

'What of it?' Ross came to a halt beside Lock.

'The Sheikh has a fleet of them.'

'Yes?'

'And Lord Shears has been driving around in one for the past few days.'

'Has he, indeed? Interesting.' Ross frowned.

'Any news, sir?' Lock said, changing the subject.

'Yes, bad . . . and good. This army of Wassmuss's . . . it's been spotted by a routine patrol, encamped to the west of here. It's a smaller force than the one Robinson engaged to the north of Ahwaz, but it includes nearly five hundred cavalry. Yet, for some reason, the main body of Turkish troops have halted outside of Ahwaz. They haven't moved and show no sign of doing so. Damned curious.' Ross's expression turned grave. 'And the brigadier general's injured. Took a bullet during the retreat. Means the chap in there is in overall command of the troops here. But I used my White Tab influence and secured a gunship to get us to Basra.'

'Did you raise Basra and warn them?'

'The telegraph lines are cut. I fear the natives sense a turn of the tide.' Ross pulled out his pipe and began to fill the bowl.

'What about here in town?'

'Oh, they'll behave, as long as we show calm and strength.' Ross finished filling his pipe and rummaged in his pockets for a light. 'Have you a—?'

Lock handed Ross a box before he could finish his question. 'So when do we leave?'

Ross lit his pipe and puffed away until it began to smoke. He put the box of matches away in his own pocket. 'The gunboat will be ready at dusk. So we have some time to kill.'

The two men started to walk back across the courtyard towards the main thoroughfare.

'How do you know Lord Shears has been driving around in one

of the Sheikh's motor cars?' Ross asked, as if he had only just heard what Lock had told him a moment ago.

'He was here,' Lock said.

'Hmm?' Ross still seemed distracted.

'Yes. He was off to meet the Sheikh before leaving town.' Lock paused to see if Ross had anything to say. 'He was concerned about Wassmuss.'

'We are all concerned about Wassmuss, my boy.'

'Yes, but it was something he said . . .' Lock trailed off.

Ross glanced at him. 'You look tired. And why in God's name are you still wearing that bloody winter tunic? Didn't you have any of your own in your trunk?'

'Only a mess jacket, sir. Didn't have much time in Karachi to get a full set of uniforms.'

Ross shook his head. 'Come on, let's find a place in the shade to have a drink where you can sit in your shirtsleeves. I'm parched after all that negotiating, I can tell you!'

Lock smiled. It was, he thought, the best suggestion Ross had come up with since they'd set foot in Persia.

The garrison commander had been true to his word. When Lock and Ross arrived at the dock, not only was there a boat ready and waiting, but what appeared to be a large amount of ammunition and supplies were being loaded on board, too.

'When do we sail?' Lock said.

'Not sail, Lock, steam!' Ross said.

Lock could see a funnel amidships, belching smoke into the late afternoon air, but the three sail masts pointing proudly to the heavens puzzled him.

'Ah,' Ross said, 'I see your confusion. But despite the rigging, she was never fitted with sails.'

'Looks pretty smart for a gunboat.'

The captain, a tall, broad man in his mid thirties, with a red complexion so familiar on men who had spent years at sea, and an even redder set of whiskers, was standing at the end of the gangplank. He was puffing contentedly on a pipe as Lock and Ross made their way on board.

'She's actually an old sloop, gentlemen, one of the Cadmus class. But rest assured I can handle all 1070 tons of her like a pleasure yacht. Hayes-Sadler. Welcome aboard the HMS *Espiegle*, Major.'

'Thank you, Captain. Are the men on board?' Ross said, stepping on deck.

'They are. All settled down. And that's the last of our supplies being loaded now. I'm afraid I can only offer you a shared cabin with the first officer. I was going to give you mine, but we have an unexpected dignitary as an extra passenger.'

'Oh?'

'Yes. Lord Shears. Came aboard about half an hour ago, with a bloody Arab manservant, too. Fellow was even dressed in a uniform.'

Ross glanced at Lock and pursed his lips.

'Hope that'll suffice?' Hayes-Sadler frowned.

Ross turned back and smiled. 'Of course, Captain. As long as I'm not on deck, I don't mind where I sleep.'

'Your . . . companion,' Hayes-Sadler said, raising an eyebrow at Lock's sheepskin jerkin and slouch hat. Lock had conveniently left the SD jacket behind at the bar he and Ross had spent the afternoon refreshing themselves in.

'Lieutenant Lock,' Ross said.

'The lieutenant will have to kip on deck.' Hayes-Sadler gave a quick smile.

'That will be fine,' Ross said before Lock could comment.

Hayes-Sadler nodded. 'Shouldn't be a bad trip, about ten hours in all. The Shatt's an easy waterway and we may get up to a top speed of thirteen knots. Should reach Basra well before dawn tomorrow.' He stuffed his pipe back in his mouth and waved down to the dockhands on the quayside to cast off.

'Splendid.' Ross gave a cheery salute, and he and Lock strolled over to the stern.

'What the hell is Shears doing here, sir?' Lock whispered. 'I thought he was on his way back to Karachi.'

'So did I.'

Ross fell silent, and Lock peered out over the guard rail to watch the sun slowly setting over Mohammerah. He was taken by how peaceful Arabistan, and beyond it, Persia, looked; no gunfire, no shells, no thick clouds of black smoke. Not yet, anyhow.

Footsteps approached and both men turned to see Lord Shears.

'Gentlemen. Good evening,' Shears nodded curtly.

'Lord Shears.' Ross bowed his head slightly in greeting. 'Forgive me for being so blunt, sir, but where we are going could be extremely dangerous for you.'

Lock could detect a touch of annoyance in the major's voice. Shears stood by the guard rail and fished out his cigarette case. He carefully pulled out a cigarette and waited expectantly.

'Oh,' Lock said, patting his pockets, realising what Shears wanted. He tutted softly as Ross politely struck a match for Shears.

'Thank you. I am well aware of the dangers, Major. Besides, do you think Mohammerah will be any safer? I was originally on my way to Basra, if you recall. But I must get there now. Mohammerah is cut off and there are no ships leaving for India. This is the only vessel going anywhere.'

'Why must you get to Basra, if I may ask?' Ross said.

Shears drew heavily on his cigarette, then exhaled long and drawn out, keeping his gaze fixed out on Mohammerah. 'Well, Major. After my brief chat with Lieutenant Lock this morning, I realised that it was pointless my returning to Karachi. I'm needed on the front line, to advise and secure our oil interests. That's what Churchill appointed me to do, after all. I'm sure that you could use my support and influence once we arrive.'

Ross narrowed his eyes. 'You were appointed by the First Lord of the Admiralty? Personally?'

'Official oil business, Major,' Shears said, tapping the side of his nose. 'That is all I can say.'

There followed a moment of awkward silence, then Shears gave them an insincere smile. 'Would you care for a game of cards in my cabin after supper, Major? And you, Lieutenant? Quinto or *Le Truc* perhaps?'

Lock looked to Ross for a response. He was keen to do so. But was the major? It would be a good chance to study Shears up close, that's for sure.

'We'd be delighted, Lord Shears,' Ross said.

Little happened over the next few hours. Lock strolled the deck, keeping the stiffness from his knee. It had begun to ache of late. He put it down to the amount of riding he'd been doing, but he couldn't help but worry that it was to do with his old wound from the Hindu Kush. Then he smiled. For the first time in ages he felt his mind was free to think of Amy. He wondered how she was faring as a nurse in the hospital in Basra. Was she safe, or fearing for her life each day? No, she would never be so selfish. Lock had no idea what kind of situation the city was in. Still, he would be able to see for himself in less than twelve hours. But how easy would it be to see her? Would she even want to see him? Surely the incident with Bingham-Smith was forgotten, forgiven? Bingham-Smith. Now there was a man he was happy never to see again. Lock laughed to himself. It was ridiculous, but whenever he thought of Amy, bloody Bingham-Smith popped into his mind, too. Bollocks to the man, bollocks to his pompous, cursed arse.

Whilst the *Espiegle*'s crew went about their duties, Lock checked on his platoon. The recently demoted Dunford seemed happy enough; he had buddied up with one of the sailors and they were playing cards, and Underhill was sitting nearby meticulously cleaning the SMLE he still possessed from the late Lance Corporal Connolly. The sepoys were mostly asleep, or chatting quietly amongst themselves, and Singh was reading a tatty prayer book.

The big Indian jumped to his feet as Lock approached.

'How are the men?' Lock said, glancing over to the group of sepoys.

'They are glad to be on the move, sahib.'

Lock removed his slouch hat and wiped his sweating brow with his upper arm.

'Apricot, sahib?' The big Sikh offered a bulging paper bag to Lock. 'They help the thirst but not the bowels!' Singh grinned.

Lock took one of the fruits and chewed it in silence. Singh made to move away, but Lock put his hand up to stop him. 'Do I make you uncomfortable?'

Singh frowned and looked in Underhill's direction. Lock followed his gaze. The sergeant major had been watching them and, when he caught their eye, he grunted his disapproval and returned to his cleaning.

'Sahib . . . I . . . do not understand.'

'Am I too familiar with you, Singh? Would you prefer me to be as the sergeant major? Or perhaps you'd like the stern, white colonial landowner, as my uncle would have been? He would have whipped you for offering him an apricot, you know. "How dare you address your superior!" he would have bellowed.'

Singh shifted uneasily and glanced over to the sepoys again, but Lock just carried on talking.

'I was brought up to believe that you are an inferior people, Singh; all Indians, all castes and religions. "Useless, black, darkie scum. Good for fetching and carrying, nothing more."'

Lock paused, wondering whether to continue. Singh had a scowl across his brow.

'That was my uncle's view,' Lock said. 'He owned a tea plantation in Assam. But I didn't share, don't share, his views. We had a wonderful family living in the servants' quarters. Now I come to think of it, they were Hindus not Sikhs, as I thought before . . . They were kind to me. I grew to respect them. Of course, when my uncle found out I was treating his staff as equals, he shipped me off to England for a "proper education".'

Lock fell silent and stared off into the middle distance.

Singh made to leave again. 'I best check on the men, sahib.'

'Why did you join the army?' Lock said, indicating for the big Indian to be seated.

Singh smiled shyly and sat down, crossing his legs. Lock joined him.

'I was a clerk for a cotton company in the north of the Punjab, near to a place called Hasan Abdal. Have you heard of it, sahib?' Lock hadn't. 'It is where Panja Sahib is, the shrine to Guru Nanak, the founder of Sikhism. It is not far from Murree, where the British spend their summers. This you know? Yes? Well, I was not happy in my job, sahib. Then a friend suggested joining the army. I was a young man. I was restless and had . . . well, I found myself with no family to care for.' He paused here as if about to elaborate, but changed the subject instead. 'When the war broke out, I saw it as a great opportunity to do my duty for the generous-hearted sovereign, King George.'

'So you're alone? No sweetheart? No arranged marriage?' Lock said.

Singh shook his head. 'No, sahib. The woman promised to me was killed . . .' He trailed off, lost in memory. Then he smiled. 'But the women of the Punjab are most beautiful and I would like one for my own one day.'

Lock smiled. 'What do you think about European women?'

Singh gave a gentle shake of his head. 'They are most beautiful, sahib, particularly the ones with hair the colour of wheat dancing in the sun. But they have no devotion to God and, if I may be permitted to say so sahib, they are shameless.'

Lock laughed. 'Shameless?'

'Yes, sahib,' Singh answered in all seriousness, 'how they mingle so freely with men.'

Lock grinned and got to his feet. 'It was good to talk to you, Lance Naik. I'll let you get back to your book.'

Singh jumped up, too, and nodded his head. 'Thank you, sahib.'

Lock made to move away, but he suddenly stopped dead. Something was niggling at his mind, and he turned back to Underhill. What was it? By Christ, the bastard!

'Hey!' Lock said, storming over to Underhill and snatching the cloth he was using to polish his rifle with from his hand. It was Amy's handkerchief. 'Where the hell did you get this?'

Underhill scowled back at him. 'Found it on the deck o' the *Lucknow*.'

Lock opened the handkerchief up. It was stained with grease and dried blood, but he could still make out the dainty flower monogram of Amy's initials stitched in the corner. 'Look at the state of it!'

'It's only a bleedin' bit o' rag,' Underhill said.

Lock glowered down at him, stuffed the handkerchief in his pocket, and wheeled away.

'Bastard,' Underhill said. But Lock just carried on, happy at least to have been reunited with Amy's keepsake once again.

As the sun slowly sank on the horizon, the light began to fade and the shadows lengthened. The gunboat chugged smoothly along, but there was precious little of the surrounding country that sparked an interest. Lock could see nothing but thick reeds and date palms dotted along the bank, and a vast, barren land beyond.

Lock was relieved that the weather remained calm, although it became increasingly sticky as the evening progressed and the further west they travelled. Irritating flies gave way to insufferable mosquitoes, but Lock's spirits were lifted briefly by a cloud of delicate moths flittering about the navigation lamp at the stern.

He thought of Amy and tried to imagine her here with him now, holding her hand out, as he did, into the weak light, watching in fascination as the insects delicately brushed their fingertips. His eye was drawn to a small fishing boat further upriver, returning, no doubt, with the day's catch and Lock wondered if they even knew a war was going on around them.

Time ticked by uneventfully, until just before nine o'clock when Lock was startled out of a doze by a gunshot from the north bank. He strained his eyes into the dark, as a few of the sepoys were stirred to their feet by the noise. Lock could make out the odd muzzle flash coming from the bank quickly followed by the crack of rifle fire. He and the other men instinctively ducked down as bullets pinged off the hull of the ship. There followed a flurry of commotion from the starboard bow and then all hell broke loose as the *Espiegle*'s machine guns opened fire on the north bank.

A familiar voice piped up next to Lock. 'Bloody Marsh Arabs,' Underhill scoffed, 'they never learn.'

Lock nodded in agreement, but he didn't really understand what the sergeant major meant.

'Still, gives these sailor boys a bit of target practice!' Underhill moved away and left Lock watching the Marsh Arabs flee in panic. It looked like a picture show, with the opposite bank flickering in the glare from the machine-gun fire. Lock stayed at the starboard guard rail until the *Espiegle* drifted out of range and the guns fell silent once more. There was a smell of cordite and hot metal on the air and Lock felt strangely impatient for the battle to come.

CHAPTER ELEVEN

After the evening meal, Lock and Ross joined Shears, as arranged, in the captain's sparse but comfortably furnished cabin. They sat in awkward silence around the wooden table in the centre of the room, Shears opposite the door, then Lock, with Ross to his left.

'We must get you a proper jacket in Basra once and for all, lad,' Ross said out of the blue.

'I'm growing rather fond of it, sir,' Lock grinned, as he peeled the sheepskin jerkin off his shoulders and made to hook it over the back of his chair.

'No, no, no! Outside with it! Go on!' Ross said, waving to the door. 'I can abide the stench no longer.'

Lock picked the jerkin up again, just as Hayes-Sadler came bursting in with a bottle of rum clutched in his hand. Lock went outside and spotted a lifebuoy attached to the bulkhead. He threw the jerkin over it, then returned to the cabin and sat back down at the table. Shears was smoking his habitual cigarette, and Ross and Hayes-Sadler had both already stoked up their pipes. Soon the cabin became heavy with tobacco smoke.

'Well, gentlemen, shall we play? May I suggest *Le Truc*?' Shears opened his hands to invite comments.

'Sorry, sir. I don't know that game,' Lock said, lighting himself a cigarette.

'Quinto then?' Shears said.

'Sorry,' Lock said.

Ross sighed. 'What *do* you know, Lock?'

'Hearts, sir,' Lock said.

'Hearts! Too straightforward,' the major scoffed.

'Well, I prefer a stakes game, sir,' Lock said.

'What about skat, gentlemen?' Shears said.

Hayes-Sadler shook his head. 'I know hearts, but I'm afraid I don't know that game, my Lord. Skat, you say?'

'It's similar to hearts, sir,' Lock explained before Shears could, 'but more skilful. The Turks on my old engineering crews before the war used to play it. A German card game isn't it, sir?' Lock directed the question to Shears.

'Is it? I didn't know that,' Shears said.

Ross turned in his seat and stared at Lock, puffing thoughtfully on his pipe. 'It amazes me the things you come out with sometimes, Lock.'

'I aim to please, sir.'

'Then how about rummy?' Shears said, as he removed his glasses and began to polish the lenses with his handkerchief.

'If Lock knows the rules?' Ross said.

'I do, sir. Rummy suits me fine.'

'Ah, rum,' Hayes-Sadler said, 'that reminds me. Here.' He stretched from his chair to a nearby shelf, grabbing four thick tumblers. He poured out four measures from the bottle resting at his elbow, and placed them in front of each player.

'Very apt, Captain,' Shears said, pushing his glasses back on and stuffing the handkerchief into his breast pocket. He leant forward and picked up the pack of cards from the table. 'Shall we say seven deals per game? And may I suggest a penny a point to make it more interesting?'

'Fine by me,' Ross said.

Hayes-Sadler nodded in agreement and downed his rum in one. Lock sipped at his. It was harsh stuff, and burnt his throat. But it left a pleasant fiery feeling in his chest, and he didn't refuse the offer of a refill when Hayes-Sadler poised the bottle over his glass.

'And you, Lieutenant?'

'Let's make it a shilling.'

'Lock!' Ross said.

'It's quite all right, Major,' Shears said. 'A bob it is. Captain?'

'Agreed.'

'Very well,' Shears said, 'we will need pencil and paper to tally up the points. Do you have a notebook, Captain? Major?'

The question was innocent enough, but Lock's ears pricked up at the mention of 'notebook'. He glanced at Ross, but the major appeared not to have noticed Shears' request. Hayes-Sadler lifted himself out of his chair and went over to a small wooden cabinet in the corner. He opened a drawer and noisily rummaged around inside until he found what he was looking for. He returned to the table and placed a notebook and pencil in front of Shears.

'Good,' Shears said, and with a watery smile, he began to shuffle the cards. 'Shall I deal?' It wasn't a question.

Lock watched with interest as Shears dealt out seven cards apiece; all the time his mind kept returning to the comment about a notebook. He didn't know what it meant, but he had a feeling that Shears' presence on this boat was no accident. Shears was a powerful man and he could easily have secured some form of transport to get him back to Karachi. No, he wanted to be here and he wanted to get to Basra, Lock was certain of that. But why? He couldn't believe that it was at the behest of Churchill. Or perhaps it was? The British were after the majority share of APOC, so was he merely protecting their investment?

Shears finished dealing and Lock took up his seven cards and carefully fanned them out. It was an excellent hand. He already had a book of three nines.

It wasn't long before Lock found himself racing ahead in the game, making sets quickly and easily. Shears was running him a close second, but Ross and Hayes-Sadler seemed to be just enjoying themselves, and not too bothered as to how the game went. Hayes-Sadler did, however, reward himself with a tot of rum with each set he managed to lay down. But the drink appeared to have no effect on the man other than to accentuate the red veins in his nose.

After a while, the game changed in Shears' favour. He had a miraculous rummy within four hands and Lock began to feel irritated. Not only by his luck changing, but by the smug look on Shears' face. Play carried on, with each man taking his turn at dealing. But there were no great changes in fortune. More rum was consumed and tobacco smoked and, after an hour, the cabin became stifling. Jackets were removed and sleeves were rolled up.

All except for Shears, that is. He seemed content to just sit and sweat. Hayes-Sadler threw open a porthole, but the warm air from outside was little better.

When play moved to Shears once more, Lock spotted that he drew the top card from the discard pile, the jack of diamonds, the last jack, and after a brief show of sorting, discarded the same card again. This was the second time he had done so. It was a dishonest play, to discard the same card drawn from the discard pile in the same turn. Shears was ensuring that he wouldn't have to finish and that he was also not left with a high-points-value court card in his hand should the game end.

Lock looked at Ross and Hayes-Sadler to see if they had spotted the same, but neither man made any indication that they had done so. Lock pursed his lips. If there was one thing he hated more than losing at cards, it was losing to a cheat. So he decided that the only option he had was to adopt Shears' method and, as soon as he did, he began to gain ground again.

After four more hands Lock drew level and Shears became twitchy. The smug look vanished, to be replaced by a tic at the left-hand corner of his mouth, as he angrily totted up the points in the notebook. He broke the lead of the pencil twice, obliging Hayes-Sadler to sharpen it again with a pocket-knife.

On the next hand, with Ross dealing, Lock made it obvious that he had discarded the card that he had just picked up, and Shears noticed. His face flushed with anger as he looked up into Lock's eyes. Lock just stared calmly back.

Go on, you bastard, Lock thought, say something, I dare you.

Shears wisely kept his lips tightly shut. Lock placed his final four cards down in sequence, the four, five, six and seven of diamonds, winning the hand and going 'out'. Play ceased and the deal passed to Shears again.

But instead of shuffling the cards, Shears pinched the bridge of his nose and stood up. 'Excuse me, gentlemen. I have a dreadful migraine and need to take some air.'

'Perhaps we should call it a night?' Ross said.

'Nonsense,' Shears snapped, and then he smiled thinly. 'I just need a little break. Besides you still have money I wish to relieve you of, Major.'

Hayes-Sadler chuckled at that and Shears made his way out of the cabin. Lock swivelled in his chair. Should he follow?

'Something bothering you, Lock?' Ross said, before necking back his rum.

Lock turned back. 'No, not really, sir.'

'Not even Lord Shears' cheating?' Ross raised an eyebrow.

'I was beginning to think I was the only one who noticed.'

Hayes-Sadler snorted. 'Bloody aristocrats. Always the same when you play them at cards.'

Ross smiled. 'But Lock is giving him a good run, aren't you, my boy?'

'Playing him at his own game, sir. That's all.'

'And should you win, you'll reimburse the captain and I, won't you?' Ross said.

'Of course, sir,' Lock said.

Ross grunted and went to pour himself another drink. But the bottle was dry.

'I'll get a refill.' Hayes-Sadler pushed his chair back.

'No, let me,' Ross said. 'I've got a fine bottle of Armagnac in my cabin. Let's all take a short break.'

'Good idea. I'll go and check on the first officer, see how we're progressing,' Hayes-Sadler said, slapping his cap on his head and throwing his heavy jacket back over his shoulders. 'Shall we, say, meet back in fifteen? I'll let Shears know, if I see him.'

'Very well, Captain,' Ross said, standing and rolling down his shirtsleeves. He pulled on his jacket as Hayes-Sadler left the cabin. 'Why don't you come with me, Lock? Clear your mind.'

Lock nodded and followed Ross out onto the deck. There was a three-quarter moon high above them and the sky was littered with bright stars. Everything had an eerie, silvery glow to it, from the ship's deck to the palm trees lining the riverbank. Persia and the war was like a half-forgotten dream to Lock, such was the tranquillity of the night. He took a deep lungful of warm desert air and stretched.

The ship itself was very quiet, with nothing to be heard but the gentle chug of the engines, the lapping of the water below, and the chattering of conspiring insects on the hunt for sweat and blood.

'The whole ship's asleep. Must be later than I thought,' Ross said.

They made their way forward to the first officer's quarters where the major was bunking. As they approached the door, Ross froze and held his hand up. Lock started to speak, but Ross hushed him.

'When I left my cabin earlier this evening,' he whispered, 'I turned the light out.'

Lock looked to the door. There was a sliver of light showing through the porthole. He strained his ears, but couldn't hear a sound coming from the inside. 'Aren't you sharing?' he said.

'Aye, with the first officer. But he's on duty at the helm. Have you got your pistol?'

Lock nodded. 'Where's yours?'

'In there.' Ross indicated towards the cabin.

Lock silently unclipped his holster and, wiping his damp palm down the seat of his trousers, withdrew his Webley. He held his breath. Ross slowly pressed down the handle and softly pushed open the door.

Inside, the cabin looked as if it had been hit by a whirlwind. Furniture was upturned, clothing was strewn across the beds and floor, and books had been torn apart with their pages littered everywhere. Cups were smashed, a trunk was on its side, the contents scattered. Even the mattresses had been tossed over and cut open, their innards ripped out.

'Jesus!' Ross said, quickly moving inside.

Lock followed, stepping into the cabin and pulling the door closed behind him. Broken glass crunched under his boots. 'Careful, sir,' he hissed, Webley raised, eyes scanning the room.

Ross kicked through the papers and bent to pick up one of the books. Its cover had been torn, and the spine ripped away. 'The letters are gone. Damn.' He got to his feet and moved over to the bunk on the far side. He picked up the pillow and put his hand inside. 'My, my, that is a surprise!'

'Surely . . . ?' But Lock stopped short when Ross pulled out a pint bottle of brandy.

'Good God, lad, I keep the notebook on me at all times,' the major said, patting his breast pocket. 'Just amazed the brandy's still where I put it! Come along!' he added, moving over to the door. 'We'd better raise the alarm and set about searching the ship. Can't have a spy roaming around free. Well,' he smiled sheepishly, 'not one of theirs, anyhow!'

Lock held up his hand, stopping the major. 'Sir,' he said indicating to the other side of the room.

'What? What is it?' Ross said, frowning.

'The mattress.' Lock could see a hand sticking out from underneath.

'I—' Ross started to say something, and then he too spotted the hand. He picked his way across the room and pulled back the mattress. A body was lying on its front, like a discarded rag doll. Ross knelt down and turned it over. It was Lord Shears.

'Is he dead?' Lock said.

'Yes. Looks like a stab wound to the heart.' Ross got to his feet again. His hand was smeared with blood.

Lock holstered his Webley and moved over to take a closer look at Shears. The dead oilman had already taken on a waxy pallor and there was a look of indignant surprise frozen on his face. 'Do you think . . . ?' Lock trailed off.

Ross gave him a sceptical look. 'What, that Wassmuss is on board this very ship? Perhaps,' he said. 'But if not him, then one of his agents is, that much is certain. Poor Shears must have stumbled on them ransacking my cabin.' He shook his head. 'I've had my suspicions about Lord Shears and the activities of Anglo-Persian Oil for some time. But it appears I was barking up the wrong palm tree, as it were. I realise now that they're nothing more than a greedy, corrupt corporation out to maintain their profit and supply, no matter who controls Persia.'

Ross moved to a slatted door in the corner. 'I think I'd best wash this blood off my hands before we go.' He pulled open the door. 'You know Lock, I—' He stopped short and stepped back into the cabin, slowly raising his hands.

A figure was standing in the shadowy doorway of the water closet. Lock made to spring forward.

'Careful, Lock,' Ross hissed, 'he's got my gun.'

'Yes, Lieutenant, careful,' the figure said, moving into the room.

Although Lock didn't recognise the figure, other than as Shears' Arab chauffeur, he did recognise the voice. 'Wassmuss,' he said, and instinctively made for his Webley.

'Dear me, no, Lieutenant,' Wassmuss said, aiming his gun at Lock's chest. 'Don't be so stupid. Hands where I can see them, *bitte*.'

Lock slowly raised his hands. He was standing close to the main door to the cabin and, on lifting his arms, he took a subtle step closer to it.

'That is better. Now, gentlemen, I believe you have something that belongs to me.' He swivelled the gun back towards Ross. 'Or rather, I believe you do, Herr Major.' Wassmuss gave a quick, perfunctory smile.

Lock could scarcely believe his own eyes. Wassmuss bore little or no resemblance to the Bedouin Arab he had sat across the table from in the cafe at Daurat. He was clean-shaven except for the typical curled Persian moustache under his nose. The face, though mostly obscured by tinted-lensed driving goggles and a peaked chauffeur's cap, was still angular, but seemed a little thinner, as did the man as a whole. His grey uniform was well tailored, down to the highly polished black boots. And, remarkably, he was shorter by an inch or two. If he had not spoken, Lock would never have known.

Ross didn't move.

'Come, come, Herr Major. I know the notebook is in your breast pocket. I heard every word.'

Ross lowered his hand. Wassmuss jutted the pistol forward and shook his head. Ross slowed his movements down and carefully began to remove the notebook from his pocket.

'Very good. It was careless of me to let it out of my sight,' Wassmuss shrugged. 'But I have so much on my mind these days. I think I need a secretary, no?'

Lock was itching to make for his gun, but despite the German's cavalier attitude to the situation, he knew that if he made one sudden movement he'd get a bullet in his gut. He flicked his eyes to the light switch on the wall by the door. It was tantalisingly close. If he could just reach it, then the sudden darkness would give him all the time he needed. But it was a risk. Ross was in the line of fire and Wassmuss could just as easily shoot him.

And then the major made Lock's mind up for him. As he held the notebook out for Wassmuss, he made a sudden lunge towards the German's gun.

'Now, Lock!' Ross shouted.

Lock seized his chance and dived for the light switch, plunging the cabin into darkness.

Wassmuss opened fire. There was a flash, and the major cried out. Lock threw himself to the floor, fumbling at his holster again. A second shot rang out with a deafening clang, ricocheting off the bulkhead to his right ear. Lock shifted to his left, lifted his Webley and pulled the trigger. The shot smacked against the wall, but the muzzle flash revealed that Wassmuss had stepped to the cabin door. The German fired his gun wildly once more, then threw the door open. Moonlight spilt into the cabin, and then the German was gone. There was a shout of alarm from outside and Lock could see a wavering beam of light cutting through the darkness.

Lock exploded out of the cabin to give chase. 'Stop that man!' he bellowed.

'Oi!' Underhill yelled, pulling himself up. Lock could see Wassmuss had barged through the sergeant major and a group of sepoys. An electric torch was spinning on the deck like a Catherine wheel.

'Stop him!' shouted Lock again.

Wassmuss spun around and let off two shots in quick succession. Lock, Underhill and the sepoys threw themselves to the deck as the bullets screamed by them.

'What the bleedin' 'ell are you up to?' Underhill fumed.

'It's Wassmuss, the spy!' Lock hissed.

'What, 'ere? Bollocks! You're tight, sah! I can smell the rum on you!'

Lock clambered to his feet and aimed at the fleeing German. But as he pulled the trigger, Underhill clumsily knocked his arm and the bullet smacked harmlessly into the bulkhead.

'He shot the major, you stupid bastard!' Lock shoved Underhill away from him and ran on after Wassmuss.

Rounding the corner, Lock saw the German approach the very stern of the gunboat and athletically jump up onto the guard rail, grabbing hold of the ensign mast to steady himself. He turned, jammed Ross's pistol into his trouser belt, and raised his hands to remove the driving goggles.

'Hold it right there, Wassmuss,' Lock said, Webley aimed at the German's head.

Wassmuss slowly raised his arms.

'I've got you now,' Lock snarled. 'You've led me a merry dance, but it's over. Turn around!'

The German twisted around, using the ensign mast to steady himself.

'Up!' Lock jerked the Webley, indicating for Wassmuss to keep his hands raised.

'Quite the hero, aren't we, Lieutenant? Is the general's daughter proud of you?' Wassmuss said.

Lock didn't reply, he just kept his gun aimed at his foe.

'But, tell me, Herr Lock,' Wassmuss said, 'will you be able to protect this one? She is very close is she not? At the hospital in Basra, *ja?*'

Lock licked his lips. He wasn't going to let himself get riled by the German's taunts. 'Shut up and step down. Slowly.'

Wassmuss dropped his goggles to the deck but remained where he was. 'You cannot protect your women, Herr Lock, can you? Your mother, your Chinese lover, and now that pretty little nurse. Amy, is it not? Perhaps I will pay her a visit.'

'I said, shut up!' Lock's finger tightened on the trigger. How the hell did the bastard know all this? Know about Amy? Know where she was? Sod it, just shoot him and be done with it. Get the notebook. He began to squeeze the trigger. Wassmuss must have sensed some change in Lock, for his face seemed to tighten up. Then Lock eased off slightly. He could hear Underhill and the sepoys nearby, their boots thundering on the deck as they rapidly approached. Then a torch beam struck the German. His blue eyes sparkled as his face broke into a smile.

'Never hesitate, Lieutenant! You lose!' He then winked, turned, and dived overboard.

Lock let off a shot at the same instant and ran towards the guard rail. He stared down into the inky-black waters and cursed. Wassmuss was gone.

'Christ, Lock! What the hell is going on?' Hayes-Sadler gasped, as he, Underhill and the sepoys came storming up to the guard rail next to him. The captain peered down into the water below. '*Iggry!* The light! The light!' he called back over his shoulder.

Singh pushed forward with the electric torch, and directed it down into the water. The beam cut through the darkness, but searched in vain for any sign of the German. 'Do you think he was cut up by the propellers, sahib?'

'Possibly,' Hayes-Sadler said. 'Wait . . . what's that?'

Singh moved the beam through the frothing water of the ship's wake until it fell upon a chauffeur's cap floating on the surface.

'Our dignitary's manservant, that Arab chauffeur . . . was a Fritz spy, Captain,' Lock said, stuffing his Webley back in its holster. 'He killed Shears and shot Major Ross.'

Hayes-Sadler stared back in shock. 'Are they both dead?'

'No, Captain, I'm very much alive. He just wounded my pride a little.' Ross shuffled forward. His left arm hung loosely at his side and his shoulder was matted with blood. He spotted something on the deck and bent down to pick it up. It was the German's driving goggles.

'I can't believe he duped us, sir,' Lock said.

'Did you get the notebook back?' Ross leant over the guard rail and scowled into the water below.

Lock gave a shake of his head. 'Why would he risk exposing himself like that, sir?'

'Who knows? Panic, perhaps? I guess Shears stumbled on him searching my cabin for his documents. One thing's for certain, though, we're close to Basra and he's worried. I managed to copy out some of the contents; we could still thwart his plans if I can decipher it. Maybe find this rat in the White Tabs. Or perhaps he meant to kill us all before we reached Basra . . .' Ross turned to Underhill. 'Sergeant Major?'

'Sah?' Underhill saluted stiffly.

'Best search the boat from top to bottom for any signs of sabotage. A bomb, a leak, anything suspicious. Can't be too careful. This chap has form.'

'Very good, sah!' Underhill saluted again. 'Right lads,' he said, turning to the sepoys, 'follow me!'

'I'll go with you,' Hayes-Sadler said, and led Underhill and the sepoys back towards amidships.

Singh remained with Lock and Ross, directing the torch over the river.

'Did you get him?' Ross said.

'I don't know, sir. I think so.' Lock continued to watch the beam of light scanning the river. 'He knows about Amy, where she is.'

'We'll get to Basra before he does, see she's safe,' Ross said.

'I hope so, sir. I hope so.'

Ross smiled weakly, tossing the goggles over the side and taking the bottle from his pocket. 'At least he didn't shoot the brandy.'

CHAPTER TWELVE

'What do you think, sir?' Lock said, lowering his field glasses.

He was standing alongside Ross on the bridge of the *Espiegle*, with Hayes-Sadler, Underhill and the first officer, looking up the wide, open, flat water of the Shatt al-Arab towards the legendary city of Basra, the Venice of the East. It was eerily still and Lock could make out the line of the city wall and the jagged rooftops of the buildings beyond, as well as a Babylonian tower and a magnificent dome that reminded him of St Paul's in London. All were dark and still, giving the impression of a theatre set, particularly as the far-off, thumping gunfire had turned the sky behind the city to the west into an artist's palate of pulsating reds, oranges and yellows.

'It's like the aurora borealis,' Ross almost whispered. 'Have you ever seen the Northern Lights, Lock?'

'No, sir, I can't say that I have.'

'A must, Lock, a must.'

Lock turned back to stare in wonder at the light show.

Would Amy be standing somewhere, on a balcony perhaps, looking at the same thing? Would she be as captivated? Or would she be nervous and full of apprehension? Perhaps she was up to her elbows in blood, tending to the wounded. Lock smiled. She would make a good nurse, he thought; strong, brave, stubborn. He couldn't wait to see her again. So close now. He fingered her handkerchief deep inside his pocket. Not long now.

'That artillery fire's coming from Shaiba, the fort a few miles further west,' Ross said. 'Those letters you intercepted were right, Lock. Do you remember? "*Split the attention of our enemy from Miralay Subhi Bey's offensive at the shadow of the crescent moon.*" Well, look to the sky.'

Lock glanced up. Ross was right; it was as the letter said. This moon, he recalled from schooling, was known as a waxing gibbous; not quite full, and the crescent on its left side was, indeed, as a shadow.

'I don't think we're too late, though. Wassmuss's army can't be here yet. But we need to get into the city and contact the garrison,' Ross said, his voice thick with strain. His left arm was in a sling and his face was pasty and glistened with sweat. Lock could see that the major was struggling to stay alert.

'Did you get any clues from the notebook, sir, about what Wassmuss had planned?'

'He has agents in the city, Arabs, although I wouldn't put it past him to have a man in British uniform, too,' Ross said. 'He's a cunning fellow.'

Lock knew that all too well. Twice he had come face to face with the German now, and twice he had surprised him. He knew he hadn't shot the bastard when he dived overboard and his instincts told him that he'd escaped the propellers and made it to the shore. But which side? Ross had told him that Wassmuss was a master of disguise, that he'd been living and working among the Arab people for years. Well, Lock could easily believe that. The German's ability to blend in was astounding, and he knew their customs and languages. Lock had to admire the man, and that worried him. Wassmuss could pass himself off as anyone: British, Arab, Indian, Turk . . . He could slip into the city and disappear. But then again, Lock knew him to be arrogant. He'd want to lead his army to glory, that's what he believed. But he was also troubled about how much the German knew about him, about Amy.

Ross wiped the sweat from his brow and frowned. 'Why is the city so qui—' He broke into a coughing fit and winced, grabbing hold of the guard rail to steady himself.

Lock moved to help, but Ross waved him away.

'Did the MO get the bullet out?' Lock said.

Ross shook his head again. 'Lodged in my shoulder. But I'm fine. You'd best get ashore and reconnoitre. Signal from the city wall when you've assessed the situation. We'll steam on through to the quays. We don't want to get sunk by friendly fire now, do we?' Ross's eyes flickered and he began to sway on his feet.

Lock grabbed hold of him. 'Steady, sir. We really should get you to that hospital.'

'Do as I say!' Ross snapped. He checked himself and smiled apologetically. But his grey, damp face looked ghostly and drawn in the moonlight.

'Very well, sir,' Lock said. 'Singh, gather the lads, make ready to go ashore. Sergeant Major, you're to stay with Major Ross. I'm leaving Private Dunford and Bombegy with you.'

'I should be going with the landing party, sah,' Underhill said through gritted teeth.

Lock pulled the sergeant major aside. 'I need you to get the major to the military hospital in the city. You can see he's in a bad way. Dunford and Bombegy will act as stretcher-bearers. I'm putting the major's welfare in your hands. Understand?'

Underhill nodded reluctantly, and Lock turned back to Ross.

'If you jump off on the west bank you can make your way up to the city directly,' the major said.

'No, the east,' Lock said. 'I want to find out how Wassmuss is planning to get his army across the Shatt. It may be its narrowest point here, but it's still a little over 750 feet to the other side. Remember, they are on foot, or horseback, travelling over land. They must have some plan as to how to cross the river.'

'It's probably in that damned notebook,' Ross winced. 'But I couldn't work it out. Very well, Lock, get going!'

Half an hour later, Lock was hidden with Singh amongst the date palms on the eastern shore of the Shatt al-Arab as the river ran towards the north, scanning the opposite bank through his field glasses. Despite Basra's tranquil impression, he knew things weren't right. There was the flicker of flames and a worrying amount of smoke billowing from just behind the city walls further upriver. He prayed it wasn't the hospital. Beyond that he could make out the unending series of quays where shadowy forms of boats and steamers lay berthed at the wharves.

Lock turned his glasses back. The whole corner of the city directly across the wide expanse of water, just above the gaping mouth of a large creek that headed south-west, looked deserted. There were no fires. There wasn't even a light shining. 'I can see no sign of life. Not so much as a sentry on the walls . . .' He glanced at Singh. 'I don't like it.'

A distant gunshot rang out and Lock fixed his attention back on the city.

A second shot.

'What the hell is going on over there?' Lock hissed in frustration. 'We must get across!'

'Sahib! Sahib!'

Lock and Singh turned to see one of the sepoys scrambling along the bank towards them, waving his hand excitedly. Singh called out to him in Punjabi. He received a staccato response, interspersed by breathless gasps, until the scrawny Indian was kneeling down beside them, grinning from ear to ear. He saluted Lock.

'Sepoy Ram Lal reporting, sahib!'

'Well?'

'Many, many boats, sahib!' Ram Lal said, waving back down the river to the south.

'What!?' Lock snapped his gaze to the river. But all he could see was gloom. A thin mist was now blanketing the water's surface, and even the *Espiegle* had been swallowed up by the shadows of the palm trees lining the shore on the opposite bank.

'Sahib, I have found boats,' Ram Lal said. 'Bellums, sahib. Downriver in a lagoon, hidden in the reeds.'

'Bellums?' Lock said.

'Yes, sahib, Arab boats.' Ram Lal bobbed his head.

'Transport for our troops?' Lock said.

'No, no, sahib, they are on this side of the river!' Ram Lal said excitedly. 'There is an Arab man with a rifle. He did not see me, but he was most definitely a guard. I am certain, sahib.'

Lock raised the field glasses back to his eyes and scanned the riverbank to the south. There were innumerable lagoons and backwaters all along the edge of the river, all covered in large areas of tall reeds that ranged from slight rushes by the water, to canes nearly twenty foot high further up the bank. But he could see nothing of the boats Ram Lal mentioned. 'How far?'

'Five-minute walk, sahib. I was going to turn back, but I heard the wood of the boats knocking in the current. Most odd, I thought. So I follow the sound away from the main river, sahib, to a lagoon. I circled around and made my way down to the water's edge to take a look-see.'

Lock nodded slowly. 'Good work, Ram Lal, good work.'

Ram Lal grinned with delight.

'Singh, this must be how Wassmuss planned to get his army across the Shatt and into Basra undetected,' Lock said. 'What with the shelling to the west and what looks like some action to the north, I'd say that Wassmuss's agents have been hard at a regime of sabotage and distraction. The south-east of the city looks totally deserted.'

Lock paused and rubbed his chin distractedly. 'The south!' he said. 'Of course! No one would expect an army to invade from the marshes. Singh, we are looking to the east of the city from this point here, the south-east, you understand? Well, where we are now is the best place to cross. The river's at its shortest point here. From what I recall of Major Ross's map, it's only some seven hundred feet across. Head a little to the south, swing round and you come to the Southern Gate of Basra itself.'

Singh bobbed his head. 'I believe you are on the right track, sahib.'

'Let's take a look at these boats, then. Ram Lal, lead the way!'

Lock and Singh, with Ram Lal a little ahead of them, crept quietly down the riverbank to where the reeds became denser. Ram Lal slowly led them through a seemingly impenetrable forest of canes to the edge of one of the lagoons, thick with smaller reeds. They changed direction here and waded through the water, away from the main river, until they hit a sandbank choked with yet more reeds. They crawled along as quietly as they could, the lapping water, the soft rustling of the reeds and the distant thump of the guns at Shaiba covering their movements. The growing mist was a stroke of luck, too, for the Arab guard would find it harder to see them as they approached.

There was an explosion of feathers and squawking right in front of them, as a couple of nesting birds took startled flight.

The three men froze, and lay flat.

'Bollocks!' Lock hissed.

'No, babblers, sahib,' Singh whispered. 'We will have to be careful. There will be many of the birds in here.'

'That's just great!'

They remained still, and Lock listened for a moment to the beating of his heart, expecting to hear the clunk of a rifle bolt, or the sudden crack of gunfire. But there was nothing. No shouts and no sound of an approaching man.

Ram Lal raised his head cautiously. He beckoned to the others; the coast was clear.

They crept on, keeping their heads low, until the mist finally revealed the first of the long flat-bottomed bellums. Lock thought that they looked like punts, although these vessels narrowed at each end to a point, and the stem and sternpost ended in a high curved piece more in keeping with an Italian gondola. As Lock got closer, he could see that the boats were made of coarse timber, and that they all had a number crudely painted on their side. He estimated that they were about twenty feet long, each one more than capable of carrying ten or more soldiers.

The trio continued to move onwards, and more and more of the boats came into view, all tied together, bobbing and knocking gently in the current.

Ram Lal pressed Lock's shoulder, and all three men stopped. The sepoy indicated over to the left, and Lock slowly lifted his head above the reeds. About thirty feet away, an Arab was sitting in one of the boats, facing out to the main river. He appeared to be dozing. His chin was resting on his chest and a rifle lay across his belly.

Lock lowered his head again. He rolled onto his back and raised a finger to Singh, who nodded then drew his dagger and began to creep around the other side. Lock removed the sheepskin jerkin, his belt and holster, slouch hat, and slipped off his boots. He handed them to Ram Lal and signalled for him to stay put. Lock drew his bayonet and, placing it between his teeth, slipped down into the water beside one of the bellums. He stifled a gasp, surprised at how cold the water was, and then, after composing himself, carefully pulled himself along the edges of the bellums, inching closer and closer to the dozing Arab.

The breeze picked up slightly, and the rustling reeds seemed impossibly loud to Lock. He paused and watched Singh move nearer and nearer to the bellum the Arab was sitting in. The Indian lifted his head. All of a sudden there was a squawk and a flurry of feathers right in front of his face as another brooding babbler was disturbed. The Arab jumped up, startled, and spun round. Lock exploded from the water and, in one swift movement, threw his bayonet. It struck the Arab in the side of the neck with a dull thud, like a faraway axe striking wood. The Arab cried out, twisted in surprise, and collapsed heavily to his knees. Singh rushed forward and jumped into the boat just as the Arab toppled over like a felled tree. Lock waded over and hauled his sodden body from the water and clambered into the boat.

'Pukka throw, sahib,' Singh said, pulling Lock's bayonet from the Arab's neck. Blood oozed from the wound. The Arab twitched, and then was still.

'I was aiming for his back,' Lock said, taking the bayonet from Singh. Both men crouched down. 'Any more, do you think?' Lock said, wiping the blade clean on the dead Arab's aba. Singh shook his head. 'Good,' said Lock, pulling himself up again. 'Call Ram Lal.'

Singh whistled for the sepoy. Ram Lal's turbaned head popped up from the middle of the reeds. He waved and quickly made his way over to them, with Lock's kit cradled in his arms.

Lock sat down and started to pull his boots on. 'Right. Ram Lal, go back and fetch the others. Lance Naik Singh and I will take care of these boats.' Ram Lal saluted and hurriedly made his way back through the reeds. 'We had best scuttle all but one of these, Sid.' Lock buckled his belt and scowled. 'If only we had an axe.'

Singh drew his kirpan and grinned at the hefty blade. 'Better than any axe, sahib!'

Lock smiled. 'I'll get rid of this chap, you get chopping!' He bent down and grabbed the dead Arab by the arms, and started to drag his body from the boat.

While Singh made quick work of chopping below the waterline on the other boats, Lock continuously scanned the reeds and the bank, his Webley drawn and his ears straining to hear anything other than the distant shelling. A few minutes passed with nothing but the sound of splitting wood filling Lock's ears.

'Well, my German friend, "check again".' He scoffed at his chess analogy. But it was all beginning to feel like a game. Wassmuss had gained the upper hand, but then Lock had managed to thwart him. 'Well, now I've got the upper hand,' he said to himself. 'Try crossing the river without boats!'

A different sound stopped Lock's thoughts. He snapped his head to the left and whistled softly for Singh to stop chopping. The Indian froze and Lock gave a second whistle. After a moment, the whistle was returned, and Ram Lal made his way forward with the rest of the sepoys following close behind.

'Hurry!' Lock said, and jumped down from the boat. He gathered the sepoys around him on a nearby muddy clearing, and pulled a thin reed from the ground. He crouched down and began to scratch a crude map of the river, the bank and the city of Basra in the mud.

Singh made his way over to them. 'All done, sahib,' he said, wiping the sweat from his brow.

'Good,' Lock said, before returning his attention back to the map. 'Now, we don't know what we will find on the other side of the Shatt, or at the Southern Gate for that matter. Maybe Johnny is already here, or the place has been abandoned, overrun by Marsh Arabs, left to its fate, which I doubt. But keep your heads, skirmish order through the marsh dwellings here . . . careful of dark doorways and possible hostile natives. I know it's a British-held city, but we cannot take any chances. Keep focused and cover each other's backs. There's an observation tower just inside the city wall, so keep an eye out for snipers, too. Even if they're our own chaps. Remember, we're not expected. Got it?'

There was a muttered 'sahib' as the sepoys indicated their understanding.

'I don't plan on losing any of you now!' Lock said, getting to his feet. 'When we get to the city gates I will scout ahead with two men.' He tossed the reed aside and studied the sepoys thoughtfully. Singh stepped up.

'Not you, Lance Naik. I need you to lead the rearguard. Besides, what if I got shot? Who would take charge then?' Lock said with a smile. 'Ram Lal . . . and . . . you . . . Sepoy . . . ?' He pointed to a slender young Indian with eager eyes and a fuzzy moustache. Christ, he was young, Lock thought, no older than eighteen. But he looked sprightly enough.

'Sepoy Indar, sahib!' The young Indian saluted, as did Ram Lal, who could barely disguise his pleasure at having been hand-picked.

'All right, lads,' Lock clapped his hands, 'in the boat! *Iggry! Iggry!*'

CHAPTER THIRTEEN

Nearly an hour after Singh had set about scuttling the bellums, Lock's platoon loaded up into one of the flat-bottomed vessels intended for Wassmuss's invasion force. They clumsily set off across the quiet Shatt al-Arab towards the south-western bank and into Mesopotamia itself. Two of the sepoys, one at each end of the bellum, punted as best they could. The going was slow and meandering, and out on the water visibility in the ever-increasing mist made navigating worse. Lock saw or heard no one on the journey across, except for the continual rumble of the distant guns at Shaiba.

What seemed like an age passed before they struck the muddy bank on the far side. Singh was the first ashore, leaping off the front of the boat and helping to run her aground so that Lock and the others could scramble off.

All of Lock's senses were alert as he waded through the last of the sharp reeds and pulled himself up the bank. Ahead were a number of traditional Marsh Arab dwellings, little more than simple fishing huts. They were primitive mud structures with domed roofs made from reeds, and dotted haphazardly about amongst the date palms. Lock pulled his Webley from its holster and crouched down, with Singh and the sepoys behind him. There was no sign of life, no livestock roaming free, not even the customary mangy dog.

Lock strained to pick out anything, anything at all. But there was nothing, only the incessant chatter of insects. He waved his hand to the left and right and the sepoys spread out.

Lock crept closer to the first of the dwelling houses. He paused and leant against its rough wall, cool to the touch, and looked over at the city perimeter, standing about five hundred yards away. He licked his lips and watched the darkness. The breeze suddenly picked up and a fishing net, hung out to dry, knocked against its wooden supports. Lock indicated with three fingers to his left, and then did the same gesture to his right. The sepoys separated and picked their way past the marsh huts.

Lock moved forward and made his way up the tree-lined central track that led to the Southern Gate of the city. Singh and two sepoys followed close behind. Lock's eyes were alert, searching every shadow, every possible hiding place for a telltale sign of a hidden foe: a gun nozzle, a bayonet tip, a glimpse of a kabalak or a flash of colour from a kufiya. But there was still no sign of life.

As they neared the city perimeter, the dwellings thinned out and a crumbling wall of about ten feet in height came into view. It didn't have any battlements like that of a castle, but seemed to be there more as a defence against the floodwaters than as a protection against potential invaders.

Something crashed through the undergrowth near to the wall making Lock, Singh and the two sepoys swing around in alarm. It was a cow. Lock let his breath out slowly. The creature stared at the four intruders for a moment, chewing mournfully. It flicked its tail, defecated, then lumbered away. Lock signalled for the men to move on.

Two minutes later, Lock and the sepoys were opposite the southern entrance to the city, a large open archway in the wall big enough for an ox-drawn cart to pass through. Two pillars, elaborately decorated with stone carvings of exotic animals and plants, were standing either side. Lock crouched down next to one of the date palms clustered around the last dwelling. He rubbed his stubbly chin thoughtfully. There was still no sign of life, and there was no barricade across the entrance. It was just an open, dark passageway. The city beyond was vulnerable.

Singh was at Lock's shoulder now. 'Well, Sid? What do you think?' Lock whispered.

The big Indian shrugged. 'It is very strange, sahib. But there is no evidence of any roughhousing. No cartridges scattered about, or bullet holes in the walls. No bodies, not a thing.'

'Exactly,' Lock said. 'So why are there no sentries? No checkpoint? No natives?' He looked over to his left where three of the sepoys were crouched beside a wooden slatted fence. Indar was at the head of the small group. He caught Lock's eye and nodded his readiness. Lock leant back and tried to spot the three sepoys to his right, but he couldn't see them anywhere. Singh tapped his shoulder and pointed over to a darkened doorway about a hundred yards further on. Lock could see a rifle nozzle sticking out. He whistled softly. The turbaned head of Ram Lal appeared briefly, and the Indian waved back.

'Well, time to find out what exactly is going on. I'll see you on the other side,' Lock said, and he ran across the track to the gateway, bearing left as he went, and leaving Singh under the cover of the trees. Ram Lal and Indar followed quickly, scuttling over to the boundary wall.

Lock pressed his back against the left-hand pillar and waited. Indar appeared beside him, breathing rapidly but softly. Ram Lal was pressed against the opposite pillar. He raised his hand to Lock signalling that all was fine. Lock paused, listening. Still there was nothing but the breeze in the trees, and the lapping of the water on the riverbank and, as a reminder that there was actually a war on, the boom of the distant guns.

Lock tapped Indar on the arm, and then both men slipped inside the entrance, with Ram Lal close behind.

It was very dark on the other side of the wall, the moonlight only illuminating the tops of the buildings opposite. Lock crouched down, letting his eyes adjust to the gloom, ears alert. The eerie stillness continued. Nothing moved. He could make out the occasional crack of a gunshot in the near distance. It sounded as if there was a sniper picking off targets. But they weren't coming from the nearby observation tower. It loomed above them to the left, dark and foreboding, but silent and empty. Lock gripped his Webley tightly and set off down the narrow street opposite, with Indar and Ram Lal at his heels.

At the corner of a crossroads they stopped. Lock indicated for Indar to head off to the left, across a large expanse of lawn towards a row of flat-roofed two-storey buildings. He signalled for Ram Lal to take the road to the right. It would take the young Indian by a grand-looking residence with a loggia-style upper gallery, and over to an area of what appeared to be brick warehouses. The sepoys nodded and set off quickly and quietly.

Lock crossed the deserted street, and headed north, towards the gunshots. He came to a bridge that led over and through a long, two-storey building lined with barred arched windows. He paused, gripping his Webley tighter. Then, crouching low, he scuttled across. His nose twitched as he passed over a foul-smelling canal. He ran under a stone archway and emerged onto another narrow street, the surface of which was made of hard mud. He could now see that the walls of the buildings were constructed with rough, mud bricks. Every now and again there was a doorway, crowned by an elaborate archway, cut into the wall, but there were no windows on this level. He looked up. Jutting out over the street on both sides, like enclosed balconies, were quaint latticed windows. They overhung the narrow road and nearly met in the middle. Lock was reminded of the Tudor windows of certain houses back in England. The sound of flowing water pulled his gaze down. There was an open gutter running down the centre of the road.

Lock glanced back the way he had come. The road was mostly in shadow, but there was a sliver of moonlight seeping down through the narrow gaps between the balconies above. He had the uneasy impression that he was being watched and then the quiet was broken by the sound of running footsteps echoing around the walls. They were close by and getting nearer and nearer. Lock remained frozen to the spot, listening to the sound bouncing around his ears. He glanced behind him again and thought he saw a figure step into a doorway. He pressed himself as flat as he could against the wall, the bricks cold against his back, and breathed heavily, listening to the blood pulsate in his ears.

A gunshot rang out. The running footsteps stopped abruptly.

'Sahib!'

Lock span round. Indar was standing half in shadow at the end of the street. Lock lowered his Webley.

'Sahib!' Indar hissed again, and beckoned Lock over.

Lock glanced behind him once more and darted over to the young sepoy. He was now crouched down facing away from the street towards the east.

'Was that you running, Indar?' Lock said, kneeling down behind him.

'No, sahib. But there is some activity over there, near to the church.' He nodded over at an old building bathed in moonlight that was about two hundred yards away across an open courtyard.

'Ram Lal?' Lock said.

'I have not seen him, sahib.'

Lock peered over to the church. It was a stone-constructed building, square, with a flat roof. There was an open bell tower in the middle, with two bells, one smaller than the other, and a simple cross on top. On the right of the roof was what looked like a hut with a doorway to one side. Below the bell tower was an arched window and a set of heavy wooden double doors. Two smaller arched windows were situated to the left and right. There was a path leading up to the doors with neat railed gardens either side, planted with well-tended ornamental shrubs. And in the garden on the left was a large palm tree that reached up to and obscured part of the roof.

A movement beside the bell tower caught Lock's eye. He saw the tip of a rifle barrel and the crown of a topi briefly appear.

'One of ours?' he wondered out loud. 'Indar. Go back and fetch Lance Naik Singh and the others. Be swift, but be cautious. I saw movement behind me. Maybe it was a local, but I'm not sure . . .'

Indar saluted and was gone, running on his toes. He was barely audible.

Lock pulled out his field glasses and scanned the church roof. The figure was no longer in sight. He adjusted his focus to the front of the building. There was a body lying in the shadow of the railed garden on the right. Lock adjusted the focus again, but in the gloom he couldn't tell if the corpse was Turk, Arab or British.

Or an Indian? He strained his eyes to see if the figure was wearing a turban, thinking of Ram Lal and those running footsteps. But it was no good; it was too dark among the bushes to make out.

A rifle shot rang out and Lock jumped back as part of the wall above him shattered. He looked at his left hand. There was an angry gash below his knuckles. 'Bugger,' he hissed through gritted teeth. He pulled Amy's soiled handkerchief from his trouser pocket, and then bound the injured hand as best he could. 'Sorry, Amy,' he said, 'needs must.'

He poked his head out and the wall inches above him cracked again, showering him in debris.

'Bloody hell!' Lock dodged back into the cover of the street as the sound of another rifle shot echoed around the courtyard. He cursed again as he smacked the back of his head against the wall and his slouch hat fell to the floor. He briefly thought about retrieving it, but it was in clear sight of the sniper. He turned and looked back up the street. It was empty. He pursed his lips, and then moved off back the way he had come.

After about fifty yards, Lock came to one of the doorways cut into the wall that he had passed earlier. It was slightly ajar, but he paid the dark gap little attention. He stopped and turned to check back up the street towards the church. No one was following him. Something grabbed his shoulder. He spun around, startled, Webley pointed at the gaping shadow in the doorway.

'*Maalesef doluyuz!*' a voice whispered from the darkness.

Lock reached with his bound hand into the shadows, grabbed hold of the figure that was cowering there, and yanked him out into the moonlight. It was a wild-eyed Arab with a patchy goatee beard and shiny burn scar tissue down the right side of his face. Three fingers were missing from his right hand, which was also scarred and little more than a claw. He was younger than first appeared, too, no more than thirty years old. Lock noticed that the man's left arm was stained dark with blood.

'*Lütfen*,' the Arab croaked.

Lock's mind was racing. He was momentarily shocked at the surprise of the man appearing from nowhere, and at his own stupidity for not remembering the figure he saw dart into the very same doorway earlier on. But he was together enough to notice that the Arab was speaking to him in Turkish and not Arabic or English. But it was what he initially said: 'I'm sorry, we're full.' A code? Had he mistaken him for someone else?

Then he remembered, he'd lost his hat and he was still wearing the sheepskin jerkin. This Arab clearly thought that Lock was a German, or possibly a Turk. There was nothing about Lock's appearance that said Australian or even British officer at all, save for his Webley, and he doubted whether the frightened, wounded Arab would notice the model of firearm he held.

'*Who are you?*' Lock said in Turkish.

'*Abdullah Al-Souk, effendim,*' the Arab said. '*Darf ich ein schluck wasser?*'

Lock remained still. '*You are Al-Souk?*' he said, ignoring the German and sticking to Turkish.

Abdullah switched back to the same tongue. '*Yes, effendim. I have been expecting you . . . Are you with Herr Doktor Wassmuss?*'

Lock, who was still holding the Arab's collar, pushed him up against the door frame. '*I am alone.*'

Abdullah Al-Souk waved his hand weakly. '*But you are his scout? I was watching you enter the town. There is a British sniper . . . on the Syrian church around the corner. I saw him . . . shoot at you. That is when . . . I knew who you were . . . effendim . . . I remembered the code "I'm sorry, we're full" . . . I . . . there are others . . . Indian soldiers. I . . . Water . . .*' he said.

Lock let go of Abdullah Al-Souk's collar and gave him his water canteen. The Arab nodded his thanks and drank thirstily, gulping the water down noisily.

'*Has everything been arranged?* Lock said, continuing his bluff.

Abdullah Al-Souk wiped his mouth and gasped. He handed the canteen back and nodded. '*Shokran, shokran. Yes, effendim. The bombs set off to the north, near to the docks, caused great confusion at the stroke of midnight. Many of the British men guarding the Southern Gate were called there. My men and I then dealt with those left behind. Except . . .*'

'*The church,*' Lock answered for him.

'*Yes, effendim, the Syrian church,*' Abdullah Al-Souk nodded. '*Yes. I am glad you are here. The sniper has killed many of us. I am shot also. My arm.*'

'*Surely he hasn't killed you all?*'

'*They are weak-hearted, effendim. Cowards, no better than worthless women*,' he spat. '*They have fled back to their homes to cower in the dark and to wait for you*.' He paused. '*When does the Doktor come, effendim? For I fear the British garrison will send out patrols and reman the Southern Gate once they see they are abandoned*.'

'*When I give the all-clear. But he is ready, outside of the city walls with a thousand men at his side*,' Lock said.

Abdullah Al-Souk nodded satisfactorily. '*Good. Quick!*' He yanked Lock back into the darkened doorway. There were footsteps approaching from the south. '*It may be a British patrol!*' the Arab said.

They waited in the darkness, hardly daring to breathe. Lock was close enough to the Arab to taste him. He reeked of fear, of stale sweat, of rotting meat and of blood. But he also reeked of good fortune. Good fortune for Lock. This was one of Wassmuss's key men in Basra, he was certain of it, and he had stumbled into his hands. Perhaps the game really was in his favour, he smiled to himself; perhaps he really was going to stop the German in his tracks.

The footsteps came closer and the Arab began to tremble. Lock almost felt sorry for him, but then he saw the faces of all those dead soldiers murdered at their posts and pity was quickly replaced with anger.

'Lock, sahib!' It was Singh.

Lock roughly pushed Abdullah Al-Souk out into the street. 'Here, Lance Naik!' he called.

Singh, Indar and the six other sepoys were standing just to the right, rifles raised in surprise as Lock and the Arab tumbled from the darkened doorway. Lock pressed his Webley into the Arab's neck. The Arab's eyes were wide with confusion as he tried to twist out of Lock's grip.

'Lieutenant Lock, at your service!' He spoke in English and touched his forelock mockingly. '*Now move!*' he said, switching to Turkish, and shoving the Arab in the back.

Abdullah Al-Souk spat and cursed in Arabic, but Lock just smiled.

'*I said, move!*' he repeated, this time using Arabic.

Singh pulled the Arab by the scruff of the neck and shoved him forward. 'You have been busy I see, sahib,' the Indian smiled. He glanced down at Lock's injured hand and frowned. 'Are you badly hurt, sahib?'

'What?' Lock asked. 'Oh, nothing . . . just a scratch. Any sign of Ram Lal?'

'No, sahib,' Singh said. 'But we found many British sentries, all with their throats cut.'

'I hope that bloody Tommy sniper on top of the church hasn't shot him!' Lock said to himself. He didn't react to the news about the sentries. He already knew whose handiwork that was.

Lock pushed Abdullah Al-Souk forward roughly, making him lead the way back up the street, with Singh and the sepoys close behind. The noise of their boots echoed off the surrounding buildings, and Lock knew that there was no way that the sniper on top of the church could not fail to hear them approaching. He halted his men at the end of the street and waited. He could see that his hat was still lying on the street corner, within clear view of the sniper.

'You on the church!' Lock bellowed. 'Hold your fire! This is Lieutenant Lock of the Australian Imperial Force. I have nine men with me, including one Arab prisoner!' He waited to see if there was any response. 'Do you hear me?'

Still there was no reply.

'If you fire on me or my bloody hat again, I'll come up there and throw you off that bloody roof! Do you understand?'

Lock glanced back and could see that Singh and the sepoys were amused by his threats. However, Abdullah Al-Souk was petrified, bent low, with his clawed hand held up as a shield.

'We are coming out!' Lock called again. 'Abdullah, you lead the way! Right, men. Forward, march!' With that, he shoved the Arab out into the open. Abdullah Al-Souk gave a yelp and threw himself to the ground. Lock stepped out into the courtyard, halted, and looked up at the church. A small part of him expected a bullet to strike him, but he was met only by silence. He bent down and picked up his hat. He brushed it off, pushed it back into shape, then placed it on his head. Singh and the sepoys followed him out, then stood to attention and waited.

'Soldier!' Lock shouted once more up at the church roof.

Very slowly the sniper on the church roof raised his head above the edge. Footsteps suddenly approached from the right of the church and Lock was pleased to see Ram Lal marching across the courtyard, rifle held low across his belly.

'He's one of mine!' Lock quickly shouted to the sniper. 'Good to see you alive and well, Ram Lal.' But as he got closer, Lock could see that the sepoy's arm was bleeding. 'How bad?'

'Just a flesh wound, sahib. The sniper Tommy, a most bloody good shot. I have been pinned down over by that water fountain for a long time!'

Lock raised his own wounded hand and smiled knowingly as

he patted Ram Lal on the shoulder. 'Not a Blighty one either, alas!'

The door to the church opened with a loud creak of rusty hinges, and the sniper cautiously stepped outside.

Lock glanced over to him. 'Good man!' he called.

The sniper saluted tentatively. 'Sir!' he shouted back across the courtyard.

Lock looked round at Singh. 'Have you that flare gun, the one Captain Hayes-Sadler gave you?'

'Yes, sahib. Here.'

Lock took the gun and aimed it at Abdullah Al-Souk's temple. The Arab cowered back, whimpering, and then Lock grinned, pointed the gun skywards and let off a flare to signal for the *Espiegle* to make its way up to the wharves.

'Right,' Lock said, passing the flare gun back to Singh, 'let's find out where the hell this bloody garrison has got to then.' He kicked Abdullah Al-Souk to his feet, and led the way over the courtyard to the Syrian church.

CHAPTER FOURTEEN

'General Barrett was evacuated sick three days ago, Lieutenant. Besides, General Nixon is in overall command,' the staff captain said, looking Lock up and down from where he sat, and swatting irritably at a moth that danced around the gas lamp on his desk.

Lock could see the weaselly officer scowling as he reread the letter Ross had provided as a form of identification, the doubt about whether he was telling the truth, or that he was even an officer at all, clearly written all over his face. Lock still wore no officer's jacket, only the increasingly foul-smelling tunic made of animal hide, and his Billjim slouch hat. In fact, the cross belt and the holstered Webley was the only thing 'officer' about his appearance.

'Where exactly did you get this letter?' the staff captain frowned.

'I told you, sir, Major—'

'Yes, this Major Ross . . . a fellow you claim to have seen or heard not so much as a dickie bird of since leaving the . . . *Espiegle* . . .'

Lock squeezed his wounded hand. It was sore, throbbing, and the makeshift bandage Singh had made for him was already soaked with blood, blood that now dripped onto the highly polished floor. 'What about General Townshend? Has he arrived yet?'

'No—'

'Then let me see General Nixon!' Lock was getting increasingly impatient, and all the tact that Ross implored him to use when engaging with higher ranks, particularly those with red tabs, had well and truly been forgotten. He didn't have the time or the patience for niceties or, as Ross would have put it, the proper protocol. He felt like drawing his Webley and giving the bastard a fright, but there was the staff sergeant and the sepoys outside the office door to take into account. He wouldn't be able to do anything locked up in the guardhouse.

'Out of the question, Lieutenant. The general is not to be disturbed until morning.'

'But he *will* be disturbed, and very soon!' Lock said.

'Calm yourself, Lieutenant. Remember where you are!' the staff captain said, rising to his feet, face red. 'Now, sit down and report to me!'

Lock glared at him for a moment, but he knew that he would get nowhere if he continued to argue like this. 'I prefer to stand, sir.'

The staff captain glowered at him, but said nothing and sat back down again.

The silence between the men stretched out, and Lock found himself listening to the sounds of distant artillery fire as the Turkish guns kept up their shelling of the British positions at Shaiba, nine miles away. According to the church rooftop shooter who had pinned Lock down on his entry to Basra, the shelling had been going on continuously since the previous morning.

The sniper was called Alfred Elsworth, a young private, it turned out, from the 104th Wellesley's Rifles. He said he was eighteen, but Lock suspected that he was younger. However, he was a fine shot, and Lock told him to come along with them. Elsworth was more than happy to do so, having seen his squad wiped out by one of Al-Souk's bombs.

'Major Ross and I left Brigadier General Robinson's force at Mohammerah and raced here,' Lock said, returning to the matter at hand. 'My orders are to warn the commanding officer here of the second Turkish force that has circled down from Persia.'

'Yes . . . this force you never saw . . .' the staff captain said.

Lock ignored the remark. 'There was word before we left that the lines were cut and that Ahwaz was overrun. It was my job to get that information to Basra as quickly as possible, and that is what I'm trying to do—'

'Hmm. And this Buddoo you brought in with you?'

'As I have already explained . . . a saboteur we captured on our way in. You have spoken to the men on patrol in the south-east of the city? You know of the explosions and the skirmishes there?'

'Yes, Lieutenant. It is all being looked into as we speak. Only, you see,' Winslade laughed nervously, 'we know Abdullah Al-Souk. He's a hospital orderly. Well known as an informer for the provosts. So, Lock, you are clearly mistaken about the Arab's guilt.'

Lock shook his head. This man was a fool.

'And the boats we discovered? Enough for an army to cross the Shatt—'

'Yes, yes . . . Now you say you were part of a special reconnaissance team under the command of Major Ross . . . but we have no record of a Major Ross here, on the list of personnel newly arrived from Karachi,' the staff captain said, leafing through his papers. 'And no record of Australian personnel either, for that matter.'

'Then I must be a figment of your imagination, sir,' Lock said.

The staff captain glared up at him briefly, then returned his attention to his list. 'Ah! Here's mention of a detachment of the Australian Flying Corps,' he said. 'Perhaps you're here . . . Is Ross an Australian, too?'

Lock was becoming more and more frustrated. This was getting him nowhere and all the time he wasted here was time for the Turks to breach the poorly defended south of the city which, it turned out, was actually the port area known as Ashar. Old Basra city itself was a mile south-west of the Shatt al-Arab. However, he had managed to rally together a few stragglers from various units, the stunned remnants of the patrols who'd been guarding the section of the wall when Al-Souk's men struck. But they were only a handful. They needed more soldiers, artillery too, and to send patrols out to the east bank of the Shatt al-Arab to raise the alarm when Wassmuss's Turks arrived en masse.

'Captain?' Lock said.

'Hmm?' the staff captain muttered, continuing to leaf through his papers.

'It is imperative that you strengthen the southern walls of Ashar. If Basra falls then the oilfields are in danger. There will be nothing to stop the Turks march—'

'Yes, yes. I heard you the first time, Lieutenant. Now, you claim that you are attached to the 2nd Mendip Light Infantry . . .' He raised his head and regarded Lock. 'Where is your regiment now?'

'Shaiba. But—'

'Then you and your men must return there immediately.'

Lock took a deep breath, and clenched his right fist. 'I cannot return, sir. The barrage . . .' He felt he was stating the obvious.

The staff captain frowned and rubbed his thin lips thoughtfully. He picked up his telephone and wound the handle. He waited for a few moments until the exchange answered.

'Captain Winslade here . . . Get me Lieutenant Colonel Godwinson . . . of the 2nd Mendips . . . Yes, at Shaiba . . . What? . . . I don't care . . . Well, keep trying!' He scowled and put the receiver down. He gazed at Lock impassively. 'It appears the line is cut to the fort. The shelling I presume . . .' He picked up the receiver once more and wound the handle. 'Major Hall, Dorsetshire Regiment, please . . . Certainly . . .' He began to drum his fingers on the tabletop. 'Ah, sir, Winslade here . . . No, sir . . . Yes, sir . . . I . . . Yes, Lock, sir . . . No, Lock . . . L-O-C-K . . . Yes, sir, like a canal . . . Beg pardon, sir . . .' Winslade was scowling as he listened. 'Very good, sir . . . At once. Thank you, sir.' He placed the receiver down and smiled thinly up at Lock.

'You are to report to the Western Gate in Basra city, you and your men, where you will be transported to Shaiba—'

'Look,' Lock said, 'I can't just leave—'

'You can and you will, Lieutenant. Those are direct orders to you from a senior commanding officer,' Winslade said.

Lock pursed his lips and squeezed his injured hand tighter, dripping more blood onto the floor.

Winslade glanced at Lock's bandaged hand. 'Run along to the

hospital first and get that hand seen to. And while you are about it, get yourself properly dressed! You are a disgrace to the uniform, man!'

'And the southern wall at Ashar?'

'Yes, yes.' Winslade waved his hand dismissively.

Lock stared down at the staff officer in disbelief. But what could he do? He couldn't force the captain to act. He was powerless. Where was Ross? Even Underhill would be a help. But Lock had no idea where the sergeant major was either. He uttered a foul curse and turned on his heels.

'What did you say?' Winslade spluttered after him. 'Lieutenant!'

Lock ignored the captain and moved towards the door just as it opened. A staff sergeant entered. Lock barged past him.

'Sarnt! Stop that man!' Winslade yelled shrilly.

'Sir? Sir?' the sergeant called after Lock, pulling him back by the shoulder.

Lock spun round. 'Sod off!' he said.

The sergeant stared into Lock's eyes and held his palms up, stepping back a pace.

Lock smiled wryly. 'Nothing personal, Sergeant, but that . . . base-wallah behind the desk hasn't the first idea of what's going on, or what he's doing. Now, I'm leaving to go and fight the Turks. If he or anyone else gets in my way, I'll kill them. Now, you best get Captain "Yes Yes" . . . another cup of char.' He mockingly saluted Winslade, who was standing with his mouth agape. 'Sir,' he said, then turned, pushed past the two watching sepoys, and left.

'I'll report this . . . this insubordination. Not befitting of an officer . . . even a damned colonial one . . . if you are an officer at all . . . Report to the Western Gate, or you will be arrested! Do you hear me, Lock?' Winslade shouted after him.

Once he stepped outside, Lock hesitated, took a deep breath, then kicked at the dirt on the ground. 'Bollocks!' He needed to find someone who would listen, who had the power to do something. He needed to find Ross. And Winslade's comments about him looking like a Buddoo irregular were right. To get himself taken seriously, and listened to, in this damned fool army, Lock at least needed to look like an officer.

He made his way over to a covered walkway where Singh and the others were gathered. The sepoys dozed whilst Elsworth blew gently away on a mouth organ. Lock grunted, recognising the ditty. It was 'I Don't Want to be a Soldier'. He slumped against the dusty wall and threw down his hat. He winced. His hand was getting stiff.

'You best get that cleaned up, sahib,' Singh said. 'The hospital is not far from here. I saw some sisters whilst you were inside talking with the brass hats.'

'I didn't get to talk with the general,' Lock said. 'Bloody staff officers! Bloody army protocol! I'll have the provosts after me now.'

'But what of the southern wall, sahib?'

'Well, I guess we will have to use our own initiative, won't we?' Lock said. 'Take the lads back there, find some buckshee supplies on the way: lanterns, ammo, anything you can lay your hands on. Oh, and a couple more star lights for that flare gun I gave to Indar. Go and set up an observation line. Cajole as many other men as you can find, stragglers, whatever. Say it's a direct order from Major Ross if you get any backchat. I will be along as soon as I get this hand sorted.'

'And the major, sahib?'

'Sweet FA. I'm hoping the sergeant major got him to the hospital. I'm going there now. There's someone else I want to see, too.'

'Sahib?'

'Never mind.'

Singh and Lock got to their feet. Singh shouldered his rifle and went and spoke a few words in Punjabi to the resting sepoys. They groaned, but wearily pulled themselves up.

'Sorry, lads,' Lock said. 'Private Elsworth, you tag along with me. I need someone who knows his way around this bloody place.'

Elsworth tapped the spit from his mouth organ and jumped to his feet. 'Where to, sir?' he said enthusiastically.

Lock raised his injured hand. 'Hospital. To repair your damage. Ram Lal . . . you best come with us.'

Ram Lal looked to Singh.

'What's the matter?' Lock said.

'Sahib, Ram Lal should report to the Indian hospital,' Singh said.

'Nonsense! He's coming with me. That's an order!'

Singh nodded, then Ram Lal picked up his rifle and moved over to Lock's side.

Outside the main entrance to the British Hospital, which looked more like a grand Victorian railway station than a medical centre, with its cupolas, porticoes, large arched windows and entranceway, Lock watched as the true horrors of war unfolded before him. A pretty nurse, her uniform splattered with blood, ran out from the main entrance to where a number of ambulances were beginning to arrive in the courtyard. The headlamps of the vehicles were shining brightly, casting eerie shadows upon the walls of the building. A group of wounded khaki-clad figures stumbled by, wrapped in blankets, bandaged, mostly caked in dried blood, dust and salt sweat. Labels were attached to their tunics. Curious, Lock stopped one private, who gazed back at him vacantly. Lock turned his label over. It gave brief details of the man's injuries, scribbled in pencil. Lock let the soldier shuffle on.

'Wounded from Shaiba, sir,' Elsworth said grimly. 'Can't believe there's so many. The Turk offensive is barely a day old! And this is just one of three hospitals.'

Lock watched the nurse with the blood-splattered uniform move from soldier to soldier, reading their labels, trying to smile at the men reassuringly. One man, his left leg bare and bound with blood-soaked bandages, stumbled as he tried to make his way from one of the ambulances to the hospital door. The nurse reached out and steadied him, then all but carried him inside. Lock, Elsworth and Ram Lal followed them into the already crowded reception hall. The nurse helped the wounded soldier through the stone-floored foyer and into the first ward. She guided him down into an empty chair next to one of the occupied beds.

The ward was full yet eerily silent. It had an overriding stench of death, a sickening cocktail of sweat, blood, pus and mud. It was all Lock could do to stop gagging. Most of the soldiers were pale and shivering. Nobody complained or cried out, no one even seemed to have the energy to talk; they all appeared to be utterly spent and, Lock guessed, glad to be away from the fighting. Most simply looked numb. Even the soldiers without a bed or a seat just leant against the walls, clearly so exhausted that they somehow managed to sleep without toppling forward.

Lock called out to the nurse but she didn't appear to hear him. He followed her through to the next ward. Here, the smell of antiseptic was the first thing he noticed. He glanced at the uncomplaining men laid out on metal frame beds in neat rows, and tried not to focus on their shattered heads, or their hideously disfigured faces and their blind eyes that would never see a sunrise again.

'Miss?' A soldier, half his face bandaged, stretched out his hand weakly and the nurse stopped and leant over him. 'Can you spare a smoke?' She shook her head and Lock stepped forward.

'Here.' He handed the pasty soldier a cigarette and struck a match for him.

'Thank you,' the nurse said. She was so young, hardly more than a schoolgirl. Then she spotted Lock's blood-soaked, bandaged hand. 'Are you hurt?' There was concern in her voice.

'It's nothing,' Lock said with a gentle smile. 'Actually, I'm looking for someone, an officer. He's about—'

The nurse smiled wearily. 'I'm sorry. You'll have to go back to reception. Perhaps at the desk? Or even the Officers' Hospital.' She turned and paused at the door at the far end of the ward. She took a deep breath, and pushed it open.

Lock followed, with Elsworth and Ram Lal a few paces behind, and peered through the glass observation window. It showed another ward, again full of men all lying neatly on beds, again in neat rows along the wall, like graves in a cemetery. Some of the patients were conscious and watched, their mouths drawn at the corners, while the newly arrived nurse conferred with her colleague, who was seated at a desk in the middle of the ward. She looked ashen as she talked and indicated to the men under her charge.

Lock turned away. 'Come on, let's find the major ourselves.'

Elsworth glanced at Ram Lal, who just shrugged. Both men followed Lock down the crowded corridor further into the hospital. They passed through a set of double doors and came out onto another corridor. Only this one was deserted. A sign pinned to the yellowing wall said that it led to the operating theatres.

A door opened a little way up the corridor and a nurse wearing a cotton mask over her nose and mouth rushed out with a bowl in her hands. She disappeared through another door further down.

'You lads sit and wait here,' Lock said, seeing that there were a couple of chairs pushed up against one wall. 'I'll go and speak to that nurse.'

Elsworth and Ram Lal slumped into the chairs, and Lock continued along the corridor to the room from which the masked nurse had appeared. He put his face to the small observation window in the door. Blood covered most of the surfaces inside and a soldier was lying on the operating table. A masked doctor was sawing away at his patient's leg above the knee. Lock's gaze was drawn to a dark and bloody pile in the corner of the room. It reminded him of a compost heap, only, as he stared, he could make out familiar shapes: a hand, a foot, a leg. He realised with horror that it was a pile of severed limbs.

'Jesus,' Lock muttered, 'this isn't a hospital, it's a slaughterhouse.'

'What are you doing here?' the masked nurse snapped, purposefully striding up to Lock, brown eyes wide and full of fury.

Lock smiled. 'I'm . . . er . . . was told to report here.' He raised his bloody, bandaged hand.

The nurse scowled at him. 'To be amputated?' she said, her voice tinged with a Lancashire lilt. 'In there. But you'll have to wait.'

She indicated to the room further down the corridor and quickly brushed past Lock and darted back into the operating room. The sound of the saw briefly assaulted Lock's ears. He winced and walked away.

Lock sat quietly in the treatment room as the nurse, the same nurse who had scowled at him earlier from behind her mask, dressed his hand. He watched her with interest: a brown-haired girl in her early twenties. Her face was as pale as milk and she had a delicate, small nose and beautiful, sensual lips. They were slightly open and Lock could see her tongue move across the tips of her teeth as she concentrated on what she was doing. Lock was filled with a sudden desire to pull her to him and kiss her hard.

The nurse glanced up and caught Lock staring at her. She dropped her eyes again. Lock wondered what she was thinking, but any unspoken question was lost when a familiar voice called out his name from the corridor.

He looked up to see Lady Townshend standing in the doorway. She was wearing a sister's uniform of grey and scarlet, with a red shoulder cape and white veil, quite different from the glamorous woman he had first met at Amy's party. How long ago was it now? It seemed like years. But she was still a handsome woman and her eyes, those same emerald green eyes, were her daughter's.

'It is all right, Nurse Owen, I will take over now,' she said softly, as she entered the room. '*Bonjour*, Lieutenant Lock. Fancy meeting you here.'

Lock made to pull himself to his feet, but Lady Townshend waved him back up onto the treatment table.

'Sit, sit. Let me finish that dressing.' She held her hand out and Nurse Owen gave her the bandages and scissors. 'Nothing too serious, I hope? *Merci*, Nurse. Go and take some refreshment.'

Nurse Owen smiled warmly at Lock then left. Lock recalled Amy mentioning that her mother was a sister with the VAD, but he was surprised to see General Townshend's wife here in Basra without her husband. Then again, Captain Winslade could have been lying about the general . . .

'I . . . Madame . . . Lady Town . . . Sister . . .'

'*Bon*, that looks fine.' Lady Townshend snipped the excess bandage away and put the tray with the iodine and scissors aside. 'Lady Alice, Sister Alice if you prefer,' she smiled, 'but less formality, *s'il vous plaît*, Lieutenant Lock.'

'Is the general with you? Here in Basra, I mean?' Lock said, getting stiffly down from the table.

'*Non*, not yet, I am afraid. In a few days, perhaps. I sailed on the troopship after yours. I thought it best to be near Amy sooner rather than later. Her father is still furious with her for joining the VAD, and furious with our Commandant-in-Chief, Katharine Furse, for letting Amy be posted to the front,' she said. 'Although it had nothing to do with her. But that is of no consequence, my husband wouldn't dare write or say anything to *Mme* Furse, Amy would never forgive him!'

Lock had to smile at that. 'How is she?'

'Well, under the circumstances. I fear she is a little young for this kind of work, but then all the nurses are, not to mention the poor boys being stretchered in from the front. Young ladies shouldn't have to see the horrors that go on in this place. *Mais*, Amy . . . Well, you know her well enough, Lieutenant Lock.'

Something in Lady Townshend's expression made Lock wonder if she knew about their feelings for one another or, at least, the feelings that had developed on the *Lucknow* before the incident with Bingham-Smith.

'She is off duty now, but I am sure she will welcome a visit from you.' Lady Townshend leant forward and lowered her voice. 'She seemed a little troubled at first and I am inclined to think that she may be having doubts about her suitor, young Monsieur Casper. You remember him? Lieutenant Bingham-Smith? *Non?* Although he is an assistant provost marshal now, I believe, here in the city.'

Lock was stunned by the news. Bingham-Smith promoted. How on earth had that happened? And in the provosts, too.

'I'm sure that suits him fine, Lady Townshend. Keeps him away from the fighting,' Lock said.

Lady Townshend gave Lock a disapproving look. 'Someone has to protect the city, Lieutenant Lock.'

Lock scoffed inside. He'd already seen first-hand how well the city was protected. He also knew that that wasn't what the provosts did. They were the police, the lawmen to watch over the soldiers, and they were about as popular as syphilis in a brothel. A perfect career path for Bingham-Smith, he thought.

Elsworth appeared at the door with a jacket over his arm. 'Beg pardon, sir,' he said shyly.

'Come in, Elsworth. Lady Alice, may I present Private Elsworth, one of the finest shots in the British army.'

'How do you do?' Lady Townshend said.

Elsworth blushed as he stood there in silence. 'Ma'am,' he eventually blurted out before turning to Lock. 'Er . . . sir, a jacket for you. Australian, too. Found it in the . . . er . . . well, it's a spare.' He handed it over awkwardly.

'Thank you, Elsworth. How is Ram Lal?'

'All patched up and waiting for your orders, sir. He's in the corridor.'

'Will you rejoin your regiment?' Lady Townshend asked, turning back to Lock.

'No. The shelling makes it impossible at the moment. I guess we are stuck here for the time being. Besides, I need to find my major. Major Ross – you remember him?'

'Of course.'

'Well, I seem to have mislaid him.'

'My, that is rather careless,' Lady Townshend said. 'I will see if I can track him down for you. He may well be in the Officers' Hospital, a different building. Now, I must be getting along. But tell me, have you boys had anything decent to eat recently?'

'Not for days, your ladyship,' Elsworth blurted out. He coloured again.

'Well, wait here and I will get one of the nurses to rustle up some bread and cheese and hot tea for you.'

'Thank you,' Lock said.

'*Bonne chance*, Lieutenant.' She nodded to Elsworth and made her way out of the room.

Lock rolled down his shirtsleeve and opened and closed his

injured hand. The bandages were restrictive, but it felt better. He picked up the found jacket Elsworth had passed him. It had the bronze 'Australia' badge on the shoulders and a purple square below it, which meant 'the Engineers'. But there was no white flash this time. However, the cuff badges of rank had two stars instead of one. It was a full lieutenant's jacket. Lock smiled to himself. So he'd been promoted for the time being. Then he stopped and stared. There was a hole above the left breast pocket and the area around it was stained. Someone had attempted to scrub off what he could only presume was blood. He put his finger through the hole.

'Where did you say you got this, Elsworth?' Lock was rather horrified.

'Er . . . there was a pile near the operating theatre. The owner won't be needing it any more . . . sir . . .' He trailed off and lowered his eyes, embarrassed.

Lock didn't say anything and pulled the jacket on. It was a near-perfect fit. He tugged the cross belt from the foul-smelling sheepskin and looked back at Elsworth.

'You and Ram Lal eat some food. I'm going on a little errand. If I'm not back in half an hour, make your way to the Southern Gate and report to Lance Naik Singh. And save me and the others some of that cheese!' He fastened the belt about his waist and up over his right shoulder, and stepped out into the corridor.

Ram Lal, who was sitting on the floor with his eyes closed, scrambled to his feet.

'Wait in there with Private Elsworth. I'll be back later,' Lock said.

'Sahib.' Ram Lal saluted and went to join Elsworth.

As Lock walked down the quiet corridor he spotted Nurse Owen at the far end. Her back was to him and she was bending over a soldier who was in a wheelchair. She turned on hearing his approaching footsteps. Their eyes met and she blushed.

'Nurse Owen . . .'

She smiled. 'Mary, please.'

'Mary, can you tell me where Nurse Amy Townshend will be?' Lock said.

'Yes. Not very far, in the Street of Allah's Tears. We share rooms there.'

'Really?'

'Well, it helps to be friends with a girl from the aristocracy,' she smiled. 'It's a small place, cosy. We have to share a bed but we're rarely there at the same time. Her father arranged them, I believe.'

'And she'll be there?'

'It's her rest period. She'll be sleeping, I guess. We've had an exhausting time of late.'

Lock nodded and was about to turn away when Mary took hold of his arm.

'You're Kingdom, aren't you?' she asked, looking from one eye to the other.

'Yes.'

She suddenly grabbed his face, kissed him passionately on the mouth, before breaking away again. Then she turned and quickly pushed the soldier sat in the wheelchair away back down the corridor.

Lock stood and watched her go as he rubbed his lips. 'What is it about nurses?' he said, smiling.

* * *

Lock made his way out of the hospital and, following Mary's instructions, soon found the Street of Allah's Tears. It was conveniently labelled in English as well as Arabic. It didn't look like much, another claustrophobic, enclosed alleyway, barely wide enough for a cart to pass through, but it was quiet. Dirty brown water was running down the open gutter in the middle of the hard mud road, but it lacked the pungent odour of some of the streets Lock had passed through when he'd first entered the city. He moved swiftly along, conscious that he didn't have a lot of time to be away from the city wall, from Singh and the others. Just half an hour, he told himself. Time enough. Enough for what? To make love to her? To Amy? Is that what this was? He didn't know, wouldn't know, until he saw her again.

He moved on down the street, counting the doorways softly under his breath. 'One . . . two . . . Here we are, third door along on the left.'

Lock paused at the entrance, his hand instinctively going to his Webley, remembering his encounter with Abdullah Al-Souk. There was a bell pull and three nameplates, two in Arabic, the third, the top one, in English. He could just make out the words in the dim dawn light. Written in pencil, already fading, were the names Owen and Townshend. His hand hesitated at the bell pull, then he tried the door instead. It opened with a soft creak.

There was a sudden flash of movement and Lock stepped back as something small brushed past his leg. It was a cat.

Lock cursed at his own nervousness and stepped inside. There was a long, dark corridor with a door to the left and a staircase going up. Lock's nostrils twitched at the acrid smell of cat piss. He pressed the electric light switch on the greasy wall and a dim bulb flickered into life on the landing ceiling. He swiftly made his way up the stairs, taking two at a time.

The first floor had a door with an Arabic nameplate and six pairs of shoes neatly parked outside. They were well worn and looked to belong to a family: two adults and four children. There was a smell of cooking coming from the other side, but no voices Lock could make out. He climbed the final flight and came to the door marked with Amy and Mary's surnames, once again in pencil, but clear and bold this time.

The stairwell light went out. Lock tried the door. It was unlocked. He moved inside and closed the door softly behind him.

'Amy?' he whispered, and waited, letting his eyes adjust to the gloom. He was standing in a cramped square hallway. It was lined with coats, hats and jackets on one side, and some shelving overflowing with books and pot plants on the other. There was a small tiled room opposite in which Lock could just see part of a tin bath. Off to the right, at the end of the corridor, was a second door. A strip of light was showing underneath.

Lock made his way forward and pushed it open.

The room he entered was like the hallway, cramped and over-furnished. There was a small dressing table over in the far corner, and a pot belly stove to his left with an iron kettle on top, and a table and two chairs in front. A line was strung across this part of the room, with a number of undergarments hanging from it. Lock could smell the damp. An elaborate carved screen partitioned the room down the middle, at the end of which was a pair of large French windows, open, showing a lattice-shuttered balcony overlooking the street. To the left of the screen was an old leather armchair, horsehair stuffing spilling out in a number of places in its torn and worn upholstery. But on the right of the screen, illuminated by a standing lamp with a yellow frilled shade, was a large wooden bed, pushed up against the wall.

And here was Amy, sleeping, as Nurse Owen said she would be. She was lying fully clothed in her uniform, even with her shoes still on her feet. Her face was angled towards him. Her auburn hair was loose and tumbling over the pillow and she was breathing softly, every few seconds making a small whimpering sound, like a puppy dreaming. Her eyes flickered open and stared at him unfocused for a moment. She frowned, and sat up.

'How long have you been standing there?' she whispered, voice half asleep.

Lock flung his hat aside and moved forward, taking her in his arms and kissing her breathless. She pushed him away and slapped his face hard. It stung, but Lock didn't react and just stared back at her. She hesitated, then pulled his head to hers and kissed him passionately.

They didn't speak as they began to strip each other of their clothes, kissing, biting, nibbling at each other. Lock eased Amy back on the bed. Her skin felt good against his, and she pulled him to her hungrily until they both collapsed, spent, exhausted and drenched in each other's sweat.

Lock rested his head on Amy's naked breast, and she held him tight, combing her hand through his hair. He began to feel aroused again and moved up to press his lips against hers once more. Her mouth opened and his tongue brushed against her teeth. She began to moan, at first in pleasure, but then he felt her begin to struggle and twist away from him.

'Stop!' she gasped, pulling her face away from his. 'You left without a word. Again. And after what you did. Is that how you treat your women, Mr Lock?'

He gently turned her face back to his and stared into her emerald eyes. They were no longer dreamy, but alert and angry. They were the eyes he last saw her with, when he had fought with Bingham-Smith.

'Amy . . .' Lock said.

'Get off me!' She thumped his bare chest hard and he rolled away from her. She then snatched the blanket up over her nakedness, and jumped off the bed.

Lock stared up at her, momentarily bewildered. Why the sudden change of mood? 'What have I done?' he asked.

She scowled back at him, then abruptly turned and padded over to the hallway, depositing the blanket over the armchair on her way. Lock heard her go into the bathroom. There was silence and then he could hear her urinating. He sighed. He should be getting back.

'Amy,' Lock said. 'I need to tell you something.'

She didn't reply and he continued to listen to the sounds of her moving about, to water splashing. She began to brush her teeth.

'I have to get ready,' she called. 'I'm on duty again at six.'

'Come back here,' Lock said. 'So we can talk.'

Amy emerged with only a towel around her head. Lock drank her in, his eyes moving up and down her body. She seemed to suddenly realise she was naked and made a lame attempt at covering herself with her arms and hands.

'Don't look at me like that,' Amy said, snatching up the blanket again and wrapping herself in its rough veil. 'You took advantage of me,' she said. 'Why are you here?'

Lock pulled himself up off the bed and began to gather up his discarded uniform. He didn't hide his nakedness and, as he started to dress, he could tell that she was watching him.

'I came to find you. To say "I'm sorry if I hurt you." To say . . .' But he couldn't say it, those words he wanted to say, those words that could offer so much joy, yet so much pain.

'To say what?' Amy said.

Lock looked at her. She was very beautiful, he thought. 'Nothing. It doesn't matter.' He pulled on his jacket and was arrested by Amy's sudden expression of horror. Then he remembered. He glanced down at his left breast where the bullet hole was, and smiled ruefully. 'Not my jacket. A young Persian girl has mine.'

'A young girl?'

Lock noted the tinge of jealousy in her voice and laughed. 'Another time. I must go. I've spent too long away from the wall as it is.' He buckled his Sam Browne belt and picked up his slouch hat. As he stepped towards the door, he turned back.

'Amy, listen to me. Please be careful.'

'I can look after myself, Kingdom,' she said.

'That I don't doubt. But I worry about you, and there's a man—'

Amy scoffed. 'Another suitor? Are you jealous?' It was spiteful, but her face didn't match the words. Lock knew she was trying to be deliberately aggressive.

'Stop, will you, and listen. There's a German agent, he's—'

'Kingdom,' Amy interrupted, stepping forward, 'I don't care about that. I have something I need *you* to hear, something about Casper.'

Lock sighed impatiently. 'I don't want to talk about Casper Bingham-Smith. He deserved what he got. But if it means so much to you, then I'm sorry – sorry that you saw it.'

Amy shook her head. 'No, it's something else. I have to tell you that—' But she didn't finish, as someone was coming rapidly up the stairs outside.

The footsteps paused, then there came a hammering at the door.

'Lieutenant! Lieutenant! Are you in there? Amy? It's me, Mary . . .'

Lock walked out into the hallway and pulled open the front door. Nurse Owen was standing there looking flustered.

'I'm sorry, but I've located your major!' Mary said.

'What? Where?'

'At the hospital,' she said, catching her breath. 'And not in the Officers' Hospital, but the British one. He's in one of the operating theatres. Come, I'll take you.' She glanced at Amy and shrugged as if to apologise for interrupting.

But when Lock looked back at Amy, she had turned her face away.

'I'm sorry,' he said, 'I have to go.' He waited for Amy to say something, but she seemed determined to make herself not catch his eye again.

'Goddamn you, Amy,' Lock said. 'Just be careful.' And he walked out after Mary, slamming the door behind him.

Lock paced the corridor outside an operating theatre, smoking cigarette after cigarette, waiting for news of Ross's condition. He kept glancing through the observation window, seeing the doctor leaning over the still body of the major, surrounded by nurses. Lock wanted desperately to go back to Amy, but he couldn't leave, not until he had news of the major's chances. What if he died? Then what? He'd be on his own with no ally to keep him away from fools like Captain Winslade. Without Ross's word he would have trouble convincing Command that Basra was under threat from the east. Not that Command would listen to him. In fact, he needed Ross to talk to Command for him. They would listen to the major.

Lock stopped pacing and ran his hand through his hair, shaking his head. 'Stop being a bloody fool!' he told himself. 'You're on your own, like always. So do what you do best, act for yourself!'

Eventually the door opened. Lock tossed his cigarette aside and grabbed the doctor's arm as he emerged with the nurses from the operating room. The medical man's unshaven face was drawn and he looked exhausted, with heavy black circles under both eyes.

'How is he?'

The doctor stared blankly back at Lock, then down at his arm. Lock let go and the doctor forced a tired smile.

'Touch and go, Lieutenant. He's lost a lot of blood. But we managed to remove the bullet. Saved the arm. Just have to wait.'

'Can he talk?' Lock said.

'Still unconscious. Will be for a while. Then he'll be moved over to the Officers' Hospital. Quieter there. Now, you'll have to excuse me.'

The doctor walked off, and Lock smacked his bandaged fist against his thigh. 'Bugger!'

Lock peered through the observation glass. Ross was still lying on a table in the middle of the room. If it weren't for the slight rise and fall of his chest, Lock would have said that the major was dead, such was the pallor of his skin. Lock cursed again. There was nothing for it. He would have to convince Command himself. Somehow. Even if he had orders to report to the Western Gate. That would have to wait. And if Winslade got in his way . . . Well, it would be the last time that he did.

CHAPTER FIFTEEN

Lock left the hospital, moving south. He passed the now silent presence of the Syrian church, and quickly made his way to the outskirts of the city, back to the Southern Gate at Ashar where he hoped Singh and the others were keeping an eye out for Wassmuss's army. But as he moved on, it became all too clear that Captain Winslade had done nothing with regard to Lock's report. The area was still deathly quiet and worryingly devoid of soldiers. When eventually the city wall loomed up ahead of him, he spotted Sepoy Indar crouched down beside the open gateway. Well, that was something. Good old Singh, he thought.

'Where's the lance naik?' Lock said.

'In the tower, sahib.' Indar pointed to the Babylonian watchtower a little further along the wall.

'Any sign of the enemy?'

'None, sahib. As quiet as the graveyards.'

‘Good, keep alert.’ Lock moved over to the watchtower and began to climb up the damp, cool stone stairway inside. It was claustrophobic and silent, with no sound other than the breath in his throat and his boots scuffing on the worn steps. When he came to an open doorway at the top, he stepped out onto the roof and paused, momentarily taken aback by the view. The sun hadn’t appeared above the horizon yet, but it promised to be a glorious day as the sky was already an artist’s palette of blues, rose and gold.

Lock pulled out his field glasses and crossed to the ramparts where Singh and Elsworth were standing. Singh was squinting into the fading gloom, while Elsworth knelt, the scope of his rifle pressed to his eye as he scanned the opposite bank. Down beside the water’s edge, the mist had thickened and was now enshrouding the entire length of the Shatt al-Arab. Every now and then there was a break in its low blanket, and it was in these patches that Lock could make out the plain beyond and the cluster of date palms along the bank. And beyond them, like a sinister shadow, lay the darker mass of Wassmuss’s troops.

‘How many?’ Lock said.

‘About six, maybe seven hundred men, sahib. There are cavalry, too.’ Singh indicated to the south where a large group of horses were corralled together.

‘Have they discovered where their bellums went?’ Lock said, studying the bank, trying to find the lagoon where they had earlier destroyed the boats.

‘Oh, yes, sahib. There have been riders going up and down the riverside for the past quarter of an hour. I am guessing that they are searching for any vessel that will carry them across the water.’

‘Did you have any luck with rounding up some more help?’ Lock said.

Singh shook his head. ‘None, sahib. Ram Lal and the rest of the boys are positioned near to the Southern Gate, but we are a thin line, sahib.’

Lock grunted. He’d had a feeling that it would be futile sending Singh to rouse any men, and he’d been proved right. He inwardly cursed the attitude of the white man to their Indian brothers, and cursed his own naivety at thinking a white soldier would take orders from an Indian in the first place.

‘Where the hell is Underhill when you need him?’ Lock said, continuing to watch the Turks for a moment. He moved his glasses to the bank on his side of the river and stopped at a group of moored boats. ‘They will try to get across to those fishing boats down there; send over a couple of swimmers, I guess. Best put a few of our boys down near the bank. We could do with a machine gun there actual—’

‘Sir,’ Elsworth said, ‘I can get you a Vickers.’ Lock lowered his field glasses and raised his eyebrows. ‘A Vickers gun placement was knocked out by the saboteurs,’ Elsworth said, ‘but I think the machine gun itself is undamaged . . . It’s down near to the Syrian church.’

‘Right, Elsworth, go and bring it back! Take Indar with you.’ The private jumped up and made his way back down the tower. ‘And don’t forget the ammo!’ Lock shouted after him. He removed his hat and sat down against the ramparts. ‘Christ, I could really use a drink right now.’

The sound of liquid swilling around made him look up. Singh was standing over him holding out his canteen. ‘I can only offer you water, sahib. Most refreshing.’

Lock smiled wearily and closed his eyes. 'Not really what I had in mind.'

He pictured Amy. She was supping wine. Then she put the glass down and lay back, naked, in front of him. She pulled him towards her, lips parted in anticipation. Then her expression changed and her hands turned to fists and her lips peeled back to reveal snarling teeth. Her eyes, her beautiful emerald eyes, were glowering hatred. 'Is that how you treat your women?'

'Of course not. I adore you,' Lock could hear himself saying.

'Lies, lies!' But although it was Amy's lips moving, it wasn't her voice he was hearing. It was Wassmuss's.

'You cannot protect your women, Herr Lock. Townshend's daughter, the pretty nurse . . . Perhaps I will pay her a visit. Amy is her name, *ja?*'

'Touch her and I'll kill you,' Lock said. 'Now get out!'

Wassmuss laughed. 'You will be too late, once again, Herr Lock,' he said through Amy's mouth.

'I said . . . leave her . . . alone!'

Lock woke with a start. He was still on the roof of the tower.

'Sahib?'

Lock rubbed his eyes. 'What?'

'Elsworth has returned, sahib,' Singh said.

Lock pulled himself up and leant over the ramparts. He could see Elsworth and Indar lugging the bulky, cumbersome Vickers gun between them. There was a second sepoy close behind that Lock hadn't seen before, carrying a couple of boxes of ammunition. All three men were making for the Southern Gate. Lock's gaze moved back to the Shatt al-Arab.

'I don't like the look of that mist,' Lock said. 'Stay here. I'm going to set the Vickers up down by the riverbank.' Lock put his hat back on, thumped Singh's shoulder, and made his way down the stairwell.

The mist became denser down by the water. It was as thick as fog, damp and clammy, and smelt of rotting vegetables. Lock could hear the river, but he couldn't see it. He checked over the Vickers gun position. It was nestled behind a crumbling wall at the boundary of the fishing huts, hidden at the point where the reeds met the date palms. He nodded to himself in satisfaction. Indar and the new soldier, Mirchandani, a gaunt, dark-skinned Indian with bulging eyes, were eager and ready.

'Elsworth, get back to the watchtower and rejoin Singh,' Lock said. 'These two can handle the machine gun.'

Elsworth saluted and Lock watched as the young marksman dashed off. Lock then headed off in the direction of the water, his boots squelching in the swampy, muddy ground as he went. He halted. It was eerily quiet now; even the river was still. He fished a cigarette from the crumpled packet in his pocket and turned away from the water to light it. He sat down at the base of a tree and smoked in silence, wondering if Captain Winslade would come marching down the road with a couple of provosts and a warrant for his arrest. Oh, the irony if the provosts were led by Bingham-Smith.

But that wasn't what was really troubling him. What he couldn't shake was the feeling that something terrible was going to happen to Amy. Perhaps it was the guilt at how he had behaved, those last harsh words he'd said to her. But he was angry, concerned about her being so close to so much death, about Wassmuss's shrouded threats. How did the German know so much? Was there a . . . How did he put it? A rat in White Tabs? A leak? A traitor? Maybe Wassmuss was bluffing; after all, General Townshend would be well known to German and Ottoman intelligence. They would know he had a wife, children. But would they know where they were? That his eldest daughter was a VAD nurse posted to Basra? Surely, if they had knowledge of that, then they would know about Townshend's wife, Lady Alice, too? Yet Lock knew, knew deep down that it was a personal threat to him about Amy. Wassmuss was a clever man. He was playing with him, trying to get inside his head, to distract him. Well, it won't work, Lock said to himself. I'm one step ahead of you this time. You'll have trouble getting across the Shatt without those bellums, my German friend.

Movement to Lock's left caught his eye. Indar was waving his arm frantically and pointing over in the direction of the water. Lock tossed his cigarette aside and hurried down to the very edge of the river.

The bellum that Lock and his platoon had used to punt across only hours previously was still resting half on the muddy bank and half in the water. He crouched down and strained his ears, staring into the haze ahead of him. After a while the pins and needles in his legs made his squatting position uncomfortable and he unsteadily got to his feet to ease the sensation. The mist in front of him swirled and began to clear in patches. A bellum, not a hundred yards out in the water, was heading straight for him. Lock cursed. Either he and Singh must have missed one of the boats, or Wassmuss had managed to repair one.

He dropped back down to his knees and drew his Webley from its holster. He couldn't be sure if the men in the boat had seen him, but he heard no shouts of alarm before the mist enshrouded them once again. He slowly broke into a smile. Good God, he thought, the gall of the man! He only had a fleeting glimpse of the boat, but the figure standing at the front was undoubtedly Wassmuss, now dressed in the white summer uniform of an *erkan*, a general, in the Ottoman Army, complete with a grey fur serpuş cap and a sword at his hip.

'Well, Herr Doctor, I've got a little surprise for you,' Lock muttered to himself and he scrambled to his feet, and darted back over towards the Vickers gun.

'Indar, have you got that Very pistol?'

The sepoy rummaged in his haversack, and handed the cumbersome flare gun to Lock along with a couple of flare canisters.

'Wait for my signal,' Lock said. 'A shot from this, then open fire directly in front of you, towards the water. Sweep from left to right, but whatever you do, and whatever you hear, don't fire until you see the flare. Got that?'

Indar bobbed his head enthusiastically and tugged the heavy bolt back on the Vickers gun. Mirchandani, who was holding the ammo chain ready to feed it into the weapon, bobbed too, indicating his readiness. Satisfied, Lock left them to it and made his way back to the bank.

Once there, he crouched down and listened. After a minute he became convinced that he could make out the rhythmic 'plock' of punts pushing the bellum along. Lock was certain that a small party was on its way over, more than likely to do a quick raid on the fishing vessels that he had spied earlier. Tightening his grip on the Webley, Lock crept closer to the water. He glanced from left to right and once over his shoulder, then hissed Turkish into the mist.

'*Maalesef doluyuz.*' It was Al-Souk's code word.

Silence.

Again Lock called, slightly louder this time. '*Maalesef doluyuz!*' He paused, glancing behind him again, hoping that Indar wouldn't get an itchy trigger finger. '*Effendim Doktor?*' he called, louder still, back into the mist. This time he could hear the unmistakable sound of water sploshing. There was no doubt that a boat was heading straight for him.

'*Abdullah Al-Souk?*' came a hissed voice in return.

Lock smiled wryly. His ruse was working. And the voice was unmistakable.

'*Effendim Doktor?*' Lock repeated softly, squinting into the mist. Still he could make nothing out.

'*No, I am Erkan Feyzi of the Imperial Ottoman Army,*' the voice came back. Lock shook his head and smiled at the German's lie. '*The Doktor has sent me on ahead. But Allah be praised you are here! The bellums are all scuttled! We must get boats for my men to cross the river!*'

Lock raised the Very pistol high and pulled the trigger. 'Allah can't help now, you German bastard!' he said in English, throwing himself to the ground. The flare rose up into the dawn sky and burst. Indar immediately opened fire.

Cries, curses and shouts rang out from the water as the rat-tat-tat of the Vickers boomed into life. All around, the foliage exploded as hundreds of bullets pierced the air. Lock lay as flat as he could, hands over his head, gritting his teeth. That was stupid, he thought, and laughed. He just hoped that Indar kept his aim high.

Lock dared to raise his head. He could hear the Turks splashing frantically as they tried to get out of the water and reach the bank.

'Time to move, Kingdom!' Lock said, and began to crawl as fast as he could down to the water. He dropped into the river just as the bank above him exploded into life, hot lead peppering the mud. Indar had adjusted his aim.

Lock waded upriver, keeping his head down and his Webley up out of the water, pulling himself along by the reeds that lined the bank. The mud was clawing at his boots, but he had to keep dragging himself away from the Turks. A swimming figure loomed out of the fog to his right. Lock turned, aimed and fired his gun in one swift movement. He half expected, half hoped, that it was Wassmuss. But it wasn't. It was a Turkish soldier. The *Mehmetçik* gave a gurgling, choking cry as the bullet ripped open his neck, and he sank back into the water. Lock could hear other men splashing towards him and he felt a sudden surge of urgency. He cursed himself for getting into the river in the first place.

Up above him, the machine gun kept up a relentless, deafening spray of death upon the bank and the water. Lock waited for its arc to pass before popping his head above the reeds. There was a native hut about a hundred yards away. He hauled himself out of the water and ran. Indar must have spotted Lock's movement, as bullets suddenly danced at his ankles. But he made it to the cover of the hut uninjured and threw himself through the open doorway. Gasping to catch his breath, he stayed low as the machine-gun fire rattled back towards the river. Then he remembered the Very pistol. He pulled it out of his tunic, shook and blew the water from the chamber, and loaded another flare. He pointed the pistol out of the doorway and fired up into the air.

A moment later the machine gun stopped, leaving nothing but the smell of cordite, freshly cut wood, and newly churned earth. The wails of the Turkish wounded sliced through the eerie silence.

Lock gathered himself up and poked his head gingerly out of the hut. All seemed clear. He remained low, and darted from the building back along the edge of the palms towards the Vickers gun post.

'Who goes there?' came a faint cry from up ahead.

Lock peered out from behind a palm tree. 'Lieutenant Lock,' he called out. 'Hold your fire, Indar! I'm coming in.' He holstered his pistol, stepped out from the tree, and headed back to the machine-gun post.

The two sepoys saluted as Lock approached.

'Jolly well done, sahib,' Indar said.

'No, jolly well done to you!' Lock patted the Indian's arm. 'Proper shooting, although it was a close thing; you nearly got me! Any sign of Lance Naik Singh and the others?'

Indar shook his head.

Lock couldn't understand it. Surely they heard the shooting?

'Sahib!' Mirchandani cried out, snatching up his rifle.

Lock and Indar spun round just in time to see a white-uniformed figure sprinting for the fishing huts. It was the same uniform Lock had glimpsed through the mist, the one that the Turkish officer at the head of the bellum was wearing. Only it was no Turkish officer – Lock knew that it was Wassmuss.

Mirchandani got off a shot. It seemed to hit the runner, knocking him off balance, but not stopping him. He kept on going, and disappeared from sight.

'Indar, stay with the Vickers. Mirchandani, come with me!' Lock pulled his Webley from its holster and scampered back over to the fishing huts, in the direction the figure had fled.

As they neared the first hut, the same hut Lock had sheltered in only minutes before from the spray of Indar's bullets, Lock held up his hand. Mirchandani stopped dead still. Lock indicated for the sepoy to check the inside, and motioned that he would check the blind side. Lock held three fingers up and lowered each one in sequence, then both men sprang forward, Mirchandani into the hut, Lock around the corner.

The scraggy ground yawned back at him.

Mirchandani appeared at Lock's shoulder and gave a shake of his head. The hut was empty, too.

'Where are you, you bastard?' Lock said under his breath. He stepped forward, then stopped.

At his feet the ground was scuffed and disturbed, as if something heavy had fallen there. He dropped to his knees. There was blood on some of the grass. He put his fingers to it. It was fresh. So Mirchandani did hit him after all. Good. Wassmuss may well still be alive, but he was wounded and trapped on the wrong side of the river.

Lock moved slowly forward concentrating on the ground at his feet. There were more spots of blood heading off in the direction of the city wall. He turned back to Mirchandani.

'Go back to Indar. Stay by the Vickers and keep a sharp eye out. I'm heading for the city gate. I'll send reinforcements.'

Mirchandani gave a sharp salute and dashed off back to the machine-gun post.

Lock followed the spots of blood on through the fishing huts, as still and as empty as they were when he first arrived. The trail began to head east, away from the Southern Gate, and Lock paused at the edge of the huts. There was the same path of open ground leading right up to the city wall where, looming high above it, stood the Babylonian tower. Lock slowly scanned the area. There was no sign of the German anywhere.

Then a sudden grating of metal and a dull clang made Lock snap his focus back to the wall. He moved to his right and spotted a dark doorway at the foot of the tower. He checked his left and right, then made a dash across the open ground, and slammed into the wall. He raised the Webley up, took a breath, then jumped out, gun pointing at the doorway.

A rusted gate overgrown with weeds barred the way to a dark tunnel that ran as far as he could see under the tower. It smelt of damp soil and rot. He rattled the gate, but it was solid. He listened for any movement, but there was only the sound of dripping water. He considered shooting the lock away, but the bolts were embedded in the rock of the wall both top and bottom.

Lock cursed and was met by a ripple of laughter coming from the darkness beyond.

'You're beaten, Wassmuss. Do you hear me?' Lock shouted, pulling at the bars.

The laughter continued, then quickly faded away.

'Bastard!' Lock said, and ran back, following the line of the wall, towards the Southern Gate.

But as he got closer and closer to the entrance he knew that something was wrong. There was no sign of his men, that was until he rounded the corner and approached the city side of the Babylonian tower.

Singh, Elsworth, Ram Lal and the rest of the sepoys were all sitting, looking decidedly dejected, to one side. There were two

British corporals Lock hadn't seen before standing over them, pistols drawn. They wore SD caps with red tops and black cloth armbands bearing the letters 'MP' in red. Bloody provosts! And it looked as if they were holding his platoon under arrest.

'What the hell?' Lock said, as he marched towards them. He could see Sergeant Major Underhill to the left, standing talking to an officer. And then Lock realised who the officer was. Despite the fact that he had his back to Lock, he recognised his spiteful form immediately. It was Bingham-Smith, the man Lock had last seen nursing a smashed nose on the deck of the *Lucknow*.

Underhill nodded, just as Bingham-Smith turned to face him. His mouth dropped open in surprise, but Lock wasn't going to stop.

The sergeant major had his usual smirk written across his face and Lock knew that he had been stirring up trouble for him. Not that he could make matters worse. He knew why his men were being held and why Bingham-Smith was there. The man's uniform was evidence enough, pristine khaki drill with the same red cap, the same MP armband, but with badges of rank and the powers of arrest. Lock had been told to report to the Western Gate and then to the front, and he'd disobeyed the order. He regarded stopping Wassmuss as a priority. And, if he didn't hurry, the German would slip through his fingers again.

'Lieutenant Lock! Stop right there!' Bingham-Smith shouted, putting his hand up as if trying to halt traffic. But Lock ignored him and hurried on determinedly.

'Lieutenant Lock! You are under arrest for dereliction of duty. It is in—' Bingham-Smith made to grab Lock's arm.

'Bugger off, Casper,' Lock said, shoving Bingham-Smith aside and storming past, on towards the tower.

'Halt! Halt!' Bingham-Smith screamed, firing his weapon in the air. The gunshot echoed loudly around the walls.

Lock stopped and slowly turned his head, and glared back at Bingham-Smith.

'You're a bloody fool, Casper.'

Bingham-Smith's face was crimson red. But it still bore the scars from the glassing Lock had inflicted upon him. He was no longer a pretty young officer.

'And you, Lieutenant, will address me as "sir". I am the assistant provost marshal, the same rank as captain, and therefore your superior officer!' Spittle sprayed from his mouth as he spoke. 'You and your men will be taken to the Western Gate where you will report for duty on the front lines!'

'Tell me, Casper,' Lock said, stepping closer to Bingham-Smith. 'Why is the sergeant major not under arrest? He's one of my men.'

Bingham-Smith's mouth dropped open and snapped shut again. He looked to Underhill for help, but the sergeant major was just staring back at Lock, with the same look of gleeful hatred across his face.

'You really are a first-class bloody idiot, Casper. Assistant provost marshal? Where's *your* superior? I'll listen to him, not to you! There's a whole army of Turks the other side of that wall and they need to be stopped!' Lock said. 'So let my men go, you dungheap, so they can do their duty!'

'Captain Winslade has taken command of the situation and reinforcements are on the way,' Bingham-Smith said, voice trembling with doubt.

'Winslade? That fool! Where? Where is he?' Lock said.

'In the tower, but—'

Lock turned away. 'Right, we'll see what he has to say!'

'I won't warn you again, Lock!' Bingham-Smith said shrilly, and Lock heard the hammer of his Webley being cocked.

Lock paused again, chest heaving with rage. 'Shoot me in the back? In front of all these witnesses?' He glanced over to his men and to the two provost guards. They looked nervous and unsure. Lock caught Singh's eye and winked.

'Sir?' Bingham-Smith suddenly shouted.

Lock looked up and saw whom he presumed to be Captain Winslade emerge from the darkened entrance of the Babylonian tower and march quickly off in the opposite direction. Lock broke into a run.

'Hey, Lock! Captain Winslade!' Bingham-Smith shouted, but he didn't fire his gun again.

As Lock passed the entrance to the tower he came to an abrupt halt. A pair of boots was sticking out of the doorway. Lock peered inside. The boots were attached to the legs of a provost NCO. He was dead, a single stab wound to the heart. Next to him, lying in a pool of blood, and slumped up against the inner wall, was another body, semi-naked, dressed only in underclothes. Lock turned the body over. It was Captain Winslade. His throat had been cut.

'Idiot,' Lock muttered. The officer he saw leave, it had to be Wassmuss. He'd killed these two men and had stripped Winslade of his uniform. He'd be able to move in the open dressed as a British officer. 'Damn him!' Lock said, and turned straight into Bingham-Smith's Webley.

'Out of my way, Casper!'

'What have you done?' Bingham-Smith gasped, staring wide-eyed at Winslade's dead body.

'Don't be a bloody fool! It's him, the German spy. The man dressed as the British officer you thought was Winslade!'

Bingham-Smith was shaking his head. 'You killed him!'

'Oh, for Christ's—' Lock slapped Bingham-Smith's gun aside, and hit him square on the jaw. The blond assistant provost marshal's head snapped back and he dropped to the floor unconscious. Lock shook the stinging sensation from his hand and burst out of the tower.

Underhill was standing just outside. ''It 'im, did ya?' He shook his head and tut-tutted.

'Where the hell have you been, Sergeant Major?'

'With the major, at the 'ospital.'

'You're lying, Underhill. I was at the hospital earlier. I saw the doctor who was operating on Ross. Didn't see you there.'

Underhill shrugged. 'Told to clear off, we was, me and Dunford and the nignog cook. Then bumped into the provost marshal there and was told we were being escorted to the front.'

'Well, now you're here, get the men together, and guard this gate. Until the reinforcements arrive.'

'Guard against what?'

'There's an army waiting on the opposite bank, Sergeant Major. And you and the lads are all that stands in their way.'

'Bollocks. Sah.'

Lock grabbed Underhill's lapels and pushed him up against the wall. 'Go up the tower and take a look! Then come back down and argue the toss.' He shoved him away and stormed over to his men, who were still sat under guard.

'Lance Naik Singh! Here, at the double!' He clapped his hands. '*Iggry! Iggry!*' he bellowed. 'On your feet, man! All of you, up, up! What the hell do you think you're playing at?'

The two provost corporals glanced at one another, then stepped back a pace, lowering their guns. Singh signalled for the others to hurry to their feet, and the provosts nervously shifted, unsure whether to stop them or not.

'You, there!' Lock said to one of the provosts, the older of the two, who had a neat, small moustache and a pockmarked nose. 'The assistant provost marshal has had a funny turn. Go and help him, then assist my men in holding this position. Sergeant Major Underhill is in charge until I return! Or until reinforcements arrive. Clear?'

The provost nodded. 'Sir!'

'Singh?' Lock said, turning to address the big Indian.

'Sahib?'

'The sergeant major is at the top of the tower getting the shock of his life. If he comes back down and tries to leave, you have my permission to belt him,' Lock said. He snapped open his Webley, checking it was loaded. 'I'm going back to the hospital. I'll be back when I can.'

Lock began to run. He knew where the German was heading, he just hoped Amy would be sensible enough, vigilant enough, to not be fooled by him. She could handle herself, he knew that, he believed that. But he also knew Wassmuss was a snake. A very clever snake.

CHAPTER SIXTEEN

Gone was the caution of earlier, as Lock burst into Amy's apartment building on the Street of Allah's Tears and tore up the stairs, gun in hand. There was a scream, followed by a tirade of angry Farsi as Lock pushed past a woman and three or four children coming out of the flat below Amy's, and climbed higher. Lock paused at the top of the stairs. He put his ear close to the main door, but could hear nothing above the cackle and squawking of the voices from below. He tried the handle. It was unlocked. He stepped to one side and put his back to the wall, then reached over and pressed down the handle. He pushed the door, and it swung open.

Lock paused, then stole a glance into the hallway. The coast was clear. He went inside. He could see the bathroom opposite was empty, so he moved to the living-room door. He paused, trying to make out any sounds of life from within. Silence. He tightened his grip on the Webley, stood back, then shouldered the door open, ducked and rolled, and sprang up.

Nothing and nobody was there to greet him.

Lock released the hammer on his gun and stuffed it back in its holster. The room was as before, unkempt, with a slight smell of damp, but showed no signs of a struggle.

'Bugger.' Lock realised that he had made the wrong choice. He should have gone to the hospital first. So convinced was he in Wassmuss's intelligence network that he presumed the German would know where Amy's digs were. Maybe he did, but he also knew Amy was a nurse and would more than likely be on duty.

Lock turned and ran back out of the flat and down the stairs. What a fool he was! He knew where Amy would be, she had told him herself. 'I have to get ready. I'm on duty again at six,' she had said.

The hospital was as chaotic as before, only more so. The injured and the dying were everywhere, and the stench of death was impossible to avoid. Lock pushed his way through the glazed-eyed soldiers and headed for the wards. He looked in room after room, but couldn't see Amy anywhere. Where could she be? The treatment rooms? Assisting an operation?

He ran along the familiar corridor, passing the operating rooms. He glanced in one observation window after another, but it was impossible. There were nurses in each one, yes, helping a doctor operate on some poor battered soul, but each one was masked. They could be anybody.

'Amy!' he shouted. 'Amy Townshend!'

He moved on down the corridor banging on each door,

shouting her name as he went. Soon some of the doors opened and masked faces peered out.

'Amy Townshend!' Lock called again and again.

A commotion of voices started up, then one single voice, louder than the rest, cut across the bewildered atmosphere.

'What is the meaning of this outburst? Quiet, I tell you, quiet!'

Lock ignored the request. 'Amy Townshend!' he repeated, louder still. 'Amy!'

'Quieten down, young man, this instant!' A matronly sister marched up to him, pushing her way through the curious nurses. 'There are operations going on. Be quiet!' She was a dumpy woman, all bust and hips, and had fierce grey eyes.

Lock grabbed hold of her. 'I need to find Amy Townshend, she's one of your nurses. Now!'

'Take your hands off me, young man, and calm yourself!' the sister said, pulling at Lock's hands. But Lock didn't budge.

'Listen to me, Sister, she's in mortal danger and I must find her.'

'We are all in mortal danger, Lieutenant,' the sister said, trying to wriggle out of Lock's grip.

Lock let go of her and pushed by. 'Amy!'

'Lieutenant Lock! Lieutenant Lock!'

Lock turned and strained his neck to see over the sea of faces. A hand was waving at him. And then he saw Lady Townshend.

'Lady Alice.' Lock pushed by the sister.

'I'll take care of this, Sister Gladys,' Lady Townshend said to the matronly sister as she approached.

'Very well,' Sister Gladys said with an air of disapproval. She turned and clapped her hands. 'Back to work girls, chop-chop!'

The nurses quickly dispersed, leaving Lady Townshend alone with Lock in the corridor.

'Where is she? Where is your daughter?'

'I . . . I do not know, Lieutenant Lock. Why, whatever is the matter?' Lady Townshend's voice was calm, but there was panic in her eyes.

'Where did you see her last?'

Lady Townshend frowned.

'Come on, ma'am, think. She's in danger!'

'I saw her in one of the treatment rooms attending to an officer. He had been shot in the leg. We said he should be taken to the Officers' Hospital, but he insisted on staying here. Quite a charm—'

'Show me!' Lock said.

Lady Townshend turned back the way she had come. 'This way.'

Lock grabbed hold of her arm and hurried her along.

'Tell me, Lieutenant,' she pleaded, pushing through a set of double doors at the far end of the corridor.

Lock was reluctant to do so. He didn't have time to deal with possible hysterics. He needed to find Amy, and quickly. 'Just lead the way, Lady Alice, if you please.'

She nodded, but Lock could see the tears welling up in her.

They rushed down the next corridor. 'This one,' Lady Townshend said, and put her hand to the door handle.

Lock grabbed her wrist and pulled her back, away from the door. He put his hand up, motioning for her to be still, and pulled out his Webley. Stepping aside, he reached down for the handle, slowly twisted it, then flung it open. He swiftly moved out and dropped low, gun levelled, facing the room. It was empty. Just as empty as Amy's flat was. Lock got to his feet.

'Just once I'd like that move to pay off,' he muttered to himself, and holstered his gun.

He scanned the room. There was a tray of bloodied bandages, scissors and a hypodermic needle on the treatment table, and a smashed bottle on the floor. The air was heavy with the smell of iodine. He was too late. Thrown over a chair next to the French windows at the far end of the room was a pair of blood and mud-soiled, torn white trousers. Wassmuss's trousers.

Lady Townshend came into the room. 'Lieutenant. What *is* going on?'

'That man, Lady Townshend,' Lock said, moving to the treatment table, 'was no British officer.' He picked up the bloodstained bandages, sniffed them, then saw the metal kidney dish underneath. There was a pair of tweezers in the bottom next to a bloodied bullet.

'I assure you he was, Lieutenant. I spoke with him,' Lady Townshend said. 'He introduced himself as Captain Winslade. He told me he was shot while defending the Southern Gate.'

Lock glanced at Lady Townshend. 'Captain Winslade is dead. That man who was with Amy, who has her now, is a German agent called Wilhelm Wassmuss.' Lady Townshend put her hand to her mouth and gasped. 'Yet, what I can't understand is how he knew what Amy looked like,' Lock said. 'Or even where she would be.' He paced the room racking his brain. Surely he had missed something.

'Were they alone? Amy and Wassmuss?' he said.

Lady Townshend nodded. '*Oui.*' She hesitated.

'Well?' Lock said.

'Except for the orderly,' Lady Townshend added.

'Orderly? What orderly?'

'Abdullah. But he has been with the hospital for years.'

Lock stared back. 'Al-Souk? Is his name Al-Souk?'

'*Mais oui*. Abdullah Al-Souk.'

'Bugger!' Lock blurted out. 'He's one of Wassmuss's agents. That's how he knew where to find Amy. How in the hell did he get out of custody?'

'But why, Lieutenant? Why would this German risk coming here? Why would he take Amy?'

'She's a bargaining chip, to aid his escape. But there's more to it than that.'

'Which is?'

'Me, Lady Alice, because of what she means to me.'

Lady Townshend regarded Lock, her eyes searching his face. 'Then if that is the case, Lieutenant Lock,' she said, 'you had jolly well better go and save her!'

Lock shook his head. 'Where do I start? He won't lie low, not with a hostage. I wager he will try to flee the city.' Lock tapped his lip with his finger, trying to second-guess the German. 'He can't go west because of the fort at Shaiba and the sheer volume of troops there, and he can't go south, we've blocked that way. East, back across the Shatt al-Arab into Persia? Or north, up the Shatt to the Tigris and the safety of the Ottoman lines?' Lock paused. Wassmuss could go east, he thought, try and circle back to his forces? But why take the risk? Wassmuss knew the battle was lost. No, if it were him, he would head for the safety of Turkish-held territory.

'North, he'd go north.' And he knew he was right. 'They wouldn't have gone out of the front of the building,' Lock said, trying to picture Wassmuss's movements. 'He wouldn't want to risk bumping into me, and I don't believe Amy would make things easy for him, even with a knife to her side.'

Lady Townshend smiled bravely. '*Oui*, you are quite right. She will not be going quietly.'

Lock moved over to the French windows at the other side of the room. He pulled them open and pushed back the slatted shutters. It led out onto a sun terrace that dog-legged and then ran the length of the rear of the hospital. It was edged by waist-high railings in part and with wooden benches set out along the rest. Beyond this was a narrow rocky bank that led down to the dirty waters of the Shatt al-Arab itself.

It was a busy waterway, littered with boats, mostly bellums, some beached, some tied to the rickety wooden jetty at the edge of the hospital perimeter. There was the ferry, which Lock could see was heavily laden with natives as it made its way across the river. But Lock knew Wassmuss wouldn't risk that. Besides, it was going the wrong way. To the south there was a large white hospital ship, a huge red cross painted on its hull, anchored a little offshore. Various small vessels were toing and froing, helping to load up the seriously wounded to return them to Karachi. But no, that would be an even bigger risk for Wassmuss to hide there; he would never be able to keep Amy under control for long enough. North it was, away from the commotion.

Lock walked down to the river's edge. There were plenty of creeks and waterways feeding off the Shatt, and it would be easy to weave one's way up to the dockyards and Makinah Wharf. From there Wassmuss would have no problem commandeering a motorised launch, not dressed as a British officer.

Lock turned his attention back to the hospital terrace. It was dotted with tables and easy chairs, some sheltered by canvas awnings to keep the blazing sun off the recuperating patients. But at present they were all unoccupied. However, further along the terrace, two soldiers, both amputees from the knees down, were sat on one of the benches. Both men wore topis as protection from the sun, and both men were quietly contemplating the waters and what, no doubt, their lives held for them when they returned home to England.

Lock walked up to them, but neither man paid him any heed. Lock fished out his cigarettes and offered them out. The soldiers perked up and grunted their thanks as they took one each.

'Keep the pack,' Lock said.

'Thank you, Lieutenant,' the nearest one said.

'Did you happen to see a British officer, a nurse and an Arab come by?' Lock asked, striking a match and lighting up the men's cigarettes.

'Aye, we did. Loopy trio for a boat trip. And the nurse . . . Cor, she was a cracker, weren't she, Bert?'

'She was that, Ollie, she was that. Only she didn't look none too pleased to have to be puntin'. Bitchin' away at the officer, she was,' the second soldier said.

'Which way did they go?' Lock said, smiling at the picture he had of Amy chastising the German, even as a prisoner.

'That a-ways.' Bert jerked his thumb upriver.

'How long?' Lock said.

'Reckon about ten minutes,' Ollie said.

'Take it easy, lads,' Lock said, nodding, and hurried back to Lady Townshend.

She was waiting, looking exhausted, nervously rubbing her hands together as if washing them in imaginary soap and water. She tried to force herself to smile as Lock approached. 'Any news?' Her voice was shaky.

'Yes, ten minutes ago, in a bellum heading north. I think they will make for the main wharf by weaving through the canals, avoiding the Shatt,' Lock said. 'I'm going to grab a horse from out front. It'll be quicker than me trying to row after them.'

'Good,' Lady Townshend said, putting her hand to his chest. 'Take care, Mr Lock, and bring my daughter back safe and sound.' Her voice trembled with emotion.

'It's beginning to become a habit, ma'am,' Lock smiled, as he moved back to the door of the treatment room. He paused at the threshold and turned back. 'But she's a strong girl and that German bastard, forgive my language, ma'am, is already finding that he's bitten off more than he can chew picking her out for a hostage.'

He tipped his hat, and was gone.

Lock rode like the wind, pushing his mount on through the narrow alleyways of Ashar. He twisted left and right to avoid the many pedestrians, Arabs, off-duty soldiers, walking wounded, and children who littered the streets, still going about their daily lives despite the war raging beyond the walls. On he pushed the mule, galloping through the bazaar, ignoring shouts of protest from the woman who skipped out of his way, spilling the fruit-laden basket she was carrying on her head. A whistle blew somewhere to his left and he heard the shout of a provost ordering him to stop.

Lock powered on, whipping the mule with the reins, its hooves echoing off the wooden wall to his left opposite the stalls and street cafes that blurred by to his right. He banked right, thundering over a slatted wooden bridge, and turned the corner, only to be met by a stationary lorry. Its cargo of wooden crates was being unloaded by four sepoys, under the direction of a British sergeant, into one of the store huts that ran the length of the road. Lock gritted his teeth and pulled back on the reins trying to slow the mule. It snorted a protest. Lock yanked it to the left and then kicked his heels into its side. The mule leapt over the pile of crates, the sepoys and the sergeant diving out of the way. There was a dead end ahead, the road coming to an abrupt halt at a strip of water. But Lock spotted a store hut to the left with its doors wide open. He turned the mule and clattered through the hut, passing the rows of shelves stacked with supplies, and headed for the daylight gap at the other end. A soldier loomed up ahead but quickly skipped out of the way as Lock and his mule burst out onto a wide-open wharf.

On Lock pushed, head low, the waters of the canal to his right, the low buildings of the telegraph office and GPO, with their roofs lined by the familiar telegraph poles, zipping by to his left.

'Move, get out the way!' Lock shouted at the Arab and British telegraph workers, who scattered in all directions, throwing fists and curses after him.

The mule was beginning to grunt, its body soaked in the acrid sweat of exertion that now drenched the seat and legs of Lock's breeches. The beast had probably done little more in its life than pull the milk cart he stole it from, Lock thought.

The wharf and the buildings were rapidly coming to an end, with only the wide open waters of the Shatt up ahead. Then, to his left, a series of jetties and moored launches and other river craft came into view. Lock eased back on the reins and sat himself up tall. He pulled out his Webley and slowed the mule to a trot, eyes scanning the vessels bobbing against the wooden jetties. He listened to the water lapping and the gulls screeching overhead. There was a strong smell of rotting fish, garbage and diesel oil coming from the water. An engine was putt-putting a little way out, but he could see it was manned by a lone Arab.

Lock stopped, gun raised. Three Arab fishermen were preparing their bellum just below him, two hauling up its mast to an upright position, the third loading nets into the bow. They hesitated on seeing Lock and the weapon pointing in their direction, but carried on when he clicked his tongue and urged his mule to trot on. Lock continued to search the boats for any sign of movement. A few yards further on he stopped again. There were raised voices. Two men and . . . a woman. Lock reined the mule in and slid off its bare back. He tied it to a jetty post and patted its neck.

'Good boy. Whoever said mules were stubborn was an idiot,' Lock whispered and edged forward.

Masked by a couple of bellums and a dilapidated river craft, with a ripped and torn awning flapping in the warm breeze, Lock could make out a smart motor launch. It had a white hull and its deck and the deckhouses were in some natural wood. It had two masts either side of the funnel and a small dinghy suspended above midships. It must have been at least fifty feet long, maybe more. It was quite the gentleman's vessel and Lock knew instinctively that it was Wassmuss's. How typically arrogant of the man, he thought, and guessed that it had probably been berthed here for months.

Lock crept forward using the torn awning of the river craft as a screen. He could only see two people on deck, Amy and Al-Souk. The girl was standing by the funnel, just outside the wheelhouse, and appeared to have her hands tied. She looked dishevelled, but otherwise unharmed. Al-Souk was busy with something on the forward deck. There was movement from the rear of the boat and a third figure appeared from the deckhouse. He adjusted his cap, pulled his jacket taut, and made his way forward, edging the gunwale, limping slightly. He barked an order to Al-Souk, who raised his hand in reply and began hurrying up his task.

Lock adjusted his position to get a better view. The officer was Wassmuss, clean-shaven now, but unmistakably him, still dressed in Winslade's uniform. Al-Souk moved to the gunwale and began to release the mooring rope. Lock jumped down onto the deck of the river craft and raised his Webley.

Al-Souk froze momentarily, then threw the heavy rope into Lock's face, making a dive for something behind him. Lock put his arm up to deflect the blow of the rope, but it still stung like hell, sending a numbing judder from his elbow to his wrist. Al-Souk sprang up, a Muscat rifle in his hands, but the weapon was awkward and Lock was quicker. He sent a bullet ripping through the Arab's right eye. Al-Souk collapsed dead to the deck.

Amy shouted a warning, then cried out in pain, and Lock swung round. Wassmuss was standing behind her, using her as a shield, his left hand wrenching her hair back, his right holding Winslade's Webley to her temple.

'So, Herr Lock, you have finally caught up with me, no? Yet you are once again too late,' Wassmuss said.

Lock stepped closer to the edge of the jetty, inching away from the cover of the river craft. He kept his gun raised, pointing directly at the German's head, and tried to avoid catching Amy's eye. He didn't want to see the fear there, for the worry that it would cloud his judgement. He would wait, patiently, for the German to make one mistake, to take a step too far from the shelter of Amy's body, and he would finish him.

'You are the one who is too late, Herr Wassmuss,' Lock said. 'There's no escape this time. Checkmate, I think!'

'Nonsense, I have your queen, Herr Lock, check to me. Mate in . . .' He shrugged. 'Two?' He pressed the barrel of his pistol harder into Amy's head. She winced.

Lock couldn't help himself. His eyes met Amy's. But she wasn't scared. Far from it. She looked positively enraged, and Lock found himself wanting to laugh.

'I'm glad you find this all so . . . amusing, Lieutenant.' Wassmuss gave a shake of his head. 'But I assure you, I am deadly serious. Move, move!' he shouted at Amy, pushing her forward. Her hands were bound at the wrists, but her legs were free. 'Lower your gun and step back,' Wassmuss said.

'I lower my gun, and you shoot me. No deal,' Lock said.

'There, the rope, unfasten it and toss it away,' Wassmuss ordered the girl.

'With my hands tied?' Amy sneered.

Wassmuss yanked her head back hard and she cried out in pain.

'Bastard!' Lock lunged forward, but stopped when Wassmuss cocked the hammer on his gun. Lock stepped back, but kept his own weapon level.

'Tisk, Herr Lock. But the girl is quite right. And I cannot possibly untie her. It appears that the poor, dear departed Abdullah was rather a necessity in getting my little boat underway. Stalemate again, no?' Wassmuss said, raising his eyebrows.

Lock shook his head. 'Checkmate. I already told you.'

'I tell you what, Lieutenant. I'll make you a deal,' Wassmuss said. 'I don't doubt that you will try and shoot me if I so much as move out of the shelter of this pretty thing. But then again, you may hit her. A tragedy, no?' Wassmuss pouted his lips mockingly. 'Another poor Mei Ling for you to grieve. So, I offer this . . . My life for her life.'

Lock didn't say anything. He just held Wassmuss and Amy in his sights, willing the German to move.

'I have one bullet left, Herr Lock. It is true. You let me go and I give you your precious nurse. But you have to trust me. Drop your weapon.'

Lock could feel his mouth go dry. He didn't trust the German an inch. Wassmuss could so easily have shot Amy already out of spite, and he hadn't. So, perhaps he did just have the one bullet. If the German killed Amy, he was spent, and Lock would then kill him. But if he lowered his own weapon, Wassmuss could then shoot him. It would give Amy the vital seconds she needed, though, to get away . . . No, Kingdom, he told himself, shoot the bastard now, take the chance. But what if he did hit Amy? He would never forgive himself. He cursed, and reluctantly lowered his gun.

'Good. See, Herr Lock. I am not shooting you. Now, I need you to uncouple the last tie rope for me.'

Lock bent down to unknot the mooring rope, but was struggling with one hand.

'Alas, Herr Lock, you will need both of your hands,' Wassmuss said.

Lock glared up at him.

'As soon as you uncouple me, I shall let Miss Townshend go.'

Lock hesitated, then dropped his Webley, and began to pull at the ropes. They were rough, stiff and heavy, but he soon had them free.

'Good, Lieutenant. Now, toss the line to me,' Wassmuss said.

Already the launch had begun to drift away from the jetty. Lock gathered the line and threw it onto the forward deck. But just as Lock was at full stretch, arms flung forward, Wassmuss pulled himself away from Amy and turned his gun on Lock.

Anticipating the betrayal, Lock was ready, and as soon as Wassmuss moved, he used his swinging momentum to throw himself to one side. He slammed heavily into the jetty just as Wassmuss pulled the trigger. There was a crash as the bullet smacked into the damp wooden floor inches from Lock's head. Lock rolled over, blood pouring from a cut in his cheek where a thick splinter had embedded itself just above his jawline. He sprang up, eyes and shoulder smarting with pain, only to see the barrel of Wassmuss's gun pointing right at him. Suddenly Amy smashed the German's arm aside and a second bullet fizzed past Lock's ear.

Wassmuss swore in German and swung out at Amy. She tried

to dodge the blow, but the German's gun caught her temple and she staggered and tipped over the side of the boat and slammed into the water. Lock scrambled forward, snatching up his gun and let loose. One, two, three bullets smashed through the glass of the wheelhouse where Lock could see Wassmuss cowering in front of the boat's controls. Then a thick plume of black smoke spat into the air as the launch's engines coughed into life. The boat began to power forward leaving a foaming wake in its trail. Lock held his Webley level. His eyes flickered down to the water. Amy was floating face down, drifting. His eyes flicked back up to the wheelhouse. He licked his lips. His eyes flicked back to Amy again. She still hadn't moved.

Lock's eyes went back to the launch. He saw Wassmuss peer out of the wheelhouse door, and he fired. The German's head jerked back and he slumped out of sight. The launch motored on, out towards the middle of the Shatt. Lock ran forward to the very edge of the jetty, tearing off his Sam Browne belt. He threw the belt and hat aside, and dived in. He powered towards Amy, praying that he'd get to her in time. He grabbed her arm, pulled her towards him and, treading water, turned her over. He brushed her wet hair from her face, but she looked pale and lifeless. There was a deep cut in her hairline and blood was running down into her eye sockets. He cradled her head, and turned and swam back to the wharf.

The three Arab fishermen Lock had seen earlier were there at the edge, waiting for him, and they helped to drag them both up out of the water.

'*Shokran jazeelan, shokran,*' Lock gasped. He felt Amy's neck. Nothing. He pressed his head to her chest, and then quickly stuffed his fingers in her mouth to sweep out any foreign objects. He tilted her head up slightly then, pinching her nose, began to blow air into her mouth.

'Come on, Amy!'

Lock clamped his lips to hers once more and breathed again for her, pushing air deep into her lungs. He felt for a pulse. It was weak, but it was there. He breathed into her four more times, and suddenly felt her heave beneath him. He jumped back as she spewed up water and began to cough violently. Lock gently helped her sit upright and held her.

The three fishermen began to laugh in relief and patted Lock on the shoulder, chattering away in Arabic. One of them removed his tunic and wrapped it over Amy's shoulders.

'*Shokran*,' Lock smiled up at them. 'Thank you.' He held Amy tight and felt her body heave with deep sobs. 'It's all right, darling, you're safe now. I'm sorry,' Lock said. 'Sorry about what I said. I love you.'

But this made her body tremble even more.

Lock lifted her face up to his and kissed her. She responded, and it felt as it was before. But then she pulled away, burying her head in his shoulders.

'Oh, Kingdom. I'm . . .' she moaned, but let the sentence hang.

The rattle and hum of a motorised vehicle filled the air, and from around the corner Lock saw an AEC 'YA' Type three-ton truck come rumbling towards them. He helped Amy to get to her feet. The fishermen quickly dispersed as the vehicle juddered to a halt, throwing a cloud of dust into the air. The rear tailgate swung down and four armed provosts piled out and stood facing Lock and Amy, pistols pointing at them.

'What is this?' Lock demanded. He was met by stony silence.

The front passenger door opened with a teeth-jarring creak, and Bingham-Smith stepped down from the cab. He adjusted his cap and glared at Lock for a moment without saying a word. He bore a nasty, fresh bruise below his right eye. Then he indicated for his men to move forward. They grabbed Lock away from Amy and marched him to the rear of the lorry. Lock struggled to turn and caught a glimpse of Bingham-Smith taking Amy in his arms. She was sobbing.

Lock was roughly bundled into the back of the vehicle and thrown down onto the hard metal bench inside. The four provosts jumped in with him, and then the tailgate was slammed shut.

CHAPTER SEVENTEEN

There was a clang of metal and then a squealing grate as if a rusty blade was being dragged across an iron girder. Lock looked across from the rough wooden bench he was stretched out upon. Two eyes were staring in at him through the narrow observation hatch in the cell door. The eyes stayed there momentarily, then the grate slid shut again, and Lock was left alone with his thoughts and the distant, yet constant, drip-drip from some unseen tap.

Lock had been confined to the 6ft-by-6ft room for nearly two hours now, judging by the way the shadow of the sun coming through the barred window, high up on the wall opposite the door, had moved across the floor. He had an urge to urinate, but had been given no slop bucket and refused to ask for one. If the feeling became unbearable he would piss up against the door and hope that his water would ooze underneath and out into the corridor, rather than back across the cell floor. That would teach them to be so uncivilised. He allowed himself a smile, then rested his head back on his folded arms and closed his eyes.

The provost truck had driven him to the western edge of Basra, where he had been roughly bundled out and then across a deserted courtyard and into a faceless mud-brick building. He was passed over to two more provosts, both lance corporals, and they had uttered not a single word to him, and neither had he to them, as he was led first through a vast echoing hall, occupied by a lone provost sergeant sat at a sterile desk, writing in a ledger, and into an empty antechamber. This, in turn, led down a series of worn stone steps to a long corridor which was lined with metal doors all bearing faded tin numbers. At the one reading '7', they came to an abrupt halt. One of the two provosts unlocked the door, stepped aside, and nodded for Lock to enter. He did so, and the door was slammed shut and secured behind him. Lock listened to their footsteps fade away, then turned to assess his new accommodation.

The cell was damp, airless and sparsely furnished. A single wooden bench was set along one wall and a small semicircular shelf was screwed to the wall in the opposite corner. This was empty, bar a thick layer of dust. High up, near to the cut-stone ceiling, was a barred window. The sun was blazing through, but it was too far up for Lock to see out of.

Pushing his hands through his hair, Lock fished a cigarette from his pocket. He lit it, tossed the match aside, and inhaled deeply. He exhaled and swore bitterly, then removed his jacket and went to sit on the bench. His Sam Browne belt, holster and pistol had been confiscated when he was in the truck.

'Now what, Kingdom?' he muttered.

He hadn't seen his men, but he presumed that they were being held under arrest somewhere within the same walls. That made him feel angry, for they had done nothing but obey his orders, and he had got them into serious trouble. Well, he'd stand by them, Ross would stand by them, if only the major would recover in time.

Lock finished his cigarette, dropped the butt on the floor, and rolling his jacket up as a pillow, lay himself down on the bench. No point wasting the opportunity for forty winks, he thought, and closed his eyes.

But sleep wouldn't come. Wassmuss's grinning face loomed up at him, peering around the door of the launch's wheelhouse, and his laughter echoed in his ears. Then he saw Amy's drowning face. He could taste her lips. Then he remembered her unfinished sentence. What was she trying to say to him? He had told Amy that he loved her, those dangerous words that can cause so much pain and sorrow. Did he? Did he really love her, though? He thought he did. He knew he had feelings for her that he hadn't experienced since he was with Mei Ling in Tsingtao. But did she love him back? Could she love him? Christ, he needed to get out of here, to talk to her, to get her away from Bingham-Smith. And then he saw Bingham-Smith holding her, caressing her, protecting her. How he despised the odious little prick.

Had he failed? Lock wondered. Had he made the right choices? With Amy? With Wassmuss? Yes, he had, he had thwarted Wassmuss's invasion plans. But at what cost? Ross would understand, wouldn't he? If he ever saw the major again.

Lock's battling mind was distracted by the grate opening in the door. He waited until it closed again, then he heard a key in the lock. The door opened and someone stepped in.

They stamped to attention. 'If you'd be so kind as to follow me, sir,' they said.

Lock opened his eyes and sat up. It was a guard, a different one, but still a British provost lance corporal. He was standing, waiting at the open doorway, staring back at nothing in particular, and was holding Lock's slouch hat in his hands.

Lock swung his legs off the bench and got to his feet. He picked up his jacket, shook out the creases, and pulled it on.

'I believe this is yours, sir,' the guard said, handing Lock his hat. 'It was picked up when you were arrested.'

'Yes. Thank you,' Lock said, brushing the hat down, adjusting its shape, and slapping it on his head. He walked out of the cell.

Something had changed, Lock guessed, judging by the fact he'd been spoken to and called 'sir', and his spirits lifted slightly. Maybe Ross had recovered after all.

The guard closed the cell door, then led the way back along the corridor and up the worn stone steps to the antechamber. They stepped out into the vast echoing hall, passing the same solitary sergeant who was still scratching away at the ledger opened up on the sterile desk, and made their way to the main door.

As they left the building, Lock squinted up at the baking midday sun. He pulled the brim of his hat down to shield his eyes and then followed the guard further still, out of the courtyard and into the beginnings of a large military encampment. The sounds of war were closer now, like an approaching thunderstorm.

Lock and the guard carried on down through the bivouacs, passing not only tent after tent, row upon neat row, but hundreds of soldiers, all busying themselves with the monotonous tasks they were undoubtedly ordered to do. At the head of the camp they came to a large sector-command tent.

The guard spoke with a youthful-looking adjutant. He was seated at a card table at the entrance with a sheaf of papers in front of him. He did little to hide his distaste for the Australian uniform Lock was wearing as he looked him over. The guard turned, saluted Lock, then marched away again.

The adjutant frowned at Lock, then using the pencil he had been writing with, indicated for Lock to enter the tent.

'Wait inside, Lieutenant,' he said, then returned to his writing.

Lock did as he was told and entered the tent.

Regimental colonels and their battalion commanders occupied the tent, nine officers in total, all of similar ages, backgrounds and breeding, all British aristocracy. Not one of them paid Lock any heed, as they stood around conversing and drinking out of delicate china teacups. Lock knew that to them he was just another minion, slightly older and more worn than the usual pimply boys, no doubt, but young all the same, and just as expendable.

He continued to wait, standing at ease, but with hands behind his back. He knew not to put them in his trouser pockets, not in this company. Eventually he found himself drawing circles in the straw-lined floor with the tip of his boot, his mind numb with boredom.

After half an hour, Lock was struggling to keep his eyes open. He had swayed once already, having nodded off on his feet, and despite trying to focus on the officers' idle chat of hunts and estates to keep alert, was finding it hard to concentrate and was now convinced that he had been forgotten about completely. He was about to turn and leave when everybody suddenly stood to attention.

A hush descended on the tent; a middle-aged general had entered. Lock watched this new arrival toss his cap aside, smooth back his neatly trimmed slate-grey hair, and go to stand by the table at the rear. He sifted through a few papers piled on one side of the tabletop. He picked up a large tube that he unrolled and spread out across the surface, using a teacup, a Webley and two books to hold it in place. He then picked up a cane and, after a moment, looked up, passing his steely eyes over the room.

'At ease, gentlemen. Gather round if you would.' His voice was gruff, but he waited patiently, stroking his pencil-thin moustache between his index finger and thumb while the officers noisily put down their teacups and circled around his map.

'You'd better move forward, too, Lieutenant.'

Lock turned to see that a rotund officer with sharp, intelligent eyes was addressing him.

The officer smiled affably. 'I'm Major Hall. The gentleman at the table . . . General Delamain, section commander. You'll be interested in what he has to say.'

'Sir?'

'Don't look so worried, Lieutenant. You are no longer under arrest. I have Major Ross's report. I know all about you.'

'Sir. Is Major Ross here? How is he?' Lock was lifted by the fact that Ross had managed to speak to someone at last.

'On the mend, I gather. But no, still confined to bed. Anyhow, best listen up!' Major Hall jerked one of his chins towards Delamain.

Lock had more questions, but the major had already stepped away. So Lock followed his advice and edged closer to the tight group of senior officers, all staring down at the map. It was a detailed drawing of the area surrounding Shaiba.

'. . . just come from a briefing with General Melliss,' Delamain was saying. 'The situation south-west of Shaiba is precarious. We have lost nearly a thousand men since this morning and Johnny is showing no sign of buckling. They are continuing to march towards the south, and there has already been two attacks by the 104th in an attempt to stop them.' He paused, looking from one man to the next. The mutters of approval died down. 'But both have been rebuffed . . .'

As Delamain continued, Major Hall leant into Lock. 'It seems your regimental commander, Lieutenant Colonel Godwinson, took it upon himself to send his men charging into the Turkish mob,' he whispered. 'A complete disaster. They were hopelessly outnumbered.'

'The 2nd Mendips, sir?' Lock said, peering down at the map through a gap in the officers' bodies.

'Yes, son. Decimated. General Melliss sent the 7th Hariana Lancers to their aid, but a Turk machine gun cut the lot to ribbons. Total carnage. Not to mention a morale-boosting victory for the Turks, too.'

'Is Colonel Godwinson here, sir?' Lock peered at the crowd. He was yet to meet his immediate commanding officer.

'Good God, no. He's had a major dressing-down. If I had any influence on the matter, he'd be court-martialled and stripped of his regiment. But, alas, he's too well connected for that to happen. And he knows about you. Which I will tell you about later.' Hall pressed a finger to his fleshy lips, putting a stop to any further questioning, and turned his attention back to Delamain.

'. . . we are still managing to hold the line,' the general continued. 'I have been given the task of attacking this mound here . . . and the buildings in its vicinity.' He pointed to the position on the map with the tip of his cane, tapping it lightly as if he hoped it would make it disappear. 'This is the mound from which the 2nd Mendips and then the 7th Hariana Lancers failed to eject Johnny and his Buddoo chums. But they are thick on the ground there, and God knows how many are actually on the other side of the mound. Swarming like ants, no doubt, and stretching as far back as the eye can see.'

Delamain paused, and let the officers briefly confer with one another, before tapping on the desk with his cane to get their attention once more.

'I have been ordered to send in three battalions, two of my own, as well as the 24th Punjabis, to help. I want the Dorsets to handle this. Think your boys are up to it, Chitty?' He turned to his left.

Lock strained his neck to see who the general was addressing. It was a tall, youthful lieutenant colonel with a shock of white-blond hair and a flushed expression.

'Glad to be of help,' Chitty said, voice warm and distinctively well spoken.

'Hmmm. I will remind you of that when this little scrap is over!' Delamain smiled wryly, and the other officers chuckled. 'But fear not, we have got Colonel Cleeve's guns to lend us a hand. They will be moved . . . here . . . to opposite the mound. He is under orders to support all the infantry below . . .'

Lock pinched the bridge of his nose. He didn't want to get caught up in a battle. He needed to get to Amy.

'. . . if we can push Johnny back then the rest should tumble like a pack of cards. Questions? No? Good. Return to your posts and make ready. Kick-off is scheduled for 8 a.m. tomorrow. We'll cross to Shaiba within the next few hours. Give the men some well-earned rest for the remainder of the day, hot food and a rum ration this evening. Good luck, gentlemen.'

If any of the officers had a question, they were given no opportunity to ask it, and Delamain began to roll the map away. The briefing was over. The officers mumbled their goodbyes and, in a murmur of conversation, drifted out of the command post. Chitty stopped at the entrance and briefly conferred with Hall. He indicated to Delamain. Hall nodded and Chitty placed his cap back on his head, gave Lock a cursory glance, then left.

'Come with me, Lieutenant,' Hall said to Lock, walking back over to where Delamain was standing. 'Sir, may I have a word?'

Delamain looked at the major and frowned. Then his face lit up. 'Hall, isn't it? Well?'

The general didn't even acknowledge Lock's existence.

'Yes, sir. Compliments of Colonel Chitty, sir. He asked me to remain behind and talk to you, as I . . . er . . . know more about the . . . er . . . What I mean to say is, what about the floods separating Shaiba from Basra, sir?'

Delamain raised a quizzical eyebrow. 'What about them?'

'Well, I believe the Turks are planning to outflank us, sir, by sending a section into that area. Or attempting to.'

'Oh?' Delamain said.

Hall pointed to the map. 'May I?' he said, and Delamain waved him to continue. Hall opened up the map again and quickly ran his eyes over it. 'This is the point here, sir, between us and Basra, where I believe that they may head for.'

Delamain frowned. 'But the floodwaters are ankle-deep there,' he said. 'Heavy going for an army to march in. And there has been no report of any boats being transported by their column. Besides, we shall be crossing it ourselves in a matter of hours.'

'I would say it would be cavalry, sir,' Hall said. 'Sometime over the next forty-eight hours. That would be good support for the force planning to march on Basra. If so, then we would be outflanked and cut off.'

Delamain brushed his moustache thoughtfully as he listened.

'This section of the fort further east,' Hall continued, 'to that southerly point, is covered by the 24th Punjabis, with the Dorsets situated next to them. You have ordered us to attack the Turkish positions at the mound immediately opposite, to the west. But it is possible that a cavalry battalion could use the cover of confusion during the assault and sneak around out of range of our artillery, loop back, and begin their ride between the fort and the city.'

Delamain stared at the major. 'And what makes you think that this is about to happen?'

'That would be me, sir,' Lock said.

Delamain turned and glared at Lock. 'And just who might you be, Lieutenant?'

'Lock, sir,' he saluted.

Major Hall cleared his throat. 'Seems the lieutenant here is with some special unit . . . the White Tabs?' He paused to let Delamain comment, but the general remained silent.

'The lieutenant was responsible for stopping a surprise attack on the south of Basra, sir,' Hall said. 'Scuttled dozens of bellums hidden on the Shatt that were meant for a Turkish column.'

'What!?' Delamain said. 'This is the first time I have heard of this.'

'It appears that a German spy planned to cross the Shatt with a force of nearly a thousand men,' Hall said. 'Working with Arab agents within Basra they plotted to take the south of the city by surprise. I believe that troops from the Turkish force to the south were to march to their assistance.'

Delamain stared down at the map. 'The White Tabs, hey? They're something to do with Intelligence, if I recall correctly. Don't rightly know, though there was mention of some operation or other going on in Persia under a . . .' He clicked his fingers, and pursed his lips. 'What was his name? Rose? No . . .' He frowned again.

'Ross, sir,' Lock said.

'What? Oh, yes.' Delamain studied Lock properly for the first time, his gaze looking from eye to eye, and then his attention fell on the bullet hole above Lock's left breast. Delamain's eyes widened in surprise, but when he looked back up Lock's own gaze was at a point above the general's right shoulder.

'Or are they Communications? The White Tabs?' Delamain said. 'Was that it? Did you intercept a signal?'

'Sir?'

'You're part of the AIF, are you not? One of their engineers? That's the insignia there on your shoulder, Lieutenant.' It was Delamain's turn to frown. 'I know there's a section of the Australian Half-Flight around somewhere. But you're no pilot, that I can see.' He paused. 'There's a rumour that the 1st Australian Wireless Signal Squadron will be joining us soon. Perhaps that's it?'

Lock nodded, but didn't confirm or deny the general's presumption. He didn't know about the Signal Squadron. He'd heard that the Australians had been asked to provide air support in Mesopotamia. It was quite apt, really, if it was true about the Communications Company, seeing as he himself had been involved in telephones before the war. He wondered if Ross knew this about the AIF. It would be typical of the major not to have let that vital bit of information slip, holding his cards close to his chest as always.

'Tell me, Lieutenant, you're not from a Dorset family originally, are you?' Delamain said, breaking Lock from his thoughts.

'Er . . . No, sir. Somerset.'

'Oh. Really?' Delamain scowled. 'Hmmm. And you're attached to a British regiment, is that correct?'

'Sir.'

'Where are they now?'

'Apparently they were decimated, sir.'

Delamain shot Lock a black look. Then he turned to Major Hall. 'Right. I will inform General Melliss of this new information personally. We reinforce that section. Stop any cavalry in their tracks. Major, you had best return to your company at Shaiba.'

'Sir,' Hall saluted. 'Come along, Lieutenant, we have things to discuss.'

Outside the tent, Hall led the way back down through the ordered canvas streets of the Dorsetshire Regiment's encampment. There was no provost guard waiting for them, and Lock hoped that what the major had said to him was true, that he was no longer under arrest. Still, he'd find out soon enough.

'Here we are,' Hall said, and he turned to one of the many nondescript tents.

An NCO, a man in his fifties, with a lazy left eye, was seated on a garden chair outside, and he quickly jumped to his feet and saluted. 'Sir, all ready for you!'

'Thank you, Pike,' Hall said. 'Right, come along, Lieutenant.'

Inside, the tent was bare, save for a large table serving as a desk with four chairs and a made-up bunk bed in the far corner. A steaming black kettle and two tin mugs were sat on top of the table next to a holstered Webley and the obligatory aristocratic officer's cane. There was an overriding smell of paraffin oil and hair lacquer in the stuffy air, and something stronger. Lock was oddly reminded of Christmas.

'Come in, Lieutenant, come in,' Hall said. 'Tea?'

'No, thank you, sir.'

'With rum . . . to give it some flavour?' Hall smiled slyly.

Lock grinned. Hot rum. That was the festive smell. 'My favourite variety, sir. Thank you, I will.'

Hall poured Lock a mug of brown liquid and handed it over. Lock nodded his thanks and had a large sip. There was barely any tea in it at all. The steamy aroma enveloped his face and the drink, hot on his tongue, filled his belly with fire as he supped it down.

'Now, Lock, I've been reading a detailed report that will be of interest to you,' Hall said, taking a seat and waving for Lock to do the same, 'about your regiment.'

'But, sir,' Lock said, sitting down opposite the major, 'we have no way of joining them. Too far across the fort and through the

Turkish barrages. Not worth the risk.' He knew he didn't sound all that convincing.

'Just listen,' Hall said. 'Although I don't like it . . . not proper protocol and all that . . . Well, there is a good possibility that the 2nd Mendips may no longer exist.' He paused, but Lock didn't make any reaction to the news. 'You don't seem overly concerned as to their fate, Lieutenant?'

Lock shrugged. 'Any more news of Major Ross, or Mohammerah, sir?'

'None.' Hall eyed Lock for a moment. 'I've heard conflicting reports about you. Outrage from some blustering staff captain about your insubordination and disobeying orders to report to the front, accusations of striking an assistant provost marshal, striking a superior officer, suspicion of murder . . . which, quite frankly I'm at a loss to comprehend . . . You do realise, Lieutenant,' Hall scowled, 'the seriousness of these . . . charges? Penal servitude, cashiering or imprisonment and even death. That's what you and your men could face.'

'My men were following orders, my orders,' Lock growled. 'To accuse them of anything other than that, sir, is a total fabrication.'

Hall held up his hand and Lock stopped ranting. 'And then you thwart that Turkish attack on the city from the other side of the Shatt al-Arab. You trouble me, Lieutenant.' Hall scratched his forehead. 'You can't even say "sir" with any proper conviction.' His eyes fell on the bullet hole in Lock's breast. He frowned. 'There seems to be some confusion over your rank as well. Are you a subaltern or a lieutenant?'

Lock took a slurp of his rum to avoid answering.

Hall gave a deep sigh. 'Still, it's of no matter. You and your men have been ordered to the front. You have little more than a section, but they will be a useful addition in the attack that the Dorsets have been ordered to carry out.'

'But, sir, I have a mission to complete. I need to pursue—'

Hall was shaking his head. 'I'm sorry, Lieutenant. That will all have to wait.'

'What about General Townshend, sir, he—'

Again Hall interrupted. 'General Townshend is somewhere on the Persian Gulf and cannot be contacted. So, for now, Lieutenant, you are to report for active duty on the front lines. Clear?'

'No, sir. My orders are to catch and stop a German agent. He was making his escape on a launch when—'

Hall held up his hand to stop Lock once more, then leant forward and rifled through the pile of papers on the table. Lock noticed his previously confiscated Sam Browne belt and holstered Webley were on there, too.

Hall pulled out a single piece of paper. 'While you have been resting in your cell a number of things occurred near to the wharf where you were arrested. A launch, a very smart gentleman's launch, was found run aground only a few hundred yards upriver. It was abandoned and empty. There was a good deal of fuel oozing out of a hole just above the waterline, and despite signs of damage from gunfire on board, there was only one body, that identified as Abdullah Al-Souk, hospital orderly and a known informant for the provosts.'

'No one else?' Lock said.

'No one else,' Hall said. 'And then a British officer was reported to have stolen an ambulance, which was later seen heading for the front.'

'That's him,' Lock said. 'That's the man I'm after. But he's no British officer, sir, he's a German spy.'

Hall studied Lock's face for a moment as if assessing his sanity, then returned his attention to the report he had been reading from. 'However, I also have a report about another officer, judging from the description of his unusual hat, an Australian officer, having stolen a mule from outside the British Hospital.'

'Sir, I—'

Hall rubbed his forehead and sighed. 'Theft from a native to add to your list of crimes, Lieutenant. And for what? There's nothing to corroborate your story about this spy.'

Lock slammed his fist down on the table. 'Christ, ask Amy Townshend. She was kidnapped by the bastard!'

'It's of no matter anyway, Lieutenant,' Hall said.

'Yes it is, sir. I need to get on his trail.'

Hall shook his head. 'Afraid no can do, Lieutenant. Orders.'

'Sir, I—'

'Orders from your commanding officer.'

'Ross? But he knows how imp—'

Hall shook his head again and handed Lock a second slip of paper. 'Orders from your regimental commander, Lieutenant Colonel Godwinson.'

'But, sir, you told me yourself what an ass the man is, that he should be court-martialled himself!'

Hall grunted. 'My opinion, Lieutenant, but not my decision. And the last time I looked, a lieutenant colonel outranks a major. Godwinson wants you to abandon your mission and report to him at the front. I'd advise you to forget about this spy and do as you're told. Things are bleak enough for you as it is. Besides, what harm can the German do now? You said yourself that you thwarted his plans. He's trapped behind enemy lines, with no hope of escape.'

'With respect, sir, you don't know what the hell you are talking about,' Lock said. 'This German is a positive Houdini.'

'Be that as it may, Lieutenant, you will report for duty as ordered. There's an escort waiting to take you and your men across the floods to Shaiba. Once there your weapons will be returned to you and you will be placed in position. Understood?'

Lock understood. He was trapped, being forced under armed guard to report to the front line. They knew he would try to make for the city to pick up Wassmuss's trail if left to his own devices. He could still do so, but there were his men to think of. Their lives really were in his hands now. If he disobeyed Godwinson's ridiculous countermand of his mission, then he had no doubt that Singh and the others would face courts martial and possible execution. They were in the British army after all and therefore subject to British military law. He was cornered, he was checked, and without Ross or Townshend to intervene, he was at Godwinson's mercy. He cursed and got to his feet.

'Here, Lieutenant,' Hall said, handing Lock the Sam Browne belt and holstered Webley. 'It's not loaded. You'll be issued with bullets in Shaiba. If it's any consolation, I think this is ridiculous, too. But orders are orders, and where would we be if we didn't follow orders?'

'At peace?' Lock said, buckling his belt around his jacket.

Hall glared back at him. 'Hopefully you and your men will all be killed and we shall not have to worry about any courts martial at all. Nasty business, executing one's own. Now, get out of my sight, Lieutenant.'

Lock gave Hall a stiff, mocking salute, and turned on his heels and exited the tent.

Sergeant Pike was waiting for him outside, with two armed provosts, the same lance corporals from earlier.

'Hello, fellas,' Lock said. 'Fancy seeing you again.'

'We're here to take you down to the floodwaters, sir,' Pike said. 'See you safely on one of them bellums and off to Shaiba.'

'Bollocks, Sergeant,' Lock said. 'Bollocks.'

CHAPTER EIGHTEEN

The fort of Shaiba may only have been nine miles out of Basra, but it was also located across nine miles of flooded desert, and the only way to get there was by mule or by boat. So, once again, Lock and his platoon found themselves in a bellum punting their way towards a possible violent death.

Sergeant Pike and the two provost lance corporals had escorted Lock down to the edge of the floodwaters where already a large task force was either wading or ferrying across to Shaiba. Singh, Underhill and the others were there, under the armed supervision of a provost sergeant and a corporal, waiting beside two bellums. Lock caught the sergeant major's eye, but he just turned to the side and spat. That was his only comment on the situation Lock had gotten them into.

'Welcome back, sahib,' Singh said, and Lock gave him a half-hearted smile in reply.

'Elsworth, how did you manage to stay with us?' Lock asked.

'Told the truth, sir,' he said. 'That you recruited me into the 2nd Mendips. Seemed to believe me. So here I am.'

'Good lad,' Lock said. 'All right, chaps, in the boats. We have an appointment with the devil to keep.'

There were a few grunts, but nobody laughed. The men piled aboard, seven in one bellum, eight in the other, with a provost also sat in each one, the NCO with Lock's boat, the corporal with Underhill's.

'I'll see you on the other side, sir,' Pike said to Lock, helping the two provost lance corporals to push their bellums out.

Lock nodded, then turned to face the direction of travel.

There wasn't a landmark in sight and in every direction the plain, stretching to the horizon, flat and still, was nothing but open water. Lock and his platoon arduously poled across the mosquito-infested, foul-smelling sewer-brown water, with each man taking it in turns to do the punting, Lock included. The provosts just kept a watchful, if bored, eye on them. Underhill was the only one with a timepiece and at twenty-minute intervals he would shout across from the other boat, 'Change!' The work was monotonous, but after a while Lock fell into a kind of trance.

He tried to picture Amy again. But the more he did, the more his mind kept pulling him back to Wassmuss. He was certain that he'd shot him. But the report said there was only Al-Souk's body in the launch. And if so, then where did the German go? How far would he get in an ambulance, if that was him who had stolen it? But if he was still dressed as a British officer then he could easily make it to the Turkish lines and then slip across. He desperately wanted to go after him.

Lock glanced at the provost NCO sat next to him on the gunwale at the rear of the bellum. He could easily overpower him, push him overboard, and then turn this boat around and head north. But what about the men, his men? They were his responsibility, Major Hall had made that perfectly clear. Prison, penal servitude and possibly death awaited them if he deviated from his orders to report to the front. That fool Godwinson's direct orders. Lock cursed. It really did look like he had little choice but to join the regular troops.

It was not what he had in mind on accepting Townshend's 'offer' of a commission within the AIF. Keeping away from the front lines, working for the White Tabs, was the kind of war he hoped to keep on fighting in. But now, sat in this boat and heading for the fort under armed arrest still, despite Major Hall's reassurance to the contrary, Lock feared that he would soon become mere cannon fodder after all.

A tap on his arm brought him back to the moment, and Singh took his place at the pole. Lock slumped down on the wooden cross-beam and massaged his aching biceps. He opened his canteen, swilled his mouth out, and spat over the side. Then he had another sip and swallowed. The water was warm and stale.

'Time, Sergeant Major?' Lock called across to the other bellum, which was about ten yards away.

There was a pause before Underhill gruffly replied. 'Ten after five. Sah.'

Lock grunted. They had been travelling for a little over two tedious hours now, but it felt more like ten. He should try and sleep as he could feel his legs twitching. He closed his eyes, then cursed and slapped at his neck.

'Here, sir.' Elsworth was holding out a pack of Navy Cut. 'The smoke'll help to keep the mosquitoes away.'

'Thank you, Elsworth.' Lock took one of the cigarettes and the offer of a light, and sat back.

'What do you think we'll find there, sir?' Elsworth said.

Lock stared ahead and exhaled softly. There was the beginning of land just about visible on the horizon. 'More bloody mozzies, no doubt.' He slapped his neck again. 'Bloodsucking bastards!'

Elsworth grinned. 'How about a tune, sir?'

'If you must,' Lock said.

Elsworth put his mouth organ to his lips and started to play. The tune to the familiar recruiting song 'I'll Make a Man of You' filled the boat, and Lock found himself humming along to the music. The others began to join in, and then Underhill's group softly took up the tune. With a grin across his face, Dunford sang with gusto,

On Monday I touched her on the ankle.
On Tuesday I stroked her on the knee.
On Wednesday a sweet caress,
And I felt inside her dress.
On Thursday she was smiling sweetly.
On Friday I had my hand upon it.
On Saturday she gave my tool a tweak.
And on Sunday after dinner
I had my dingus in her.
Now I'm paying seven and six a week.

Those who were familiar with the words joined in heartily, even Underhill, who found great pleasure in shouting out the dirty lines towards the end. The others whistled and hummed, and the song floated around like a welcome breeze in summer, carrying them on to Shaiba. Lock tossed his cigarette stub over the side and closed his eyes.

He awoke with a start as the boat bumped into something. Blearily looking about, Lock saw that they had arrived at the British fort of Shaiba.

It was an ancient, crumbling structure of sandy bricks made of stone and mud, with reinforced walls of sandbags everywhere. The buildings looked like something from the Crusades; so ancient and decrepit were they that Lock could not see how the place could be called a fort at all. Surely one direct hit from a Turkish artillery shell would send the whole thing back into the dust from whence it came.

'Time, Sergeant Major?' Lock said thickly.

'Just after six, sah,' Underhill said, clambering out of his bellum.

Lock did the same, and as he waited for all his men to disembark and collect their equipment, he gazed out across the shore of the fort to where hundreds of bellums were tied up, bobbing together in the water. He thought of Wassmuss's plan and of the boats Singh had scuttled, and scoffed.

'Lead on, Sergeant Major,' Lock waved.

'Right, let's get a move on!' Underhill snapped, and the men fell into line, and with the two provosts bringing up the rear, they began to march up the makeshift wooden dock, over to the sentry point and the fort itself.

They halted at the closed barrier, and the provost NCO marched up to the British corporal sentry on duty. He spoke a few words to him, then turned back to Lock.

‘I’ll be leaving you here, sir,’ the provost NCO said. ‘You are to report to the western perimeter.’

‘And then what?’ Lock said.

The provost NCO hesitated. ‘I don’t know, sir. Wait for further orders, I presume. Sorry, sir, that’s all I was told.’

‘Very well, Sergeant. What will you do now?’

‘Wait by the bellums, sir.’

‘Guard them you mean.’

The provost NCO averted his gaze.

‘Off you go then, Sergeant,’ Lock said.

The provost NCO snapped a smart salute, then he and his colleague marched back down towards the bellums.

‘Bloody Red Caps,’ Underhill spat. ‘Now where? Sah.’

‘The western perimeter,’ Lock said.

The British corporal sentry lifted the barrier pole and eyed them suspiciously as they walked through, but saluted smartly when Lock glowered back at him.

On he and his men wearily trudged, along the mud-caked road, through the entrance arch and into what Lock could only think of as total bedlam.

It was a nightmare place overflowing with British and Indian troops, most belonging to regiments Lock didn’t recognise. There were hundreds, if not thousands, of khaki soldiers there, all similar except for the varying colour flashes of their topi patches. The troops that did stand out were the Scots in beige and tartan kilts. There were just as many Indians of all castes, from infantrymen to lancers, as there were British, and there was even a small squad of Australians, sweating away as they rolled a number of cumbersome fuel drums in the opposite direction.

One of the men tipped his slouch hat at Lock. 'G'day, Loot,' he said with a jovial smile as he passed by. They must be part of the Australian Half-Flight General Delamain mentioned, Lock thought.

There were flatbed field ambulances carrying haunted-looking wounded back from the front, travelling in the opposite direction to the ox-drawn carts full of artillery shells, their smooth iron casings glinting in the sun. These were closely followed by donkey trains. They were lugging tin barrels of water, and what appeared to be kitchen paraphernalia. The traffic had turned the earthen tracks between the sandy-coloured walls of the fort to sludge. The noise was grating, a shrill symphony of motorised, animal and human cries, underpinned by the continuous thump and whine of battle in the near distance. The air was thick with the smell of explosives and rot, and Lock could see rats scuttling along the foot of the walls. But whether they were retreating or just arriving, he couldn't tell.

A frazzled-looking subaltern was rapidly approaching, carrying a clipboard and weaving in and out of traffic. Lock grabbed his arm and yanked him back as he passed by.

'Sir?' the subaltern said, his face a picture of exasperated impatience.

'We were told to report here and to set up camp for the night.'

The subaltern shook his head. 'I'm sorry, Lieutenant, I haven't a clue.'

'To Lieutenant Colonel Godwinson?' Lock said.

The subaltern frowned, pursed his lips, then just shook his head again.

'The western perimeter?' Lock said. He was beginning to get annoyed himself.

'Ah, keep on heading the way you're going,' the subaltern smiled. 'At the wireless station take a sharp left and go all the way down. You will see the bivouacs. Find a space,' he shrugged, 'and wait.'

Lock nodded and let go of the young officer's arm. The subaltern saluted briskly, then darted off, narrowly avoiding being crushed by one of the Australian Half-Flight team's oil drums.

'Mind where yer bloody goin', ya drongo!' shouted an Aussie private after him.

The subaltern gave a wave and a shout of 'sorry', but didn't break step.

'Right, lads,' Lock said, 'some hot food and a good kip's in order. We've a busy day tomorrow.'

Lock stared into the fire Bombegy had made at their temporary camp in their designated spot by the western perimeter, and watched as the pot of sweet-smelling curry bubbled away over the flames. It was early morning now, a little over twelve hours since they had arrived, and nothing much had happened except that their weapons had been returned to them. So, his platoon were still sat around the fire, and each man was now meticulously stripping and cleaning his rifle under the watchful eye of Underhill. Singh was sharpening his kirpan with a whetstone, the rhythmic to and fro of the scraping of the blade melding with Elsworth's soft voice as the young marksman gently sang another of his army ballads.

I've lost my rifle and bayonet,
I've lost my pull-through too,
I've lost my disc and my puttees,
I've lost my four-by-two.

I've lost my housewife and hold-all
I've lost my button-stick too.
I've lost my rations and greatcoat –
Sergeant, what shall I do?

So lost was Lock in watching the dancing flames that he didn't notice the subaltern with the clipboard from earlier walk right up to him.

'Sir?' the subaltern said. 'Sir?' he repeated.

Lock started. 'Sorry . . . Yes?'

'Your men are fully armed? Their weapons returned?'

'Yes, although my lance naik is not happy at the condition of his kirpan,' Lock said, getting to his feet.

'Sir?'

'Never mind. What's that?' Lock indicated to the upturned topi the subaltern was carrying.

'Oh, yes. This is for you, sir. Standard issue on the front line for officers in the Dorsets.'

'I'm not in the Dorsets, I'm in the 2nd Mendips.'

The subaltern hesitated. 'You and your platoon – well, section – are attached to the Dorsets, Lieutenant Lock, sir. For the time being Lieutenant Colonel Godwinson, your regimental commander, he's been told the same, sir, with what's left of his er . . . regiment after the . . . er . . .'

Lock nodded. 'Yes, I know all about that.'

The subaltern smiled nervously. 'Very good, sir. Here, you'll be needing these.' He handed Lock a watch and a whistle on a chain. 'Compliments of Major Hall.'

Lock studied the watch. It was a silver-cased François Borgel trench watch with a wide leather strap and steel pin buckle. He strapped it over his wrist and placed the nickel-silver trench whistle in his breast pocket.

The subaltern then handed Lock the topi. 'There's going to be a hell of a barrage, sir. You'll be needing more than that slouch hat to protect your brains, sir.'

Lock reluctantly took the cumbersome helmet. 'And the lieutenant colonel? Where is he?'

'That's still not terribly clear, sir,' the subaltern said.

Lock shook his head slowly. This was ridiculous.

'Well then, if you're ready, sir?' the subaltern said.

'For what?' Lock said.

'It's time, sir.'

'Already? Then I guess I am. Right, lads, jump to it!'

Lock placed his slouch hat in his jacket, put the topi on his head, and brushed down his uniform. The bullet hole above his left breast was still prominent, and everyone he'd met for the first time since arriving at Shaiba had their gaze drawn to it. He quite enjoyed the feeling. It made a pleasant change from the looks his eyes were usually subjected to. The men handed their packs to Bombegy, who would stay behind until the attack was over, and then formed an orderly line, two abreast. Lock nodded his satisfaction, and joined Underhill at the head.

The subaltern led the way out of the camp, along the perimeter wall, and out into a communication trench. This ran the length of the other side of the wall and Lock guessed it was an old dried-up moat. Despite the extensive flooding on the other side of Shaiba, here the ground was dry and dusty. The trench came out into a flat open area crammed with equipment, soldiers and heavy artillery.

The land ran flat for nearly half a mile, until it came to a low wall, about four feet high. This was lined with troops, but there was a gap ready for Lock's platoon to spread out along. Underhill began to direct the men into position, and Lock glanced back over to his right at a small rock hillock. This had been tunnelled into, with battery points around its base, and obviously there was a stairway of some kind inside for there were men on the summit. It was an excellent observation point.

Lock shaded his eyes against the rising sun. He could make out that the men were some of the company commanders that he had seen in General Delamain's command tent. Major Hall was up there, too, as was Lieutenant Colonel Chitty. He was carrying something circular under one arm, and from where Lock was, the colonel looked like some ghoul from a Brothers Grimm fairy tale.

'What's that under his arm?' Lock said to the subaltern, and jerked a thumb in the direction of the senior officers.

The subaltern grunted. 'Oh that. It's a leather ball. The colonel's a big football fan. He's from Liverpool. Owns a business there, I'm told. Some factory or other. Anyway, he loves the game. Believes it bonds men like no other sport. Right, sir. I'll be leaving you now. Have to report back to my own platoon.' He saluted.

'What's your name, Subaltern?'

'Mitchell, sir.'

Lock returned the salute. 'Thank you, Mr Mitchell. Good luck.'

Subaltern Mitchell nodded. 'And to you, sir,' he said, and hurried off.

Lock turned his attention back to the commanding officers and tracked Lieutenant Colonel Chitty as he made his way from the observation point and out across the open space to the low wall. He watched as Chitty began to walk along the lines of troops, nodding and chatting affably to the men, reassuring them undoubtedly about the job to come.

All along the section of the defences where Lock and his platoon were sheltered, the soldiers of the 2nd Dorsetshire and the 24th Punjabi Regiments were poised, bayonets at the ready, waiting. He checked his watch. It was a little after half past seven. The guns from both sides had fallen silent a few hours before dawn, and apart from a low general murmur from the ranks, it was now eerily quiet again.

Lock pulled the heavy topi off and wiped his already sweating brow. Despite it still being early spring, he could already feel the heat from the sun begin to prickle his skin. He pushed the topi back on, then scanned the land in front of him, away from the fort. It was an appalling scene, like something out of a nightmare. Wherever he looked, the churned-up ground was littered with the dead men of the 104th, the 7th Hariana Lancers and the 2nd Mendips. Between gun equipment and all the paraphernalia a soldier had to carry on his back, bloody limbs, formless torsos, severed heads still wearing helmets and, worst of all, butchers' cuts of flesh from both man and beast were strewn everywhere. It was like hell's own refuse dump.

A pack mule lay nearby, its feet in the air and its belly torn open. Carrion circled overhead, squawking and flapping blackly down to feed on the cadavers. The stench of charred, rotting flesh caught Lock's throat making him gag. He began to breathe through his mouth and forced himself to look beyond the carnage to where he would run when the time came. He could make out bushes, rocks and the shattered remains of carts that men had used as cover from the Turk gunfire. Soldiers were still lying behind them as if firing upon the enemy. Only now they were dead, forever frozen in the act of battle. An Indian was sprawled a few yards ahead. His turban had unravelled, revealing long, greasy hair matted with blood. His arms were outstretched as if he'd been crucified. Lock turned his gaze away.

From where Lock was standing, the scorched land ahead of him slowly rose up a steep incline to the mound, five hundred yards away. Dotted all the way up were bombed-out, wrecked dwellings, broken walls and gnarled tree stumps, until it reached the summit where more buildings were clustered. This was where the Turks were dug in, and this was where Lock and his men had to go.

The silence was broken by the British artillery. Delamain had stuck to his promise as Colonel Cleeve's guns began to pound the Turkish positions mercilessly. Smoke and dust filled the air, coupled with a sudden rush of machine-gun bullets and the crack of rifle fire. The fight back had begun.

Lock passed down the line of his men. He said a few brief words of encouragement to each one, firstly to the Indian boys, the serious Ram Lal, the ever-eager Indar, and the reliable Mirchandani, on to Prajit Pahwa and his ridiculous waxed moustache, the nervous Chopra and his bosom-buddy Toor, to the serious Daljeet Kapoor, the black-toothed Harbir Sagoo, and Kulveer Ram, the old man of the group. Next along the line were the English lads, the clumsy Private Dunford, and the musical Elsworth.

'Still glad you came along with me, Alfred?' Lock said.

Elsworth smiled nervously. 'Hope so, sir.'

Lock winked and moved on. He passed Sergeant Major Underhill, but neither man looked at the other. Lock finally came alongside Singh.

'Well, Sid, think I'd rather chance an arm in a bellum again than this.'

Singh nodded in agreement, keeping his gaze on the open, scarred ground before them. 'Sahib, I think you are right. And thank you, sahib.'

'For what?'

'For calling me "Sid", sahib,' the Indian grinned.

Lock patted him on the shoulder and smiled.

All of a sudden the shelling intensified, drowning out all sound of the retaliating Turkish guns. Lock checked his wristwatch. The minute hand was ticking ominously towards eight. He produced the whistle from his breast pocket and put it to his lips. He pulled his Webley from his holster, tightened his grip on the handle, and took a deep breath. He looked back along the line of his men: all stooped nervously, bayonets glistening in the morning light. His eyes met Underhill's and the sergeant major gave a curt nod, then turned his gaze away. The shelling stopped and an eerie quiet descended on the battleground. Even the Turk guns had ceased firing.

'Keep low, make for the first house on the right!' Lock said. He checked his watch one last time. The second hand clicked to the hour.

'Tally-ho, boys!' came a cry from behind, cutting through the silence. Chitty stepped forward and booted his football high into the air towards the Turks. He drew his sword, and bellowed, 'Next stop Crystal Palace for the final!'

The company commanders blew their whistles in unison and then, like a wave crashing over a sea wall, the men of the 2nd Dorsets and the 24th Punjabis, with Lock's platoon from the 2nd Mendips amongst them, poured over the defences.

Cleeve's artillery started to bombard the mound and the houses ahead of them once again. Lock knew this would keep the Turk heads down and give the British and Indian troops a few valuable seconds to cross the marshy, open plain before them and make for cover.

Lock ran. His heart was thumping in his chest, and his boots were slipping and sliding as he weaved in and out of the debris of the previous engagements. On he pressed, head instinctively ducked low between his shoulders. Already the chinstrap of his topi was beginning to chafe.

When he and the rest of the charging, screaming soldiers were within about one hundred yards of the first mound, the trajectory and range of the British shells altered, and the first Turkish heads popped up from their shelters. They opened fire.

Blinded by the smoke from the artillery guns, Lock stumbled over corpse after corpse as he continued his way forward. A cacophony of noise pounded in his ears, and time seemed to slow as hundreds of boots thundered on. The bullets came relentlessly. They cut up the ground at Lock's feet and buzzed around his head like a swarm of angry bees.

A bombed-out house loomed up ahead, and Lock felt relief that some shelter was near to hand. There were only a few more paces to run now. He headed for a low wall and jumped over the carcass of a horse that was slumped at its base. To his horror the other side of the wall was piled with the dead. His boot squelched sickeningly as he landed, releasing a cloud of black flies and an acrid stench. He gagged and held his arm up over his mouth and nose.

Quickly he gathered his bearings and saw that he was in some kind of corral, a dusty square enclosed by a low wall. It was a grim morgue open to the elements, piled with animals and soldiers from both sides. Lock forced himself onwards, slipping and stumbling over more cadavers, to the wall on the opposite side. He caught a muzzle-flash in the corner of his eye and something hot passed his neck. Slamming against the pockmarked wall, he breathed deeply and put his hand up to his throat. There was no blood but, feeling lower, he discovered that a bullet had cut the collar of his tunic and grazed his neck.

Leaning against the wall, only a few feet away from where Lock was crouched, was a fair-haired lad from the 104th. He was painfully young and appeared as if he was kneeling in prayer, hands clasped together. Lock was about to call out to him, but the words stuck in his throat. The soldier's face told him it was pointless. It was twisted and red and his eyes were open but glazed and unseeing. An ugly gash was cut across his temple.

A deafening clatter burst forth from the house on the other side of the wall, not fifty yards from where Lock sheltered. It was as if the Turks had decided to attack with a fleet of motorcycles, such was the mechanical din. Bullets struck the top of the corral wall sending shards of stone raining down on Lock, forcing him to duck down lower.

From his position Lock could only watch helplessly as the Turk machine guns callously cut into the still-advancing Indians of the 24th. He prayed that the masonry in the wall about him would hold, and then there was a blinding flash and a deafening thump. All the sound was sucked from his ears. His eyes smarted. His lungs filled with suffocating dust, and he began to cough uncontrollably. He spat and, without thinking, went to stand. Heat from a nearby flame hit him. He was thrown to the floor as the house where the Turk machine guns had been dishing out their mortal punishment disintegrated into a ball of fire.

After a few moments, Lock tentatively raised his head. His ears were singing with a high-pitched tone. He coughed and slowly sat himself up. Pressed against the wall, not five yards away, was Singh. He still had his hands over his head. The big Indian coughed and cautiously straightened up, dusting himself down. He looked up and spotted Lock. His lips moved, but Lock couldn't hear the words.

Lock put his hand to his head. It was bare. He scanned the ground for his topi. He found it, but there was a gaping hole in the crown. He shook the dust from his hair and pulled his slouch hat from inside his tunic, knocked it into shape, and put it on. He scrambled to his feet and picked his way through the debris over to Singh, passing Mirchandani on the way. The sepoy was bleeding; a piece of jagged shrapnel was sticking out of his arm above the elbow. But the Indian indicated that he was all right, and Lock moved on.

Singh was saying something.

Lock shook his head. The ringing in his ears was subsiding, but he still couldn't hear properly.

'Sahib,' Singh shouted, 'do the British artillery know that we are here?'

'I bloody well hope so, Sid,' Lock bellowed in return, slumping down next to the Indian. 'That was too bloody close for my liking!'

Through the billowing dust Lock caught snatches of the other men from his platoon, scattered about the corral. He spotted Elsworth, Ram Lal and Indar on the far side. They, as did the six other sepoys, seemed shaken, but miraculously unharmed. There was no sign of Underhill or Dunford.

Lock hacked and spat thick and brown. His wrist ached from the kickback from his Webley, and he sucked his teeth as he changed the weapon from one hand to his injured one. As he stretched and flexed the fingers of his right hand, he thought he could hear cheering. The sound was faint but distinctive. He pinched his nose, closed his mouth, and blew. It didn't help. He couldn't make out where the noise was coming from above the constant ringing in his ears.

Singh tapped Lock's arm and pointed. As the dust settled, Lock could see Underhill pulling Dunford along behind him. They were in the middle of the men of the 2nd Dorsets and the Indians of the 24th Punjabis, who were all pushing on. A stretcher-bearer was attending to Mirchandani's wounded arm.

'*Jildi*, Sid,' Lock shouted, pulling himself to his feet. 'No time to dawdle!'

Singh, Elsworth and the sepoys all scrambled up. They moved on to the pile of smouldering rubble that was once the house on top of the mound, and stopped.

All around lay Turkish and Arab dead. There must have been ninety or more enemy bodies there. Only their uniforms showed that they were any different to the British and Indian corpses, just as hideously broken and twisted, just as ghostly silent, like so many discarded rag dolls. But the mound was now clear and the British and Indian boys were cheering. Lock looked beyond them at the plain below. The artillery had turned what other buildings there were into bombed-out shells; black, smouldering and dead. And further on still was a small belt of trees. They acted like a barrier or a border to a farmer's field. After that was another large stretch of exposed ground, about half a mile across, which eventually came to the main body of the woods, a huge bank of trees that filled the horizon. It was here where the Turkish defences lay, stretching all along the length of the woods. And heading towards this was a throbbing grey mass. The enemy were pulling back.

Whistles calling the men to order echoed around the mound, and soon the troops were marching on towards the trees. Lock, his ears still humming dully, signalled for his men to follow, and he too set off towards the enemy.

Miraculously, he had lost none of his platoon so far; even Mirchandani's wound had proved to be superficial as the Indian had caught up with them again. Lock's gaze fell on Underhill's back. The sergeant major was a little way ahead, striding purposefully forward. He was caked in dust like the rest of them, but otherwise unscathed.

Behind Underhill marched Dunford, nervously glancing to his left and right. Elsworth was at his side, as jovial as ever, whistling 'Hanging on the Old Barbed Wire'. Singh was next in line with Indar beside him. Ram Lal, Mirchandani, Kapoor, Sagoo, Pahwa, Chopra, Toor and Kulveer Ram followed behind them in twos. Bombegy had joined them now, bringing up the rear, walking with an equipment-laden mangy camel.

Lock rubbed his neck. It was beginning to feel prickly. He removed his hat and fished Amy's soiled handkerchief from his pocket. Tying the corners, he placed it on his head, drooping it down to his collar, and put his hat back on. The handkerchief offered a little shade, but not much. He stumbled as his boot tangled in the rapidly thickening undergrowth. The landscape was starting to change the nearer they got to the treeline and the barren ground was giving way to a covering of harsh bracken and spindly bushes.

A rifle shot rang out and one of the Tommies from the Dorsetshires collapsed in a heap only a few feet to the left. Lock swore and instinctively ducked down. Immediately the air was angry with bullets again. They hadn't reached the belt of trees yet, but had come upon the first of the new line of Turkish defences. The enemy machine guns opened fire and Lock, with the mass of British and Indian troops, began to move off at the double. NCOs bellowed and company commanders blew their whistles. Lock fumbled for his, but when he put it to his lips, he didn't blow. Already there was too much confusion. Voices cursed and cried out in pain as all around men were cut down. But on Lock ran with the soldiers, weaving in and out of the bushes, desperate to remain under cover. They were running fast now, screaming as they headed straight for oblivion. Lock couldn't see the Turk guns, but he could feel their hot bullets fizzing about his ears.

He looked across the jagged line of troops just as Major Hall took a bullet in the thigh. One minute he was there, standing tall, revolver out, waving the men onwards, the next he collapsed to his knees, gasping in pain. And still he kept waving the men on. Lock urged his own men onwards and glanced back to see Sergeant Pike helping Hall to his feet. Then a spray of Turk bullets hit both officers.

Lock roared for the soldiers of the Dorsetshires to continue moving forward, and then he ran on after his own men as the bushes around him were shredded by enemy gunfire.

The blood was throbbing in Lock's ears. He mentally counted the seconds he and his platoon were out in the open. He could see a machine-gun nest up ahead, the dark mass of foliage with the gun turret sticking out like a deadly metal arm, and he could make out the Turks manning it, two men and an officer. The gun was firing to their right and as it began to arc back, Lock levelled his Webley at the officer. The Turk spotted Lock's small group of British soldiers running straight for him. Lock could see the officer's mouth open to shout a warning, and the soldier at the machine gun start to look in his direction. A bullet from Lock's revolver smashed through the officer's left eye, and the Turk's head kicked back. Bullets peppered the Turkish gun post and both enemy soldiers jerked in death. Lock heard Singh yell on his right, and heard a distant whistle and roar as Chitty's men stormed forward. And then Lock was at the gun post, jumping over the bracken and sandbags, with Singh in front of him, his kirpan flashing down and cutting into a Turk soldier who had his hands raised in surrender. But it was too late for him. There were three other Turks in the machine-gun nest, huddled in fear, unarmed, begging for mercy. Underhill shot one in the chest and the rest fell in bloodied heaps under Singh's slashing blade.

Lock pushed ahead with his platoon, on through the dense bracken, and came to a line of tents pitched at the very edge of the treeline. Equipment was scattered everywhere: not just weapons, but pots and pans, and sacks of grain. It looked as if it was a field kitchen. A fire of twigs was burning under a large dixie with what appeared to be burghul bubbling away inside. Kulveer Ram paused to dip his finger into the oatmeal mixture. He crumpled to the ground as he was shot.

'Take care!' Lock shouted, and fired blindly into the trees.

Harbir Sagoo tripped over a tent rope. As he pulled himself up again Lock heard the sepoy's shoulder crack from the impact of a bullet. The Indian cried out, then was immediately silenced as a second bullet struck his forehead.

Lock cursed and fired again into the trees. But this time the hammer fell upon an empty chamber. He swore and ran on, zigzagging his way through the bushes to the nearest tree. Only a few feet more, he thought, and then he could reload.

A bullet whistled hot by his cheek. Diving to the ground, Lock rolled, and slammed hard against a tree trunk. He pressed his sweat-soaked back against the rough bark, and swiftly reloaded his Webley. As he slid each new cartridge into its chamber, he watched his men pushing on, firing as they went. He could not see him, but he could clearly hear Colonel Chitty urging the soldiers forward as they moved across the open ground and into the safety of the treeline.

Lock peered around the trunk. He could see Turks fleeing through the thin line of trees. They were heading to the open stretch of plain, beyond which, maybe a half a mile across, was the thicker mass of the woods themselves.

Lock lifted his Webley and followed the run of one of the Turkish soldiers. He watched the man weaving in and out of the trees, getting further and further away. The soldier was an easy target and all Lock had to do was pull the trigger. He watched him until he disappeared from sight, then lowered his gun. He couldn't bring himself to shoot a man in the back, even if he was the enemy.

Whistles blew and Lock could hear the NCOs calling the men to a halt. He spotted Sergeant Major Underhill on his right kneeling over a soldier. The soldier was screaming with pain. Lock made his way over to them, but stopped before he got too close. The soldier was Private Dunford. He had been shot in the stomach and blood had soaked the lower half of his tunic. Underhill was whispering to the wounded man, softly comforting him. Two stretcher-bearers were hurrying towards them.

Lock caught sight of Singh and Elsworth. He beckoned them over.

'You all right?'

'Sahib,' Singh said.

Elsworth, though looking grey, forced a smile.

'Any sign of the others?'

'None, sahib. We all got separated very quickly.'

Underhill, his hands stained red with blood, slowly walked over to them. He shook his head when Lock indicated to Dunford, who was being lifted onto a stretcher.

'Did we lose many?' Lock said.

'I'm not sure, sah.' Underhill crouched down and began to wash his bloody palms in the sandy soil.

'What do we do now, sir?' Elsworth said.

Lock took his hat off and wiped his forehead with his sleeve. 'We need to find the remainder of our platoon, assess the damage, check ammunition and make our way to the edge of this small belt of trees. This isn't over yet.'

CHAPTER NINETEEN

Lock lay flat at the foot of a tree, with Singh close behind and Sergeant Major Underhill to his right. He watched the destruction of the woods ahead with bitter satisfaction as the British artillery gave the Turks sheltering there a good pounding. Smoke, fire and debris filled the air, creating a blanket of choking dust that was illuminated sporadically by the colourful explosions of more and more shells. The atmosphere was thick with the smell of freshly chopped wood and newly upturned earth.

Lock's platoon had shrunk to eleven men now, ten being stretched out along the treeline nearby, and Bombegy safely back at the rear with his camel, making do with the abandoned Turk field kitchen. Further on, the remnants of the Dorsetshire Company were dug in, along with a precious Vickers gun placed under cover of some bracken. The belt of trees they were all sheltered in was fortunately on an incline, and there was a slight ridge at its edge before it flattened out again. There, the trees thinned and gave way to a second flat and open area, before it too came up against the thicker mass of the woods. The plain between was grassy and dotted with tree stumps and small thorn bushes.

Shrill whistles cut through the still air as all along the line the signal was given to advance. The shelling was over.

'Now, lads,' Lock said, 'don't bunch up! Twos and threes. Keep your heads down. Any sign of the enemy, fire, cover, reload. Keep it simple!' He steadied his grip on the Webley, blew his whistle and scurried forward. He was thankful for the smokescreen that the artillery bombardment had created. If there were any Turks left alive within the woods then they would not be able to see the British and Indian soldiers. Not until it was too late, anyhow.

Lock and the others advanced carefully into the open. It was oddly peaceful there, just the sound of his own heartbeat and the swish of hundreds of feet passing over the carpet of long grass. He glanced along the line. The Dorsetshires were a little advanced to his left and the 24th Punjabis were over to his right.

Lock turned his attention to the smoke up ahead. It was beginning to thin out. Something made him stop. He raised his hand. The men halted. He waved them down, and Underhill quickly moved to his side.

'What is it?'

'There!' Lock pointed. He could see a figure through the smoke. It was running. 'And there!' He turned to the Dorsetshires to warn them, but they were already too far forward. 'Christ.'

Lock looked back at the smoke. It was rapidly dissipating

and he could see a number of figures rushing towards them, then dropping down as if disappearing into the ground.

'Holy mother of God, trenches! Fall back! At the double!' He waved the men back.

Underhill shoved Elsworth back to the trees, pushing past the hesitating sepoys. On his left, Mirchandani knelt down to give covering fire.

'Move!' Lock screamed, taking a blind shot at the Turk positions.

Singh cursed at the sepoys in Punjabi. They got the message, and wheeled about and ran back towards the belt of trees they'd just left.

Lock blew a warning with his whistle. But just as he did, the Turks opened fire and the smoke in front of him turned into a deadly firework display as muzzle flashes lit up the entire line of the woods. Lock dived flat and began to crawl as fast as he could between the tree stumps and bushes, his jacket snagging on the thorns, back to the relative safety of the first treeline. Bullets whizzed overhead shredding the trees and branches nearby, sending debris showering down on his back.

'Retreat! Retreat!'

Lock could make out the screams of the platoon leaders as the other companies were cut down by the Turk gunfire.

Then Turk shells fell among the British troops trapped in the open and in the treeline, and beyond.

Lock scrambled back to the first of the trees and dived into a foxhole surrounded by bracken, low branches and raised roots. Underhill, Singh, Ram Lal and Elsworth were already there.

'The others?' Lock said.

'To our left, sahib,' Singh said.

Underhill swore. 'Bloody farce, this! I thought we'd smashed Johnny's bloody artillery?'

Lock didn't answer. He had thought the same thing only moments earlier.

'Definitely trenches, sir,' Elsworth said, scanning the Turk line through his scoped rifle.

The shelling continued for what seemed an eternity, as the ground shuddered around them and the air became thick again with the smell of wood, earth and blood. The five men kept their heads down and Lock prayed that a shell wouldn't land in their foxhole.

Ten long minutes of continuous pounding elapsed and then the shelling came to an abrupt halt. There was a moment of stillness, followed by the sporadic crack of rifle fire.

Lock raised his head and peered through the bracken. There was nothing to see except another scarred and battered field. He could make out bodies, but it was impossible to tell who they were. He looked to his left, along the line of undergrowth at the edge of their treeline. About seven yards or so away he thought he could make out a turban. 'Mirchandani?' he called, and waited.

'Perhaps—' Underhill started to say.

'Shh! Listen!' Lock hissed.

A twig snapped and there was a sudden movement in the undergrowth as Mirchandani's grubby face peered over the edge of the foxhole.

'Bloody 'ell!' Underhill spat, lowering his rifle. 'Could've blown yer bleedin' 'ead off!'

Mirchandani sniffed and crawled down into the foxhole. He looked tired and there was a criss-cross of scratches across his cheeks and hands. 'Sahib,' he said, and saluted Lock.

'Well?' Lock said. 'How many?'

Mirchandani frowned. 'Two, sahib. Pahwa and Indar. Kapoor's dead.'

Lock cursed. 'Pass the order down the line, Sepoy. Dig in. Pick targets. Don't fire willy-nilly! Then you get back to your foxhole. Stay alert and keep your heads down! Got that? Good, now go!'

Mirchandani grabbed his rifle, clawed his way up out of the foxhole and darted down the line of the ridge.

'You are getting the hang of this, sahib!' Singh smiled at Lock.

'Of soldiering?'

'Of leading, sahib.'

Underhill grunted.

Lock fell silent. He was surprised by Singh's words; but, yes, he had to admit to himself that he was getting used to leading. And, if he was honest, he was even starting to enjoy it a little.

They ducked down quickly as the ridge just above their heads jumped with machine-gun fire sweeping over their position.

'Can you make out that gunner, Elsworth?' Lock said above the clatter.

Elsworth waited for the bullets to pass by, then cautiously lifted his head and gently slid his rifle between a raised tree root. He fixed his eye to the scope and waited.

The Turk machine gun rattled away as it continued to spray the British positions. Elsworth licked his lips, took a deep breath and held it. He paused and then squeezed the trigger. His rifle kicked back into his shoulder and, at the same time, the spent shell flew out of the chamber.

The machine gun stopped.

Elsworth grinned and lowered himself back down.

'Good man,' Lock said.

Then the machine gun started up again.

Elsworth shrugged. 'There's always someone else to take their place, sir.'

Lock sighed. He didn't like being pinned down. It felt hopeless. He wanted to press on. He checked his watch. It was just after noon.

Lock stifled a yawn and shifted his aching limbs. It was now three in the afternoon and the British had been trading blows with the Turks for nearly seven hours. The sun had arched to the right of their position and was now shining directly on the treeline opposite. Elsworth, Underhill, Singh and Ram Lal were still with him in the claustrophobic foxhole and they were keeping up a sporadic fire on the entrenched Turks opposite. Bombegy had crept up and provided them with some welcome coffee and foul-tasting but hunger-stifling burghul, before scuttling back to his precious camel. 'Most nervous, sahib,' he said, with an anxious bob of his head.

Lock opened and shut his right hand, trying to get some life back into the stiff joints and ligaments. Was it all from the shooting he'd been doing? Or was it still smarting from when he gave Bingham-Smith that right hook? He scoffed and told himself he should have hit the assistant provost marshal harder. He holstered his Webley and took out his field glasses, blew on the lenses, then pressed them to his face and slowly scanned the terrain in front of him. He could make out three howitzers hidden deep within the thick canopy of leaves, and the occasional flash of a white uniform worn by the Turk artillerymen. He adjusted the focus, trying to get a better look at the officer directing them. Lock couldn't be certain, but he appeared to be wearing a German uniform. His stomach tightened and he momentarily thought it could be Wassmuss. But he did know that was impossible. He may well have escaped, but there was no way he could be here. Still . . .

'Elsworth?'

'Sir?'

'In the trees, about eight, maybe nine hundred yards in . . . eleven o'clock . . .'

'Sir. I see them.'

'Can you hit that German officer by the second gun?'

There was a brief pause.

'I don't know, sir. Range is a little far for an accurate shot.'

Lock heard Elsworth pull back the bolt of his rifle, and then the young marksman swore. He turned to see Elsworth slump down from the lip of the foxhole. 'What's the matter? Target too difficult for you?'

Elsworth was sucking his fingers. Lock could see that they were raw and blistered.

'Bloody barrel's on fire, sir. And the bolt's stuck fast. Jammed, sir.' He impatiently tore at his weapon. 'No good, sir. Firing mechanism is fouled up with grit. It won't budge. Sorry, sir.'

There was a sudden boom, like distant thunder, and a high-pitched whine filled the sky.

‘'Ere we bloody go again!’ Underhill said, pulling his topi tightly down over his head.

The others pinned themselves to the edge of the foxhole and froze as the Turk artillery unleashed hell upon the British sheltered in that first line of trees. Lock closed his eyes and tried to block his ears from the noise, but it was impossible.

‘Jesus H. Christ!’ Elsworth screamed, as all around them the trees were lit up like Christmas decorations. At the same moment, the earth trembled beneath Lock's body and their little foxhole was showered with hot clods of soil and splinters of wood.

On the shells came, raining down like angry hail. The ground shuddered and thumped and all sound was drowned out by a string of explosions. Lock peered up briefly and saw a tree disintegrate into a million matchsticks and others around it smashed to the ground. He ducked his head lower and waited. He allowed his thoughts to turn to Amy. Christ, if only this would end, so he could get back to her, to see that she was all right.

The shelling continued for another five minutes, then abruptly stopped. Lock tentatively raised his head. The air was thick with dust and the smell of smoky bonfires. There was a pattering like rain on his head and, looking up, he watched captivated as the sky was filled with floating charred leaves and ash. A hush fell and the distant, plaintive cries and groans of the injured and dying rose up from all directions.

‘Stretcher-bearers!’

‘Sergeant!’

‘Mother!’

Lock spat the dirt from his mouth. 'Christ! The Vickers gun!' It was silent now and Lock knew the Turks would soon seize the opportunity to move out without its firepower pinning them down.

'Singh, go check on Mirchandani and the others. The rest of you, stay here!' Lock said, then scrambled out of the foxhole and picked his way over burnt and shattered trees to where the Vickers gun was dug in.

But when Lock got there, he was met by more destruction. The Tommy who had been manning the machine gun was lying on his back, eyes staring blankly ahead. His companion, a lance corporal, was next to him, head resting on his arms, leaning forward as if asleep.

Lock shook the soldier's shoulder. He toppled to the side and Lock could see a bloody hole the size of a cricket ball where the lance corporal's ear used to be.

Lock swore bitterly and flung himself on the Vickers gun. He pulled at the trigger. Nothing. He hit it hard, and pulled at the cocking handle. But it was jammed fast. 'The bloody magazine won't rotate!' he spat. He rattled the gun and slammed his fist into its hot metal.

'Sahib?'

Lock was aware of Singh crouched at the edge of the foxhole, but he didn't turn to face him.

'Sahib, Mirchandani and Pahwa . . .' Singh trailed off.

Lock looked back at the big Indian.

Singh shook his head. 'They are gone, sahib.'

'Gone? Gone where?'

'Just gone,' Singh whispered and lowered his head. 'There is nothing there, sahib, not even a turban or a topi or a weapon. I think they took a direct hit. It is just a blacked-out hole, stinking of scorched earth, sahib.'

Lock swore again and again, feeling the rage explode in his chest, as he repeatedly thumped the Vickers gun in frustration.

'Chopra and Toor are all right, though, sahib. They were in a foxhole further over,' Singh said. 'And so is Indar. He moved just before the barrage.'

'If you've finished your little tantrum, sah, there's more pressin' matters over the way.'

Lock jerked his head to the side. Underhill was sheltered behind a nearby tree stump, coolly looking down on him. He threw his chin to the Turkish trench across the grassy opening. Lock could see that there was a lot of movement from that direction now. As he feared, by silencing the Vickers gun, the Turks seemed to have gained some fresh courage.

Lock tried the cocking handle one last time, willing it to work. Then he ran his eye along the barrel casing to the sights and stopped. The muzzle was frayed and splintered. The gun was dead.

'We had best be getting out of here, sah. Retreat back to our lines,' Underhill said.

'No, Sergeant Major, we are not going anywhere,' Lock grimaced, getting to his feet. He glanced across the grassy opening towards the Turk positions, and then grabbed Singh's offered hand and let the Indian haul him up out of the foxhole. 'Follow me!'

With Underhill and Singh close behind, Lock scampered back to his own foxhole, where Elsworth and Ram Lal were continuing to keep up a constant fire on the trench opposite.

'Fixed your rifle, Alfred?' Lock said.

'Pumped ship in it, sir,' the young rifleman smiled wryly. 'That soon shifted the grit. Stinks to high heaven now, though!'

Lock picked up his field glasses. 'Oh, bollocks.' They were torn open and a six-inch piece of iron shrapnel was sticking out of the left-hand eyepiece. He tossed them aside. 'Alfred, how many men would you say are over there, in the section of trench we're facing?'

Elsworth squinted through his scope, sweeping his rifle slowly across the Turk line. 'I'd say . . .' He squeezed the trigger. 'No . . . now I'd say . . . twenty, maybe a few more . . . I don't know . . . hard to tell . . . It's not straight, though. The trench, I mean.' He threw the bolt and loaded another cartridge into the chamber.

'Probably a dry river bed, or gully,' Lock said. 'According to my map this entire area is riddled with them.' Lock studied the Turk line and rubbed his stubbly chin thoughtfully. 'That section there, to the right . . . hidden by the bracken . . . Is that where the machine gun is?'

'Yes, sir, that's the spot. But I think there are two of them there. I can make out at least seven men around and about them. No clear shot, though.'

'Well, stay here and keep your sights focused on that. Keep their heads down. The rest of us . . . we're going for a little walk.'

Elsworth nodded. He opened his mouth to ask where, but Lock turned away pulling Underhill and Singh to one side.

'How long 'til sunset?'

Underhill shrugged. 'Three hours . . . maybe. I think we should scarper, sah, before it gets dark. Johnny'll sneak up on us if we're not—'

‘The trees,’ Lock said, indicating over to the Turk position and ignoring Underhill. ‘They’re rather high, aren’t they? So this whole clearing will be thrown into shadow earlier when the sun drops below the treeline to the west.’

Underhill scowled. ‘Maybe.’

Lock raised an eyebrow to Singh.

‘It is possible. Yes, sahib,’ he said.

‘Right, well, listen,’ Lock lowered his voice, ‘we can’t just sit here. It’s pointless.’

‘Can’t argue with that, sah,’ Underhill said. ‘Lets get go—’

‘We’re taking a right beating,’ Lock said. ‘One more barrage like that and you’ll be able to put what’s left of us in a matchbox. We need to press on.’ Underhill was shaking his head in disagreement. ‘Unless we can get our own artillery up here, that is,’ Lock continued. ‘But Christ knows how long that would take. We need to capture that wadi and those machine-gun nests and force those bloody Johnny howitzers to turn tail and run!’

Singh nodded grimly. ‘I agree, sahib, but what can we do? We are pinned down here and there is very little ammunition left.’

‘True, but I reckon that the Turks are as short on ammo as we are, especially artillery shells. Why stop that bombardment? Remember, they were on the run after we pushed them back from Shaiba, and we’ve seen tons of abandoned Turk equipment from there to here already.’

‘What are you sayin’, sah?’ Underhill frowned.

‘Look, we can sit it out and be pounded to oblivion while we wait for the rest of the bloody army to catch up, or we press on. Retreat is not an option. But we need to make a move before the next barrage. So, what I'm saying is, let's charge their positions . . .' Underhill gave an incredulous snort, but Lock ignored him still. 'We wait until the sun falls below the trees. If I'm right, the Turks are just as rattled as we are, only they're spread out fairly thin and they know it's only a matter of time before we break through in numbers. I believe if we push them, they'll panic. And under cover of darkness, they won't know how many there are of us.'

Underhill grimaced. 'It's not enough. What about those machine guns?'

'They'll be taken care of by Elsworth and a selected bunch of sharpshooters. We'll give them enough ammo to continually pick the Turks off. We line up a few more crack shots along the trees here to keep any Johnny head, trench periscope, whatever, down. A continuous fire. Then, as soon as it's dusk, we leave the trees.'

Underhill shook his head. 'I dunno . . .'

'Sid?' Lock said.

Singh studied Lock's face. 'Yes, sahib, we can do it. The artillery spotters will hopefully be unable to see our movement in the dusk. But we need something loud to put the frighteners up them, sahib, something more than just sniper fire.'

'Bah, bloody stupid idea,' Underhill spat.

Lock slapped Singh's arm. 'No, Sergeant Major, Sid's right, and I have just the thing in mind. Elsworth?' he called back. 'Stay put and don't let those buggers get any rest! Ram Lal, you come with us!'

Elsworth raised his hand in salute and, returning his attention to the Turks, began to nervously whistle a few bars from 'I Don't Want to be a Soldier' again.

Lock rubbed his hands together and grinned at Underhill and Singh. 'Right, we've got some jam tins to find!'

Lock and Singh were sitting on a burnt-out tree trunk with a pile of pitted and battered jam tin grenades spread out before them. 'Not very good, is it, Sid? Can't do much with twelve of the buggers.'

'It does appear as if Ram Lal has had better luck, sahib.'

Lock could see that Ram Lal and a grubby, stocky British corporal were approaching. 'What have we here? Funny looking jam tin,' he said.

Ram Lal saluted, as did the corporal.

'Sir. Corporal Pritchard, sir. Didn't quite understand your man here so I came myself.'

'We need jam tins, Corporal. Nothing to understand. Do you have any?' Lock was rather curt.

Pritchard stared at Lock.

'Well?' Lock snapped.

'Oh . . . sorry, sir . . . Here . . .' He slipped the sackcloth bag off his shoulder and handed it over. 'Eight. Made them myself, with my pal Freddie, sir. He's dead now, though. Caught one in the chest.'

'Excellent! Sid.' Lock beamed at Pritchard and handed the bag to Singh.

Pritchard was now staring at the bullet hole above Lock's left breast. 'Er . . . proper bombs they are, sir,' he said, as Singh knelt down and began to sort through them, examining each one carefully. 'Packed with gun cotton and nails.'

'What is the fuse, Corporal?' Singh said.

'Two seconds.'

'You sure?' Lock said.

'Yes, sir. Tested them, I did.'

'Because I don't want one going off in my hand.' Lock looked the corporal up and down as if sizing up his honesty. He was little older than Lock and held himself proudly. His face and hands were tanned, lined and scarred with experience. He looked like a reliable enough fellow.

'What company are you with, Corporal?' Lock said. 'Alpha?'

'Yes, sir. But we're scattered pretty thin. That nasty bit of shelling earlier . . . lost contact with the whole bunch. Been waiting for word from Sergeant Pike. Have you seen the sarge, sir?'

Lock glanced at Singh. 'I'm sorry, Corporal. He bought it, along with Major Hall.'

Pritchard's face dropped.

'Have you any idea how many men you have left . . . in Alpha Company?'

Pritchard was silent.

'Corporal!' Lock barked.

Pritchard gave a start. 'Sir . . . I . . . No, sir, I don't. Two dozen . . . thirty at the most . . . Could be more. As I said, we're pretty thin now, spread out I mean.'

'Take Ram Lal here with you,' Lock said. 'Round up as many men as you can and meet me back here in twenty minutes. But leave two men, the best shots, about every ten yards or so along our line. Make sure each one has got enough ammo to maintain a steady fire on the Turks.'

Fifteen minutes later, Corporal Pritchard returned with twenty men, all from the Dorsetshires. Singh was sent in the opposite direction and he managed to round up thirteen more, all sepoys from the 24th Punjabis, along with a jemadar, an Indian second lieutenant.

'Do you realise that you're the most senior man any of us have seen since the charge led by Colonel Chitty?' Lock said.

'And you for me, Lieutenant sahib,' the Indian officer said, forcing a strained smile. 'Jemadar Pahal at your service. I am sorry we are not more. But we are ready for any do.'

'Excellent. Now . . .' Lock paused. Sergeant Major Underhill was making his way towards him. He looked mean and pissed off, more so than usual.

'Well?' Lock said, as Underhill came over.

'Waste of bloody time, if you ask me.'

'I didn't ask you that.'

Underhill shot him a black look, then composed himself. 'Three sniper rifles, two good shooters. I placed 'em like you said, along the line either side of Elsworth. But—'

'Good, let's get down to business, then.' Lock got down on one knee, and with Pahal, Underhill, Singh and Pritchard standing over him, he began to scratch his plan in the dirt with a stick.

'We'll split into four squads of . . .' Lock looked to Singh for clarification of the arithmetic.

'There are forty-four men, sahib, including us,' the Indian stated helpfully.

'Good . . . so four squads of . . . eleven. Singh, you're with me. Pritchard, you're a sergeant now.'

'Yes, sir!' Pritchard said, his chest puffing up proudly.

'Jemadar Pahal and you, Sergeant Major,' Lock said. 'Each of us gets five jam tins. Sorry it's not more. Now, the trench immediately in front of us seems to be a kind of wavy line, so it's probably a reinforced old wadi, a dried river bed. Directly opposite our position it's rather like a bend in a river.

'Our three shooters will take care of the machine gun and any inquisitive Johnnies. Fingers crossed those howitzers remain silent. As soon as the sun drops below the treeline, the clearing between our two positions will be plunged into shadow. All four squads will move out simultaneously. We'll be about fifteen yards apart with a sharpshooter between us and on either side. Each squad will advance in an arrowhead formation, one man at the tip of a triangle of two, then four, followed by two and two.

'The man with the jam tins will be in the row of four, shielded by the tip. He and the man next to him will have lit cigarettes. Remember, keep them cupped in your hand. These will be used to light the fuses. Got it? The man on the left will carry, light and pass the bombs to the man to his right, who will throw. Everybody else will have rifles set, bayonets fixed. But hold your fire. Move quickly, quietly, but fast. I'll throw the first bomb from about thirty yards.

'These tins . . .' Lock glanced at Pritchard, 'I'm reliably informed have a two-second fuse. A good strong throw from fifty paces should do it. But count. Timing is essential. We want mayhem in that trench; confusion, smoke and agony to hit the bastards. Light them and throw. Don't delay. If the man with the tins goes down, replace him quick.

'We'll take that part of the trench, then squeeze out left and right. If the Turks try to get out on our side the lads on the ridge will finish them off.' He smiled wryly. 'Once in there, keep your heads down. I just hope our shooters have good eyesight. Wouldn't want to buy it from a friendly, now.'

Singh handed a sack of jam tins to Underhill, Pritchard and Pahal, and left one for Lock.

'So remember, wait for the first bomb. When it goes off, charge like hell! But no whistles, no screaming. Just deathly quiet. I want those bastards over there to fear us. I want them soiling their breeches and running from us in blind panic, and hopefully taking those howitzer teams with them!'

The men nodded their understanding.

'Good,' Lock said. 'Let's go and pick a fight!'

Lock and his men stepped out from the cover of the treeline like an army of ghosts, silent and cautious. As Lock had predicted, the sun had dipped below the treetops behind their right shoulders, throwing the open ground in front into deep shadow. For the entrenched Turks the sky would be yellow above the black silhouettes of the trees and they wouldn't be able to see anything else. Lock knew this, knew the difficulty of making things out in the twilight, of trying to see when your eyes are still adjusting. But he also knew he and his men wouldn't have long to get within range so as to throw the jam tin bombs. He prayed that Elsworth and the other marksmen stayed alert and ready. He prayed, too, that the Turks would be tired and unfocused.

Lock moved on, quickening his step, the men around him keeping in the arrowhead formation he had described. With each yard covered Lock counted, counted down in his head, to the moment the attack would begin. To his left he could see the young Indian officer Pahal calmly leading his group forward, and to the right Underhill and his ten-man squad. Pritchard's squad would be further over still.

Lock hardened his grip on the pitted jam tin in his hand and counted down softly, '. . . eleven, ten, nine . . .' He rigorously puffed on his cigarette, encouraging the tip to burn and glow red hot within his cupped palm, then he put the fuse of the jam tin to it. It caught instantly in a fizz of sparks and smoke, and Lock threw the jam tin as hard as he could. It sailed through the air, sizzling like a firecracker. Lock's heart was in his throat as he watched the bomb pitch then drop just in the bracken before the line of the trees ahead. It exploded in a ball of flame and a deafening thump, thrusting mud and splinters and a mushroom of smoke into the air.

Screams of pain followed, and then Lock was running, running with his men, all in disciplined silence, like wind rushing through a field of barley. Indar passed a second jam tin, fuse already lit, and Lock lobbed it after the first. Now, to his left and right, the other jam tins were being ignited and hurled at the Turks. Single cracks of rifle fire broke out from behind, methodical and deadly. Elsworth and the marksmen had started their covering fire. The air became thick with smoke, as one after the other of the jam tins exploded along the line of the Turkish trench.

Lock was ready to duck down, ready to retreat if need be, but his plan was working. There was no return fire from the Turk lines, and no sooner had the doubt begun to play on his mind, than he was jumping over a wall of split sandbags and down into the enemy trench.

Thick smoke stung his eyes and burnt his lungs. The smell of explosive and cordite and hot metal, as well as burning cloth and worse, roasting flesh, assaulted his senses. He dropped to his knees, Webley at the ready. The trench floor was dry but littered with spent shells, discarded equipment and the dead. Everywhere Lock looked he could see Turkish *Mehmetçiks*, hideously disfigured, some with their guts spilling out over their tunics, most with their eyes wide with shock, and mouths half open as if pleading for mercy.

Lock turned to his men. 'Careful now,' he said. 'We clear this section. Then up and into the trees!'

An explosion, extremely close, went off to Lock's right. More smoke and gritty, choking sand billowed out. A muffled cry was suddenly cut short. Lock fired blindly into the smoke. But the shouts and the cries continued.

Lock paused. He could now hear shouts of confusion and panic coming from the trees beyond. He waved his squad on, hurrying to his left, and headed towards the noise of close combat. He stumbled. Something was lying across the floor of the trench. The dust cloud cleared briefly and Lock could see that it was a headless soldier. One of the enemy. Lock looked up at the smoke and saw that they had come to a junction in the trench. Harsh voices and the crack of gunfire came from every direction.

'Indar, follow me,' Lock hissed. 'Singh, take the others down there!'

Lock and Indar carried on forward and Singh and the rest of the squad moved off to the right.

Another explosion jolted Lock, the flash suddenly illuminating the trench a few yards further on. He could make out figures close together, running towards him. A shout from behind made Lock turn, but there was no one there, just more formless smoke.

‘Indar?’

A blood-curdling cry from within the blankness ahead made Lock’s skin crawl. He slowly levelled his Webley and stood his ground. He was alone.

As he peered into the smoke it swirled and began to thin. The explosions had ceased. Lock could make out two, no three figures heading straight for him. He had no idea whether they were friend or foe. But he didn’t call out; no sound would rise from his throat. As the figures came nearer, Lock’s finger tightened on his trigger. There was a blinding flash and he was blown from his feet.

Lock’s ears were ringing when he came to moments later. He thought he was back at the mound again, just as the building housing the Turk machine guns had been destroyed. He gave a shake of his head, trying to clear the cloud blocking his ears, but there was no sound other than a dull tone that seemed to come from somewhere further up the trench. It was as if he was underwater and a steamboat was passing overhead. Groggily he dragged himself upright again. He steadied himself against the rocky trench wall, and cautiously raised his head. He remembered the approaching figures. He looked about, but they were no longer there. He coughed. The Webley was still in his hand. He snapped it open and stared down into the empty chambers. He was out of cartridges. He shakily passed his bandaged hand over his bare head, and knelt down to fumble on the ground beneath him. His hand passed over a boot, a warm body, a broken rifle butt, and then his slouch hat. He slapped it back on his head and turned to face the dense smoke once more.

The rifle fire was sporadic now and the cries had ceased, but

Lock had no idea if they had overrun the Turks or had failed. A noise over his shoulder made him spin round. Standing behind him, enshrouded in smoke like a ghostly apparition, was a Turkish officer. He was swaying unsteadily and staring at the ground. The officer put his hand to his head and pulled it away again, and stared in horror at the blood on his fingers. Lock could see from the markings on the officer's uniform that he was a captain, a *yüzbaşi*.

'Hey!' Lock called, but the Turk officer didn't seem to hear him. Lock stepped hesitatingly forward, hand outstretched. '*Yüzbaşi?*'

The Turkish officer was looking at his feet as if he had lost something, then he crouched down and picked up an automatic pistol. He stared at the handgun in his palm as if he was unsure as to what it was. Lock stood motionless and watched, while the nearby crack of gunfire seemed to fade away to nothing. Lock called out again, softer, and this time the Turkish officer heard him. His head snapped up and he slowly rose to his feet.

Lock stepped closer, left hand outstretched, his right low down by his thigh, but still holding tightly on to his empty Webley. He looked into the pair of brown eyes staring back at him, but they were glazed over, as if in a trance. Blood was trickling down the officer's haggard face.

'*Yüzbaşi, let me help you*,' Lock said in Turkish, hand out in offering. He took another step closer. '*Please*.'

The Turkish officer blinked again and frowned. He was momentarily transfixed by Lock, looking from one eye to the other. He blinked again, shook his head and stared down at the automatic. He looked back up at Lock.

'*Give me the gun, Yüzbaşi. Surrender. We can get you to a doctor*,' Lock said.

The Turkish officer shakily raised his pistol and pointed it at Lock's heart. Lock froze. He was about to speak when the officer pulled the trigger of his gun. Lock flinched, but there was no explosion of hammer on bullet. The Turk pulled the trigger again. Click, click. Still there was nothing. No kickback, no bullet. He looked from the gun to Lock's chest, and frowned again. Lock glanced down and realised that the officer was looking at the hole in his tunic, the bullet hole in his left breast. Lock looked up again.

'No!'

But he was too late. Underhill had thrust his bayonet into the officer's back.

The Turkish captain coughed blood. His arm went limp and the automatic fell from his hand. Four inches of steel were sticking out of his chest. He tried to raise his hands to touch the foreign object, but he appeared to be paralysed. Then Underhill withdrew the bayonet.

'No,' Lock said again, and the sound of the war came rushing back to him. The gunfire had died down and in the distance he could hear whistles blowing and the sound of men shouting in triumph.

The Turkish officer stared back at Lock in hurt surprise. Their eyes held each other for a moment and then the Turk collapsed at Lock's feet. Singh came out of the smoke, with Chopra and Toor at his heels. Singh glanced at Lock and Underhill, and at the dead Turk on the floor, then the three Indians pushed on.

Underhill spat at the Turkish officer, and glared up at Lock. 'Well don't bleedin' thank me then, will ya, sah?' He scowled, then a grin spread across his lips. 'Oh, I see. One of yer ol' pals from the telephone lines, was 'e?' he sneered. 'Never mind. I could so easily

’ave missed. ’Ard to see who you’re skewerin’ in this coal box, eh?’ Underhill hesitated, but when Lock didn’t react, he just grunted and made off down the trench after Singh and the others.

Lock stood where he was and stared down at the twitching body of the Turkish officer. Blood was pulsating from the man’s chest. Then the Turk let out a gentle sigh and was still.

Lock’s gaze fell on the officer’s gun. He bent down to pick it up. It was a new type of sidearm, one he hadn’t seen before. The engraved markings along the barrel read,

Selbstlade-Pistole “Beholla” Cal. 7.65 D.R.P.

The Beholla 7.65 automatic was smaller and lighter than Lock’s Webley, and it was a handsome gun. Lock turned it over in his hand and studied it admiringly. Then he straightened up. He stretched out his arm, aimed into the trench wall, and pulled the trigger.

The gun fired.

CHAPTER TWENTY

Lock arched his back and pulled himself to his feet, away from the fallen tree he had been sitting on. He patted his pockets and fished out a packet of cigarettes. Opening it up he groaned. There was just one left. He put it between his lips and tossed the empty packet aside, struck a match, and stood smoking as he stared into the glorious sunrise of a new day. The sky was burnt orange with hints of pinks and light blues. As far as his eye could see, British and Indian troops were tramping back towards Shaiba. They had beaten the Turks, pushed them from the woods, forcing them to retreat and regroup back at their base near Hammar Lake, a large body of water some fifty miles to the west along the Euphrates River. Or so he had been informed. What he did know for certain was that the fight was over, for now. And he was glad. He was weary, hungry and itching to get back to Amy at Basra.

'You must be very proud, Lock sahib,' a voice called.

Lock turned to his left to see Pahal approaching.

'Proud of what?' he said with a smile, shaking Pahal's hand. The Indian officer was bloody and bruised, and his left arm was in a sling.

'Your plan, Lock sahib. It made a breakthrough and carried the Turks' first line of trenches some five hundred yards, I believe, in front of the woods. Three howitzers were captured, along with the German officer commanding them.'

'And so?' Lock shrugged, drawing on his cigarette. He knew the German officer wasn't Wassmuss, so he didn't really care.

Pahal grinned. 'Modesty, Lock sahib, if I may be so bold to suggest, is not becoming of you. And so, seeing your success, the rest of the bloody British along the line followed suit. Your attack inspired them, and the Turks . . .' Pahal flung his good arm up, 'scarpered pretty damned quickly, like headless chickens. All positions abandoned. The Battle of Barjisiyah Woods is won!'

Lock took another puff on his cigarette. 'It was all *our* doing, Pahal. Without you and the others, we'd still be stuck in those damned foxholes,' he said, exhaling. 'And will you stop calling me "sahib"? You're the same bloody rank as me!'

Pahal bobbed his head in the familiar Indian way and smiled.

'Barjisiyah Woods, you say?' Lock said, looking back at the trees.

'Yes, Barjisiyah Woods, Lock sahib,' Pahal said.

Lock grunted, and at the sound of creaking wooden wheels and shuffling feet, turned his gaze to the wounded men who trundled by in the loaded ambulance carts.

'When did they get here?'

'The ambulances, sahib? A few hours ago,' Pahal said. 'There are many, many dead and wounded, I am sorry to say. But the men will find hot food and dry clothing waiting for them back at the fort.'

Behind the carts trudged those troops who could still walk. They looked dishevelled and exhausted, but relieved to be heading away from the battlefield.

Marching amongst the soldiers Lock could see the survivors of his platoon: Elsworth, Singh, the three sepoys, Ram Lal, Chopra and Toor, as well as Bombegy and his mangy camel. And Sergeant Major Underhill. Eight men, including himself, Lock thought bitterly, that was all that was left. He let out a deep sigh of tobacco smoke.

'Good God! You there! Hey, you!'

Lock turned to see what the shouting was. An officer on horseback was cantering towards them.

'You'd best be getting along, Pahal,' Lock said. He threw his half-smoked cigarette aside, and he and Pahal shook hands once more and the Indian officer rejoined the walking wounded.

Lock watched the approaching rider, then muttered a curse under his breath as he recognised the distinctive red cap, and pushed his way into the line of dusty troops. The officer on horseback called out again, but Lock didn't break step, which forced the rider to turn his horse sharply about. The officer began to trot alongside the marching men.

It was Bingham-Smith, still dressed as an assistant provost marshal. 'What the hell are you doing here, Lock?' he said. 'You are supposed to be in custody awaiting court martial.'

'I was,' Lock responded blankly, continuing to march and keeping his eyes facing forward.

'Captain Bingham-Smith! Captain Bingham-Smith!'

A second officer on horseback was calling out as he cantered over to join them. He was using Bingham-Smith's military rank, not his provost title. Lock stopped and regarded the older man, a silver-haired colonel in his late forties, who, considering there had just been a major battle, appeared to be in pristine condition. He was short of stature, but sat erect in his saddle trying to give the impression that he was taller. His uniform was bright and shiny, and even the cane he carried in his gloved hands was polished. His grey-blue eyes flicked towards Lock and hardened immediately.

'Don't you eyeball me, soldier!' he blurted, slapping his cane against his highly polished boot. 'I'll have you put on a charge, by God! Who are you?'

'Unc . . . er, sir, this is Lieutenant Lock,' Bingham-Smith said. 'I told you about him. Don't you recall?'

The colonel stared down at Lock. 'The bloody colonial! But you are due to be court-martialled for assaulting a British officer!'

'That's what I was saying, sir,' Bingham-Smith said. 'Seems he has wormed his way out of trouble again.'

'We will see about that!' the colonel blustered. 'You may think that you're protected by Australian law and that White Tab chap, that upstart Major Ross . . . Be still!' He suddenly jerked at his reins to steady his frisky steed. 'And you think you can run around the country when you should have been here, on the front line. Just as Captain Bingham-Smith has been.'

Lock glanced at Bingham-Smith. 'Been scouring the dead and wounded for potential misdemeanours have we, Smith? Checking that the men are in the correct attire whilst dying in the face of the enemy? You bloody cowards,' he said, addressing both men, and turned away to rejoin the march. There was a murmur of amusement rippling through the surrounding soldiers.

'Halt, damn you!' shouted the colonel, as he moved his horse dangerously close to Lock. 'You will not talk to a superior officer like that! And just where the hell *have* you been, Lieutenant? I believe I ordered you to report to me.'

Lock stopped and turned back angrily, grabbing hold of the bridle of the colonel's horse and pulling its head aside. 'I've been fighting a war. Sir. And I lost seven good men today. Sir. What did you lose, apart from the shine on your boot leather? Sir.'

'How dare you, soldier! You will not get away with addressing me in that manner, not in the Mendips. There's no special treatment for White Tab men in my regiment. Or colonials, for that matter. Do you hear me?' He smacked his cane against his saddle with such force that Lock saw Bingham-Smith flinch out of the corner of his eye. 'You don't even sound Australian. There's something fishy about you, boy, and I intend to see you put straight. D'ya hear?'

As the colonel spoke, Lock noticed two more officers on horseback rapidly coming up the line towards them. Bingham-Smith spotted them, too. He cleared his throat. The colonel glanced up, saw the two riders, and gave a snort of satisfaction. Lock let go of the bridle and stepped back.

The two officers, one Lock recognised as the football fancier Colonel Chitty, the other being a fresh-faced adjutant sporting a blond moustache, pulled up in a flurry of dust. They returned the salutes of Lock and Bingham-Smith, and the nod of recognition from the colonel.

'Ah, Godwinson,' Chitty said to the officer who had been

scolding Lock, 'I see you have caught up with your man!'

Lock raised an eyebrow. So the blustering lieutenant colonel was his infamous and legendarily incompetent regimental commander. Now he really was in trouble.

Bingham-Smith noted Lock's look of surprise and grinned. Lock glared back, but the assistant provost marshal had averted his gaze and was giving a nod of recognition to someone amongst the marching men. Lock saw that Singh, Underhill and the rest of his platoon had stepped out of the march and were standing, watching the confrontation. Lock's eyes met Underhill's. The sergeant major looked, as was his habit of late, to be highly amused.

'Yes, Chitty,' Godwinson said, 'my nephew, Captain Bingham-Smith here, has filled me in on . . . Lock's record and I'm about to—'

'Congratulate him, I hope,' Chitty said, cutting Godwinson short. 'You should be mighty proud. Lock is a stout fellow and a credit to your regiment. Considering their earlier disaster. Mentioned in dispatches and all that. I've recommended him for promotion. He did a splendid job for us today. Deserves a medal.' He smiled down at Lock. 'Only you White Tab chaps can't accept baubles, can you?' he added. 'Glad to see you made it, Lock.'

Lock tipped his head in thanks, then glancing at Bingham-Smith, he smiled to himself. The blond officer's face was a picture of disbelief.

'Chitty, I . . .' Godwinson frowned in confusion.

'I've had word from your Major Ross,' Chitty said to Lock.

'Sir?' Lock was worried it was bad news.

'He's making a speedy recovery, and is waiting to debrief you back at Basra. Get back there as soon as you can. Borrow a horse.'

'I'm sorry, Colonel Chitty,' Godwinson said, 'but the lieutenant here is to make a full report to me in my command tent at 7 a.m. on the dot tomorr—'

Chitty shook his head. ''Fraid not, old chap. General Townshend has finally arrived from Karachi.'

'I know that, Colonel. Casper and I had supper with the man,' Godwinson blustered.

'He's requested to see Lock in person,' Chitty continued. 'Hush-hush and all that. Your report will have to wait.'

Godwinson was now bright crimson, but he remained tight-lipped.

Chitty looked back to Lock and indicated up the line at Singh and the others.

'So, Lock, who's that little rabble?' he said.

'All that's left of my platoon, sir.'

'Well, you should be proud of them, Lock,' Chitty said.

'I am, sir. Lock, stock and gun barrel.'

Chitty snorted. 'Jolly good. Well, don't let me detain you . . . Captain Lock. Carry on!' He winked, and lifted his cane in salute to Godwinson and Bingham-Smith. 'Gentlemen.'

Bingham-Smith saluted. Chitty pulled his horse about, and he and his adjutant cantered off back in the direction of Shaiba.

Lock lowered his own arm. He had been ordered to return to Basra, to see Ross and the general. But it also meant that he could seek out Amy and try to get things right with her.

'You can wipe that smile off of your face . . . *Lieutenant*,' Godwinson barked.

Lock didn't respond, he just slowly raised his eyes and fixed them to the colonel's.

Godwinson twitched uneasily. 'Look at the state of you,'

he blustered. 'When was the last time you had a shave? And what the hell kind of hat is that?' He pointed with his cane. 'It's not befitting of an officer in my regiment to set such a poor example. I don't care if you are in the damned AIF, you are attached to me and will dress accordingly. I still want a full report from you, in person, in my command tent at 7 a.m. on the dot tomorrow. Balls to what Colonel Chitty says. You're under *my* command, and you will obey *my* orders. Do you understand, Lieutenant?'

Lock still didn't say anything as he held the colonel's glare. Then he slowly, mockingly, raised his hand and saluted. 'Yes. Sir.'

'Come, Casper,' Godwinson snapped. He steered his horse furiously around, nearly knocking Lock off his feet, and cantered after Chitty.

'You're finished, Lock. Do you hear?' Bingham-Smith said with a sneer.

'Do you know, Casper, I don't give a bog-floating turd what you think. I'm going back to Basra, I'm going to take a long, hot soak, find a fresh uniform, and then I'm going to take Amy . . .' Lock stopped. Bingham-Smith's face had broken into a wry smile.

'Oh, my dear chap. You haven't heard, have you?'

'Heard what?' Lock had a sudden ill feeling that something had happened to Amy. Wassmuss?

Bingham-Smith chuckled. 'Why, about Amy, of course.'

'Smith . . . What?' Lock said. 'What about Amy? Is she all right?'

Bingham-Smith slowly shook his head. 'You'll find out soo—'

Lock made a sudden grab for Bingham-Smith's stirruped boot and shoved the blond officer off his horse, sending him tumbling unceremoniously to the ground. Lock pulled himself up into the saddle, yanked the horse around, and kept it pacing about the prostrate Bingham-Smith. The assistant provost marshal remained on his backside, scrambling desperately from side to side to keep out of the way of the menacing hooves.

'Lock, please . . . Stop it!' Bingham-Smith coughed as the dust rose about him. By now a good number of the marching soldiers had stopped to watch the confrontation.

Lock smiled wryly down at the blond officer. 'You heard Colonel Chitty, Smith. Borrow a horse. I choose yours.' He tipped his hat. 'Much obliged.'

Lock twisted in the saddle and called back to Singh and the others. 'You lads get a well-earned rest, food and drink on me. I'll see you in a few days, back at Basra. Any trouble, ask for Major Ross. He's back on his feet. Sergeant Major?'

Underhill scowled up at Lock. 'Sah?'

'You heard me . . . Food and drink for everyone. You see to it. And if those boys come to any harm, end up in a provost cell, you will have me to answer to. Understood?'

Underhill licked his lips and glanced down at Bingham-Smith. 'Sah,' he said.

'Good. Elsworth?' Lock said.

'Sir?' The young sharpshooter stepped forward a pace.

'Music for the marchers, I think.'

'Yes, sir!' Elsworth said, and he put his mouth organ to his lips and began to play.

Within moments the marching soldiers around them took up the tune and they began to sing with new-found gusto,

Here's to the good old beer.
Mop it down, mop it down!
Here's to the good old beer.
Mop it down!
Here's to the good old beer that never leaves you queer.
Here's to the good old beer.
Mop it down!

Lock wheeled the horse about again, and with a loud 'Ha!', he kicked his heels into the beast's flanks, and tore up the line of troops, leaving a trail of dust in his wake.

It was early afternoon by the time Lock arrived back in Basra, sweat-soaked, thirsty and saddle-sore. His journey to Shaiba and then out across the floodwaters was uneventful, if laborious, but he chose to remain in the saddle rather than find a space on one of the many bellums. As it was, the boats were heavily laden with the wounded, as hundreds, if not thousands, of troops were ferried back to Basra. Nobody bothered him, nobody stopped him, and so he guided his horse towards the British Hospital and to Amy's digs in the Street of Allah's Tears.

He climbed the stairs to her rooms at the top, and hesitated. What was he going to say? Declare his love? Tell her he'd never leave her side again? That he'd never leave her vulnerable and exposed? Maybe not. That would more than likely annoy her.

The door opened before he could knock. It was Nurse Owen, dressed in her uniform.

'Lieutenant Lock, you startled me!' she gasped.

'Mary. I'm sorry. Is Amy here?'

'No,' Mary said with a shake of her head. 'I haven't seen her.'

'Please, Mary, I need to speak to her. Can I come in?'

'I was just on my way out. I'm on duty in twenty minutes.'

Lock could tell she was hiding something by the way she wouldn't look him in the eye. 'Mary?'

She lifted her face to his. 'You look awful.'

'I feel awful.'

Mary smiled hesitantly. 'She's at CHQ. With her father and your Mr Ross. I—'

Lock turned on his heels. 'Thank you, you're an angel,' he called over his shoulder, hurrying back down the stairs.

'Kingdom!' she shouted after him. 'Don't go. Don't try and see her. You won't like what's happened.'

But Lock wasn't listening. He came out of the entrance, back onto the narrow street, and made his way to the main thoroughfare where he had left his horse in the care of a young boy.

The lad, no more than ten years old, all grinning teeth and matted hair, jumped up and handed Lock the reins.

'Very tired horse, as-sayed,' he said.

Lock ruffled the boy's hair and handed him a coin. 'Very tired as-sayed.' He pulled himself back into the saddle, and made his way down to the banks of the Shatt where the Command Headquarters building was situated.

It was of a similar construction to the British Hospital, two storeys with a flat roof, a shaded balcony running the length of the first floor, with porticoes below. Lock dismounted and tied the horse in the shade of a palm tree next to a water trough. He made his way past the bored Indian sentries, who stood sweltering either side of the entrance, and stepped into a blissfully cool and dark hall. A desk rested in the centre, behind which a uniformed clerk sat busying himself reading through a number of papers. Beyond him was a pair of highly polished oak doors.

Lock approached, and the clerk looked up.

'Yes, Lieutenant?'

'I'm here to see General Townshend. The name's Lock.'

'Ah, yes. Thought it might be,' the clerk said, looking Lock up and down. 'I'll let him know you're here.' He picked up the receiver of the black telephone at his right elbow, and waited for the phone to be answered. 'Ah, sorry to disturb you, sir. That fellow . . . Lieutenant Lock . . . He's here . . . Righto, sir.' The clerk put the receiver back in its cradle and gave Lock a quick smile. 'Take a seat, Lieutenant, he'll be with you in a jiffy.'

Lock nodded and glanced around. Set well away and opposite the desk were two hard wooden benches, one behind the other. Lock took his hat off, sat down on the front bench, wiped his brow with his sleeve, and watched the clerk at work, methodically signing each paper before placing it in the metal tray on the left-hand corner of the desk. A sigh over in the shadows pulled Lock's attention away.

To the clerk's right, over against the wall near to the oak doors, were two chairs. A uniformed woman occupied one. She was dark-haired, and even from across the hall, Lock could see that she radiated a sultry beauty. Subconsciously she was rubbing her slender neck. As she lowered her hand, Lock's gaze fell on her tightly buttoned jacket front. He looked back up to see that she was staring back at him. She smiled briefly then averted her gaze again.

Lock frowned trying to ascertain what her uniform was. She was no nurse, he could see that. The uniform was military, but nothing he was familiar with. The arm of her jacket bore an emblem of an eagle or similar bird sat above crossed swords, below which were three chevron stripes. The collars and cuffs of her white blouse were folded up over the jacket, and her skirt reached down to her ankles and a pair of polished, heeled black booties. On her head she wore a straw hat, which, like her uniform, was navy blue. There was a band with gold lettering around the hat, but Lock couldn't see all the letters. He could only make out 'val reser'.

'Hello, Val,' Lock said to himself.

Then the double oak doors behind the clerk opened and Amy and Lady Alice emerged, closely followed by the general and Major Ross. All four were laughing gaily.

Lock jumped to his feet and walked towards them. But Major Ross, arm in a white sling, quickly intercepted him.

'Ah, Kingdom, there you are!' he said.

'Sir,' Lock said, but he was looking at Amy.

Major Ross stepped into his line of sight. 'My boy, you look frightful. You could have freshened up a little.'

'Sir, I thought it best to come straight here.'

'Well, now that you are here, we need to talk about our German problem. Before we speak to the general.'

'Wassmuss?' Lock said, his eyes still on Amy. She was avoiding his stare.

'Lock,' Ross said sternly, grabbing his arm. 'This is important.' He began to walk him back towards the benches.

'Well, goodbye, my dears,' Townshend was saying to his wife and daughter.

Lock watched the two women bid their farewells, and begin to move away.

'Is she all right? Amy?' Lock said.

The major glanced over at the departing women. 'A little shaken, nasty concussion. But she's a strong one and has proved most helpful in our pursuit of Wassmuss. She's corroborated your story about Winslade, too. So you are off the hook there. But the German has still eluded capture. My reckoning is that he'll be heading for the Turk lines at Nasiriyeh, or perhaps Ctesiphon. But while I was in my sickbed, I did a little reading from the parts of the notebook I'd copied out. Very interesting. And I may have a lead on our rat in White Tabs, too. Thanks to Sergeant Boxer there.'

Lock wasn't really concentrating on what the major was saying; all the time his focus remained on Amy and Lady Townshend. 'Sorry, sir? Sergeant Boxer?'

'My American girl,' Ross said, indicating over his shoulder.

Lock looked over at the woman in the navy uniform. 'Who, Val?'

'Val?' Ross frowned. 'Elizabeth. Elizabeth Boxer. Yeoman 1st Class, in the United States Naval Reserve Female Division—'

'Lock, my boy,' General Townshend said, stepping over to them. 'My, you are a godsend when it comes to my daughter. Come, let's go into my office and toast the bride!'

'Bride?' Lock said, catching the look of dread on Ross's face. 'What bride?'

'Why Amy, of course!' Townshend beamed. 'She's accepted young Casper's proposal of marriage. And not a mo—'

'Excuse me, sir.' Lock broke away from the two officers and hurried after Amy and Lady Townshend. They had just stepped out of the hall, and had disappeared from sight.

Lock emerged out into the shaded covered walkway, looking to his left and right. 'Amy!' he called.

The two women were at the end of the portico. They stopped. Lady Townshend, face a hard mask of disapproval, was about to approach Lock, but Amy pulled her gently back, said something, and then walked towards Lock alone.

They met halfway.

Lock put his hand out to take hers, but she pulled away from him.

'Is it true?' he said.

She stared back defiantly. 'Yes, Kingdom, I told you we could never be.'

'I don't believe you mean that. You're a rebel at heart, like I am. You're a suffragette, an independent woman, and you said that fate had thrown us together. This is not who you are.'

Amy's face remained blank. 'You don't understand, Kingdom,' she said. 'I've known Casper all my life. My family, his family . . . It's what we do . . .'

'You don't believe that,' Lock said. 'I know you don't. Run away with me, now. Marry me.'

Amy tried to keep her composure, but she was struggling, and her eyes were beginning to well up. She put her hand up towards Lock's face.

'*Venir, enfant.*' Lady Townshend had walked up and she snatched Amy's hand away. 'I am grateful to you, Monsieur Lock, grateful for saving my daughter, but she cannot see you any more, and I would be thankful if you would respect that.' She gave a quick, nervous smile, and steered her daughter away.

Lock stood and watched them go, for now. But it wasn't over

between him and Amy Townshend, that much he knew. This was merely another obstacle in his way, a challenge laid down. And he had always thrived on a challenge.

'The general's waiting. If you're not too busy chasing skirt.'

Lock turned to see the major standing beside him.

'I'm not sure I want to toast the bride, sir.'

'Nonsense, we're toasting you.'

'Sir?'

'Your promotion,' Ross said. 'He's signed the order. All approved and official.'

Lock shrugged. He didn't care about that. 'Must we?'

'Oh, come, my boy,' Ross said, taking his arm and guiding him back. 'I like the sound of it. Suits you.'

Lock gave a wry smile.

Ross paused at the entranceway, and threw out a smart, teasing salute.

'After you, Captain Lock.'

AUTHOR'S NOTE

A note on the languages used in this book:

On many occasions a translation is provided within the text. The Arabic words and phrases are interpreted in familiar Roman letters and follow an imitated-pronunciation system. For consistency, the main source of reference was the Dorling Kindersley *Eyewitness Travel Guides Arabic Phrase Book* (2003).

I. D. ROBERTS